FROM THE STARS

KIKI TOWNLEY

Book Cover Artwork by © Melinda Lee

First edition 2026

ISBN (paperback): 978-1-7644864-0-8
ASIN (eBook): B0GFQ85MB6

AUTHOR'S NOTE

I have made a playlist on Spotify called 'From the Stars,' which encompasses moments within the trilogy. I've assigned them to characters or scenes, and will be disclosing more information on this over time.

Andy and I have also written and recorded an official From the Stars Anthem, with Matty producing the Instrumental. Listen to it before you start each book, and again afterwards. Each time you listen, you can picture it from anyone's perspective and delve deeper into their mind through the song.

PLAYLIST QR CODE

Thank you so much for reading this book! Some of the content might be triggering to some readers. Please review the following potential triggers: Sexual Assault references, Sexual Harassment references, Suicidal Ideation, Control of society, Violence and mutilation references, Mental Health – Anxiety and depression, Torture and captivity references, coarse language, and intimate scenes.

LANGUAGE

Language translations and pronunciation:

- Lremi* (*wait till book two for translation*)
  - Reh-mee
- Farr de huro batie – Get her cleaned up
  - Fah-r deh hew-roh bah-tee
- Youhi – Thank you
  - Yew hee
- Ghana – family, dear friend
  - Gah nah
- Rus teyez ug farr – Go easy on her
  - Rooh-s teh-yeh-z uhg fah-r
- Mihl'e dahn – Good Morning
  - Mihl eh dah n
- Mihl'eh dask – Good Night
  - Mihl eh dah sk
- Treh'sa – be gentle/calm
  - T-rare-sah
- Avah – Go on
  - Ay-vah
- Ruhsa – My girl
  - Roos-sah
- Terf'gs – Bathroom, toilet
  - Turf-x
- Ist – It's okay/I'm okay
  - Ee-st
- Kesah – Hello
  - Keh-sah
- Juf'ua – Safe place for the spirit
  - Juff-wah
- Uhi bergano tsui et hera swoar, e tsui et dask. Uhi bergano tsua et belesah et dre's du – You belong where your heart can soar, and where it can rest. You belong when you believe you deserve to.
  - Ew-ee bur-gah-noh ts-ew-ee eht hair-ah sw-oarh, ee ts-ew-ee eht dah-sk. Ew-ee bur-gah-noh ts-su-ah eht beh-leh-sah, eht dreh's dew

Dedication

This is for you, and all those times
you thought you were hard to love.
You aren't.
To you, who thinks there must be more
than this.
There is.

CHAPTER 1
DESPITE HOPELESSNESS

What the—

"Fuck."

I stumble backwards, swiping urgently at my face to get the blanketing web of film off me. Holding my hands inches from me, I scour them vigorously.

What?

Confusion roars inside my mind, finding nothing in my palms but days-old dirt settled into the creases.

A warning flares in my gut, pulling my attention behind me.

You're not alone.

The forest feels alive, holding its breath as it watches me— waiting for me to do something. With wide eyes, I comb through the scattered trees, my stomach plunging as I do a double-take on something in the distance.

What is that?

Leaning forward, I try to discern the shape. A sharp exhale leaves my body. *Surely it's just more forest.* But then it moves, and everything in creation halts—all but the figure in the distance, moving toward me.

Shock pierces through my gut; all thoughts abscond to oblivion and my breaths come in too slowly. *I'm seeing things. Surely.*

But then, the figure steps from the shadows as a break in the canopy casts a beam of light upon them. Our eyes lock.

A man.

Time moves slowly as I take him in: unruly hair and beard, spear clenched in his fist, and a deadly look in his eyes.

Run.

My rigid muscles refuse.

As if out of thin air, others emerge from behind him, moving toward me as this unspeakable force. A dawn of impending threat slithers down my spine, and all I can do is stare.

The warriors that look like they're from a lost civilization documentary glare at me, raking over every inch with sharp appraisal.

My mind screams at me, urging me to move. I know I need to, but I can't. Fear winds its way around my ankles, immobilizing me.

There's hardly a sound in each careful and predatorial placement of their bare feet on the forest floor. I can't breathe, and I can't look away.

One step. Take one step backwards. I manage to retreat a foot of distance on unsteady legs, but as I do, a pulse beats through the forest's stillness. Readiness gleans in their honed and measured strides.

I swallow hard, my jaw clenching as they inch closer. I know I'm running out of time. Fight, yell, plead, throw a damn rock at this guy's head, I just need to do something. Now.

But I don't know how to fight.

Defeat threatens to unroll over my mind like a blanket, telling me I don't stand a chance against them. But I hold the feeling back, pushing against it with shaky fingers.

The dirt gives a soft crunch beneath my boot as I take another step back.

Oh, shit.

Their muscles engage as they dip their chins in an unspoken promise: that if I run, they'll chase. *Daring* me to. Warning me *not* to.

A slow, controlled breath fills my lungs.

Screw it.

Despite the hopeless state of my life, I press my toes into the soles of my boots. Despite leaving my job, home, and everything I've known, I turn. Even with an angry heart, my shoe digs into the dirt and I push off into a sprint.

I run like I have something to live for.

As my feet pound against the earth, a string of words circles my mind—the words that have consumed me to the point of burning my life down: that if I get lost enough, maybe I can be found.

Clearly, this is not what I envisioned.

Shoving at branches and leaping over netted tree roots, I gasp humid air through my chapped lips, releasing it back even hotter.

Wait. The thought is a whisper in my mind, but I'm quick to disagree. *For slaughter? No thanks.*

I know I'm not supposed to turn and look—that this is exactly when the main character in a film trips and the pursuing creature catches them, but I have to know. I have to see how close they are. Dread coils around my ribcage when I glance over my shoulder, and they're nowhere to be seen.

My feet slow as I whip my head around, the burn in my legs competing with my strained lungs for attention. Shoving my back against the trunk of a tree, I peek back at where I last saw them in the dense forest, slapping a hand over my mouth to try to quieten how fucking loudly I'm gasping for air.

A rustle to the right sends panic through my chest, but when I look, nothing's there. Not even a breeze. Dragging my focus left, I blink too quickly to know if I imagine seeing movement, or if it was really there.

The forest seemed bigger before—expansive—where being lost in it felt like an adventure. Until I became prey. Now it's too small, drumming its fingers while watching my fate unfold.

Fear sinks her teeth into my chest, threatening to take a bite of my racing heart. *This is not happening.* This is not my life. *My* life is predictable. Stagnant. Even if I was nothing more than a vessel for someone else's will, I can't deny the creeping regret of chasing freedom only to be right here, days later.

Clenching my fists, I lean sideways inch by inch to peer behind the tree again, wondering if I hallucinated the whole thing. I release a breath, conceding that I've definitely lost my mind, but when I turn back around, I see three of them an arm's length away. A gasp rips through me and I jump away, turning to run in the opposite direction, but skid to a halt as three more surround me.

Static fills my brain as I assess exactly how screwed I am, absorbing everything about them all at once. Their downturned lips, weapons readied, primal gazes... I surmise with an internal nod—*very* screwed.

Dread tightens my muscles, but I push past it to raise my hands in surrender. The man in the back tenses at my sudden movement. My forehead puckers in confusion. I'm alone, unarmed, and clearly can't run more than a couple hundred meters without wanting to vomit. Yet he looks afraid... of *me?*

Fool.

As Spearman steps forward, I fight the urge to collapse into a ball and cry at the authority and violence in his gaze. I'm a hair's breadth away from saying something, but it's probable that all I'll manage is gibberish as anxiety holds my tongue hostage.

From behind me, an arm wraps around my chest, snapping me from my stunned stupor.

"Woah!" I attempt to turn my head to look. At the same time, I swipe my hands at the arm, but a cold sharpness presses against my throat. My chest heaves up and down.

"What are you doing? Let me go!" I yell out, squirming to free myself.

Whoever holds me from behind pushes the sharp tip deeper into my neck, a slight movement away from breaking the skin.

"Stop." Spearman gruffly voices the man's nonverbal command, sauntering closer.

What accent is that?

Spearman inclines his head, commanding a defense line to form around me. He shares a glance with one of the women, their stern expressions communicating in silent conversation.

My eyeline zips around the group, over their shoulders, and to the endless expanse of forest. Worry starts to make my mind drift and my awareness dull. The only thing keeping my consciousness attached to my body is the pounding sound of my own racing heartbeat.

"You!" he barks, stepping into my field of vision, inches from my face.

Alarm bells ring in my mind and I shake my head, barely able to get a full breath in as I rapidly blurt out, "What did you say?"

Fuck, that droning sound I barely registered through the static buzz in my ears was him talking to me.

The others watch me warily, sizing me up and sharing glances.

"Who are you?" Spearman's voice grates out each word through a locked jaw.

I blink at him, numbness overtaking me. "Nobody. I'm just out here walking."

So many eyes on me, yet not a single mouth moves.

In the silence, I reappraise the group, confused with the contradiction. Their clothes are in tactful shades of camouflage, but there's a refinement that feels imperfect. Handmade. Their weapons of choice are ancient, promising threat or death, yet are decorated with beads and colored strips, each personalized. Some have hair long and unkempt, while others braid it tightly or cut it close to skin.

Do they live outside? Have they always?

"Who are *you?*" The question was meant to stay in my head, but it slips past my lips.

Eyes narrow and heads jerk back—surprise and offense from all but the singular woman who doesn't react. She just watches me.

Spearman spits out words to the woman in a foreign language, lifting his spear in one swift move and hovering it in front of my heart.

Well. That's not a good sign.

Apprehension elicits a tremor to roll through me, and my only choice is to try intellectualizing, to calm down, to look unafraid. *I can't come across vulnerable and weak. But I also can't come across as a threat.*

Fuck me.

Dragging my eyes from the tip of the spear, I meet the woman's firm stare. "I'm sorry. Can you please tell me what's happening?"

Sweat rolls in threads down my temples, over my cheeks, and drips from my jaw to my half-soaked shirt. The afternoon sun seems pissed at me, too.

The woman studies me, absentmindedly fiddling with the ethereal turquoise necklace hanging just below her collarbones. The bow and arrows strapped to her back look as sharp as her energy feels. Her piercing eyes spark a flare of unease in me, a silent tell that I'm being examined as prey. She lifts her hand, lightly pushing the spear away with the tip of her finger to stand in its place.

Intimidation urges me to shrink back, as if I'm safer with the man holding a knife to my throat from behind me. I can feel the steadiness of his heartbeat as my back presses against his chest, and as fucked up as it sounds, I feed off how calm he is. But then I think about the eeriness of him being so at peace in this insane situation, which unnerves me all over again. *Ugh.* Being trapped and so close to this stranger, so at their mercy—it all makes me want to recoil and peel my skin off.

I plead with my eyes, looking at the others as if one of them might see me and my harmless intentions. That they'll say, "Oh, you're actually alright. We apologize for the confusion, Milady," and send me on my way. Maybe with a banana as a parting gift. Only if they have one to spare. *I'm starving.*

Turquoise Necklace speaks firmly over her shoulder in that language, never looking away from me as if she knows her pinned attention is paralyzing me. Spearman's eyes rove over her face as she speaks, absorbing every word like he needs it to breathe. The transformation in his expression when his focus slides from her to me is jarring. I don't need Spearman's razor-sharp reply translated to know all hope of escape has been sliced away from me.

A spark of surprise shoots through my stomach as the man holding me loosens his grip. *Am I being let go?* A second later, I feel the tug of my backpack straps. *Fuck… no.* My backpack has my phone, my journal that acts as my friend, and my tether to sanity. Swiftly, I hunch over and grip the straps firmly in my hands. Everyone steps toward me, half of them squinting in skepticism while the others maintain a withering scowl.

Turquoise Necklace drawls, "Let it go."

With a chest rising and falling quickly in angsty resistance, my mind tells me I don't have a choice. I drop my hands, and they maneuver it from me, eyeing me as if *I* were the unidentifiable mystery.

"Come," Turquoise Necklace orders in a tone that demands no follow-up questions.

My mouth barely opens in protest before she gives a curt 'no' with her head. Without waiting, she turns on her heel to walk, and they all follow, clearly expecting me to do the same.

I don't want to. I'm scared.

Recklessly, my feet stay planted as I lift my chin and ask, "Where are you taking me?"

The person behind me pushes the tip of the knife to my back, urging me forward, and I arch away from the sharp stab, my fear switching to anger as I throw him a side-long glare.

Turquoise turns to stand in front of me again, the impatience in her expression stealing my attention, disorienting me. "Walk, or we carry you unconscious."

My head jerks back. "Why would I willingly go with you to die in a change of scenery? Just kill me now and do it quickly. Or let me go, and I swear I'll pretend I never saw you."

Spearman grits out, "Enough," and flecks of spit hit my cheek. The conviction in his eyes terrifies me, and that's the only reason I don't wipe it off.

Turquoise Necklace murmurs something to him in that language.

As a last-ditch effort, I turn to logic. "If you were on a hike, and strangers threatened you, demanded from you at knife point that you follow them to some random place, would you just... go? No questions asked?"

Her nostrils flare, eyes darting between mine in thoughtful analysis. "I wouldn't be stupid enough to be in unknown territory alone."

I swallow, turning stiff as stone as she severs my reach for connection.

Impassively, she supplies, "You will be interrogated first. That's where we're going."

The crumb of information isn't nearly enough to ease the intensity of my nerves, especially when I register a key word she said. *First.*

So, they want a quick chat before spearing me to a spit? The gentleman of people-eaters.

Confusion settles into my features, my voice a little squeaky as I question, "Interrogated? I'm nobody, and you'll realize that as soon as you take a second to know me. You can ask me your questions right here."

She crosses her arms, fingers drumming along her bicep at my tone. I swallow in regret, watching as she does a once-over of me. "I'm not the interrogator."

I feel the sudden urge to expire as fear tightens my throat, locking every atom of my being.

Dipping her chin and taking a small step toward me, she asks again, "Will you be walking, or are we dragging you there?"

Defeatedly, I finally answer, "Walk." The word is barely audible.

They part to form a walkway, lined up and expectant.

Forcing my locked muscles and blistered feet to move, I trudge past them. In the time it takes for a slow blink, a numbness spreads through me. It falls over my features and carries on through my bones. Their stalking eyes hold judgement, as if they know me.

But they're as uncertain as I am.

This is the largest, most unexplored forest in the world, only offering guided tours around the skirts twice a year on designated trails. I overheard the Elites of the company I work for talking about how their experience here was raw and mystical. If this is a healing place, Creations knows I needed to come here.

A day and a half on a plane, two days with the random hiking group, and three days spiraling alone because this innate pull told me to sneak away when they fell asleep. To go deep into the forest by myself. I ventured slowly and curiously at first, then came the balled-up crying on the gnarled forest floor. The journal remained clenched in my hands—rereading the scribbled entries that are the inked version of my bleeding heart kept me grounded. When rain suddenly bombarded me, I laughed sardonically while walking in sloshed socks, thinking, *of course*. But then I felt bad for being angry at the sky. Maybe the clouds are sad too, without knowing exactly why. I climbed a tree and binge-ate two-thirds of my food rations while completely dissociating, wondering what love felt like. To put it simply, feelings that I've been too busy to feel were felt. I convinced myself I needed this—needed to come here. Explore. My instincts told me to go soul searching. *Good to know my instincts are a piece of shit that will get me eaten by a village of cannibals.*

A scoff escapes me, and the hand around my arm tightens in response. I glance over my shoulder, but I can't see my captor.

Always a captive.

Flashes of memories bombard me. Being trapped in greyness, living a life that wasn't mine. Empty, repetitive, and commercial.

I try to focus, get out of my head and note landmarks to track the path we've come, but it all blurs into the same twisted vines, looming branches, and moss creeping over fallen logs.

Doom settles in the pit of my stomach, just as it did walking through the bustling city back home. Once, I walked for hours—my knees and feet aching then, too. I didn't want to stay out, and I didn't want to go home.

The echoing tweets of birds pull my eyes upward. Their freedom spikes my envy. I realize I didn't escape being trapped and controlled. *I just swapped one prison for another.*

I roll my eyes at myself. I can hear it, how miserable and negative and frustratingly repetitive I sound, and I fucking hate it. How do I stop feeling sorry for myself? How do I find peace in my own mind? *Why is peace and freedom always dangling ahead of me, as if it's a mystical thing I can work toward, but never attain?*

A protruding root trips me, and I smack one knee against the ground. But before I can get a mouthful of dirt, I'm yanked to my feet and steadied.

A relieved smile touches my lips. I turn to thank the man, but rocks form in my throat from his dismissal, pushing me to keep walking. I do, watching the ground carefully.

My eyes lift for only a second, skimming the others. They exude this... energy of confidence, self-assuredness. Even though they're different ethnicities and ages, they share this cohesive disposition—like a family.

Memories flash of sitting at birthday parties, family dinners, work social outings, and it always felt so prudently clear that I was an independent outsider sitting amongst an established group. I felt like life was one big inside joke, and I sat there nervously laughing, hoping they wouldn't catch on that I wasn't there when they made it up. I mean, I could have fun. I got along with people—I even loved them, but I never moved and breathed with someone like they do with each other. These people are so sure that they belong. *I'm literally jealous of my captors. How low is my lowest?*

Releasing a breath, I continue tracking our movements, trying to map our route. *Why? Delusional optimism.*

The ground here is less damp as the canopy thins out, letting rays of light shine through. The hold on my lungs relaxes as I find myself distracted by the buzzing of insects and how they're much louder than before. The vines seem wilder as they wrap around the floor and trees, like untethered souls excited about having a form. The brightness of those little red berries and the vibrance in the ferns seems edited, or visually enhanced. I'm sure I'm in the same forest, but it feels like I've stepped into a dream version of it.

Awareness wrenches me from my thoughts and shoots through my veins as I hear distant voices. *Could they help me? Do I call out?*

Wait.

A realization washes over me, and my whole body sags with despair. They don't even flinch at the voices.

They know them.

Panic leaks into my already-tense muscles as I know that escaping whatever this is, just became impossible.

CHAPTER 2
NO ONE

To remain calm is a feat as my thoughts thunder against my skull, trying to process what I'm seeing. The instant I cross the treeline into a clearing, the scent of food cooking crashes into me. My hollow stomach begs me to inhale the aroma, like it might somehow satisfy the gurgle demanding whatever's on that fire. Smoke curls lazily into the sky, the pit surrounded by smiling faces and laughter. My eyes wander, taking in the scattered tents varying in size and colored a beige-brown to hide within the environment they fill. I watch as an aliveness vibrates through the people, carrying it with them through every foot of the space as they create, craft, build, or rest.

Spearman whistles a tune, pulling every set of eyes toward him. A haze blurs my vision as they all hone in on me. A hand presses into the middle of my back, pushing me to keep walking. The shock is seizing me, and I fall into an autopilot left-right-left-right daze. Turquoise announces something in their language, and mistrust laces itself through each of their expressions before they abandon their things and go into their tents.

The sense of unease these people radiate forces my heart to pound viciously. Plus, they just don't make sense. There's a poise—

a familiarity in their shared glances that feels aware of social norms, but this couldn't be further from any society I've seen. For starters, they're outside in nature.

The loose fabric door to the tent is yanked open, and I'm roughly pulled inside. Dread swirls with shock as I scan the room.

Tent isn't the right word, because it would diminish the structure to something bare and feeble. Nothing like this. The floor and walls are made with that thick canvas material, held up by posts and shaped in a yawning circle. The roof is the same material reinforced with some kind of interwoven large leaves, peaking upward as it builds to a point in the middle. Surprise jolts through me when I notice the red, orange, and yellow hand-crafted blankets and pillows stacked in the corner, then my eyes drift over the unique and rough-edged trinket hanging from the ceiling. I marvel at how it catches the light, reflecting tiny star-shaped rainbows onto the walls.

Everything I've endured in the last few days—even the last hour—isn't enough to stop the strange longing from beating through my heart. I stare at the wooden table and the accompanying chairs lined with cushions, then at the antique storage chests pressed up against the wall. *Cozy, beautiful, and homely.* The innocence and color of this room starkly contrast with the clinical and industrial spaces I'm used to.

Frenzying nerves shoot through me when Turquoise strides over, nodding to the man behind me. As I twist to look over my shoulder, he steps back to reveal the knife in his clutches. My curiosity is piqued—*what is that?* It's carved to smoothness, appearing as opal or marble, but I can't tell what it could be made of. *Stone, bone, or crystal?*

A firmness in the lines of his face is now known to me as the unmistakable trademark amongst all the captors. He's younger than I pictured him—or maybe it's his smooth features that allude to youth, because his hands are rough like he's been building all these tents and tables himself for decades. Spearman says a few words to him, and he nods in response, leaving without looking back.

When Spearman turns to face me, I look away fast enough to avoid that assailant's viciousness, only to just as reluctantly land on Turquoise's piercing glare. *Sigh.*

She gestures to the wooden chair beside me with an unspoken command: sit.

I try to conceal my rising anger by pressing the tip of my tongue into my molar, then, like a good dog, I lower myself into the chair. *Why do they think they can just take me? Tell me not to talk like I don't have a right to ask where the fuck I am?*

Pulling my bottom lip between my teeth works to shut my mouth for about two seconds. "Look, I don't know why you think I need to be interrogated and treated like this. I went off trail on my hike, and for some reason, that's upset you. I'm sorry, I didn't mean to. I can leave and never look back. Please, just let me—"

Turquoise raises her hand, silencing me.

My lips press against my teeth. "Yep. No talking."

Spearman stands shoulder to shoulder with her, his perpetual scowl the only predictable thing today.

Realizing there's no reasoning with them, my fingers knot in angst. I'll have to wait to convince the interrogator I'm innocent, or for an opportunity to escape.

Minutes pass while I mentally fight my way out of here. I use a series of ninja sequences that I delusionally think I could nail first try with zero experience. But even if I got away, where would I go? I can't go home to the mind-numbing existence I loosely recall as a life. But I also don't want to stay here for... Creations knows what.

Turquoise pushes off the table she was leaning on and leaves the tent. Licking my dry lips for moisture tells me that this headache brewing behind my eyes isn't just from stress, but dehydration. I stare at the door, noticing that the light peeking through is a fading orange as the sun sets. *Dammit.* How am I going to escape in the dark?

I hear her voice first, her tone sure and direct. When a male voice responds, my stomach drops. Not because he's male, not because *another* person is coming to my guard, but from a sense of recognition. I try to hone in on the source of why I might know that voice, but it vanishes at my inspection.

"She speaks English," are the only words I can discern before perking up in my chair.

Reality sets in and I don't know if I should laugh or cry, desperately clawing at any shrivel of hope that this is a bad dream I'll wake from.

The door sweeps open, and a man steps inside, the setting sun framing him in a powerful silhouette. His unhurried footfalls echo confidence, and his presence radiates a force that makes Spearman seem kind of friendly.

Turquoise follows in behind him, melting into the shadows. The interrogator stops in front of me, but I'm fixated on the others that are settling in comfortably like vultures, expecting my demise. An urge chips away at my patience, pecking at the hold on my tongue—to lash out and force their hateful eyes away. But I don't give in to it.

Instead, I decide to change tactics if there is any hope of escape. I face the interrogator and allow my expression to fall before I begin pleading. "Can you tell me what's going on? I've just been told to be quiet. I've been taken here without any answers, and I just don't understand what I did wrong... I mean, I know I'm not in a position to demand answers..." I grunt in frustration, then take a breath to ease my festering temper.

Lowering my voice, I ask, "Will you tell me what's going on? Please."

He doesn't respond, the silence deafening and rancid. Tears of frustration start to prick my eyes as I let my head fall back, a breakdown sure to overcome me any minute now.

"You're right," he assures, and my eyes dart to him. "You're not in a position to be demanding anything. But I can appreciate it's coming from a place of confusion."

I'm stunned. Relief floats through me at the full sentence coming from the man's mouth after being spoken to all day in monotonous, clipped words and grunts. Also, I definitely didn't expect him to be considerate.

His energy feels calm and reassuring, as if he's going to be the one to put me at ease. He adds, "I understand you'd like to know why you're here."

Every vowel is wrapped in compassion, but I don't know... I don't trust it. Sweet words from the Elites often veil a selfish need of theirs. But wherever I am, I don't think I'm in the company of Elites. I'm in a pocket of the forest that feels like a different world.

He takes a step toward me, and the hairs on my arms rise. *He's the interrogator; he knows what he's doing.* Trying to read his expression before replying is fruitless—the dim light and his measured movements give nothing away.

"Yes, I'm confused." My arms involuntarily lift as I lean forward, desperate to explain. "I—"

"Do not move," he clips. Any semblance of kindness vanishes from his tone, warning every cell in my body to halt. My eyes drop to his knife, unsheathed and in his balled fist as if summoned out of thin air.

No sudden movements. Got it.

The other guards take a small step toward me, and I become motionless.

He continues, "I'm here to question you. Tell me, why were you in this part of the forest?"

My mind whirrs at the absurd question. "This part of the forest? I don't understand. This is a popular hiking destination." I lock my fingers and squeeze my palms together, refraining from my usual animated gestures.

The silence stretches on, so I fill it. "I mean, yes, I went off trail a few days ago, which is illegal. Is that what this is? Am I trespassing?"

His head tilts slightly, inscrutably. A beat of silence stretches between us before I feel an intrusive warmth spread up my spine. I flinch, banishing it as he stiffens.

I stare at him, dumbfounded. *What was that?*

His head turns slightly toward Spearman, and I hold my breath at the silent conversation they have. Slowly, he turns back to me, the knife fluidly rotating in his palm as he stalks closer.

I look nervously between the knife and him. "Please, no..."

He studies me intently, then crouches down, holding the knife loosely between his legs. His whole posture is deceptively non-threatening, and I stifle the urge to shuffle backwards in my chair.

I'm snapped back to reality by his low and calm voice. "It's okay. I'm just going to ask you again..." His eyes drift shut. "Why were you found in this part of the forest?"

My breath hitches as everything about this feels wrong. *How many times can I answer this question the same fucking way?*

My teeth grind and I force my voice to sound calm. "I... uh, I know I wasn't supposed to leave the tour. I—"

He rises and strolls behind me at a nonchalant pace. A contemplative 'hmm' sounds from his chest as he rests his hands on the back of my chair.

Leaning forward slightly so his knuckles don't brush my back, I press on. "I wasn't really thinking. I just wanted to explore. Which I'm realizing *now* is completely stupid..." I throw my hands up, exasperated, but a firm grip locks around my wrists. The room goes deathly quiet.

His voice drops an octave, enunciating each word. "What did I say about moving? Hands in your lap."

His fingers loosen their grasp, and I let my arms drift down to rest on my legs in a daze of shock.

People are harder to kill if they see you having a life to get back to.

I blurt out, "My name is Stella. I've always wanted a dog. That's what I was going to do. Get a dog. But I thought, I'll do it after I come out here. Because they deserve a good life and a happy owner." My explanation quickens to a ramble as the silence of the room presses in on me. "So, I came here first. Because I wanted to see a sunrise without a giant, grey, rectangular building ruining it. Sunrises are the happiest part of my day. My favorite color is green... Well, right now it's green. Sometimes it's chocolate brown, so I came to the forest. I... I didn't mean to... I just wanted to see trees and a sunrise. Please..." I pick at the skin on my thumbnail, attempting to calm my racing heart. "Believe me."

The silence stretches on, stealing the last shred of my sanity. My foot bounces restlessly against the ground.

He walks back in front of me, angling his body toward Turquoise. I barely catch the subtle shake of her head before his voice commands my attention again.

"Stella." My thoughts trip over themselves at the way he says my name, like he doesn't trust a single letter in it. "We can't take your word on that, and we aren't willing to place unjustified faith in you."

I watch with bated breath as Spearman and Turquoise share a look with him, seemingly making some kind of decision. The group of them turn from me, arms crossed. This interrogator is barbaric, barely saying anything before he's decided he's done with the conversation.

No.

I quickly rebut, squeezing my interlocked fingers together as the words rush from me in panic. "I thought you were supposed to ask me questions? That's all I get? One question? What kind of interrogation lasts less than five minutes? Have you never seen a single movie with detectives?"

Grounding myself, I take a deep breath and whisper, "You didn't even give me a chance. You... I..." My voice is fervent enough to hide the tremor. "I know words don't mean much, but I promise I have no desire whatsoever to mess up the peace that seems to reside here."

The group of them stare at me. The only sounds are whispers of wind against the tent and unseen wildlife.

The interrogator rolls his shoulders back, stretching out his neck. Silence breaks when he starts speaking to Spearman and Turquoise in their language. *They must be the leaders.*

My focus sprints between them, trying to decipher what they're saying. The interrogator gestures to me, his voice measured at first, but a fervor starts to edge his tone as the foreign words sharpen. Shocked into silence, Spearman turns to face me. His reply cuts through the air as he gestures wildly with his hands, in what I assume is disagreement. Turquoise is weighing up what they're saying, and everyone else in the room looks at me like I'm nothing but an inconvenience with shit smeared across her face.

For my final trick, folks, I will evaporate!

...

Still here?

Fuck.

Turquoise Necklace nods, and the word "sage" is intertwined with her sentence. She paces two steps one way, two steps back. The interrogator lowers his voice, firmly delivering a line that makes Spearman exhale with a growl. A short minute of anxiety-driven hell passes before he reluctantly nods. All three of them turn to face me, and it is at this moment that I realize how full my bladder is. I wonder how much worse it would be for me if I literally pissed myself. I push the thought to the side of my mind. *Damn my luck.*

"Come with me," Interrogator demands.

Despite myself, I'm inclined to do what the rude, brutish interrogator says, and I rise to my feet. But not before a quick glance over him, to size him up and weigh my chances of getting out of here. He's a lot stronger than me, plus I'm outnumbered. Even if I did miraculously get past them, this is their turf. They know the forest, and it's about to get dark. *I'm stuck here.*

Interrupting my impending spiral, he inclines his head for me to walk first. Holding my breath, I take a wobbly step forward, sending a silent plea for mercy to anyone listening.

I look at the closed door, preparing myself. *For what? I don't know.* Tentatively pushing the door open, I squint my eyes at the direct hit of setting sun, blinking until my vision clears. It's a ghost town. *No one will help me.*

The interrogator is on my heels, barely a foot away. *Seriously? Give me some fucking space.* Instead, his hand drops on my shoulder, guiding me to walk as if I'm a child prone to running away in a grocery store. I scowl over my shoulder, and the festering rage halts as I get my first proper look at him in the light. His expression falls, and we stop still in our tracks, eyes locked. My jaw slackens as I turn to face him, recognition trickling through my blood. *But where...*

The ground rocks beneath my feet. *Breathe.* My lungs fill and deflate in slow motion. My mind scrambles to place him, *but I...*

The words slam into me, then fall out of my mouth. "I know you."

CHAPTER 3
A SACRED LIFE

His whole body tenses in a fleeting and subtle state of shock, but then it's gone as if I'd imagined it.

"Do you?" His words challenge the idea, and he waits to see my reaction.

I swallow, and my eyes trail down his face, to his lips, his jaw dusted with the new growth of a beard. *Dammit, I bet Neanderthal-Interrogator shaves his beard with a knife.*

"I—" An intrusive thought interrupts my sentence, the image hazy and unfurling in my mind. I'm standing over him, tracing the chisel of his jawline, lifting his chin with my finger. His hand closes around mine, teaching me, guiding the knife's edge for a close shave...

All thoughts dissolve when he gives me a pointed look, pulling me back to my body and heating my cheeks.

"You said you know me?" His voice is laced with disbelief and annoyance as he crosses his arms. That's when I notice the scars trailing over his skin, up his shoulders, across his bare chest. As I follow the line of scars, I notice the almost imperceptible ones along his neck. Then I meet his eyes, the glow of the sun revealing the depths.

Shifting my weight, I blink at him. "Sorry, I thought I did..."

A deep part of me stirs, and I flex my hands in response. I reach for memories that place his rough exterior, engulfing presence, and his studying stare. I search for clarity, peering into his life through the subtle creases around his eyes and mouth, but I'm left without answers. My stomach sinks. *I haven't seen him before. I know we haven't met.* Unease courses through me at the thought.

He's watching me openly gape at him, and I school my features to be carefully neutral. Mortified. But then, I realize he's doing it, too. My blood hums when he scans my face purposefully. A spec of hope flourishes when I think he might recognize me—fill in the blanks of why I feel this way, but my stomach hollows when he says, "Impossible." A statement. His tone sure, but then he watches me like he wants me to argue the point.

This is all too much.

I frown and straighten my spine. "No, I don't."

He waits—for what? I don't know. But it has me digging my nails into the palm of my hands. Angling his head barely an inch, his eyes trace down and take me in, stopping only when they lock onto something. The muscle in his jaw tenses and I frown, the light fading from my chest as his expression darkens. I follow his eyeline, the glint of gold reflecting off my left ring finger. My eyes snap up, and he's already watching me, unreadable.

I force myself to look anywhere but at him, eyeing the treeline over his shoulder, then to the abandoned dinner plates on tables. Too long has passed, and I glance at his face, hoping that if I clear my throat, he might relent the intensity of his focus on me. It does not. Instead, he asks, "You thought you knew me. Why?" The question is sharp, but his curiosity tracing my features feels the opposite.

I try to relax my shoulders, appearing less stiff than I feel as I double down. "No. I was wrong." My tone comes off unexpectedly convincing.

"That's alright," he says as if consoling me. "I'm sure it's not the first time."

The urge to hunch over and hiss has never been a thing I had to talk myself out of until now. Instead, I lift my chin slightly, refusing to give him the satisfaction of a reaction to his insult.

Voices from inside the tent get louder, coming toward us. He steps away from me, and I'm surprised by the sting in my chest.

He sweeps with his hand, commanding, "This way."

A steady breath expands my lungs as I square my shoulders and straighten my spine. I feign control as I turn, but just before my gaze shifts, I catch him noticing the ring again. *Swallow the urge to explain. You don't owe him anything.*

I try not to focus on the muffled whispers coming from within the tents as we pass them. *Look around.* There's shared spaces designed in a communal open plan, and seats of all shapes and sizes surround tables that are spread out with no rhyme or reason. There's hammocks strewn about, and gazebo-like covered areas, all illuminated by these old school lamp posts with solar panel attachments. *What is this place?*

I look over my shoulder to ask him that exact question and notice that his attention is already on me. A quizzical expression wears into his features, but it vanishes behind his collected veil.

Turning away from his prying regard, I ask, "Where are we going?"

Neanderthal-Interrogator decides to become mute, prickling my nerves like a silent, stalking cactus. A glance over my shoulder is cut short by his clipped instruction. "Stop at that hut up there on your left."

As we approach the tent—*hut*, he directs me with a terse incline of his head to enter first. I clench and unclench my hands, bracing myself before I go inside. In a flash, my brain visualizes different images of what could be in there. Maybe I'll find a table with torture tools splayed over it, a makeshift jail cell, or plastic covering the floors and walls to this killing room... *Is that a thing? What do you call a room you kill people in?*

Adrenaline spikes, and I swipe at one side of the door, ready. *Not ready. What in the not-anticipating-the-inviting-and-homely space is this?* It has a similar set up to the first hut I was in, but slightly smaller. A generous-sized bed hugs the wall, framed by a bedside table with drawers, and intimately finished with a table and chairs to the side. The sun's descent behind us casts the room with an angelic and warm glow, making it feel... comforting. The mental gymnastics of trying to figure out what's happening only adds to my pulsing headache.

Stepping into my field of vision, he announces, "You'll be staying in here. Your wrists..."

A disquieted confusion billows through me as I look down at my wrists, then I notice his outstretched hand and the rope. My mouth drops open, a realization dawning over me like a dark cloud promising a storm. I'm being forced to stay here? For how long? Why? As a prisoner? *Absolutely not.*

White-hot anger presses against my ribs, coiled and ready to unleash as I step forward. My chest rises and falls quickly in anticipation, my expression sharpening, a promise of violence etched in every muscle.

He exhales through his nose, muttering, "Don't bother." His unimpressed reaction to the scariest version of me, my unabashed rage—it suffocates the fire inside me. Utter boredom settles into his features, like he can't be bothered to douse the lick of flame behind my eyes.

I avert my gaze, stepping away from him. "I'm not staying here as your prisoner."

"You want a chance to show you're trustworthy?" He steps into my line of vision, forcing me to meet his hardened glare. "This is it."

Raising my voice, I demand, "*What* is?"

His stare drifts over my face, lingering. "These people live a sacred life. And you? Are not threatening that."

My throat tightens, his words hitting a nerve. *I don't live a sacred life.*

I spend life working toward something I don't care about for people who don't truly care about me. The grey cement society that we inhabit is soul-sucking, with the buildings stacked too close and technology stripping us of autonomy. It moves too quickly for me to even keep up.

And if you don't keep up, the world will swallow you whole.

On one day, I think I might be closer to grasping the artificially intelligent systems that are taking over our lives. The next day, it evolves. It's near-impossible trying to get soap from the fucking dispenser in the work bathroom. I nearly cracked a knuckle punching the thing, then a wide-eyed stranger closed and opened her fist underneath it and it dribbled soap into her palm. I forced a smile, mortified, as she walked away. *Oh.*

I relaxed at the reprieve of knowing what I had to do. I copied her movement, and *no* motherfucking soap came out. Something like a choked sob and laugh broke from me before I started pulling at the thing to pry it from the wall, planting my foot next to it for extra leverage, as I yelled, "You bastard!" at the emotionless tech. Security caught me red—and soap less—handed, fingers curled around the dispenser and disheveled hair from whipping my head back and forth in the way I really threw my back into my efforts. I'm genuinely surprised I didn't get fired for nearly breaking work property. I should feel lucky that I wasn't left unemployed after the artificial consciousness rollout. And that I had a place to sleep, even if the proletariats don't get the kind of space the Elites do.

But I didn't feel lucky. I felt like a ghost. And I had to leave.

My running from a jungle of concrete to a forest of aliveness was meant to fix whatever is broken inside me. Instead, I'm here, imposing on the 'sacred' life of these people. I'm ruining—no... *disturbing* something important.

Because I'm not important.

Something clicks in my mind as two words barrel into my awareness. He said 'these people' as if he isn't exactly one of them. Surveying his features, I study him in quiet contemplation, wondering if he, too, doesn't belong anywhere.

He carries on, pulling me out of my thoughts and breaking the silence. "We have gone to extremes to ensure that it stays hidden. Somehow, you managed to pass through the barrier. We can't risk exposure; people cannot know we are here. The investigation on you will continue until the next full moon, which is in three weeks. Then, you'll face the Trials of Trust."

Those words grip my heart in a clenched fist, squeezing out everything except fear.

The space between us shrinks as he takes a measured step forward, and I take one backwards. He watches me like he knows I want to run, as if he knows my instincts before I do.

In unbroken composure, he continues, "Should we find you trustworthy, you'll be allowed to leave, and with our secrets. But if you aren't... we cannot risk everything here for one life."

I stare at him. "Oh," is all I can manage. *Pass or die.*

His informative tone cuts through me, as he says, "We'll be taking you out tomorrow where you'll show us how you got past the barrier."

I hesitate, but no emotion pricks my soul. Mental exhaustion and crashing adrenaline force me to slip into a numbness that I've become familiar with over the years.

"What barrier?" I say with an exasperated edge to my tone.

He stares at me, and in a tone devoid of emotion, instructs, "Give me your wrists."

The opal knife sits in his worn-out sheathe like he's had it for a million years, and I wonder if he'll use it if I refuse. The rope in his hand waits to take my freedom with a knot, and I can feel myself slipping, my mind dissociating as I can't make sense of this.

"Now," he demands.

My lungs pinch closed as it dawns on me that letting him bind me with it is my only chance at survival. I numbly lift my hands, feeling like I'm watching everything unfold outside of my body. His rough fingers reach for mine, turning my hands palms-up. A thread of shock weaves through me at the contact, piercing through the haze and making my stomach feel like it's falling thousands of feet through the Earth. I stare at him, but if he caught my reaction, he doesn't show it. Neanderthal wraps it around one of my wrists and I drop my eyes to his cheek, tracing the small scars along it. When he stalls his movement unexpectedly, my eyes fly up to see his are already on mine—wild and capturing my full attention.

An adjustment in his stance lets in more light from outside, illuminating the inside corner of my wrist as he holds it up. Carefully, he grazes his thumb across my skin. To my horror, a shudder betrays me. *What is happening?* Curiosity deepens the lines between his brows, parts his lips, and forms cracks in his composure. An urge to tug my arm back fails as he holds on firmly. His eyes find mine, looking at me as if I've slapped him in the face.

The spot he grazed his thumb over holds the small marking I was born with. "What? My birthmark?"

The word collides with something buried inside his mind. A second later, I'm watching his face assume an indifferent expression, his lips forming a straight line and features relaxing until they're flat and unreadable.

As if nothing just conspired between us, he continues to tie the rope around my wrist, covering the birthmark with a knot. Despite his efforts to mask, I catch his quick glance over my face before turning me to secure my wrists behind my back.

When he's done, he clips, "Turn to face me." I do, but I don't know where to look. Starting with a glimpse at his eyes, I avert my attention to the floor, his chest, the drawers... the *bed*. Untamed petrification fills me to the brim, my body starting to quiver.

He announces, "I'll be staying in here tonight." *That* confirms my fear. *In the bed?* Hiding the turmoil rummaging through me is a feat, and if I say anything right now, I don't trust my voice to stay level.

When I look between him and the bed nervously, he clarifies, "In that chair. To keep guard in case you try to escape. Which will not work in your favor when it comes to proving your trustworthiness."

Better than I thought. But also not better.

I say bluntly, "I'd like to request a female guard to stay here."

He watches me with a stern expression, deliberating. "Why?"

I don't want to insult him or his character, but I don't want to be in a vulnerable position, alone with a man I don't know or trust. Men aren't known to treat women as something to be protected, and I'll be damned if I trust this stranger to be anywhere near me if I fall asleep. "I'd just prefer a woman." I know I'm not in a position to propose my preferences, but it needed to be said.

My meaning settles into a thick blanket, wrapping around him and wiping away whatever indifference was there in his expression. The inference of my words shoves a dark emotion into his features, and I'm sure I've said the wrong thing. Upset him. Offended him.

"The men here do not take what is not given. You can sleep knowing I will not come near you, and neither will any other man."

And I'm supposed to just believe that? The irony of him expecting trust from me whilst they are treating me like a raccoon scrambling through their drawers of secrets nearly makes me laugh.

Dipping my chin and clenching my jaw, I realize he could never understand how actions speak louder than words—that a captor's promise to a prisoner doesn't hold much weight. "Whatever," I mumble frustratedly.

Guess I'm not sleeping tonight.

His rough voice beckons my attention. "As we are giving you a chance to prove your trustworthiness, allow me the same."

What am I supposed to do? Allow this motherfucker, who has just tied me up, to perch in a chair and watch me while I'm unconscious? He could come near me while I'm asleep—and it would be no coincidence that he also took away my ability to defend myself. He has done nothing to assuage the unsettled feeling that's been ingrained in me—to give me any reason to not stay constantly on guard.

But I don't have another choice.

"Fine," I bite out.

He watches me, clearly seeing I don't believe a single word that drips from his mouth. The air thickens in the silence, my lips in a tight line as I meet his examining gaze with a glare.

"Fine," he snaps back.

Fuck. I recap on how severely screwed I am, looking down before he can see the defeat scrawled through my features.

There's no way I can escape with him here. *He'll have to leave at some point.* Maybe in the morning, when there's some promise of light and ability to see where the heck I'm going. *They'll kill me on the spot if I'm caught trying.*

So don't get caught.

Ha, simple.

I could sneak off when he needs to pee. *Damn, why did I say that? I really need to pee.*

Inhaling, I nod exaggeratedly like a teacher's pet. "Okay. Stay or I die. Got it."

My voice takes on something sweet as I let the words fly. "I know there are other things you've said that should be consuming my thoughts, but the most pressing thing for me right now is that I really need to pee. Can you, I mean, can I..." At his 'not buying the sweet voice' flat look he gives me, I level with him. "Look, do you want me to piss myself?"

As if I've grown a second head, he just stares at me, but then a ghost of a smile touches his lips—as if it's against his better judgement. "I suppose you're the type used to full plumbing."

Why do I feel so offended by him saying that? Why is the concept of being familiar with proper plumbing making me feel like an uptight princess? *Fuck this guy.*

His expression slips into this mystifying consideration, and for the life of me, I can't place why he's looking at me like that. I guess I'll never know, because it disappears as he turns on his heel. "Let's go."

I walk one step in front of him as he guides me toward the pod-like structures, made of something that resembles bamboo. They can't be taller than three meters, or wider than two. He calls them something else, but I'm too distracted by looking at potential escape options to ask him to repeat himself.

"I'll be here," he says, stopping a few feet away.

I meet his harsh stare, the doorknob at my back as I fumble to open it.

"Damn, I was hoping you'd wipe for me," I remark with an eyeroll. The door slams shut on his icy cold expression before a snide reply has a chance to follow.

I stare at the toilet, which mostly resembles the ones at home. And to my shock, it actually smells nice in here. There's even a flush function. I don't want to know where these people's business goes and who cleans it. *That's a battle for another day.*

After struggling to get my pants down, I finally sit, exhaling a relieved breath as the pressure on my bladder slowly reduces. The next second has me begging the Divine that a spider or snake doesn't crawl over my foot. When I'm done, I see a pile of folded cloths on a floating shelf and hesitantly sniff them. It smells like sanitizer, or mint. Shrugging, I use one to wipe my hands.

Exiting the pod in a huff, I find Barbaric-Interrogator waiting with his arms crossed, leaning against the tree.

His expression is impassive as I approach, eyes locked on mine until I walk straight past him. Even though I hear his footsteps following, I say anyway, "Come on, then." It's my feeble attempt at evoking power and gaining some semblance of footing in this foreign and terrifying circumstance. But something inside me buzzes with nerves in his silence. *Who is this version of me that has found her voice? Who plays with fire?* When I left, something was altered within me, and I'm hanging onto it with bloodied claws.

My thoughts are interrupted by a massive root that trips me, nearly sending me to the ground before a rough pair of hands catches me by the waist. I gasp, though not from the near face-plant, but from the blazing and electric sensation from his touch.

He steadies me on my feet, and I can't help myself—I turn to study his face, to see if he felt what I felt. *Mistake.*

His face is inches from mine, my heart flailing at the sight before me. *Absolutely stunning.*

Shock at my own thoughts rolls through me as I stagger away from him, quickly putting distance between us.

Speechlessly, I stare at him. His expression is unreadable, body relaxed, yet somehow also an immovable force.

"Watch where you're going," he says, voice rough and impatient.

I scoff at my momentary lapse in judgement, where I might've considered him attractive. He's an asshole, and that is detestable. "I was. I'm just used to flat paths everywhere." My body isn't accustomed to lifting my feet for protruding roots and rocks.

He doesn't respond—only lifts his chin subtly in a gesture for me to hurry up and keep walking.

Sleeping—*or attempting to sleep*—with bound hands is miserable. Add in the heavy presence of this neanderthal posted as a guard behind me, and it becomes impossible. I can't stop rotating and adjusting in this stupid bed, trying to find a sliver of comfort. When I finally think I can tolerate a position, my arm falls asleep, mocking me. The numbness forces a groan from me as I roll more onto my front. *Creations, I miss my bed.*

A low chuff escapes him. *He's laughing at me.* Annoyance spreads like wildfire, fanned by his refusal to answer a single question I've asked all night.

Exhaustion loosens my tongue and sharpens the edge of my tone. "Do you really have to just sit there and watch me sleep?"

No answer.

I resort to mockery. "You must be important to get such a job."

He taunts under his breath, "Doesn't look like you're doing a whole lot of sleeping."

He speaks.

I retort, "Well, it's really hot, I don't often sleep with my hands bound like this, and... what else? Oh, that's right. I'm a literal prisoner who's fearing for her life. I have a pounding headache from the unbearable confusion, and I'm so dehydrated I can't even cry about it. So, you tell me, are those placid enough circumstances to drift away into a peaceful sleep?" The last words slice through the air like thin sheets of ice.

Surprise, he's ignoring me.

Irritation forces me to peer over my shoulder at him, using my glare as a desperate attempt to hurt him. Unflinching, he watches me with that maddening silent look of judgement.

Returning the expression, I press, "What? Stop staring at me."

The furrow deepens, his lips forming a tight line, and I swear on everything, my patience is truly being tested.

With a slight lift of his chin, he clips, "Sleep."

A dramatic exhale deflates my lungs, my eyes rolling before I turn to face the wall. "Why didn't *I* think of that?" I mutter, sarcasm laced thick in my voice.

I hated the idea of being stuck in here with him, blinded by darkness through the night, knowing he was sitting behind me in the pitch black. So, when he brought in the sunlamp, I was internally cheering, relaxing slightly as it lit the hut in a warm and burnt shade of yellow. But now, I retract my earlier relief. I didn't anticipate how much I'd want to be invisible from his scrutiny and this awkward tension.

The chair creaks, and I force myself not to turn toward the sound. *Toward him.* My ears strain, listening to the footsteps move across the floor, steadily paced and deliberate. A light breeze spills inside and rolls over my skin, making it immediately more tolerable in here. Peeking over my shoulder, I see him pinning the material to the door back. His fingers linger on the material for half a second before walking over to the table and picking up his cup of water. For a second, I think he might drink it, but instead, he walks over to me.

"Sit up."

Tentatively, I roll onto my back and awkwardly get up without using my hands to help.

"Water," he informs as I eye the cup outstretched to me.

I look up at him through my lashes, asking, "Are you going to untie me so I can take the cup, or just hover it near me as the beginnings of my torture?"

"Neither," he says unremorsefully before bringing it towards my lips, his other hand featherlight as it holds the side of my face, guiding me to tip my head back. My chin lifts, and I swallow my first sip. *Creations, the water tastes so different here.*

"More?" I rasp the question out, licking the meager moisture from my lips. He slowly pours more into my mouth, and I don't care that he drank from this cup earlier. I'm not freaking out over the intimate way he watches my eyelids drift closed, and how he lets me gulp it down to the last drop.

He pulls the empty cup away, but his gentle touch remains on my jaw as I look up at him, a pulse of aliveness thrumming through me. *He didn't have to do that.* I'm enchanted, surprised by the kindness I see in his eyes, but then he abruptly drops his hand, returns to his seat, and doesn't spare me another glance.

Part of me is grateful; the cool air sweeping over my skin is a relief. The other part? Stubborn. I'm reluctant to absolve my sharpness for a momentary gesture of goodwill from this brute of a man. *Brutus.* My captor. My Neanderthal-Interrogator. Whatever he is to me. *No. Stop it.*

Losing the battle, I force out, "Thanks."

As I lie down and turn back to the wall, I close my eyes, squeezing away the feelings and thoughts of this nightmarish day, scrambling for a replacement feeling to restlessness.

Instead, my mind latches onto something I haven't had time to process. Images loop, recalling how hard I fought for my life today. A part of me—deeper than bone, than breath—yearns to treasure life. I guess that makes sense, seeing as I left everything for a chance at happiness. Then what of the crushing sorrow that inhabits my soul? How do the two live within me side by side?

I roll back a bit to look out the door, to the stars. Something in me knew there was more. Maybe that's what I've been searching for this whole time. It's not a place, person, job, or hobby that will save me. It's not something out there that will push me to fight for my life. It's me. I've been searching for me. *How do I find you?* A spark sputters weakly inside my chest. There's more than this. There has to be.

An abrupt yawn stretches my jaw, halting my thoughts in protest of deeper analysis. My eyelids weigh a ton, and I don't fight to keep them open. Agreeing that my mind is overworked and done with thought for the night, my ears tune into the sounds of nature. I listen to the buzz of insects, the rustle of wind against trees, and the occasional gurgle of my stomach. I hope it's not loud enough for him to hear.

Without looking at Neanderthal, I ask him, "So, you're really going to stay awake all night?"

No response.

I give myself a courtesy smile before muttering under my breath, "Good chat."

Please don't fart in your sleep.

CHAPTER 4
LIFELINE

A mystical hum teeters on the edge of my awareness, stirring me awake. I'm trying to decipher the melody, but it's hazy and warped, like I'm underwater. Frowning, I inhale deeply through my nose as a distant revelation dawns on me. *That's not my alarm.*

Despite their protest, I force my eyes open. *What the—*

I freeze, disoriented. All I see in front of me is a beige canvas wall, and the burgundy blanket of my bed. Not my bed. The hut. Taken. Captive. The reality of my situation crashes into me at full speed, apprehension and shock lifting the hairs behind my neck.

Jerking to a sitting position, I only make it halfway as I'm abruptly stopped by my bound arms behind me. Acid churns in my stomach, threatening to rise up my throat in the sheer bewilderment that what happened yesterday was not a nightmare. Images flash, pushing against my skull and consisting of Interrogator-Neanderthal—how I promised not to fall asleep with just the two of us in here. Did he stay in that chair the whole night as he said he would? Or did he...

Panic controls my breathing, chest rising and falling in shallow breaths as I roll over onto my back. Through the sliver of morning light, I take my surroundings in. The chair he occupied is empty, and he's nowhere to be seen. My focus locks on the sleeves of the door, which are now drawn closed. The lamp is turned off. *When did that happen? Why?* If it were open, I would've woken up with the sun rising. *Is he the same? Did he do it, so as to not wake me? No.* I banish the absurd train of thought, wondering why the fuck I'm thinking about that right now.

Opportunity creeps into my next thought. *He's not here.* I'm alone, and presumed to be sleeping. Suggestions of escape rapidly fire inside my mind—visualizing ideas, then analytically discarding them as nonviable in a rotation. One thing stands out as a first step though, and that's becoming unbound. *I won't get far like this.*

Searching the room with new eyes, my jaw clenches. Everything is useless and soft. I need something sharp, fast.

My eyes rove over my body, locking on my laces. A memory from a movie flashes in my mind, where the girl slipped one through her zip ties and created enough tension for it to snap.

Will that work with rope? I need my hands in front of me.

Scanning the closed door, I hold my breath, hoping Neanderthal doesn't walk through right now.

A burst of adrenaline propels me upright, knees bent up to my chest. I bite down a grunt as I try scooting backwards to get my hands over my hips. Pulling my lips into a thin line, I bite out the words in my mind. *I can't fucking get it.*

Dropping to the floor and curling into a ball, I strain to get my wrists past my tailbone. Not even close. My breath hitches at the burning collision of frustration and urgency.

This is taking too long,

Moving onto my knees in a hurry, I contort my body and stretch my fingers toward my laces.

"Ah..." I grit my teeth against the way my back twinges. "Fuck," I whisper.

An indistinct scuffle outside makes me hold still as a statue, stress nauseating my stomach.

Don't puke.

An image of Neanderthal catching me like this floods my brain, sending me into a slight panic as my heart thumps against my ribcage.

But then, it's silent once more. *Too silent.*

Slowly, I rise, melting into the hut wall and edging toward the door. Through the narrow slit, I see someone sitting in a chair, back turned, head hung forward and—*you're kidding*—asleep. Not Neanderthal. A melody syncs in tune with the way I close my eyes, willing myself to calm down. The mellow strum of a guitar and rhythmic thump of drums sounds close, but not too close. That must be where everyone is. *Where he is.*

Hurry up.

I frantically search the hut, trepidation speeding my heart, once again, unsure of how long I have. But then, my eyes catch on the wooden chair, and my mind begins roughly piecing together a potentially stupid idea.

Its legs are tapered—thin enough to wedge between the rope and my wrists. Moving on light feet like a sneaky cartoon character, I steady my breath enough to listen beyond the melody. No footsteps outside, no moving shadows beyond the hut walls.

Nodding to myself in determination, I begin by using my foot to inch the four-legged chair quietly away from the table. When it's in the open space between the table, the bed, and the exit, I kneel with the seat to the chair at my back. Slowly, I lower myself until I'm sitting between my heels, and line the front leg of the chair to the center of the rope.

A sense of urgency hisses at me, telling me I'm running out of time.

Walking my shaky fingers down to the base of the leg, I awkwardly and carefully lift it in small movements, until I get it to be in line with the small gap between my wrists and the rope. But as I try to get it in the gap without being able to see what I'm doing, the leg ends up slipping through the gap between my back and my bound wrists. Desperation to get this right wills my head to drop back as I stifle a grunt before it tears through me.

Trying again, I lift the chair, carefully balancing it on its two legs. I feel it position above the gap between my wrists, and lean my shoulders back on the chair to put weight on it. The leg inches lower, and the rope tightens around my wrists as it tries to make room for the added object between the constraints.

Inching back slightly and propping myself higher, I arch back over the chair and drop my shoulders harder on the seat, feeling the leg pop through the gap, eliciting a mild thump as it connects with the floor. I hold my breath, sure that I just woke him up. Maybe it wasn't that loud? My heart doesn't get the memo of optimism as it thrums in panic.

But no one comes in. *Thank you to the Divine that he's such a shit guard.* That doesn't mean Neanderthal isn't on his way back from wherever he went, though. I bite the inside of my cheek to depict the physical reflection of how stress is gnawing at me.

Sitting back down on my heels, I use the weight of my body to hold the chair as I pull my wrists toward me, stretching the rope. Seething at the strain against my wrists, I curse internally as the frayed edges of the rope cut into my skin. Then, I curse Neanderthal for how tight he secured this. Yanking my hands again, I feel it loosen slightly, but the chair slips an inch. My eyes shoot to the door again, but no sound comes from outside.

I need more leverage.

Wrapping my fingers around the chair leg, I hold on, rising to my knees, my face scrunched up as I try keeping it from crashing to the floor.

I did it. A brief flutter of pleasant surprise in my heart urges me along.

Once the back of the chair is parallel to the floor, I shuffle backwards until my shins are propped against the two hind legs, my wrists still attached to the front leg. Pushing down with my shins so the chair doesn't move, I lean back, bending my elbows and pulling the rope taut as I wrench my hands upwards.

Creations, that stings.

Resting for a second, I suck in air through my teeth, the pain sharp as it cuts the skin. But I go again. And again.

Please don't snap this leg clean off.

There. More stretch.

The friction is painful against my skin, the burn from the rope making my fingers tremble slightly. But it's worth it, because I think I might have enough room.

Sliding my bound wrists down the length of the chair until it slips off, I test to see if there's enough room to pull one hand out. *Just. Maybe.*

I tuck my thumbs in, pulling and pulling despite the bite of skin breaking, and then I drag my tattered hand free.

In a state of doubt, I bring my hands in front of me, staring in awe at the free one while the rope hangs loosely around my other wrist. The muffled sound I make is somewhere between laughter and disbelief.

It worked.

Fixating on the torn skin for only half a second, I drop the rope to the floor, my mind already spinning to the next move.

The door is a risk with the sleeping guard and Neanderthal somewhere out there. Licking my teeth, I turn to face the back of the hut. I scurry over and brush my fingers against the base of the canvas, trying to lift it. But it's secured, bolted to the ground somehow by these posts. No gaps to crawl through. *Stupid, sturdy, bullshit tent.*

Panic gnaws at me, forcing my hands through my hair. Okay, options. *Dig?* Too slow. *Dammit.* My feet inch toward the door and I peer through the slit, trying to see beyond the immediate area. The treeline is right there. The guard is alone, and still sleeping.

Moving stealthily, I strain my neck to see if I can catch any movement... but I can't see or hear anyone nearby, and the music sounds distant. A shot of confidence nudges me to hook my finger around the canvas, slowly drawing one side of the fabric door back an inch. When the guard doesn't stir, I press my lips together, wincing as I pull it back further to see more. Nothing. No one. Either I'm covert as shit, or I'm completely lucky. *I can sneak past him.*

My fingers release the canvas, letting it fall closed.

A tremor runs through me, adrenaline fighting with nerves. I gas myself up, shaking my hands and bouncing on my toes. *Come on.*

My heart pounds, but not enough to mask the strange pang in my stomach. Unease intrudes my awareness, flurrying in my gut—there and gone before I can name it. *Focus.*

I map out a plan. Step one, get out. The music seems to be coming from the right, so step two consists of going to the back of the hut and running left. Step three, get to higher ground and see where the hell I am. Step four, get back to the trekking trail and disappear.

Nodding to myself, I close my eyes. *Don't think, just do.*

I step toward the door, one foot out, when the guard stands up abruptly. No. *No, no, no.*

Holding my breath, I don't dare move a single muscle. I don't have time to slip back, and I can't risk making a single sound. He half-tilts his head toward me, showing me a hint of his profile but not looking at me. *It's over.*

To my shock, I watch in slow motion as he turns... away. He actually walks away. Toward the music.

Barely blinking, I track his every step. My muscles lock, refusing to loosen until he disappears behind a massive barn-like structure.

A laugh sputters past my lips and I slap my hand over my mouth. *You're joking.* Maybe I'm not an idiot for thinking I could escape, or maybe someone is looking out for me. I look up to the sky, the stars hidden behind daytime, knowing that Orion has my back. Always. *Thank you.*

A thundering beat slams against my eardrums like echoing stomps. I whip my head around. No one. Where's it coming from? Slowly, I lay my hand on my chest and feel my heartbeat pound in rhythm. *Just me.*

I fix my posture.

Focus.

Run.

How can it feel like I've been running for an instant and a lifetime simultaneously?

Bursting through the forest in a sprint, I try to remain inconspicuous, but thanks to my alarming aerobic capacity and correlated wheezing, I'm a pretty fucking loud spider monkey. Two fingers dig into my ribs, trying to dull the piercing stitch. Giving myself a minute to catch my breath, I do a sweep of my surroundings. As the seconds pass, my scanning becomes more urgent and paranoid, the sensation of being stalked creeping up on me.

A jolt seizes my gut, my breath whooshing from my lungs at the abrupt feeling of freefalling. *Something's wrong.* I hunch over, heaving with my hands on my knees as something inside me creates the urge to look in the direction of the village.

A voice flashes in my memory. Neanderthal-Interrogator. "...in case you try to escape... which will not work in your favor of proving to be trustworthy."

"Fuck," I grit out.

Panic spirals through me, and I try to categorize my thoughts to align with my best chance at survival. *Keep running; try to escape—but I don't know where I am. They can find me and kill me. Go back? Apologize. Honor the agreement with Neanderthal and the tribe. Maybe they forgive me. Maybe they wipe me away like a spec of dust and no one will hear my last words. Sneak back. Act as if I never left.* Wait. My eyes find the blood on my wrists. *How would I cover that up?*

I press my palms into my closed eyes. All options feel damning. A groan drags out as I tip my head back to the sky.

Lost. Alone.

Fear trickles in, drawing my feet to move toward a tree and forcing the back of my head to meet its scaly bark. Seeking solace and feeling defeated, my eyes drift shut. I need a way out. I need to breathe. I need to picture the list. *I love surrendering control and finding flow.* Point number... *Shit.* Anguish rips through me, spinning me toward the village. *My journal.* Pure, deep-rooted pain that I gathered over years guided my pen as I scrawled that sixteen-pointed list. The guide to loving myself. The compass of my sanity.

Every entry, every point, every reminder of who I want to be is trapped in my backpack, in that interrogation hut. I haven't memorized it. The loss of those words fills me with sorrow, from my toes to my skull. Tears brim the lines of my eyes, falling automatically—unceremoniously. I've hung onto that journal like a lifeline, as if it's the one thing tethering me to the ground.

Can I really just let it go? Will I really risk going back for it?

Slowly, I drop to a crouch, staring aimlessly in the direction I just ran from. I don't have the experience or fitness to outrun them for the days it'll take me to navigate my way out of this forest. I could ignore that, and try to go home anyway... but for some unfounded reason, I feel called to the village. Maybe the journal is the tipping point that drives my motive, maybe it's something else I can't name, but I need to go back. On the surface, it feels like a stupid decision. Not worth it. But I know I have to, and I'll just have to trust that instinct.

My adrenaline crashes. Numb and deflated, I push off the tree, rising to walk.

I zone out the whole way back, disconnected from my body by the time I see the village materialize ahead of me. The haze of tears trailing mechanically down my cheeks are the last I allow to fall. By the time I cross the treeline, I feel nothing.

Not a soul fills the space. The distant melodies keep their rhythm as if my escape never happened. Instead of feeling hopeful that the alarms aren't sounding, that I might actually sneak back in, I feel worried. *Something doesn't feel right.*

I glance over my shoulder. Nothing. My mind teeters on the edge of gaslighting, the surety of being watched dismissed.

Picking up my pace, I dart through each open space between huts, finally reaching mine. *Mine—ha. What a weird thought.*

Glancing over my shoulder one last time, I pull the canvas aside and slip in. I release a breath, turning to look for the rope, and startle in shock. The music halts. The world stops. *He's here—*

sitting at his post, holding the bloody rope in loose fingers between his legs. *I'm caught.*

Neanderthal's observance emanates controlled fury, locking my feet in place. But more striking to my core is something beneath the anger. Something I can't decipher.

My pleading eyes stay locked onto his withering stare before his focus drops to my wrists. I already know what's there. Raw skin, blood... Evidence. When his eyes meet mine again, I halt, unable to look away from the way it captures me.

This is it; he said when if I tried to escape, he'd kill me.

CHAPTER 5
ALL IS NOT FORGIVEN

I didn't realize just how delusional I was in thinking I could sneak back in or apologize, and it would be okay. His staunch, icy glare says otherwise.

The silence between us is thick and swarming with emotion. I move on instinct, my mind screaming in resistance as I step through the condensed air between us. Toward him. Slowly.

His coldness switches to something primal, more focused. Every fiber of his being zeros in on me, tracking each muscle. I can see his mind working, ranking the level of threat I pose.

I slow even more, closing the final step between us. Standing before him, I'm forced to grovel, murmuring, "I'm sorry."

His jaw ticks, and my focus drops to the rope between his fingers. The only way I survive this is by truly accepting the agreement. He has to believe I won't try to escape again.

I hate this. Breathing deep into my lungs, I swallow the injustice—choking on it. I hate that I have to stand here, suffocating in his presence, pretending there's any real choice left to me. It's this, or death.

Flexing my hands, I loathe what I'm about to do. Slowly, I reach for the rope. His expression holds, not sparing me a hint of a reaction, but that energetical ferocity of his simmers beneath his skin. My fingertips brush the fibers of the rope, and I tug. For a second, he hesitates. *Is he refusing me?* But then, his curiosity wins out over what I suspect is protocol here. He releases it.

Wrapping it once, then twice, around my wrist, I bite the inside of my lip, refusing to grimace as the frayed rope licks my raw flesh. The act of yielding is sharp in my chest and against my skin.

I lift my eyes back to his, and he's already watching me as I try to refasten it, struggling to do it by myself. True to his role, the interrogator's eyes pour over every fraction of me, collecting information, even if the rest of his face adorns a mask of blank boredom.

Before I register what's happening, he moves.

One second, he's sitting. The next, he's on his feet with the rope wrenched from my grasp and into his. I stumble back in shock, but he closes the distance effortlessly. The rope drops to the floor as silent rage ripples from his skin and wraps around me. The back of my legs hit the bedpost; there's nowhere to go. Inches from me now, I feel the full weight of his scrutiny, knowing this look could wither anyone to surrender. But if he doesn't accept my apology, I'm done for anyway, so I decide that I won't go out as a coward.

His eyes dart between mine, looking for something. The frown he wears deepens like it's just out of grasp, but something he sees disrupts the search. Only for a second, and barely noticeable, his gaze softens. He traces my features, clearly noticing the evidence of tears streaked through dirt on my face, and the puffiness of my eyes. Embarrassment rises in me like a slow burn, heating my face and forcing me to look away from him.

Shame crawls up my spine and sits on my shoulder.

Coward.

Seconds ago, I was brave, swearing not to shrink before him. Now, I'm trembling beneath his judgement.

I can't take this.

I open my mouth to speak, but he abruptly stops me before I can even start. "No." The word is lethal. Sharp. My jaw locks shut as the silence rings with his tone.

I raise my chin with a hardened expression, facing his unyielding stare. *I don't care that he knows I cried.* He's pissed I tried to escape? Well, that's idiotic, considering *escaping* tends to allude to someone being held against their will. You would think the victim had more right to be the angry one, not the one who lost their hostage. And I express that much with the way I clench my fists at my side, straighten my spine half an inch. I'm a walking dead man, who's going down with a fire burning inside—one I've searched for years to ignite, and this bastard will *not* extinguish it.

Appraising the shift in me, I see his expression melt into something else. It's a stretch, but I think I recognize the faintest hint of respect in the way he relaxes the tense lines of his face.

Without warning, I feel his fingertips graze my arm, just above the raw skin. I might be sweating, but I force my expression into impassiveness before he can see what his proximity does to me. On the inside though, my internals run wild. There's a tenderness in his touch that I want to welcome, and that thought alone shocks me into yanking my arm away. But he's faster, a warning glint in his eyes before he's lifting it so he can inspect the wound.

I hold my breath as his chest vibrates a deep hum of contemplation. The sound is more to himself than to me, as if responding to a conversation I can't hear.

The chaos inside my chest, my gut, and my brain won't cease. The storm of contrasting emotions tangles with logic until nothing makes sense. The indescribable sensation from his touch. The anticipation of death or trial. The continued scrutiny. Everything...

I can't take it.

I snap.

Tipping my head down, a short, guttural sound of annoyance rips from me. Turning a glare on him, I spit out, "This is worse than just killing me already."

His body remains unmoving, but I'm cut by the sharpness of his expression.

In turn, the words bleed from me. "You don't accept my apology, my attempt to seek atonement, or a second chance. Got it. So, just pull out that knife and shove it in my chest. I can't bear this—"

A tense, tight-lipped look stops me before I can finish. His eyes permeate an intensity that promises never to cease. "You were warned what would happen if you tried to escape. That it wouldn't prove your trustworthiness."

Fear whirls through me in a taunting motion, its blades slicing up my insides like a figure skater on ice, and all I can do is stand here and endure it.

"You thought you could escape without consequence, then realized that you couldn't manage it."

He watches me, and I absorb his patronizing insult without showing the bite it takes. *He's not finished.*

"You're back in this hut because your grand escape failed in less than an hour. Judging by the red in your eyes, I'd wager your tenacity lasted no more than twenty minutes." He looks at me unimpressed, his lips curling down at the sides. "Then, you try to re-secure the rope... to show me what? That you're sorry? Trustworthy? That all should be forgiven?"

His voice doesn't waver as he enunciates, "No. All is not forgiven."

Disgust twists my expression. His retelling, his perspective, reducing it to something pathetic... It stuns me speechless. The stupor fades as pride forces my lips to move.

"Oh yes, how pathetic of me to try to escape death from random fucking forest freaks who kidnapped me! Please tell me, exactly *how* stupid am I, *sir?*" Sarcasm drips like poison from the last word.

His voice levels as he points out, "I never called you pathetic or stupid."

I don't mean to hold my breath, but the way he says it—the way he looks at me. The danger of him. It all throws me off balance.

His head tilts. "Those are your words." The warmth vanishes as quickly as the trap was set. "And you won't get an argument from me."

Despicable ogre.

Militantly, he commands, "It's over. Sit down."

I seethe.

Raising his brows a mere fraction, he dares me to disobey.

The shrivel of civility in me fights the urge to shove him, spit on him, scream at the top of my lungs. I refuse my primitive rage and lower onto the edge of the bed.

He crouches in front of me, taking my hands in his without hesitation—inspecting my wrists closer. His callous fingers hold my quivering hands, and I watch, perplexed. *What the hell is he doing?*

My shoulders nearly touch my ears with stress, the tremble spreading to my knees.

Let go of me.

Don't ever let go.

Without looking away from me, his voice cuts through the air, startling me as he calls out a name. "Sage." It's not loud enough to bring all the dispersed noises outside to a forceful stop, but somehow it does. Staring at him is the only thing I can do right now as the power pulsating from him dawns on me anew. His voice, that name, and the melody that was playing during my escape attempt haunt my mind in a ringing echo.

CHAPTER 6
A TEST OF HESITATION

I grit my teeth, pleading for anger to overturn my trepidation.

"So, Sage is... what? The executioner? Is this the part where I get to beg the leaders for it to be quick? Where are they? Getting their interrogator to do their dirty work?"

His voice edges with warning as he says, "You're either foolish or reckless to be in this position and dare speak to me like that." His voice carries no amusement, no reveal of emotion.

The way he speaks confuses me. He sounds modern. Civilized. Despite the archaic system of rights, I can tell he's educated. *How did you end up here, Neanderthal?*

Inhaling, I rebut, "Yeah, well, dead man energy, I suppose."

A subtle lift of his brow, whilst the smallest of gestures, has the ability to immediately make the space around us pull taut. Although, it's not the tangible hate I've come to expect, but something else. *Intrigue?* It catches me off guard, but then I rationalize that my brain must be fried from the day's events. I seem to have lost the capability to function properly, and now I'm imagining things.

His eyes lower to my wrists. Subtly—and so quickly I almost miss it—his thumb brushes over my birthmark. A small muscle in my arm flinches, eyes widening and lifting to meet his, but his focus is fixed on the mark.

The small shape on my wrist is something I pondered over when I was young, in a way that was idle and dismissive. Eventually, I forgot about it. But he seems perplexed by it, and part of me is desperate to know why. I can't bring myself to ask, though...

Before I can react, footsteps sound outside the hut. The door whips open, and a woman enters. The air changes. She wears a neutral expression, moving with certainty. I marvel at her braids, how they swirl like a masterpiece along her scalp before extending down her body, past her waist. She's calm, radiating something homely and vast—a feather floating in a light breeze.

She approaches us, a bowl cradled in her hands. It looks fashioned from clay, painted with unique patterns. I process every detail of her, and the way her presence competes with Neanderthal's to fill the room. Carefully handing the bowl to him, she turns to observe me.

I gasp. A drift of wind floats through my mind, imposing. My shoulders tense. *What the hell is that?*

I'm being cracked open. I feel the layers peel back, the drift sifting through the folds of my being, shaking loose the memories and emotions I've buried deep. *She's staring through me.* Beyond me. As if she's downloading every therapy session I've ever been to. I should feel exposed—violated. I should hate it. But I don't. The transparency is a relief, as if taking off a mask I thought would never fully leave me. For a reason unknown to me, I trust her. I let her in, and float further into the trance.

The spell breaks as she turns her attention to Neanderthal, my shoulders slumping at the release of her inexplicable hold on me. I blink, the connection slipping like sand between my fingers, like I've just woken from a dream. I watch her profile as she gives him a look that I don't understand. His lips pulse into a thin line before giving a terse nod in response.

The weight of the woman's attention lands on me once more before turning to leave, but my eyes find the ground and stay there. Whatever that was, it felt out of body. I don't understand. *I don't know if I want to.*

The hut door sways open and shut as she exits, and I'm left with Neanderthal and the bowl in his hands. The white foam, potent and pungent, induces a visceral reaction as I stare at it.

"Poison?" I whisper the question aloud.

I've thought about how I'd die before—I mean, everyone does. We all hope for it to be quick and painless. Merciful. But that's not what I'm granted. I look away from the poison and aim my focus on the wall, just as a stifling thought itches for acknowledgment. *My life rests in his palms.*

I lift my chin, forcing acceptance and whatever bravado I can muster onto my face, swallowing back the acid burning my throat. In my peripheral, I catch the slight dip of his chin as he glances at the bowl. Curiosity taps at the edge of my mind, pushing me to wonder if I'll find remorse or hesitation in his expression. Instead, I find that irksome, blank look.

I mirror his nonchalance, begging the tremble to leave my voice as I say, "Let's not draw this out. You owe me at least that much."

The tense lines of his face relax as he realizes something. *Good.* He knows I won't resist, and maybe he'll do it fast.

The corner of his mouth lifts slightly. *Wait. Is this sadistic bastard enjoying this?*

Revulsion claws its way up my throat and past my tongue. "You're sick. You find this funny?"

His gaze doesn't waver as he dips the brush into the poison, coating the bristles. My pulse kicks up, rage and adrenaline knocking against my chest. I don't move. I don't cower.

He lifts the brush to my split and damaged skin, and my body betrays me. I wince, pulling away.

No point in running. No point in resisting. It'll be over soon.

I coax my hands back toward him, reality making me ramble nervously. "So, you don't do tablets? No injections? I could just eat it, take a spoonful. Seems kind of prolonged, and well, cruel to do it... Wait, how does this work exactly? Absorbs into my bloodstream through my wounds? Fuck. I guess nothing here resembles what's out there, so at least you're consistent—"

"Stay still." His instruction cuts through my words.

Licking my dry lips, I joke, "Not even a last meal?" My laugh sounds hollow and distant. "At least I won't starve to death now. That's kind of you." Resorting to humour is less about making him want to laugh, and more to do with stalling the inevitable.

The first stroke lands, cold at first. Then comes the unforgiving, fiery singe. I don't fight. I don't pull away—telling myself I'm not a coward. The truth is, I surrender to my fate. Starting to dissociate is my only reprieve from a racing mind and shallow breaths. This is it—a slow, painful death.

The burn intensifies with every passing second. Watching him apply it to my skin is jarring. The deliberate act of poisoning me contradicts how he does it with a tender and careful touch. His disdain and certainty that I deserve this is obvious. Although, it doesn't match the way he gently moves my hand to rest on my knee. Or the way he wraps his fingers around my other hand, beginning its application like brushing dust off a priceless artifact.

My eyes shut, and my focus begins to fade. I only know he stops when I hear the faint clink of the brush against the bowl, then the bowl against a table. The air is too hot and thin as I try to draw it into my lungs. *Now we wait.*

Thoughts wander through the halls of my mind, unleashable. For so long, I've fought for a sense of worth. A reason to exist. How ironic that my search for belonging led me here, to the absolute opposite. I bite hard on my bottom lip. *Do not fucking cry.* My chin trembles, and I fight the weight of emotions dragging me under, choking me. *Do not*. Turning my head away, I internally beg myself to stop.

Sorrow expands inside me as if it's alive, moving through my whole body like a snowball rolling down a mountain, collecting any feeling or memory to add to it until I'm sprinting from an avalanche of all the things that hurt me. As the snow buries me alive, and everything goes quiet and dark, I discover a feeling I never thought I'd find within myself. *Forgiveness*. I didn't fight to escape, or to keep running, because I knew I wouldn't stand a chance against him and an entire village. I can hate myself for coming back, but in that moment, it felt right. That wasn't cowardice. That was reality.

Before coming here, I fought. I invested years, money, and energy, pouring it into anything and everything that could help me heal whatever's broken inside of me. Into forgiving myself. Loving myself. All of it amounted to... *my list*. A damn list that I live by like a sworn code. And I honored it. Maybe not perfectly, and not always. Not yet in the ways I meant to. But I tried.

A small, bittersweet smile pulls at my lips, despite the tremor in my limbs.

"How long?" The whisper barely makes it out.

I don't expect an answer, or for him to stay. But then, a ghost of warmth skims across my cheek. *His fingertips*. My eyes snap open as my head jerks back. The contact is so swift that I question if it happened, until I catch the tail end of his hand lowering to his lap. The concern behind his eyes vanishes, and that practiced indifference replaces it. But I know what I felt. *He just wiped my tears away*.

I study his eyes, mapping every line of his features the way I might read the ocean for its next wave. He studies me just as intently.

Straightening, I decide to let my walls crumble, knowing there's no point keeping them up now. My voice is soft, but steady—stripped of everything but truth. "I understand why you have to do this, but I just want you to know... I would've never told anyone about this place. I didn't come to disrupt your peace."

My breath hitches as despair grips tight around my heart, filling it with coal. Averting my eyes and fighting to keep it together, I continue, "I was out here looking for my own sense of peace."

My chin trembles again, my head hanging low as tears threaten to spill again. "I really tried." My voice cracks on the last word.

He says nothing. It doesn't surprise me. In some ways, it's easier this way—talking to a wall. But another part of me is hurting, because I'll die alone.

The tension in his jaw has eased, but the expression he wears is impossible to name. Not pity. Not regret. *His eyes.* They betray him for a fraction of a second, like he's seeing me differently.

"Stella." He says my name soothingly.

He's too close. Too focused on me. Tunnel visioned.

The sound of my name on his lips, hushed and deliberate, sends a shudder skipping down my spine.

I frown at my own reaction, my mind catching on the absurd and inconsistent whirlwind of my emotions.

This man is murdering me. I should be thinking about how to survive this, but all I can think about is his stupid face and how it might feel beneath my fingertips. How my hands might trace along his jaw and trail down the center of his chest. He tracks my attention, as if he can see the fantasy unfolding behind it. The muscles in his chest tense, a sharp gasp pulling through his nostrils.

I jolt at the sound, yanked back to reality, questioning if I accidentally touched him. *I didn't.* I should not be thinking about him like this, and the certainty of that makes my pulse scarily unsteady. Because I can't stop. *What the hell is wrong with me?*

He leans back the slightest inch. Cautious. An internal conflict seems to be waging, as this magnetic force within him reaches out for me.

I hesitate to meet it. *Am I really seeing this...* The way his features are evolving to one of longing. *The cusp of death is fucking with me.* A spike of nerves tears through my desire, and I peel my eyes from his, forcing them to focus on a tiny, loose thread in the hut wall.

"I need to tell you something." His voice cuts through the daze I had slipped into, his words yanking my eyes back to his and tugging at my chest for an unknown reason.

Clearing his throat, he admits, "I can no longer—"

"Stop." The blurted word silences him.

Heat rises beneath my skin as I plead, "I don't want my final moments to be an argument, insults, or whatever else you're about to say. Just leave me to do this alone."

He has the audacity to look offended. Whatever conspired between us lingers nearby, but it's pushed aside by the heaviness of my confusion. After everything he's said to me... sentencing me to death by poison. I start to turn away, but he moves to stay within my eyeline.

"I believe you're drawing a conclusion without all the facts," he says formally, a stark contrast to the sheltered concern in his expression. Against my will, my eyes trace a line from his cheek, down along his jawline, and linger on his lips for a second too long.

He studies me, then he's adjusting his posture, subtly stretching out his neck as if he feels it, too. As if he's resisting it.

I gulp thickly. "I've accepted my fate."

The space between us changes. A rush of something wild and desperate charges the air. I'm fueled by my need to live before I die.

Convinced I see the same want in his eyes, in the barest parting of his lips as his eyes wander over my features... I consider it. Then, I decide. I don't want to leave this world the way I lived the majority of it. Right now, I'll act like who I aspired to be when I wrote that list. Valiant. Confident. Authentic.

Fuck it.

I don't hesitate.

I reach up, my fingertips brushing his cheek.

He clasps my hand, holding it mid air, but he doesn't pull away.

My heart thumps in my chest as I wait, giving him time to decide if he wants this, too. Time I don't have. At first, his brows pinch slightly, but then his eyes drop to my lips. His hand is still holding mine when he rests it back on my knee, fingers squeezing gently in a pulse of reassurance. I interpret it as he doesn't want me to touch his face, maybe because of the story behind the scars, but that's all he doesn't want.

I lean in an inch, closing the distance slowly.

He doesn't move away. Instead, his other hand lifts to tuck a piece of hair behind my ear. Bridging what little space remains, his chin dips toward me the faintest fraction.

A breath, warm against my lips. The heartbeat in my throat.

Half a second before our mouths meet, he moves.

His thumb and forefinger catches my chin, holding me in place.

My body tenses. Studying the expression on his face, all I see is hesitation. *He's rejecting me.* A blush crawls up my neck.

"Stella." He says it like it pains him. Like he doesn't want to say what he's about to.

My frown melts into a slow, understanding nod. I tear his energy off me like ripping velcro strips apart as humiliation bobs her head to the side in an 'I told you nobody wants you' way.

"I need you to listen," he rasps. Something's different in his voice. It feels like...

My stomach hollows. He's speaking to me as if we're familiar. More than strangers.

The tip of his tongue darts out to wet his bottom lip, making a *tsk* sound when he finally says, "That solution I just put on your wounds... It's medicine."

I blink once. Twice. Three times. The words unravel my sanity. Comprehension swarms through me as the entire encounter breaks into segments, replaying in my mind. My dying bravery was admirable. But without the dying part... Humiliating. *Black hole, where are you?*

"No." My voice is too loud, forged from what's beneath the word. Confusion, relief, and a supremely-awful flush creeps into my expression. "It's poison," I add with confidence—hope.

A shadow of something crosses his face before his eyes narrow at me briefly. "Is that your wish?"

He's seeing too much.

A pin drops in my empty stomach, forcing me to answer too quickly. "No."

Unease courses through me and I wrap my fingers around my thumbs, squeezing my hands into fists. If I deny wishing for that, why are his words ringing in my ears?

I'm just tired.

His mouth is firm as he exhales slowly through his nose, the lines of his face falling flat as if reading my thoughts.

Pushing my chin forward with a glare, I ask him 'what are *you* looking at?' in silent defense. I think my reaction stems from embarrassment. I'm reduced to something akin to a small child wanting to pull the covers over their head. The shame is so powerful, I have to hide it behind a reinforced mask of rage. I will not let another brick crumble and become even more vulnerable in front of him. *I've already revealed too much.*

His gaze slides away from mine. "Well, I'm sorry to be the one to tell you. You're not dying." His voice is distant. Curt. He's so disgusted he won't even look at me. Anger rises hot in my chest. *He's judging me?*

With a clear voice, the words seethe past my lips. "Don't you *dare* pretend to know me." Glaring at his profile, I let the words fly like daggers. "You're so quick to judge. Can I try? Let's review. You let me think I was dying. You let me almost kiss you, under false pretenses. You're pissed at me for having negative feelings, which by the way, surpass your miniscule understanding of me. You *manipulated* me."

When he turns his head sharply back toward me, there's a fire behind his eyes I nearly flinch at, but I catch it in time. My pulse hammers as finishing words rip out of me. "And that's just the last ten minutes. So, tell me. How high is that horse *exactly*?"

A huff. A feigned dismissal. But I saw the real reaction before he cloaked it. *Fury. Regret.*

"Nothing to say? How predictable of you." My tone drips in smug arrogance. "You let me think you were poisoning me! I spilled my..."

Oh, shit. No. My dying speech. Both hands drag down my face as the memory punches me in the gut.

A taunt glides past his tongue. "Your parting words were quite dramatic."

My jaw drops open, voice rising to become incredulous as I ask, "What is wrong with you?"

The nonchalant composure fractures as his face hardens to something militant. "If I wanted you dead, I'd slit your throat and be done with it."

I huff, making my voice overly sweet as I flutter my lashes at him. "Wow, thank you. I feel *so* much better now."

Ignoring my comment, he continues. "And I let you believe that it was poison because you were revealing relevant information—an insight I deemed vital. You drew your own conclusions, and I don't apologize for that." His voice is even, detached.

I scoff before laughing bitterly. "I'm a *person*. You write off the emotional hell that just rained down on me... because it was tactically beneficial to you?" My voice drops to a hiss. "What was the rest of it, then? What's your logical work-around for that? Or was it just some twisted cherry on top for you?"

He leans forward slightly, his voice low when he asks, "Just so I'm clear, you mean when *you* came onto *me*?" A cold shock ripples through me, sharp and sudden.

"That was a test," he informs, his tone growing more accusing. "It was incredibly telling that you were going to kiss someone else while wearing that gold band on your finger."

I lean back, face contorting in offense. "Just a test?"

"Obviously." A tick in his jaw winds the coil tighter on the tension between us until I feel my guts twisting with it.

Asshole.

I turn away in embarrassment and nod at the wall, muttering, "Right." Quickly, I push the feeling away and face him again, rising to stand as he looks up at me.

I spit out, "You know nothing about why I wear this ring." Needing distance between us, I charge a few steps away, shoving my hands onto my hips, fingers digging in. *Slow your breathing*. "You just make assumption after assumption."

Footsteps—*his*. Then he's in front of me. "Tell me."

Without meeting his moronic face, I scoff. "Why? You've already made up your mind."

He swipes my hand, bringing my ring finger up to hover between us. "There's a clear ideology around this band, on *this* finger. Deductive reasoning." His voice stays collected, an undertone of surety that pisses me off.

Snatching my hand away, I glare at him with a burn of rage so powerful it might consume me. "Your world is so black and white. For your information, since my trustworthiness is life or death, this ring is a commitment *to* myself, *from* myself." I rip the ring off, showing him the inside of it. The engraving is in a tiny cursive scrawl.

iptfm

I explain the acronym to him, my voice betraying me and coming out meeker than the matter-of-factly tone I intended. "I promise to find more."

There is a little love heart on the other side, but I don't explain that it's a symbol for something sacred to me. That one I keep to myself, letting him assume it's just simply a heart.

Without seeing his reaction, I shove it back on my finger and keep pacing. The hut feels smaller. My eyes lock on the ground, but I'm not seeing anything through the mess of emotions crashing into each other.

I whirl around, ready to yell... then freeze. He's already looking at me. Differently. Realizing it's the truth, and his mistake.

So, I shut my mouth and tread back and forth, unable to stop moving as I try to sort through my thoughts. I'm so mad at him—and embarrassed. With that said, I can't ignore the relief at the fact that it wasn't poison he put on my wrists. But I'm angry at the disappointment that flashes through me at the same time. My next thought is filled with an image of our lips close together, the way we responded to each other. That's not... I didn't imagine it. *Right?* We met one day ago. *Stop acting insane.* Slamming my eyes shut, I focus on breathing.

There's an imaginary angel on my shoulder, whispering thoughts of compassion and understanding. Their words remind me that he was just trying to help me. Maybe he did try to tell me, and I kept cutting him off. Another voice rebuts the angel, saying that I am spiraling in the first place, because of him. He's why I'm hurt and humiliated. *He let me make a fool of myself.* My hand clasps my throat as the breaths refuse to come in. Where the *fuck* am I? Why is this happening? I need to get out of here. Everything catches up to me, ramming forcefully into my chest and crushing it.

"Stop," he commands.

The order is effortless, convincing. Despite myself, I stop pacing without turning to face him.

"You'll notice the burn on your wrists has ceased. They'll heal quickly." His hand moves, trailing up the inside of my arm. A rush of heat unfurls inside me at the contact, overpowering the cusp of panic I was on. He brushes his fingers just below my birthmark, careful not to touch the red skin that's streaked with rope burn. My muscles stiffen, every ounce of attention snapping to the rough feel of his skin.

"You're okay. You're safe." His voice is low. Soothing. It stuns me enough to ease the slicing anxiety a fraction.

"Safe," I scoff.

"Look at me."

I wait until the last second before obliging.

He leaves behind a whisper of affection as he draws his fingers away. I scold myself for noticing.

For missing it.

"Killing you... is an inconvenience. Don't try to escape again." A threat and plea in one.

Before I can respond, he strides to the door, holding one side open and nodding to someone on the other side. Seconds later, they enter, but not before bowing to Neanderthal. I pull a face at the sight. *The last thing he needs is a bigger ego.* He moves to take the seat Neanderthal occupied last night. *Who is this guard? Is he temporary?*

My eyes glue to Neanderthal, and no matter how hard I try to decode, his whispered instructions to the temporary guard are foreign to my ears. The guard looks over to me, but the man who just shredded my emotional wellbeing—*semi-wellbeing*—to pieces, doesn't spare me a glance. He half-turns his head toward me, but just before our eyes meet, his lungs fill, jaw locks, and then he's gone.

CHAPTER 7
UNCIVILIZED

Temporary Guard sits in the chair, crossing his ankle over his knee.

I can feel his attention on me every now and then, and it's unsettling. I sink into the bed, hugging a pillow and sulking like a teenager—stewing over the frustrating pull I have toward Neanderthal, who clearly mentally compares me to dog shit on the bottom of his shoes.

Who does he think he is?

Halfway through replaying the ordeal with Neanderthal again, I roll my eyes like it might hit refresh on my brain. *New thoughts, please.*

A sudden sound—the clearing of a throat—surprises me. I flick my eyes sidelong at Temporary Guard, who casually looks away. If he was about to speak, he changed his mind.

Ignoring him, I sift through my thoughts, boredom settling in like a heavy fog. I startle back into the room when the chair creaks, his leg uncrossing and finding the floor in a soft thump, paired with an exaggerated exhale. This time, I pointedly look at him.

His eyes lift to mine, looking at me through his lashes. I think he might speak, because he opens his mouth like he's about to, but then he pushes his tongue into his cheek, closes his mouth, and averts his gaze.

For goodness' sake, I am not in the mood.

"Yes?" I ask impatiently, sitting up with the pillow clutched to my chest.

He hesitates, studying me.

Try again—be more approachable. In a friendlier tone, I ask, "Did you want to say something?"

Nothing. Just loaded, deafening silence.

Then, he speaks. "Can I ask you a question?"

My eyes widen a fraction as nerves pick at my ribs. *I hate that question.*

Clearly reading my expression, he purses his lips. "I don't have to. I was just curious about something. But it's okay."

I blink at him. He speaks English well. He seems emotionally intelligent, and reads social cues efficiently. In fact, everyone I've come across does. *Something doesn't make sense.*

Lifting my chin, I wager, "Only if I can ask one in return."

Curiosity gleans in his eyes, a small smile touching his lips. "You first."

Drumming my fingers against the pillow, I think over varying options before settling on one. "If you, the leaders, and I'm guessing everyone else here, speaks fluent English... What makes Neanderthal the appointed interrogator?"

He lets out a short laugh, then repeats, "Neanderthal?"

Dipping my head to the side, I rattle off the list of names I've mentally assigned him. "Neanderthal, Interrogator, Brutus..."

He frowns.

"I don't know his name," I try to recover. *Shit.* I've insulted someone he respects. But then his face lights up with amusement, a stunted laugh escaping him as if sharing an inside joke with himself. "He isn't going to like that."

The words thrill me. Worry me. *I'm clearly of sound mind.*

He straightens. "Anyway. Your question. First of all, nice phrasing. A clarifying question disguised as an open question."

He caught that. A tick of surprise lances through my body. I murmur, "Thanks."

Crossing his arms, he explains, "Most of us speak English, but not all fluently. We usually speak in our own language." He must read the confusion on my face, because he adds, "We took pieces of our origin languages and created one of our own. Everyone's included and heard. Seen."

Perplexed, I hesitate before inquiring further, not knowing if I would be overstepping. Although, I'm unsure when I'll get a chance to get information again, so I risk it. "Why not make English the universal language? I mean, the sentiment is beautiful, but why go through the effort of creating a new one instead of picking an existing one?"

"I just told you why."

Gauging his short response, I can't help but feel like there's something more. I press, "To be inclusive. And that's the only reason?"

A smirk pulls at his mouth. "No."

I was right. "So... why?" I roll my hand, suggesting he continue talking.

Slumping further into the chair and shrugging with one shoulder, he says, "Because."

"Because?" I draw the word out in a prompt for him to elaborate.

He offers a courteous smile, as if to apologize for leaving it at that. Moving on, he says, "As for why he's the interrogator... This is difficult to answer. Because you haven't proven yourself trustworthy."

Hungry for more information, I scoot to the edge of the bed and rebut, "How can I prove I'm trustworthy without someone trusting me? Doesn't that seem counterintuitive?"

A slow smile spreads across his face. "I see it now. And I don't need to ask my question anymore."

I gape at him. "Why? What do you think you've figured out?"

He purses his lips in thought, ignoring my response. "I'm still going to answer yours, though. Because I'm nice like that. He's the interrogator because he has a certain set of skills. And..." He looks at me as if wanting me to really hear him in this next part. "He's our Chief."

My composure falls through my fingers like quicksand.

"As in... he's the leader?" The words come out slowly, feeling foreign on my tongue when paired with the image of him in my mind.

Temporary Guard snorts, reading the shock on my face. "We're all equal in say, rights, and worthiness, but he and a few others are the decision makers."

I rake my fingers through my hair, only to hit a mess of knots. *What am I supposed to do with that information?* Tightening my hold on the pillow, I recall his forceful presence. The power he emanated. The intensity of when he first came to interrogate me— the way it felt like a hammer against my senses.

"Well, then." I scan the roof, as if it might display words of clarity up there. The weight of this new dynamic presses down. Something in me resists, tugging my nose into a scrunch. *But he's still... him.* Leaders I know are hidden behind walls and desks, only saying things crafted by speech writers. Neanderthal... I've seen him be real. Unfiltered. Unscripted.

As if reading my thoughts, he leans his elbows on his knees. "I'd advise you to refrain from calling him those names and start treating him with a hint of respect. He decided to give you a trial."

Respect? The only reason my life is at risk and requiring a trial is because of him. For fuck...

I bite my tongue, clamping my jaw until the frustration dulls. "I don't know what to call him. I don't know anyone's name. Except for Sage."

Nodding, he explains, "That's intentional, because they're sacred here. Connections are influential. We choose who we interact and exchange energy with. His name—that's something he can decide to tell you. Or not."

It's fascinating how seriously they take everything. The way he describes their connections feels intimate and pure. I'm not used to this. I don't know what I expected from these people, who live outside the normalcy of passing strangers in the streets on the way to work or home without a second glance. Those who could sit meters from you at a restaurant that might as well be on the other side of a cinderblock wall. Either way, I sure as fuck didn't know there was a 'Kuma tata, we are the sacred ones' place that existed.

"Hmm," I murmur, tracing my finger over the edges of my wounds, noticing the fresh skin that pulls tight. I open my mouth to ask about his earlier and unasked question, but movement at the entrance stops me.

Temporary Guard grins. "Speaking of Neanderthal..." The amusement in his projected voice is unmistakable.

Shock locks my muscles. My eyes drag slowly and reluctantly to Interrogator. A half-hearted apology sits on my tongue, but his expression kills it before it leaves my mouth.

He stands composed. Indifferent. So why does every nerve in my body scream at me to run?

He looks at Temporary Guard, then his eyes land heavily on me. "Neanderthal?" he asks, with a voice too even.

This could not get worse.

Temporary Guard leans in slightly, lowering his voice to a gossiping hush.

He's about to make this worse.

"Oh, she's got a few for you. Neanderthal, Interrogator..." He looks at me, all mock innocence. "What was the other one?"

The tips of my ears burn bright red. *Fuck.* After all his lecturing about respect, he just threw me under the bus.

My tongue rolls over my teeth, stuffing down the urge to snap. "That was it," I mutter.

He snaps his fingers in the air, a lighthearted smugness in his tone when he says, "I remember now. Brutus."

Bowing my head, my fists curl tight as I decide I must begin plotting his painful demise.

I mutter to the blanket, "I don't know what I am supposed to call anyone. Temporary Guard—or TG, because I can't be bothered saying the whole thing—says names are earned."

I can hear TG take a slow inhale, then release it with a phew. "Temporary Guard? I got off way too easy."

My head whips to him, a strained smile barely concealing my seethe. "I can certainly think of alternatives."

Raising his hands, he speaks to Neanderthal out of the corner of his mouth. "Bit angry, this one."

My features fall flat as I glare at him.

Neanderthal acknowledges him with the barest glance. "Thank you for your help." TG grins, as if he expects Neanderthal to play along. When he doesn't, his amusement wavers. Briefly, TG looks at me, his expression reserved as he turns to bow his head to Neanderthal. Without another word, he slips out, leaving me alone to face the wreckage of his mess.

Neanderthal steps closer, and I only notice what he's carrying when he sets it on the bedside table. A sliver of guilt swirls in my stomach, realizing he's brought me food while I've been teasing him, loathing him. But the guilt dissolves quickly as my mouth begins watering. I resist the urge to snatch the bowl like a possessed gremlin and scoop it into my mouth with bare hands. Instead, I watch the steam rise from the warm meal. He places a cup of water next to it, and a drop of water tauntingly slides from the rim, landing on the nightstand. *Don't you dare spill another drop.*

"That smells good," I mumble, failing to sound indifferent. My diet has consisted of granola bars, fruit, sandwiches, and nuts I packed for my hike. A gurgle in my stomach betrays my pride, letting him know I'm dangerously close to drooling. In fact, I can picture myself doing breaststrokes through a pool of this, taking mouthfuls on every dip below the surface while angels play symphonies on a nearby harp.

Once he's perched at his post, I examine his expression, desperate to steer him away from the nicknames. "Apparently, you're the Chief." The second the words leave my mouth, regret hits. My tone is too sharp, and by the stern look he gives me, he doesn't appreciate the distaste in my voice. The leaders I know rarely have a heart for the people they govern, and it's hard to see him as being the exception.

When he looks away from me again, lips sealed in a tight line, I mutter, "Never mind."

I don't want to come off as ungrateful for the meal, or anything this abhorrent male offers me. So, I lean for the bowl as casually as I can, only filling the spoon halfway like I couldn't care less that there's food in front of me. But the second it touches my tongue, any attempt at nonchalance shatters like thin ice. My eyes flutter shut, savoring it with slow chewing.

"Oh, Creations," I praise in a whisper, nearly groaning. Rice, green vegetables, and beans, all coated in a creamy, spiced sauce. It's not groundbreaking, but somehow, every bite is rich, warm, and undeniably satisfying.

The quiet and repetitive sound of him sharpening his blade fades into the background, but I watch him do it. Methodically. Intentionally. A small, yellow citrine stone is tied to the base of the handle, and I'm thoroughly confused as to why he has it. I've read about them holding spiritual and healing properties, but anyone I've spoken to considers it of equal value to a palm sized pack of plastic gems bought for five dollars. I wonder what it means to *him*.

"Why do you have a citrine stone?"

His eyes momentarily hold mine captive before he returns to his task. Silence fills the room until his voice cuts through, ignoring my question and repeating, "Neanderthal?"

Curling my lips in against my teeth, I look him over before replying. "I'm just recalling the spears, huts, living in nature... The capturing and threatening to kill me. There's also the fact that I have no rights and no say. Not to mention, you're all detached from civilization." I tap my finger on my chin. "Hmm, where would I get such a preposterous name?"

I expect a scowl or withering glare, but not the question that comes from his mouth. "You believe me to be uncivilized and unintelligent? This way of life is below you?"

The question is a blade to the heart. I'd never want to imply anyone is below me, and I have to reflect on if that is what I unintentionally thought.

With my face aimed down at my food, I reply, "I don't agree with being held prisoner, and I guess... yeah, I do think this way of life is uncivilized. But I don't think I'm better than anyone here, or that you're unintelligent. You're pretty clever, actually.

Who else could come up with such diverse ways to make me feel like shit about myself?" I throw in a laugh after the last part, but he doesn't join me. Maybe he picked up on the hurt that was hiding beneath it.

"I suppose what's considered as *civilized* is up for debate," he says. "And, I have to return the compliment, with your dexterity in finding ways to insult." His voice is rough as he replies, as if the words are layered in a context that I don't have access to.

Any snarky remark I was planning suspends in my mind right then and there. Maybe this is the closest we'll get to saying, 'You hurt me. I hurt you. Sorry.'

Tentatively, I ask, "Does me calling you those nicknames upset you? I mean it was meant to annoy you, but I didn't want to actually make you feel—"

By the glare I get as a response, I know for certain I have stepped in shit. The question was genuine, but it seems he took it as...

"I think," he interrupts, "it's offensive. Is there something wrong with living like this?"

Truth be told, there have been slivers of moments where I catch myself observing, and a warmness spreads through my chest. Those moments have dropped a tiny amount of relief into the gaping hole in my heart. *The life I knew isn't the only way.* An energy of connection and community ripples through this place, and maybe it's something I didn't know how much I longed for.

I didn't realize that calling him Neanderthal was my way of expressing that I'm jealous of them. That I'm a prisoner within this place, and not a part of it. Insulting him and their way of life is me lashing out. The village is a running river, bright and free, and I'm a grey boulder dropped in and blocking its flow.

I won't call him that anymore.

I finally reply, "No."

Apparently I'm unwilling to give him a leg up or tell him he's right.

He watches me, studying the nervous swallow I take when my mouth betrays me and goes dry under his scrutiny.

Leaning his forearms on his knees, I watch as he returns to sharpening his knife idly. "Then maybe choose your words more carefully."

Like a petulant child, I mumble under my breath, "Says *you*…"

His hands freeze, and the force of his attention makes me do the same.

I couldn't help it. The voice inside me had a mind of its own and worked its way out, telling me to pick another fight. To attack. Now, I stare at him blankly, with a hint of regret tapping me on the shoulder. Being around this man makes me so unhinged, to where I say and do the most absurd things. At home, I was perceived as a studious, bubbly, kind person. Here, I am unravelling into a heathen before him.

Muttering once again, I admit, "I don't know why I get so angry around you."

Waiting for a response that never comes, he returns to his task, and I eat the last of my food in awkward silence. *Creations, have I always chewed this fucking loud? I may as well get up and munch my last few bites right next to his ear.*

When I'm finally done, I place the bowl down on the bedside table and decide to offer an olive branch. "I won't call you that anymore. But then, I don't know what to call you."

"Don't call me anything."

A part of me wilts, not expecting the hostility in his voice.

I can't explain it, but I feel like he's angry with me beyond obvious reasons. Or maybe not *angry*, but at the very least, he's confused by my presence. Perhaps he hates not being in control, and me showing up was a spanner in the works. Either way, I don't know what to say, so I don't respond. I just stare awkwardly at my fingers that itch to fidget.

Time presses on for an eternity as we sit in this crushing quietness. Until I hear his voice. "Names have power, and I don't wish for you to have any over me."

At his genuine confession, I jerk my head up to him, but his focus remains on his task. I let out a half-laugh. "I have no power here. You don't need to worry about that." Shrugging a shoulder, I add, "You know mine, and *I* don't care."

He doesn't look at me as he replies in a clipped tone, "You gave yours away like it was *nothing.*"

I waver momentarily at the offense in his expression, my mouth going dry and driving me to pick up my cup of water. All I can hear is my greedy gulping before I mutter, "It's just a name."

"Names, to us, are a sign of trust." The weight of his attention pushes against my skin, and the hairs on my arms threaten to rise at the determination in his voice. "They're a way to say, 'here is a piece of my being.' By sharing an element of your identity, you're giving them access to you. It's a fragment—an invitation to let someone see what represents you. We walk around with an energetical dome over each of us, and inside is our individual essence. Offering your name is like extending a hand, and letting them cross over the thin film that separates you. The closer you get to someone, the deeper the impact is when saying it, or hearing it from someone else's mouth. It can change a context and influence your emotions. It's powerful." He surveys me. "Do you even know what your name means?"

I chew on the inside of my cheek, deliberating over his words. "No. I didn't realize it meant anything."

"I see."

Curiosity tugs the question from my mouth, "Do *you* know what it means?"

Breaking eye contact and sheathing his knife, he replies, "I do."

He doesn't elaborate, and I contemplate leaving it at that. Clearly, he's baiting me to ask, and I don't want to give him what he wants. He said he doesn't want me to have power over him. Well if I give in and ask, I'm feeding right into his superiority complex. Although... he knows something and, deitydamn, I don't want him to hold it over me. "Okay, what does it mean?"

"I'm not telling you." His tone is matter-of-fact.

I gawk at him, floored by his audacity. "You're not going to tell me?" I blink. "Okay, are we in kindergarten? Tell me what my own name means."

He lets out a rough laugh, studying me. "Interesting. You say a name means nothing, yet look at you. Offended that I know something about your identity. That I have access to a part of you that you don't have." He sits back, crossing his arms over his chest. "I've made my point."

I glare at him, torn between irritation and reluctant understanding. I take back the power, diminishing his point by mocking it through a sneer. "You give names way too much credit. This whole thing is stupid."

Quicker than humanly possible, he's in front of me, fists on either side of my legs.

"What the fuck?" The words race from my mouth as I jolt back, the last bit of water in my cup sloshing over my fingers.

His eyes gleam with something dark, something knowing. "*Stella.*" He draws out my name, letting it coil between us, taunting, teasing. Using my name against me.

My lips press together, as if sealing them shut will stop me from taking the bait.

His hand shoots to my throat. A spike of alarm flares in my chest, panic surging before I can mask it. His grip is firm, but not crushing. *Not yet.* His face tightens, and my heart pounds against my chest.

"What are you doing?" I rasp, my fingers wrapping around his wrist and clamping down hard.

Through gritted teeth, he growls my name, wielding it like a weapon. "*Stella.*"

I can't move.

Suddenly, he loosens his hold, his fingertips skimming the curve of my neck, my hand travelling down with his. The change is dizzying. First, I'm prey. Now, I don't know what I am, but a shiver ricochets through me at his featherlight caress. *I hate him.* But I don't tell him to stop. Moving his fingers lower, he traces slow S-shapes beneath my collarbones. Then, lower. He leans in, his breath warming my cheek as he murmurs with need, "*Stella.*"

My body responds, dragging my hand up his forearm, pulling him closer, my chest rising and falling too fast. This energy. I know this. *I know him.* The familiarity I felt before returns, threading through me with quiet certainty. His hand drops away, taking the feeling with it. All that touches my skin now is vacant air.

Taking a few steps back, he crosses his arms, watching me as pity and disapproval contorts his expression. My insides concave, and shame spirals through me, my breath snagging on the hook he set. In fact, I walked straight into it, happily. Basked in the glow of his affection. "Stella." This time, my name drips with disgust.

I stare at him, stunned. The contrast between being scared, wanted, and discarded leaves me exposed like raw nerves.

The chair lets out a soft groan as he sits in it, crossing his ankle over his knee. "Do you see now, the impact a name can have? How it can change in context? It has power—influence over emotions."

Nausea churns my stomach, sick from the violation—manipulating my feelings like I'm some kind of docile experiment. My fingers tighten around the cup, like it's the only thing keeping me attached to my body as a mess of emotions combat within me. Anger raises her hand, a merciless gleam in her eyes as she volunteers to take it from here.

I hurl the cup at his head. *The picture of maturity.*

The flash of surprise in his eyes doesn't last as he moves before it can touch him. I'm immobilized when he's suddenly crossing the hut and striding toward me. Power emanates from him, pushing against me like a thick wall, closing in until he stops a foot away—only because my arm outstretches before him, my palm an inch from touching his skin. His eyes drop to my hand, a low and swift sound from his chest warning me of his fury.

I spit out, "You made your point."

His usual, composed armor fights to regain control. I can see it in the beginning of his frown. The twitch of his chin. Common sense tells me to hide, to run, not to touch him. But our emotions are out of their cages now. A rush of my own power rises to meet his, and instinct drives my next move.

I lower my voice. "Allow me to make mine."

Purposely, I press my palm to his skin and push. He doesn't budge, not at first. But then he relents, giving me another foot of space as I rise to my feet. Like heat seeking missiles, my glare locks with his. I let lethality grow within me—let it challenge him. It's a feeling I have never felt. An unforgiving, scathing potence.

My voice is deceptively calm. "These people might trust you and follow you. But to me, you are *nothing*. Nothing but a random man who's holding me here against my will. My captor."

The weight of his stare threatens me to fold, his jaw tightening when I refuse.

I carry on, "You have toyed with my emotions. Taunted me. Invaded my space. Stolen my privacy and hope." The edge in my voice sharpens to something vaporous. "Yes, you spared my life, but you were the one threatening to take it. I guess I was right, you lead just like the others—through omission, fear, and control, and that is not something I respect. I will not be bowing to you like they do."

His glare is pure, molten lava.

Stepping forward, I level my voice. "I never want to hear my name come from your mouth again. Do you understand me? I *revoke* your access."

The air between us barely contains our shared fury. It's unbalanced and vibrating.

His lips curl in slightly before he exhales a deep breath through his nose and turns away from me. I think he's going to storm off. Instead, he faces me again, slowly. His features are a mask of something carefully restrained, tempering whatever's stirring beneath the surface.

He replies, "You seem to be well acquainted with making assumptions. Delegating blame to everyone but yourself." His voice quiets, but the weight of it isn't lost when he says, "Deciding the worst of people."

I hold my ground, lifting my chin as he continues. "You walk, talk, and act like a perpetual victim." The words slice me in half. "And that's not an assumption. It's a pattern, backed by evidence."

My stomach tightens as I brace for the next blow from him.

"Make choices and deal with the consequences. That's life. *You* came into *our* territory. One we have gone to great lengths—and lost lives—to protect. I admit, I could've handled things differently. I apologize for my part in swaying your emotions. For my part in your discomfort here, and your confusion. For not letting you leave. What you don't see is something far larger at play here, outside of your internal world. You've reduced us to a group of people who are out to get you, but can you realize how conceited that is? I have a purpose far larger than being *your captor.*"

The facade cracks at the edges when he speaks his next words. "We are risking everything for you. Giving you shelter, food, medicine, and second chances." I'm taken aback by the hint of imploring in his tone, the step he takes toward me. "We broke our rules for you."

He steps closer, and the expression he wears doesn't hold malice like I believed it would. What it holds is a yearning—like it's important that I understand his next words.

"Take ownership. You're here because of a long list of decisions you've made, alongside a force larger than you can conceptualize. Stop acting like this is the universe arbitrarily punishing you."

I jerk my head back, my nose pinched tight as I reel from his righteousness. "I know!" I bellow for anyone to hear.

He studies me, surprise hidden behind his features at my outburst.

Digging my teeth into my lower lip, I take a breath before continuing. "You don't need to get up on that pedestal and preach." I ignore the twitch in his brows and keep going. "I took ownership by leaving—to reclaim my life. But, can you pretend for five seconds that you might not know everything about me? Because my healing doesn't happen in a day, and certainly not just because *you* said so. It takes time, and having you breathe down my neck like some virtuous example I should aspire to be is not helping—"

His voice raises, an incredulous undertone leeching through it when he asks, "Virtuous example? What—"

I cut him off before he can finish his sentence. "Yes! I'll stop acting like a victim when you stop acting like some pinnacle of wisdom that will change my life or save me with a lecture or two. You telling me that I need positive change in my behavior is not going to be the catalyst in my evolution. You're not nearly important enough to play such a role in my life."

I point a finger at my chest. "I am my own damn hero. You got that, Interrogator?"

Somehow, I resisted calling him Neanderthal out of spite.

His face contorts in confusion. "I'm not trying to be your hero. I'm trying to tell you that your *clear* misery doesn't have to be the thing most prevalent about you. Realizing the world is bigger than the dark emotions inside you might teach you that other people have their own darkness. That you're only a victim if you decide to stay one. I'm sorry if you already know that. It certainly wasn't obvious."

"Apology *certainly* not accepted," I snap through gritted teeth.

He runs his hands through his hair and blinks like he's waking from a nightmare. "How did we end up here?" He lets out a deep breath, scratching his forehead as if he can't believe the direction our conversation took. "I was just trying to bring something to your attention, and it all just fucking snowballed..."

Crossing my arms, I scoff, "Whatever your intentions, your delivery sucked."

A throat clears. The moment splits in two as we turn to the interruption. TG stands just inside the entrance, his focus dashing back and forth between us. The scratching of his neck is telling of his concern, whilst the purse of his lips shows his intrigue.

TG announces, "It's time."

Interrogator's chest rises slowly before communicating something to the guard with his eyes. TG bows his head before stepping out, and a short burst of air pushes past my lips in satirical ire.

Interrogator stands deathly still, his attention fixed on the closed door. His voice is smooth as butter, as if he didn't just verbally annihilate me. "You have two minutes to compose yourself. Then we're going to see how you got past the barrier."

The words settle on my shoulders, heavy and unwanted. But I don't reply.

Turning his head to me, he assesses. A glint in his eyes dares me to ignore him.

Despite my efforts to feel nothing, a prickle of fear spreads through me, forcing a reluctant nod.

He lingers, eyes sweeping over my features meaningfully— as if seeking the part of me that doesn't want to bite him. Woven fabric meets bare feet as he turns and strides out, the door swaying shut behind him.

A sinking feeling pools in my gut. *What is he talking about?*

I didn't come through any barrier...

CHAPTER 8
A THREAD OF UNVEILING

Two minutes to collect myself and leave the hut? *Piss off.*

The emotional roller coaster he put me through over a name makes my blood simmer. Everywhere else on this planet, a name is nothing more than a throwaway add on to a greeting. Something to precede the instruction or task designated to you in an email. But here, everything is... odd. *What's his name? Why do I even care?*

Tears start to wet my lashes, unwelcome proof of my frustration. My head falls back, but I'm too slow. One escapes, trailing down my hot cheek. I wait for steam to follow, or fury to burn it away. Nothing.

Do not break. Not now. Not here.

Clenching my fists, I shove both middle fingers at the closed door, mouthing a fat 'fuck you' in a breathy scream. *As all adults do.*

I need my journal. Point number... Dammit. *What was it? I love that I know how to talk to myself... and what to do when I'm struggling to manage my emotions.* I repeat it. Again.

Emotions are not my enemy. I *feel* emotions, not judge them.

Panic edges my brain, a slow creeping threat, until I'm cracking my knuckles and bouncing on my toes. Time's up. I need to get out there. Focus on your senses. *Ground yourself.*

Stepping one foot outside, then the other, I force my focus outward. The sun is warm against my face. A breeze cools my skin, mingling with sweat.

Good. Keep going.

My stomach is full, and my tongue lingers with the taste of rich spices from the meal I ate. I remind myself that they need me alive right now. *I'm safe.* Make allies, not enemies.

Slowly, the tension in my chest loosens, anger lowering her shoulders.

I absorb the details of how my *allies* live. Wooden logs are scattered in semi-circles, some around a fire pit, others tucked under the gazebo-like shelters. Hammocks are occupied by conversing people. Swings that aren't filled with young kids sway lazily in the wind. The solar lamp posts dot the open space, or line up in pathways, charging in wait for night time to illuminate. Seeing all of this again, I can appreciate it differently. It all feels... romantic.

I spot the barn-like structure tucked near the treeline. Storage? A meeting place? Or... My stomach sinks. It's too calm out here. And delicate. Homely. The killing is obviously done in there. So, I guess that's where they'll be executing me if I don't explain how I got past this barrier. *The one I have no recollection of.*

A murmur of voices pulls me back. They've noticed me.

Conversations fade, eyes fixating. A bead of sweat trails down my spine. Composing myself, I step forward, legs feeling heavier and more sluggish than I'd like. I was so distracted, familiarizing myself with the village—and potential place of my death—that I didn't brace for the brunt of mass scrutiny.

Scanning their faces, my calmness slips, my composure cracking when I see his profile. *Interrogator.* His lips move as he speaks to TG, but then, as if sensing me, he stops mid-sentence, turning his head to me.

Barbed wire cinches around my heart, demanding it not to react.

Averting my gaze to the people he's close to, I notice the couple who first captured me: Spearman and Turquoise. Caution touches the firm lines of their features as they watch me.

Walk over to them. Just do it. I map out a straight line, but it feels eternally long, and my feet refuse to move.

A throat clears behind me and I spin, pulse quickening. It's Sage.

Memories scatter in a montage, my body tensing as I remember the way she pulled me under—gathering my mind in a bundle, cradling it in her hands, inspecting it. But I let her do it. *Why?*

Realizing she's staring at me as intently as I am her, I offer a tentative smile. "Hi," I test.

She smiles a genuine and toothy smile. "Your wrists look better."

I glance down. The redness has faded, replaced by smooth, shiny, and healing skin. *Skipped the whole scabbing stage.*

"Thank you," I say quieter than I mean to. Clearing my throat, I try again, louder. "For the medicine. They feel a lot better."

Sage dips her chin in a meaningful nod. "You're welcome."

A deep green tote bag is thrust toward me as she announces with a grin, "I made you some clothes to wear. It's not like what you're wearing—we don't have those synthetic materials."

I study her, realizing she isn't insulting me, but informing me. She wears a tight, yellow wrap of fabric around her breasts, and matching knee-length shorts that hang low on her hips and drop to her knees. *That's a whole lot of torso showing.* I internally shrivel at the idea of wearing it, and being so exposed, but her confidence in her own skin speaks volumes. I reach out and take the bag, grateful to change. Splotches of sweat, dirt, tears, and blood stains are so ingrained into my tights and baggy t-shirt, I don't think it'll ever wash out.

I peer back at her. "Thank you, truly... for considering that I might want a change of clothes."

A mirthful look remains in her eyes as she continues, "There will be some more clothes put in your hut soon, too. And there's no need to thank me. Actually, you can thank me by bathing and changing into them. Who knew someone so beautiful could smell so bad." A playful smirk edges at her lips.

Mortification washes over me. She's not wrong, I haven't bathed in days. But the spirited look on her face entices a laugh to bubble up and release from me. Until right now, I didn't realize how much I missed the feeling of finding something funny.

Her laugh meets mine as I retort, "Wow, okay. No sugarcoating?"

She perks up with a closed-lip grin. "No."

I like the fact that she's unapologetically honest. I guess it's the recipient's job to handle it well or not. It was a reminder of something I learned not long ago; we can control how authentic we are, and how we choose to show up, but not how people react to you.

I clutch the tote bag to my chest, suddenly nervous. "My name is Stella, by the way."

The lack of surprise in her expression tells me she already knows my name, and the gratitude in her expression tells me she understands my meaning. I'm doing what Interrogator said and inviting her into my dome.

"I'm Sage." Her voice is proud, sure.

My heart feels an inch fuller. "As repayment for your kindness, I will find a way to bathe as soon as possible." At this, she outright laughs, and once again, I do, too.

A sternness settles into her features when the amusement dies down. "Don't let this deter you from bathing, but my kindness isn't transactional. At the end of the day, if you're happy being the smelliest woman alive, that doesn't make me regret giving you the clothes."

I don't know if I should laugh or cry. "The sentiment does resonate deeply within me, although being called the smelliest woman alive does take the magic out of it a bit." My snort-laugh follows suit, enticing a grin from her.

Without looking, I suddenly feel aware of Interrogator. I check over my shoulder and gasp when I see him only two strides away.

"You scared the shit out of me," I spit out with my hand on my heart, imploring it to slow. Based on his scowl and general roughness, you'd expect him to stomp around like a brute, but he ironically moves with grace and stealth.

Ignoring my comment, he assesses the situation. Then as if he transforms into someone else, he nods to Sage in greeting. "Youhi Ghana," he says in their native tongue, then *smiles*. My whole body comes to a standstill at the sight: the affection crinkling the skin around his eyes, the ease of his upturned lips, the lilt of his accent when he speaks... He's truly *beautiful*. I reprimand the prickle of envy that spurs in my chest, knowing I'll never be on the receiving end of that look. *Why do I even want to be? He's a dick.*

Her voice sounds casual, at ease with him as she says, "Farr de huro batie." She gestures a thumb in my direction and smiles at me with mischief leading in her smile.

His eyes find the bag, his arms folding loosely across his chest as he wordlessly assesses the situation, wondering why she's talking to me maybe? What's in the bag? I can actually see his brain deliberating and storing information like a fucking machine.

Interrogator chuffs, his voice leaning into a friendly tenor. "Rus teyez ug farr."

My eyes are synonymous with watching a tennis match as I try to decipher their language. All I can take from it, is that I'm likely the subject of discussion.

Reading my awkward body language, Sage fills me in. "I told him you need a bath, and he said to take it easy on you. Which I won't be, but it's a nice suggestion." Heat presses against every inch of my skin as I reach a new level of blushing.

She doesn't hide a thing. Shame and embarrassment don't exist in her world. The epitome of brazen rawness. An open book. It'll take some time to get used to being around her—being completely and utterly translucent in her presence.

She smirks at me as if challenging me to rise to shamelessness. So, I stand taller. *I guess I am the smelliest woman alive. Whatever.* A slight dip of her chin acknowledges the shift in me, spurring a strange swell of pride. Abruptly, she turns on her heel and walks away, seemingly finished with this conversation. I watch as she puts her arm around TG's shoulders. They converse as he leans over the cauldron-like pot, taking her with him as they peek at the meal cooking over the fire.

I peer back at Interrogator, and we lock eyes at the same time, Moments ago, we were ready to tear out each other's throats. But now, he seems so calm. What happened? Why did he say to take it easy on me? Maybe he should take his own advice. *Can he smell me?* I go to take a step back, but remember Sage's words and resist the urge. I really would like to clean myself though, and put on clean clothes. The idea alone makes me want to melt into a puddle of joy.

He does a once-over of me before exhaling through his nose. "Before the barrier, we'll go to the stream." Only he could do a nice thing and ruin it by making it sound so burdensome with his tone. *I'm having such wonderful encounters with this man.*

I nod, readjusting the bag and putting both straps over one shoulder. I'm thankful for the clothes, but I could just get my spares. They're in my backpack along with my journal. *When is a good time to ask for it? I hope they don't read it. Or dispose of it.*

"Should we go then?" I ask, keeping my voice low, so as to not attract any more attention to me. Plus, I'm desperate not to stand here a second longer in awkward silence, with the wounds fresh in my chest from the argument we had. "I'm sure the less time you're in my presence, the better, right?"

His hand flexes, but his expression remains guarded. "I've adapted to your hostility, so there's no rush."

Clenching my teeth, I glare at him.

"See—" he points at my face "—that look? Zero impact."

I retort, "When, roughly, do you think I'll adapt to your narcissism?"

"About the same amount of time it takes for you to realize you're projecting." He tips his head to the side. "Hopefully soon."

I run a hand down the side of my face, muttering just loud enough for him to hear, "You're impossible."

His attention catches on the ring on my finger, the edge of the birthmark visible to him. His eyes feel distant, as if he's lost somewhere in thought—recalling what I shared with him, or considering whatever made him freak out when he first saw it.

I take the distraction, and use it to stare at him, hopeful I'll notice something that will reveal who he is beneath the mask. I try to see beyond his annoyingly pleasant appearance and figure out why I feel like I know him, or why I might want to.

Abruptly, I hear a... bark. The word doesn't quite compute to the guttural sound of a beast. My eyes widen in shock, scanning the area and seeking the source.

Across the village, my eyes fix on not one, but multiple creatures—one leading the pack. Onyx fur covers the beast all over, except for its face, where a silver line of fur runs vertically between its eyes. Its golden eyes... that are locked on *me*.

I don't mean to, but I can't stop my hand reaching for something to steady me as the world spins faster. My fingers latch around Interrogator's arm, but the second my grip makes contact with him, the beast's head ducks low. White, canine teeth bare at me, a snarl vibrating through the air as it prowls closer. The others follow, one by one, with red fur, brown, white, grey...

My stomach threatens to hollow as I stammer, "What-what is that?"

"That..." Interrogator begins with a teasing tone, but then he turns to me and I feel him staring at my profile.

His voice softens. "These are Okah. That one's name is Divy."

After such a big deal about names, hearing one spikes my nerves further. *I guess it makes sense, since she can't tell me her name herself.*

Also, Okah? What in the—

He steals my attention once more. "I won't let her hurt you."

A strange laugh leaves me, "You see her, right? I don't think you'll be able to stop how sure she seems about ripping me to pieces."

"She's upset by you because she doesn't recognize your scent. And because you're digging your nails into me."

He gently places his hand over mine, beginning to uncurl my fingers from his arm. I resist, pleading with a rigid grip not to make me let go as I stare at the beast. The Okah. *Divy.* She has the height and claws of a bear, the face and frame of a wolf. I consider the possibility that he's lying, and I'm their dinner. But then he gently pries my fingers off his arm, and interlocks them with his. I look down in shock at our joined hands hanging between our bodies, then back up at him.

In a calm voice, he says, "Don't look away. Keep watching her. She can sense your fear. Panic makes people unpredictable, and she sees that as a threat to me. So, take a big breath in..." Without hesitation, I do as he instructs. "Then exhale. Focus on my hand," he says as he squeezes it, and I squeeze it back. "Come back to your body."

A small part of my mind frays at the edges, recognizing those words. He has to have read my journal. He's doing point number... *Fuck, I can't remember right now*. But he knows this is what I do. He knows what I need.

His assuring voice overshadows my spiral. "Feel your feet on the ground. I won't let her hurt you," he repeats. This time, I might believe him.

Tuning into my body and feeding off his soothing voice, I calm a fraction.

Up close, my knees threaten to buckle. I've never seen anything like this creature before—anything that big, except a horse. But this sharp-toothed, giant-clawed animal is no deitydamn horse. Its nose works, assessing me through scent, and I plead with the universe that she doesn't smell the angst vibrating the blood in my veins.

"Divy." He calls to her. The other Okah stops as she approaches alone. *Breathe. Breathe.* My hand tightens around Interrogator's, and he runs his thumb over mine in tender swipes.

The Okah lifts her head slightly, her eyes leaving mine to find Interrogator's as he says, "Treh'sa." The tone of his voice sounds assertive, but I sense the love—the history of a bond behind it. I've heard it in my own voice when I sneak out to feed the stray dogs, before they start fighting over the little food I manage to bring them.

Divy watches me, her snarling subsiding only when Interrogator reaches out with his free hand, scratching under her chin. I watch Divy blink slowly, her round and moon-eyed gaze promising him something. That he will always be her person.

"Ruhsa," he coos.

Divy sits, and I force myself to breathe through the shock of her size. Standing or sitting, her head comes above both of ours. She's terrifying. Majestic.

I whisper, "How have I not seen these... Okah yet? Where did they come from? What are they?" Stealing a glance at him, I blanch at how he visibly softens, returning a deep affection as he stares at her. The expression surpasses the real smile he gave Sage. This look steals my breath. Divy's presence lowers his guard, just as he does for her.

He doesn't look away from her as he responds, "Because we told them to stay hidden the second you entered our territory. They weren't exactly happy about leaving us, or being told what to do, so I can assume that's why they came home early." Lowering his voice slightly, he adds, "There's a lot you haven't seen."

I'm too stunned and overstimulated to push for more information right now. The explanation and his civil tone is not what I expected, and I decide to accept what he says instead of fighting him on everything. For now, anyway.

I'll bring it up later. When Divy's pack, and every set of eyes in the village, are not on me.

"Okay," I say with resignation clear in my voice.

The complacency in that single word turns his head to face me, eyes squinting in a pulse of uncertainty. I wonder if it's the lack of 'hostility' that gives him pause, but he leaves it at that.

His focus drops to our interlocked fingers, and in a flat tone, says, "You can let go now."

"Oh, right." I promptly unravel our fingers, wiping my sweaty palm on my tights.

You could have let go, too.

Divy moves to his side as he inspects the crowd, then they start walking toward the warrior couple.

"Let's go," he instructs over his shoulder.

Guess I was meant to follow him.

More people join us, and I count five Okah. Inhaling a deep breath, I glance nervously at these ginormous beasts and the village warriors encircling me as we walk.

If they, too, can sense panic... *I am so fucked.*

CHAPTER 9
A SINGLE DROP

Everywhere I look, the forest stuns me. Its vivid aliveness is even more palpable than yesterday. The five petalled flowers open and arch with grace, their scent just as elegant as the off-white shade.

I graze my fingers over scaled bark, the tree's trunk twice my wingspan. When the wind blows past me, I'm convinced I hear a quiet hum. The large leaves rustle like they're waving, and I feel this absurd urge to wave back. The few plants we have in society are potted and trimmed, or fake. Nothing like this... magnificence.

I can see why they live like this, but how did they get out? How has no one found and kicked them back into the cement world? How can I go back to a reality I've known as greyness after seeing this? But it's not like I can stay, either. Where in the Divine do I go?

Something impossible draws my awareness to my feet. Deep beneath them, I feel the faint purr of the forest. Even the tiny ants and intricate spider webs shimmer with something ethereal. The birds above call out, singing a song that echoes far and wide, and their vibrancy feels animated.

An intense comfort radiates from me... That is, until Interrogator's voice beckons my attention. "Watch where you step. I don't have time to teach you which snakes and spiders are poisonous, so just avoid them all. And the leeches in the stream, and..." The list goes on. I chew on the inside of my cheek absentmindedly, nodding as I try to repeat the list back to him, but I've never even heard of half the insects he mentions.

He slows to match my pace, exhaling sharply through his nose. "Just... stay close."

I keep my eyes trained on the floor as I cautiously lift my boots over thick, tangled roots, careful not to step on the dainty orange flowers that are dispersed along the vines.

My mind drifts quickly, nuzzling into the gentle fondness of the forest. *This* is what I came out here for. To be held by nature.

Does Interrogator feel as at home here as I do?

My wandering eyes try to sneak a side-long glance at him, but he senses it and looks at me. Trying to play it off, I quickly look to the side of him, pursing my lips and squinting slightly as if something caught my eye in his general direction.

The nearing sound of running water steals me from my reverie. A few people break from the group and run ahead, a yip sounding from a joyful place in their chest.

A gust of wind whooshes to my left as the smaller Okah zooms past me. The oaky, earth scent lingers as the others follow. All except Divy.

Interrogator whispers something to her—a curt order. She prowls ahead, but not before shooting me a warning glare. The hairs rise on my arms, and I instinctively put an extra foot between me and him.

The group's energy is infectious, my fear abating for a brief reprieve as I soak it in. Creations, I'm about to be *clean*. My blood teems with the prospect.

Two people lift the hanging branches to create an opening for us, and a gasp rips through me. My feet plant to the ground as I see a glimpse of the water beyond, the branches held open framing it as an ethereal painting.

I walk toward it in a trance, the swirling combination of misty aqua and sea moss green casting a spell on me. I duck under the hanging branches and step into some kind of illusion.

This can't be real.

I've heard of places like this and seen pictures in books. Springs, they call them. They used to be free to all, but over time, the higher-ups came to own them. They claimed it was to protect the natural landscapes, but I think they knew the power nature held, and how it did something nourishing for the soul. They found a way to keep it to themselves, and profit off it. It became exclusive. By paying a small fortune to witness natural beauty, only the Elite were able to go. The benefits were reserved to those rich enough to have time and access to Mother Nature's offerings.

The few free ones were overused and littered with people. Their desperation to feel something made them seek out nature, but they couldn't come without their vices.

Scattered rubbish, broken bottles, and used drug paraphernalia became hazardous for wildlife and children. Careless and dire behavior made the water murky and the rocks crumble. Now, it's where the rebels to the system go—those refusing to be part of the society. In turn, society cuts them off. Those dirty streams are the only source of water for those without homes, no matter how contaminated. Without working income, you easily become discarded, and not many survive once those in power decide you're useless to them.

This place... I wish I could bring all those people, who've been abandoned by the ones who are meant to provide, here to see it. My eyes trail the cascading waterfall, watching how the light catches on the fine spray at the base, the mist sparkling like glitter. The plants twine around each other, sharing the space like a feral dance. Moss litters over rocks, whilst *actual* lizards and turtles perch upon them, basking in the sun. The air is crisp and clean, refreshing my lungs as I draw it in through my nose.

It's unencumbered.

Vaguely, I feel Interrogator next to me, then he's walking to stand in front of me and obscuring half my view. The weight of his presence doesn't annoy me as much as usual in the wake of this glorious place. I *barely* want to punch him.

Monotonously, he demands clarity. "You're crying. Why?"

Absent-mindedly, I touch my face, feeling the tears there. *Oh.*

"No, I'm not." I deny it without sparing him a glance as I walk past him to the water's edge.

I've cried more in the last week than I have in the last five years. People are expected to fall apart, to heal, to feel on their own—in *privacy*.

Crying is a luxury for people with time.

And the truth is, I don't know why this place feels like a cold shower on a hot day—why it soothes an aching part of my spirit.

Ridding myself of my boots, then socks, I wiggle and stretch my toes along the damp dirt. It's a reprieve of its own. Taking a small step, I let the cool rush of water glide over the red, angry blisters on my feet. When the bite subsides, I relish in the moment, closing my eyes.

Splashing nearby garners my attention, and I see the Okah. Their long tongues curl water into their mouths, trotting deeper into the stream as if they aren't terrifying beasts, but only humongous dogs.

My eyes snag on the elegance of Divy, strolling along the water's edge as it laps gently around her chest. An alpha. Regal with poise. A smile touches my lips at the sight.

Something in my peripheral catches my attention, and my eyes nearly pop from my head. I slam them shut, but the image is seared into my brain: everyone entered the stream, completely naked. Their boobs bounced and dicks flopped about as they jogged into the water, bare butts kissed the sky as they dove under. It's not just the plants that are wild and free—the people are, too. *This is illegal.* My eyes shoot open, and habit forces me to dart them around, searching for someone that's bound to come out and arrest them.

I startle at a deep, impatient voice behind me. "We haven't got all day." *Interrogator.*

Please have your pants on. Please. I turn slowly, determined to have my eyes fixed on his face, and sag in relief when I see that he's dressed.

Wait. He's waiting for me to get in the water. He expects me to get naked. Now. In front of everyone, who hates my guts.

My eyes dart to the stream, noticing a group basking under the waterfall, letting the heavy pellets land on their shoulders. I also notice the intermittent glances my way. An image flashes through my mind, imagining everyone—including him—analyzing my naked body, seeing flaws, grimacing, whispering. My recently-filled stomach threatens to chuck up its contents. *This is like that nightmare where you show up to school naked—but on steroids.* It doesn't matter that they are naked with each other, I know it'll be different with me. I don't want to be so vulnerable and *seen* by people who are primed and ready to judge.

Lowering my voice and looking just below his chin, I admit, "I know you hate me, but please... don't make me strip before everyone. I've been... made fun of since I got here. Please, don't do this to me."

His silence convinces me that he will force it to happen. That I don't have a choice. He reaches for my tote bag, and I reluctantly give it to him. Immediately, I cross my arms as if to shield myself, keeping my shirt firmly on my skin. I'm on alert, looking around to see what direction is best to flee in.

In my peripheral, I see him reach into the bag and pull out a large piece of material that kind of looks like a folded table cloth. "We don't feel shame in our own skin here. Nor do we judge others for revealing it. But I know the outside world doesn't champion this right—this freedom. And I'm not going to force you to strip. I packed this in case you needed it."

Disbelief courses through my veins as he places the bag on the ground and unfolds the large cloth.

Something confuses me. "Wait, but Sage was the one who suggested I bathe. How did you get the cloth in there before we'd even discussed going? Was coming here your idea?"

Without sparing me a glance, he states, "As I said, I packed it just in case."

Fuck two steps ahead, this brute is ten steps ahead.

In an emotionless voice, he informs me, "I'll hold this up while you undress."

I look at him through my lashes. *Is he luring me to strip, only to swipe the cloth away and expose me? Mortify me as punishment for imposing on their village? For disrespecting his authority?*

Seeking answers in his unreadable expression, I press, "What's the catch?" Mistrust edges my tone.

He sighs impatiently. "Use it to cover yourself and take it to the water with you. And do it quickly."

I give him a flat expression. "If your career in motivational speaking doesn't work out, at least you have your welcoming cheerfulness."

He stretches his neck, looking up like he's seeking patience. "Now," he says as he outstretches the cloth closer to me.

My pulse quickens as I triple check. "If you're playing me, or even try to sneak a glance—"

He interrupts, "I have no desire to do that." He pointedly looks away. "We detoured for this, so hurry up. You have five minutes to clean yourself."

Ouch. I'm getting the privacy I want, so the sting in my chest at his clear repulsion of me shouldn't hurt as much as it does. And what's with his two minutes this, five minutes that? What is he, an aspiring stopwatch? No one even has a fucking clock in sight, how would he even track time?

"I swear to the Divine, if you don't—"

I roll my eyes. "Okay, *okay.* Calm down."

As quickly as possible, I undress, balling my clothes on the ground and stepping into the cloth. I reach for the edges to wrap myself, but without even looking at me, he senses my movement and reaches around me to wrap it.

"Lift your arms," he instructs as he brings the cloth back around to my front, and I lift them to give him better access.

The backs of his knuckles touch me for barely a second, and I can tell it's unavoidable as he secures the cloth. His expression is bored, with eyes fixed on the material and not once straying to my body. Thank Creations that it also never rises to see my burning red face, which reveals what a brush of his knuckles can do.

Without warning, he drops to a knee in front of me. My heart leaps into my throat, and I jump back from him.

He halts his movement, just as I put two and two together. *His hand was aiming for my bag on the ground.*

A crack in his unbothered facade reveals a glint of concern behind his eyes at my reaction. I watch carefully as he rises, almost purposefully slow, and hands me items from the bag. "This is to wash your body, teeth, and hair." I inspect the grainy, murky green ball. "And I'm sure you're familiar with these brushes." I try not to make a face at the contraption. One side is carved and bristled into a toothbrush, the other side pronged like a comb.

I'd ogle at the design, but that would mean more time standing here half-naked in front of him. I nervously glance at his face for half a second before murmuring, "I'll be quick. About three minutes and twenty two seconds left, right?" I politely snatch the stuff from him and make a beeline for the water before he can tack off time for mocking him.

The fresh coolness kisses my hips, waist, and then shoulders, as squishy mud and weeds fill the space between my toes. I actively try not to think about the little critters that reside in this stream. Intrusive surety tells me there's likely sharks, crocodiles, snakes, and other things that will suddenly appear. *No one else is freaking out, so it's probably not dangerous. Shit.* There could be other creatures that I don't even know about. I mean, given that I've just met a pack of Okah, it's possible, right? An image is conjured in my mind, where a shark-crocodile hybrid with a knack for sucking blood like a leech is less than a meter away from me. I whip my head around scanning for the thing, then force myself to stop. *Why am I thinking about this?* Because irrational fear is my forte.

Rolling my eyes, I coerce myself to throw caution to the wind and let the water engulf me as I submerge. As soon as my head is under the water, the world falls silent, and the fear slips away. The fullness of the stream presses against every inch of me, holding me in stillness. I stay like that until my lungs burn for air, like I do in the bath at home.

When my face breaks the surface, I decide not to look around, facing away from everyone. Something tingles in my palm, and I realize the ball he gave me is dissolving. *I suppose I should start with teeth before I rub this all over my body.* Running the bristles along the ball, I tentatively smell it, and the scent of something fresh, yet foreign, fills my nostrils. I count down from three, and shove it in my mouth, brushing my teeth and tongue. Is it lemon, mint, chamomile... I'm not sure I recognize the taste, but it's crisp. Tucking the contraption between my thighs when I'm done, I break the ball in half, rubbing it against my hair and body. I scrub the dirt and blood from my skin and under my nails, going as fast as I can. I sneak a glance behind me, noticing others are already out, waiting for me. *Shit.* I try not to crumble at the ever-present loom of scorn from everyone. Except Sage. *I wish she were here.*

Quickening my pace, I marvel at whatever is in that ball. My hair feels so soft, the comb working through the tangled knots with an ease I didn't expect. *Okay. I'm done.*

Wrapping the cloth around me tighter ebbs my vulnerability as I emerge, scrubbed from head to toe. I forgot this feeling. It's wild how quickly we adapt to a new normal. A few days of being dirty, and I couldn't remember the redemption of energy that comes with being clean—something I took for granted.

Interrogator is surely about to come find me and scold the extra minute and a half I took past my deadline, and I hurry toward the tote bag. I don't allow my eyes to stray from the ground once, listening to the Okah shake water from their fur and the near-distant chatter.

I pull out the clothes Sage made for me, a smile tugging at my lips. A rich and earthy brown overall. The thin straps and scoop neck make it delicate. I turn it around, noticing there's drawstrings for the top half. I could make it tight to fit, but leave room for breathability in this heat.

My heart swells at the sight of a tiny hibiscus embroidered in royal blue over the chest area. *She could've left it plain. But she didn't. Why is she being so kind compared to everyone else? What does she see in me?*

I maneuver it on quickly around the cloth, a buzz of joy skipping through me as I pull the strings tight and secure the bow. Admiring the length and looseness of the material around my thighs, I just know it won't ride up or give me chafing if I have to walk far.

She wanted me to feel comfortable.

The smile edging at my lips doesn't fade, not even as I wring out the excess water in my hair, and then the cloth.

When I go to put my dirty clothes in the bag, I see something else that makes me stop in my tracks. Socks. *No way.* I haven't seen them wear socks, so I can't help but think that she made these just for me. The kindness, the consideration... I don't feel worthy of it.

The feeling of warmth kindles, even as I lace my boots and rise to my feet, swiping tiny rocks from my pants. Scattered whispers draw my attention, and I see glances thrown my way as they wait impatiently for me.

Find Interrogator, and let's get out of here...

I spot him off to the left, and I halt. His relaxed stance, the hands tucked in his pockets while deep in conversation—presumably about me—stop me dead in my tracks. Even though I don't have time for this, and I don't need more reasons for them to be angry with me taking so long, I stare at him. Everyone else fades to black.

I linger on those tiny scars trailing up his spine, and how they spread outward, following them up. *His hair.* It's wet—sitting as if he's dragged his hands through it to pull it off his face. Droplets form at the end of his short waves.

A single drop—it seizes me. I watch it fall from his hair, down his neck, finding its way between his shoulder blades. *If only I could be that waterdrop.* Better yet, my finger could follow the trail as it lowers down his spine, skimming the beckoning rise and fall of his body.

He tenses, going rigid, turning immediately and locking his eyes onto mine. I curse at myself; twice now he's caught me checking him out. My face is unbearably warm as I pretend to look through my bag.

Then I hear it: the earth colliding with his footfalls. Toward me. Reluctantly, I peer at him, and falter at his expression. He's aghast, or maybe angry.

Shit.

The words leave my mouth as he closes in. "I'm sorry."

He lowers his voice so only I can hear, speaking in a warning tone. "The first time you did that in the hut, I wrote it off, thinking I'd imagined it. But you just did it again. What are you doing?"

Mortified, I start entangling my fingers, struggling to hold eye contact. "I'm sorry. You're right. I didn't mean to..." *I've been scorning everyone staring at me, but I'm doing the same thing to him.*

He interrupts me and asks, "What did you do?"

He wants me to spell it out?

In a low and firm voice, I respond, "I can see that you're really angry that I was checking you out. I didn't mean to make you uncomfortable. It's hypocritical of me. I'm sorry."

I hate his use of silence.

He calibrates what I've said, taking this information in and weighing it against his own assessment. When he looks back at me, it's clear in his expression that my response is unacceptable.

"What? I said I was sorry. It won't happen again." The nerve of this guy, getting me to repeatedly apologize after everything he's put me through...

Slowly, he repeats himself. "What *exactly* did you do?"

Is he serious?

My fists clench, on the cusp of telling him to go fuck himself, but then he says, "I felt you." His voice is hushed and disbelieving.

I just stare at him. *What is he talking about?*

I shrug with one shoulder, sputtering through my confusion, "I don't know what you mean... You felt me? Sometimes I can feel when people stare at me. Is that it?" I ask.

He squints his eyes at me in appraisal, then instructs, "Tell me exactly what you were thinking."

I guffaw, unable to conceal the unlikelihood of *that* happening.

"No," I protest.

His eyes glint in what might be amusement, observing my reaction. The militant persona cracks, his lips parting slightly as he realizes I was not thinking innocent things.

Blinking the moment away, he presses on. "I'm not asking to pry, my intention is simply to ascertain something I suspect about you."

With a flat face, I remark, "That sentence is awfully contradictory."

Suspect about me? As if I'm *the enigma?*

His hand rakes through his hair, the gesture born of impatience. Straightening his spine and evening out his voice, he bites out quietly, "We don't have time for this back and forth, Ste—" He stops before saying my name.

The storm behind his eyes is my only clue to his emotions, because the guarded expression he wears is covering what lays beneath.

A single word leaves his mouth. "Please." His jaw clenches as if the word causes him physical pain to utter. I roll my eyes at him exaggeratedly. *He's so dramatic.* But I also don't think he is used to saying it. The longer we lock eyes, the more I feel inclined to do what he asks. Not because he's demanding and has authority, but because I feel like I'm talking to someone I've known longer than a day.

Pulling my lips tight against my teeth, I turn my head, cringing at the words as they leave my mouth. "Obviously I'm not going to look at you as I say this... So, I was watching a water droplet... *Ugh.*"

Pressing my palms into my closed eyes, I drawl, "Why are you making me do this?"

He encourages me to continue, a hint of urgency in his voice. "I can explain after."

My teeth might crack from how hard I'm fighting to keep this information inside.

Turning my head away, I urge the words out as rapidly as I can. "Fuck you. Fine. I wanted to trace the path of the water drop—"

He cuts in, "With as much detail as possible."

I shoot daggers at him. "You're perverted."

But his expression suggests the opposite: gentle, patient, apologetic for the imposition.

Rolling my eyes again, I stare out at the stream. "I didn't just watch the droplet; I, very rudely, was swept up in the idea of my finger replacing the water droplet, wanting to feel the skin over your shoulders, down your back. That's when you spun on me and stormed over."

Silence.

Water running.

Chatter from the others in the near distance.

This is all I hear—and now, the sound of my own heartbeat pounding incessantly in my ears.

With an ominous hint of fear in his tone, he admits, "That's exactly what I felt. Your finger tracing down my back." My head turns to face him again, and ever so subtly, as if drawing back a curtain to his internal world, he lets me in. I see something between awe and worry, but in the next second, his expression transforms— to *discovery*. My lips part as he watches me, seemingly finding a missing piece of an unsolved story. One he's agonized over.

The movement behind Interrogator draws my attention over his shoulder, finding TG and three others approaching. He turns to follow my eyeline.

When he glances back to me, my stomach tightens. The white T-shirt balled in his hands is finally pulled over his head, kindly returning a few brain cells to me in the process. But the strain between us lingers—the very makeup of the air around us is permanently altered. It's become irrevocably charged.

In a brash statement, he assures, "We'll finish this later."

Oh, joy! Next stop, Mortification 2.0.

"Can't wait," I mutter.

He slaps on that nonchalant expression and turns to give orders. But I know what's beneath that mask now.

I've seen you, Interrogator.

Have you seen me?

CHAPTER 10
TETHER

Making our way deep into the forest, I spiral over the interaction with Interrogator. *He felt me? My touch?* He also didn't say my name, respecting me when I revoked his access, even if it doesn't work like that. My emotions are scrambled eggs, burning in a pan set too high. I press my nail into the side of my thumb nervously, my mind a mess that I'm desperate to sort through. Unless it's my therapist or my journal, the world assumes I'm okay. But I don't have either to appease my burdens. No external source to witness the real me beneath my amiable smiles and 'can do' attitude. Although, that version of me doesn't seem to exist in this village. I'm... real, here. But people don't seem to like the real me here, or at home. People like the version of me that makes their life easier.

A familiar sensation of loneliness threatens to bring me to my knees, quaking from my heart and spreading through me. But I take another step. Then another. This is what I do. I push on.

Sage comes to mind. I'm sure we aren't at a place where I can confide in her, but maybe one day. She's the only one who's shared her name. *Wait.* I knew her name before she told me.

Quickening my steps to fall in line with Interrogator, I ask, "How come you told me Sage's name?

The abrupt question gains a thoughtful look from him in return. "She gave permission."

Waiting for him to elaborate is like waiting for the sun at midnight. Not going to happen.

So, I prod. "She gave permission... without even meeting me?"

Expressionless, he gives me a swift nod, then his focus returns forward. *Ice cold.*

Am I delusional, or was there a tangible tether starting to tug us closer?

I don't think I'm fabricating the way we're dancing this wearily fragile line. The more I think about it, the more inclined I am to believe that there's a mutual agreement, and neither of us are prepared to cross said line. Neither of us dare to acknowledge it aloud.

A nagging feeling tells me to forgo the eggshells I'm supposed to be walking on. When I sneak a glance at him, a strange comfort curls in my belly, telling me his rage and hate toward me isn't the whole story. Who knows why, but I think he might be warming up to me. *Luke*warming.

So, I test it.

Probing further, I ask, "Do names not mean as much to her as... everyone else?" Thinking out loud, I mumble, "No... Her reaction to me sharing my name... She seemed overjoyed, which is unlikely how someone would react if they didn't care."

Yes. A clink of his armor falls away when he sighs, realizing I'm not going to give this up.

He looks me over briefly. "Sage doesn't mind me sharing this, as she's given you access beyond what she would give most—especially someone from the outside. Sage is a Seer..."

My lips part to ask twelve follow up questions, but he holds his hand up, telling me to wait.

He adds, "She was giving me a play-by-play of what you were doing as you tried to escape."

I halt. My feet become as rooted in place as the trees around me.

Noticing I've stopped walking, he doubles back, inspecting my dumbfounded expression.

I swallow. "What do you mean?"

I knew I was being watched.

His hand finds the center of my back, gently nudging me forward. "Come on."

I try not to focus on how natural the gesture feels, or the way I relax when he looks me straight in the eyes.

When I keep walking, his hand drops back to his side, explaining, "Your escape was a test. Obviously, you failed."

I blink at him, but his focus is fixed on the path ahead. His voice feels distant as he recalls this morning.

"We left you unguarded, as people reveal themselves when they believe no one's watching. Except, Sage was."

I worry my bottom lip, listening.

Wait... Can I trust Sage? Is she pretending to be nice so I'll fall into another trap she sets without my knowing?

"There were four options: you could've tried to escape, seek us out by following the music, stay and wait for my return, or ask the guard to take you to us. Sage informed us of your every move, your feelings..."

Glancing at me for only a second, he adds, "Your first instinct was to run."

Shit.

I angle my head away from him as he continues. "The fact you were resourceful in becoming unbound raised suspicions of your innocence."

My eyes shoot to him in protest. "But did she feel my gut instinct to return?"

He watches me. "Yes, but your motive was unclear."

I want to tell him it was for the journal, but something in me tells me to wait. I thought that how he talked me down when I panicked with Divy meant he might've already read it, but surely he hasn't. If he had, he would look at me differently. Or maybe he has, and that's why he hates me. Because in my journal, you can see how weak I really am. It holds the depths of what the world did to me, scrawled across the pages. He could use it against me. He could burn it, take the list I wrote and turn it to ash along with the single shred of sanity I have left in hoping to get it back. Or, if things go badly at this barrier he keeps talking about, they might kick me out without ever getting it back.

Bile rises up my throat at the thought of never getting it back. *My only true friend.*

I decide to share a half-truth. "Something wasn't right when I left. It hardly made sense, but I knew coming back was my shot at survival, no matter how slim the chance was that I'd be forgiven."

There was also the pang in my stomach, telling me I had another reason to come back. *Him. Me. An unknown reason for why I found the village, that apparently, was never meant to be found.*

He thinks over what I've said, feeling a million miles away as he explains, "Despite your return, the others saw your escape as betrayal. They thought you were too much of a risk to keep here."

I ask tentatively, "They?"

Not him.

He doesn't spare me a glance. "Sage and I, for different reasons, fought this. I am not certain of your level of threat, who sent you, or your true intentions. And I need to investigate why you're unreadable to everyone except for Sage. I need you here for that."

I give a confused look, but he moves on to his next point. "When Sage came to give you the healing balm, she confirmed something, but refuses to share it with us. She claims you will be the one to tell us, when you know. And that we need to trust her."

He turns to me, whispering so only I can hear, "After what just happened at the stream, plus your birthmark..." He runs a hand down his tense jaw, the gesture etched with what looks like concern. *The kind that might keep you up at night.* He admits, almost to himself, "I don't exactly know what you are."

What. Not who.

Those words are like pricks along my scalp, and the answers to whatever he might mean are locked in his mind.

I stop walking, tugging on his wrist with both hands to stop him. My mouth dries as one by one, everyone stops with us. Knives are unsheathed, lethal eyes trace my grip, and Divy growls from behind.

Interrogator announces, "I'st, Youhi," before gesturing a wave for them to walk on. He turns to Divy. "Treh'sa. Avah."

Worry tugs my insides into a tighter knot as I try to keep the panic at bay.

Their skeptical and observant demeanors feel like lashes against my skin as they reluctantly sheath their weapons. He reassures them again, and finally, they turn to walk ahead. The Okah drag their feet, hovering close by before conceding and joining the group.

Interrogator turns to me, his forearm flexing underneath my clasped fingers.

I don't let go.

He doesn't make me.

His voice is low, the corners of his mouth twitching downward in a pulse. "I've overwhelmed you."

My mind spirals, replaying his words. With a chest rising and falling in quick breaths, I manage one question. "Who was playing the music?"

He scoffs, a rare smile quirking his lips. "*That's* what put that look on your face?"

Feeling the distraught expression lightly tugging at the corners of my mouth, I let it dissolve into a frown, pointedly staring at him. Suddenly, holding onto him feels weird, so I take a step back and release my grip. "I have more questions."

Retorting with a mumbled, "Not surprising," he begins to walk on as if I'd concerned him for no reason.

"Wait." I scuttle ahead and stop in front of him.

A foggy disarray of questions swarms my brain; there's too much to think about, and I'm stalling. The only thing I can think about right now is the easiest question.

I need to know who was playing the music.

It rang through my heart, even in a time as dire as the escape attempt. The sound flowed and breathed like I could only dream to. It reminded me of the version of myself I never believed I could become.

Free.

He claims I'm difficult for him to read, so why does he soften his gaze, his voice, and offer an explanation—giving me exactly what I need without having to ask? "The Muscas. Very talented musicians. The timing of it was part of a strategy, but the music itself is something else."

This time, it's my turn to be quiet—to let the silence stretch. Taking this all in, a quiet thrum taps against my skull in the birth of a headache. But I can't deny the gratitude at having information given to me, which in turn, eases my angst.

Time slows as I really look at him as an entity separate from myself. Right now, he's not a rude, prison-guard interrogator that makes my insides boil. He's just a man... with his own life, due diligence, and set of values, beliefs, and ideologies of the world. I see the lifetime of expressions that's touched his face, the thousands of ways he's used his body, the millions of thoughts that run through his mind. I see him as an individual.

I heed the profound and eloquent lesson that just because he's a pain in *my* ass, doesn't mean he's a pain in *the* ass.

Clearing my throat, I say, "Thank you. For sharing that. And for... not killing me." I scratch my forehead, mumbling, "And uh, thanks for the cloth down at the water." The words come out quick and clipped, and I look around awkwardly, sensing the weight of his scrutiny.

In a controlled monotone, he replies, "Okay."

Jackass is back, then.

My quick smile is close-lipped and doesn't reach my eyes as I stride away. He's quick on my heels, coming up next to me.

Neither of us speaks again. Not for a long time. Not until later, when the realization of where we've ended up settles in.

"We're here," Interrogator says, while the others wait and face me.

I stop walking abruptly.

The burnt-orange and brownish tree up ahead feels... familiar. I spin in a circle, scanning the vines along the floor, the slight hilling to the left.

A jolt of recognition spikes straight through me, and I turn slowly back to him.

I blurt out, "What are we doing here?" The question slices through the air as thoughts scatter in my mind, trying to understand why I'm in this exact spot. Again.

They said they were taking me to the barrier, and I was picturing a huge fence or wall... not something invisible, amongst the usual plants, trees, and soil-packed earth. This is the very spot they found me.

In a flash memory, I recall Interrogator first asking me, "What were you doing in this part of the forest?" He meant, what was I doing in the forest *past* the barrier.

I try desperately to hide the tremble of my hands, because the truth is...

I don't know.

CHAPTER 11
YOU HEARD ME

Wordlessly, the group stands in a cluster, waiting. Watching me. Seeing their expectant expressions, I lift my hands in question. "What do you want me to do?"

Interrogator takes one step toward me, drawing my attention. "When you were last here, did you feel anything... strange?"

A hollow laugh escapes me. "You're *joking*, right?"

This is where I was faced with Spearman and Turquoise. Where I was taken. Is that strange enough?

He clarifies, "Before you saw anyone. Go back to that moment and tell us what happened. Show us what you did."

The nervous energy within urges me to tuck my hair behind my ears, before letting my arms fall at my sides. "What I did? I was standing right there." My finger points near a wide-pronged tree, its veined roots the thickness of my forearm.

He nods. "When they found you, yes. But before that."

Shaking my head at the weirdness of this, I step toward the spot where I first saw Spearman. With my fingers curled into fists, I try to recall the memory.

Why was I standing there?

The memory of the sticky film that I walked right through flashes in my mind. I stopped to wipe off the... "The spider web," I murmur.

Closing my eyes, I narrate the images as they rise in my mind. "I was lost—had been for a while. I just started picking trees. I'd pick one and walk toward it. When I got to it, I'd pick the next, and that's the way I was deciding my direction, hoping I'd eventually become *un*lost. This tree..."

I start toward it. A light breeze rustles the leaves, loose strands of my hair tickling my cheeks. The sense of relief billows through me the closer I get.

My voice is sure as I recall, "I walked past it, and into this giant spider web. It wrapped around me. But... I couldn't find the web after. It felt like I was swallowed whole by sticky air, as absurd as that sounds..." My voice trails off.

Somewhere distant, I hear his voice, telling me to wait. To stop walking. But I'm drawn to the tree. I want to be close. *It wants me to come closer.* My fingers reach out toward a low-hanging branch, vaguely noticing hurried steps pounding the ground toward me.

I'm jerked backward, strong arms wrapping around my waist and hoisting me against their chest. The tree moves away. *No.* I'm being dragged away.

Blinking, I pull at the arms wrapped around me, recognizing them. "What are you doing? Put me down," I demand, my voice reaching a high pitch.

Finally, Interrogator relents, and I scramble back a few steps from him, toward the tree.

His chest rises and falls in full and even breaths. "I was trying to save you."

I draw my head back, confused. "Save me? From touching a tree? Are you not well in the head?"

Head dipping to one side, his glare cuts through the space between us, and the only sounds are from the buzzing of insects and caws of birds.

I push my chin forward with a slight wobble of my head, prompting him to explain.

Reconsidering, his mouth curls down at the edges like he couldn't give two shits. "Carry on, then."

The group looks toward him, surprise flitting over their features. Two of them share a glance, smiling at some kind of inside joke. At my expense. *Nothing new, then.*

Pulling my shoulders back, I relent in a false calm, "Fine."

Crossing his arms, he inclines his head in challenge. But when I take a step back, his jaw clenches. Another step, his fingers twitch.

When I turn and reach out, he holds his breath. *There's something I don't know.*

His unease gives me reason to hesitate, but I can't back down now. I've made it into a big deal. A challenge.

He inches forward, as if about to come pull me away again. Everyone here seems happy to have me gone, careless about my safety—but not him. My eyes stay locked on his as I stop a foot before touching the tree. Something in him awakens when he realizes I might actually do it. His expression confuses the hell out of me. It's tense and rigid. He's the stick that goes up his own ass like some kind of uptight pretzel.

I turn fully to face him as I give up my attempt at gaining power and control.

Throwing my arms out, I yell, "What? Why are you freaking out?"

Closing his eyes briefly, his shoulders lose some of the tension they hold.

No. No more people telling me what I can and can't do. He's caught off guard, and I take the opportunity to rebel, even if it's reckless.

I don't allow him time to stop me as I step backward and graze the tree with my fingertips. Nothing happens. I sag through an exhale. *I knew it.* Letting my other hand join the trunk, I spread my fingers and watch the specs of bark crumble loose and drift to the floor. Stepping around the tree, I glide my fingers along its surface, cautious to step over the roots, and reach for the tiny flower bud.

That's when I feel it. My body stalls in response. A faint hum comes from the air in front of me.

I hear the whispering behind me, but their unsure voices fade as I hone in on this *thing*.

I press forward slowly. A thick wall, and a tightness in the air pushes against my palm, but not in refusal or rejection—just a resisting force, as if something is there. An invisible energy, making its presence known. The familiar stickiness encases my fingers, and it slurps my hand deeper into its hold. Without focusing on it being a spiderweb, I'm able to relax into the sensation this time, and the way it welcomes me. It's as if an element of it stretches out to gently caress the back of my hand. *It recognizes me.*

A shiver works its way up my spine, a giggle bubbling up my throat at the strange combination of tactile fondness and internal affection. Why would Interrogator ever try to stop me from experiencing this? Does he know how incredible I feel right now? Am I imagining this strange and inviting energy web?

I draw my fingers back, a smile plastered across my face as I throw a 'told you so' look over my shoulder. Everyone stops breathing, disbelieving glances shooting between me and the tree. It causes my smile to falter.

Unsettled, I question their concern. "What?"

Interrogator watches me, seemingly unsure of something as he uncrosses his arms and moves toward me in strong and rushed strides.

The sternness in his features makes me wonder what I did wrong, and the uncertainty of what's happening quickens my pulse, coaxing me to retreat. My back presses against the tree for support, borrowing its unrelenting strength. But seconds away from colliding into me, he just... passes me, leaving my breaths quick and heart racing.

I watch with wide eyes as he walks through the energy wall, ducking and angling his head slightly, looping around the tree.

The furrow between his brows matches mine as he appears to be checking for something.

My voice gives sound to my confusion. "What the hell are you doing?"

When he stops in front of me again, he rubs his chin with his hand, processing what seems like a burdensome amount of flowing thoughts.

Mumbling to himself, I barely make out his statement. "Barrier is intact."

Before I can open my mouth to speak, he walks away, throwing over his shoulder, "Wait here." As if knowing I was about to ignore the instruction and follow, Divy comes up next to me, blocking my view of Interrogator's disappearing figure.

A minute later, she steps back, offering a grand reveal of his approach. He turns to the group, sharing his thoughts in an unspoken conversation before turning to me.

"This is the barrier. It sits over us like a dome. You shouldn't be able to approach this tree, let alone touch it."

Each time he speaks, what I think I know rattles inside my brain. The barrier, this place, these people, *him*. Nothing makes sense.

My eyes squint, lips parting silently, the impact of this information thrumming like an echo in my ears.

I unconsciously run my hand up my arm, a feeble attempt at self-soothing.

He blinks slowly. "Explain."

I'm completely lost on what he wants me to say. "You first."

The demand does not irritate him, and therefore, doesn't elicit the reaction I hoped. Instead, the side of his mouth twitches upwards in a pulse. "That wasn't a suggestion."

Why can't he just tell me what he wants to know in simple fucking words.

Dropping my head back, I whisper to the sky, "Nothing is ever straightforward with you."

"What did you say?"

You heard me.

I meet his militant disposition with my fed-up countenance. "Can you just ask me what you want to ask me? *Clearly.*"

TG approaches, resting a hand on Interrogator's shoulder, as if he knows his next moves like a shark can sense flailing fish. Interrogator physically eases, gaining the upper hand on whatever storm is brewing inside of him. Quick and foreign words are exchanged between Interrogator and TG, the other village members joining in with what I think is their two cents.

Muffled chaos is what I *hear.*

Finally, Interrogator addresses me, staring at me pointedly. "We protect our village from outsiders by using a domed barrier. This tree is the origin, communicating through an underground network to form the barrier. Coming close to any part of the dome would send a warning jolt through you, compelling you to walk away in the opposite direction, without hesitation or recollection."

I blink in surprise, not expecting that. "Well, pretending for a second that that's *not* insane, I'm not compelled to walk away."

TG and Interrogator share a glance before he continues. "To touch the tree though, the energetic protection would launch you, burning through you in vicious heat. When you wake up, all you'd remember is to return where you came from. No one knows it's here because they will never remember what happened, or have cause to come back."

His brows twitch, almost like they want to furrow, but never fully commit. "This is the first time it's ever failed. You are the only person who has ever walked freely through the barrier."

Me?

His voice takes on that authoritative tone as he adds, "I want you to explain why."

My lungs fill as I rub my hand over my sternum, trying to soothe my heart's stress topically.

"As I've told you, I'm nobody. I don't know why this is happening or why it didn't fling me away from it with amnesia." I turn to the tree. "It feels like it does the opposite."

A jittery warmth takes root in my chest, and I feel compelled to lean into it.

This feeling is... wild. Maternal. Nurturing. I struggle to recall the last time I felt this. It was sometime from when I was very young.

I let it ease me, but the rich fullness of the sensation conflicts with the gnawing feeling of eyes boring into the back of me. Turning to face Interrogator, my intuition is on point, because he's got that laser focus pinned on me.

He prompts, "Opposite how?"

I clear my throat. "I was drawn in. Answering a silent invitation, knowing it's safe."

The others start toward me, listening intently to what I have to say. *Yikes. That's a lot of eyes.*

Turning back to the tree, my shoulders relax. "I feel..." A laugh escapes my lips at the words I'm about to confess. "I feel loved by this tree. And I love it, too. Well, *her.* She feels like a her."

A smile brightens my face as I reach out again, caught up in the concentrated essence of nurture I feel from her. My palm instinctively plants itself on her trunk. "I think the barrier called me here."

My internal world is rocked the second those words leave my mouth, as if they just fell out without even forming as a thought first. *What did I just say?*

Interrogator steps into my peripheral, one word leaving his lips. "Interesting."

The unfamiliar, kind tone pulls my gaze to him. That, and the fact that I know the single word is a deceptively short summation of the streaming thoughts he's having.

"Let's walk," he announces to everyone. "Lap the barrier." Jerking his chin out, he instructs me to lead the way. So, I do.

Every now and then, I reach out, running my hand through the barrier as one would a cascading waterfall. The comforting feeling glides between my fingers, causing a tingle to dance along my spine. They wait for it to reject me, or maybe even hope for it. Instead, it signals me in a wordless whisper that I'm welcome here—supposed to be here, despite the village people's disapproval and my confusion.

"Stop. Come here." Interrogator's deep voice summons my attention. I give him an impatient and expectant look, wondering what he wants from me now. Perhaps I'm to demonstrate how meek my cartwheeling abilities are, seeing as they all stare at me like I'm a part of a circus ensemble. He inspects my expression before taking a few steps toward me, since I don't listen to him and 'come here' upon his request.

Stopping right in front of me, his eyes drift over my face, as if seeking a flaw to some kind of impersonation I'm doing. I don't shrink back under the weight of it, and instead, give him a 'look all you want, I don't care' smile.

His tone hints to incredulousness when he asks, "When you arrived, you just *walked* through the barrier?"

I catch the undertone of disbelief and awe in the way everyone shares glances.

Taking a step toward him, I lift my chin. "Appears that way. You are familiar with deductive reasoning, if I recall correctly from our earlier conversation."

Attempting to intimidate me, he scans me from head to toe. He wants to watch me quiver under his scrutinous glare. But I don't. *And he hates it.*

Studying my eyes, his low voice relays what I first said in the hut. "You were just out here exploring, and accidentally stumbled upon the village?"

Clasping my hands behind my back, I smile sweetly at him because he already knows the answer. I say it anyway. "Yes."

He licks his teeth, his gaze appraising and persistent.

Sliding his hands into his pockets, a casual smile plays on his lips as he looks away. The movement catches me off guard, my shield faltering. I stare at him in his relaxed state—the ease of his confidence. Right now, he just looks like a normal guy.

The distance closes as he takes another step forward, his eyes finding mine and holding them captive. My cheeks blush at the proximity. At the intensity of him. He's so close, his body radiates heat, warming me from the inside out.

"One more question," he drawls, raking his eyes over my face... hungrily.

Oh. *Oh. You little shit.* A sense of clarity washes over me. He can't *read* me, or interrogate me, as he would so easily others. This fucker is using my attraction to him as leverage to gain answers, seducing the truth from me. *Again.* I fell for it last time, nearly fucking kissing him. But he won't fool me twice. *He doesn't give a shit about me.* He just wants answers to protect his village.

I don't let him know I broke free of the spell, allowing my gaze to soften as I meaningfully peruse his features. "What's your question?"

His smirk wavers as I stare at him dreamily, like I long for him. His voice drops an octave as he asks, "Do you believe there is more to life than what you see?"

What? Does he mean the barrier and how it's nearly invisible? Come to think of it, what are they made of? Something I can't see...

Returning the scrutinous gaze he gives me, I ask with a half-laugh, "What, like magic?"

He doesn't laugh. No one does.

Crossing his arms over his chest, he replies, "Yes."

The smile on my face drops, and my armor wavers, recalibrating after shock.

Magic?

He doesn't move as he watches me, analyzing every single micro-expression on my face. Barely moving his lips, he adds, "Abilities far beyond what we think we're capable of."

The words reverberate through me. I'd heard of the myths—that we once had these incredible powers a time long ago. It's a far-fetched conspiracy, fueling children's stories, drunk whispers in alleyways, and blockbuster films. But any real information on it is nonexistent. It's portrayed in research as imaginary. As a concept, sure, it's entertaining. In reality? Absolutely not.

Wait. Sage. A Seer. He was already testing the waters by telling me about her. I think back to the conversation. I assumed it was some kind of gift, or...

How did I not make a bigger deal about how mind-blowing she is? How can I deny what's right in front of me? Apprehension lifts the hairs on the back of my neck as my eyes are drawn to the barrier. The trees. Slowly, I turn my attention back to the Interrogator. *What's under the skin of this man?* Distant memories tug at me, beckoning me to acknowledge them. But in the same breath, it's like remembering something that hasn't yet happened.

The word rises in my throat—*no*. Presses against my teeth—*no*. But what comes out is, "Maybe."

He gives nothing away, just watches me, waiting for me to reveal something to confirm whatever narrative he's spinning.

The group's quiet whispers draw my attention, and I sense that something is different. It's slight, and only there for a second. Long enough for me to see that a new judgement of who I might be is made.

TG glances between me and Interrogator, a half-smile tugging at his lips.

Widening my eyes, I give him a 'what are you looking at?' head wobble, earning a 'nothing' head wobble in return.

Interrogator announces, "Let's head back."

Without hesitation, everyone turns and does exactly that. Not a single word is spoken the whole journey back.

I focus on the ground, trying not to trip over winding roots strewn across the forest floor as the light fades. Every now and then, my eyes lift to the group, suspicious that I haven't had a single withering glare shot at me. Their usual animosity... it feels more subtle. I remain the outsider imposing on their lives— unaccepted—but there's another layer. A cause for reconsideration. *I'll take it.*

As we approach the village, I can see the curling smoke from the fire and smell the rich aroma of dinner. I hear the music and the signs of life existing peacefully. I'm a fiend for it, the stark contrast to the arduous reality of home.

"Avah I'st," Interrogator calls out as he slows his pace to a halt. They turn to bow their heads at him before continuing on.

My gaze swings between the departing group and Interrogator as I ask, "Do I follow them?"

My question is answered by the look he gives me. *Stay.*

The pink haze of dusk kisses the navy of night, the sky sitting between two places. Just as we do, standing opposite each other. Our minds are somewhere between mistrust and something else. *Magnetism.*

Emotions cross over his face too quickly to name, but I sense he's brewing over his thoughts, deciding whether or not to voice them. A shiver skates up my spine in anticipation.

I fill the silence. "Say it."

He looks away, licking his lips before turning an unveiled gaze on me.

"I can't read you," he admits.

Something flutters in my chest. "And... it annoys you that you can't?"

He studies my eyes. "It infuriates me."

I swallow, glancing around us.

The sky darkens as the fervor in his tone grows. "At first, I thought you were an expert at hiding your intentions—trained to shield your emotions or put on specific ones. That you were surely not to be trusted."

"And now?"

He presses on, small creases forming around his eyes as he narrows them at me. "You left and tried to escape. But then you came back. During our... discussion this morning, you revealed things about yourself that have me questioning everything." He crosses his arms. "The barrier recognizes you."

I whisper, "In a strange way, I recognize it, too."

He takes the sight of me in, as if I confirmed another one of his suspicions. "Sage sees something in you, and I see how you react to things when you think no one is watching. You're easing into this environment in ways that make you seem harmless. But in other ways, you're sharp and unreadable. Tough—not from training, but from life. You're also unpredictable, like someone who doesn't know who they are. I can't put my faith in you to leave here with our secrets yet, and not without knowing more about you."

My heart sinks. He's right; we've only just met. He couldn't possibly know me. But a whisper of a feeling from the chasm inside me questions that. Even though he says there's more to learn about me, what he just said shows that maybe he's seen more than anyone else. *What if he does know me, and just like me, he can't quite put a finger on where from?*

His tone is friendlier than I expect as he says, "Today, you have earned a small piece of trust from the village. And from me." The admission isn't what shocks me—it's his smile, barely there, but it undoubtedly takes my breath away. Steals all the brain cells that help me form sentences. What's even more strange, is that the thumping in my chest quiets, and I feel a rare sensation floating through me. *Calmness.*

"Thank you," is all I can manage.

A light sparks behind his eyes, his voice low as he notes, amused, "Another thank you."

I try to suppress my smile, but fail miserably.

"Don't get used to it," I retort under my breath. An attempt to resurrect nonchalance looks like crossing my arms and averting my gaze to the side with a shrug.

In the brief silence, I cautiously peer at him, catching the slight widening of his smile.

"What?" I ask, mirroring the expression.

Dropping his head, he sighs, moving to brush past me toward the village. But that slight lift of his lips is unmistakably still there. The sigh says I'm a thorn in his side, but the smirk tells me he might learn to tolerate it. Might even like the sharp thorns of a rose.

As we approach the center of the village, I stop just on the outskirts of everyone, observing them like an outsider. He tells me to wait while he goes to get me food, and I think this might be the first time I don't feel the urge to roll my eyes at his instruction.

I'm definitely food-motivated.

The thought of a comfort meal makes my heart skip. The emotions flooding through me the last few days have taken its toll, and the smell of garlic and rosemary has me thinking my problems aren't actually so bad. *Deitydamn, I think there's potatoes in the stew.* Now I'm salivating.

My fingers interlock behind my back as I watch the scene before me. Hearty conversation and laughter travel across the field toward me, rolling over my skin in a mocking wave. But I can't look away from the connection I long for.

Cool night air meets the small fires they surround. Their energy and shared stories lift each other's spirits, resembling the embers that float up like fire fairies.

Suddenly, gazes find mine while intermittent whispers exchange. Word is clearly spreading about what happened today. But I can't read their expressions clearly enough to know if the whispers are good, or of more skepticism.

Turning away slightly, I close my eyes. The reminder that I don't belong here looms over me. *I don't belong anywhere.*

A pair of footsteps nearing me urges my eyes open, and I turn to see Interrogator balancing two bowls and two cups in his arms. The muscles in my face relax at the sight.

Of the food. Not him.

Food back home tastes... different. Modified. But I never would've used that word before tasting the meals here.

Reaching out to collect the warm bowl and cup of water, I meet his gaze. "Thank—" I bite down on my bottom lip.

Amusement slides into his tone as he says, "I didn't catch that. What did you say?"

Without waiting to go to my hut, I take a mouthful of the delicious stew, pointing at my mouth as an excuse for not being able to speak.

The humor in his expression reminds me of a gentle breeze.

Make it stop. The silence. The watching.

Dropping my gaze to the ground, I mutter, "Well, I guess I should get back to my cell."

The joke doesn't land. I only realize this when I sneak a glance at him and see pain subtly cut through his features.

Before he can speak, I correct, "I know we have different perspectives of my situation. With that said, I didn't mean to insult you and take two steps back. It was meant to be a joke." The last few words come out in a whisper.

He nods. Whatever shadow was cast over his features drifts away, leaving something much lighter. "After you." He gestures to the hut.

Of course, he's my guard. He's having dinner with me. *Great, more opportunity to be awkward, or argue, or sit in uncomfortable silence. But maybe now... things won't be so volatile between us.*

Turning to close the distance between me and the hut, my eyes travel up to the stars blinking down at us. My feet halt right before the entrance, Interrogator stopping right at my heels.

A gasp rips through me, the clarity of the sky stealing my breath. Without all the light pollution, I can see more than an occasional twinkle. I see the universe. I see the luminescence of space. Its size and power is both daunting and exhilarating.

"Wow." I breathe the word in a whisper.

Turning to see more, I continue to gawk, feeling Interrogator's shoulder brush against mine as he stands beside me. Comfort envelopes me as we stay like this for a minute, his head tipped back and gazing alongside me.

Then, I spot it. My safety. My beacon. My oldest friend. *My constellation.* A smile splits my face, sparks dancing in my eyes just as the stars do across the navy sky.

"Orion," I whisper.

Stars always drew deep meaning for me, and I studied them from as early as I could read. The Orion constellation always stood out, and I lean on it more than I'd care to admit.

"What did you say?" he asks me, his voice low, laced with something like shock.

My eyes meet his briefly, seeing that I'm correct.

Rolling my eyes, I drawl in a teasing tone, "Come on, I'm not completely cut off from things outside the four walls of an office back home." I step closer to Interrogator, just in front of him so I can point up and guide his gaze. "The Orion constellation."

My childlike grin returns, the cluster of stars warming my chest as Interrogator's proximity heats me further.

Clearing my throat, I take a step away, my thoughts spilling out nervously as I try to rid myself of the way my senses react to his closeness. "It's always meant a lot to me, since... well, forever. It probably sounds bizarre, but I feel like I know it personally. I look for it whenever I need a sense of grounding. Ironically." A chuckle comes out as I gaze upward, knowing it's millions of miles away in the sky.

He remains silent.

Shit. I overshared. My cheeks warm as I peer over my shoulder to gauge his reaction, only to see a stunned expression. He looks at me as if he's trying to absorb every inch of my being through sight alone.

Slowly, he says, "Interesting."

I let out a nervous laugh, trying not to melt under his scrutiny. "Is it? Why?"

Without warning, he leans down to place his food and water on the ground before repeating the action with mine.

"What are you doing—" My words cut off at the sight of him standing taller, and how a surety falls over his features.

Suddenly, his hand is hovering in the space between us with his palm facing upward.

Does he want me to give him something?

Wait. Oh, he's going to introduce himself? Shit, shit, shit. My heart starts racing. Maybe he was moved by my story and wanted to give me his name in return.

My hand lies atop his, and the soft skin of my palm grazes against his calloused one. He wraps his fingers around mine, and my nerves ease a fraction, even though I've stopped breathing.

His voice comes from deep within his chest as he introduces himself. "I'm Orion."

CHAPTER 12
COINCIDENCE

Goosebumps rise on my arms and thighs, a warm fullness expanding in my stomach as if pouring water into a glass. The sensation is not quite a drop, not quite butterflies, but something born of a stark and visceral reaction to an uncovering. The feeling is a knowing flare, even though my mind has yet to catch up.

Thoughts fire like cannonballs against my skull, claiming my attention. He let me know his name. He let me in. But the name itself—it's a universal accident. Profound coincidence.

Synchronicity. No.

How is he named after my favorite constellation?

The very one that my eyes roamed across night after night, able to breathe easier because I knew I was being watched over. The stars would whisper in winks of light, telling me no matter the wrong in the world, the loneliness and worry, I must keep hoping for more. I promised Orion, and then I promised myself. I engraved it in gold and wear it every day. *I promise to find more.*

With my trembling fingers still held in his, steady and warm, I choke out, "Your name is Orion."

The fire crackling behind me reflects sparks of light to appear within his eyes, painting him truly as the picture of stars personified.

His voice is hoarse as he answers, "Yes." One word spoken through his lips, a million more in the gentle stroke of his thumb across my knuckles.

This is no coincidence. The thought spurs awake a feeling inside of me, and I rip my hand out of his grip.

He tracks the movement, and when his eyes rise to meet mine, they turn hard. Confused. *No.* Worried. "What is it? What's wrong?"

I look at him like a deer in headlights and back up a step, clearing my throat.

No fucking way.

Closing my eyes makes it worse, as the loss of a sense heightens something else. The tether I've been ignoring. Resisting the pull toward him only stirs a vision to spark in my mind. A flash of stars in a galaxy. Purples, blues, and a bright white light intertwine and snake around each other, spiraling in an ancient, eternal, and synchronized dance.

A sharp gasp pulls through the slight gap between my lips, and I try to erase the image from my mind. He steps closer, absorbing every detail of my face as he reaches out, putting his hands on my arms. I didn't realize I was unsteady until I felt his support.

"You're shaking." The statement is a stern observation, but it holds an undertone of concern.

With whatever shred of control I have available, I throw up walls and masks, relaxing my face as much as I can, until it displays polite indifference. But the crease between his eyebrows only deepens.

His voice drops low, his loaded command cutting through me. "I need you to say something."

I need some air. *I'm outside. I have been all day. But I need more. Move. Go. Get away from him.*

"I'm fine, sorry. I just..." As calmly as I can, I let the words out. "You just surprised me, that's all."

My attempt to look nonchalant, I fear, has morphed into crazy eyes and a manic smile.

I try to save it, but there's a slight waver in my voice when I say, "Thank you for sharing your name. It's cool."

I am certain that I was very chalant. Not cool.

An ache takes root in my chest as he considers me emphatically.

He knows I'm hiding something.

I am.

I don't know what, but I don't intend to find out.

But, I...

No.

A question is burning in his eyes—one I want to run from. Rough fingers run idle strokes up and down my arms, over my goosebumps as he steps in again. The simple contact stirs through me like a spoon in warm honey.

Indescribable recognition. Warm and gooey.

Without consent, the name slips through my lips in a cautious whisper. "Orion." His thumbs halt their soft strokes.

I've said the name countless times before, with my eyes locked on the constellation, imagining it looking right back at me. This is different. *Or is it exactly the same?* The name—I understand each letter and feel it rooted so deep within me, as if saying my own name.

I become suddenly aware of people staring at us, confused, and my feet take me away from him. One step... Two... Until his hands reluctantly fall from my skin.

"They're all staring—" I start to say, but he interrupts me.

"Don't look at them, look at me."

I do, and all I see is an expression filled with expectation. How he waits for some kind of explanation.

I say three words to him inside my mind, but I speak an entirely different four words out loud.

"I need to go," I whisper, barely above a rasp.

Hurt laces through his features before he schools them. "You know I can't let that happen."

My fists clench, nails digging into my palms in my familiar attempt to stay in my body. Not to give into panic.

I'm going. "I just want to go for a quick walk. I won't be long." My chest rises and falls quicker, the anxiety clawing its way through me, deciding my heart is its next victim. And so it races.

I'm sure he's noticed the sweat beading on my forehead, because he steps in to steady me again. Tiny rocks crunch under my boot as I step away from him, his jaw ticking in response.

An exasperated sound leaves him as he shoves a hand through his hair. When he takes a step back, I can't help but take one too, because if I stay too close, I might reach for him. Maybe he was thinking the same thing. The intensity of his energy, though—it's never felt more present as it pushes against mine. The tether between us vibrates as if in distress, as if reading and reflecting how we feel. I'm spiraling, and I guess that he's frustrated he can't stop it by figuring out what I'm thinking and reading me. To him, I suppose I'm the puzzle that's always missing pieces.

"Talk to me." It's not the words that pierce my heart, it's the plea in his tone. I draw my bottom lip between my teeth at the tenderness of him. I'm struggling to reconcile that this greatly rude warrior, arrogant leader of this village, finely-honed militant machine is the same man who stands before me right now— *Orion...*

Dropping my head to stare at the ground doesn't erase the look on his face; it's burned into my mind. *Be as honest as you can be right now.*

My eyes open and land on his chest. "What I need right now... is to walk. I need to think. I need a moment to breathe. At home, I'd do that. Here? I'm a prisoner. I'm panicking, and being trapped is not helping. If I stand here another minute, I'm going to rip my hair out..." I take another step back, my hands trembling, my breathing spiraling out of control.

"I promise, I will come back. I'm sorry... I can't give you more. I need to..." I force the words out between gasps of breaths.

Twisting to face away from him, my rushed steps pad atop the earth toward the heavy shadows of the forest. My fear of the dark falls second against the fear of what I feel for him.

This stranger.

A jolt spikes my stomach at the wrongness of the thought.

I hear him curse, followed by the heavy footfalls of him behind me, and then coming up beside me.

"Please, leave me alone. I can't talk to you right now." My words are equal parts gentle and firm.

Interrogator—*Orion*—informs me, "I can't leave you unattended."

I scoff, demonstrating I don't give a fuck.

His tone evens out. "Slow your steps, walk next to me. If you keep racing away like this, they'll suspect something's wrong, and we'll be followed." When I only quicken my footing, he changes tactics. "Do you really want Divy chasing you down right now?"

My head turns in his direction, but I don't dare meet his eyes. Exhaling a shaky breath, I slow my steps to an aching, leisurely pace.

Nearly there. A few more seconds.

The sounds of the village fade, the dark forest swallowing me whole as I cross the threshold. Despite the paranoia of spider webs, snakes, and other lurking beasts in here, I take my first full breath. *Relief.*

It takes a second, but my eyes adjust, slivers of light coming through the trees from the night sky.

Shin-high foliage whips against me as I pick up the pace, Orion following suit. My body tenses from even thinking of his name.

Stop.

An imploring part of me swims against the current of denial, trying so hard to address this knowing inside me. Wanting to figure it out, and investigate why I'm really here, with him, these people. Denial is too strong, the force of it shoving my desire to know under water. Suffocating it.

My feet slow as I try to blink away the black spots in my vision. *Do not pass out.*

He's silent behind me, his distance dancing the line of giving me space and keeping watch.

The burn in my legs tells me how long we've been out here, the new blisters from today angry inside my boots at more walking. Even if the socks Sage gave me are undeniably the only reason I have gotten this far, offering a slight cushioning between my skin and the week old hiking boots, I need to take a break.

Intently poring over what's around me, a pull tugs my attention toward a two hundred foot tall tree, webbing out at its base and large enough to witness my breakdown. It's sweet, patient, kind, and kissed by moonlight. *Perfect.*

When I reach it, I plop to the ground in a careless thump, leaning all my weight against her splotchy, pale bark. Raking my fingers through my hair and dragging them down my face, I beg behind closed eyes for this to be a dream. *But it's not.*

I can't explain how I know he's standing in front of me, seeking answers in that examining look he seems to love doing. I'm scared to face him, because looking into his eyes shouldn't feel so right.

I can't catch my breath around him.

"Please," I implore, "can you stop staring at me like I might suddenly combust and just... give me a minute?"

The bastard decides to ignore my words and sit next to me, his shoulder brushing against mine. A groan sounds in my throat. His physical closeness was hard to endure before, but now, it's irrevocably insufferable. *And yet, I need to be closer.*

Slowly, my eyes open, seeing him in my peripheral. *Don't look at him. Don't you dare look at him and stare at his stupid, masterful face.* I'm ashamed at how fiercely I yearn for this interrogator.

Get it together.

Maybe just a quick glance?

The back of my head is still leaning against the tree, and I cave, angling it so I can look at his profile.

Dammit.

Lost in thought, he stares ahead, arms resting on his knees and crossed at the wrists. I glance at his hands, acquainted with the feel of the warm and rough strength—wanting to know it better. They're just like the rest of him: undeniably hard on the outside, but irrefutably tender if he lets you get close. Allure personified.

The sham I've believed is that I'm simply attracted to him physically. Until now, I couldn't admit I crave his closeness. His care. His emotional affection. The complexity of him. I long to unravel and peel back his layers.

I want to see him.

I want him to see me.

My worst fear and largest hope in one.

Heaviness sags my shoulders, tears pressing to well up in my eyes at the concoction of unmet needs I have. The schema that love won't find me.

Sensing my gaze, he turns to me, but I quickly avert my attention forward, hiding the expression I wear. *Collect yourself, dammit.*

The shoulder pressed against mine shifts, and before I can stop him, his fingers are cupping my cheek, drawing my eyes to his. Half of me fights to pull away; the other half begs me to be brave. Brave enough to be seen. The firm lines of his expression make me think he might scoff at me, annoyed by my emotions. But I realize his expression means something else when his thumb catches the tear that slips past my defenses, wiping it away.

This is embarrassing.

My chin dips.

"Ste—look at me," he pleads. *Again.*

The sound of him nearly saying my name, and the need in his voice... I resist with everything I have. *Clearly, I don't have much.* This time, when our eyes meet, the words I've been trying to find slam into me. The words to describe how it feels when he looks at me like this. What it does to me. *For me.* With a single look, he can hold space for me to fall apart.

Another soft stroke of his thumb tells me he will hold my pain—he will do anything to make it stop. *Why on earth does he care for me?* Confusion tornadoes my thoughts into recalling every stark and dark interaction between us. But at the same time, it's always been charged with this incessant intensity.

"I thought you hated me." The admission meets him, stirring the air around us.

A slow shake of his head and a slight lift of his lips indicates a confession on the tip of his tongue. "Far from it."

Despite me telling him to leave, he knew that's not what I needed. I didn't want to be left, I was just afraid to break in front of him and be abandoned as 'too much'—to be reminded that I'm only worthy when I'm of use.

What I needed was for someone to watch out for me. Someone other than myself, even just for tonight. *He* is that someone.

He's the cause of so much confusion in my life right now, but his closeness is also the very comfort I need to process it. A problem and a solution wrapped into one being.

It makes little sense. It appears unwarranted. Abrupt. But that's only when I look at all the facts from the outside, and don't pay attention to the details. It's insane that only this morning, we spoke with unfounded anger toward each other, and now? It feels like two different realities. But the thread that runs through all the words we've exchanged is this cosmic connection. *There was something between us from the beginning, and it can only be described as the most natural thing in the world.*

That thought is what has my fingers wrapping around his wrist and lifting his arm over my shoulders before leaning against him. My heart pounds so loudly that I can hear it. Or maybe it's his.

His body tenses and I panic that maybe I'm only seeing what I want to see. Maybe I'm deluded and making this all up.

He's uncomfortable.

"Sorry," I quickly say, moving to put the distance back between us when he holds me firmly against him.

"Stay," he whispers.

I look at him, my throat bobbing as he lowers his legs to flatten against the ground. Then, his strong arm tightens around my shoulders, pulling me closer. My arms wrap around my knees as I cradle against him, forming a tight ball with my body.

I draw in a shaky breath, eyes squeezing shut against the rising emotion. My life. My hopelessness. The suffering in the world. The wrongness of everything. *Except this.* I cling to it like a lifeline.

He turns more into me, supporting me in his arms as I nuzzle my head into the nape of his neck, reaching one hand up and gripping his shirt in a fist.

Creations.

I fuse with him, feeding off his emotional security like a ravenous, distraught animal.

My tears mingle with the saltiness of his sweat, soaking the corner of his shirt as he strokes my back in small circles, soothing me.

This is a feeling I've always wanted. *To feel like everything is okay.* I hate how I wasn't the one to give it to myself. I hate that being in his arms for minutes has made me feel what I've been trying to do for myself for years.

It's unfair.

Still, I don't move.

The part of me waving her hand, yelling 'what the fuck are you doing?' is silenced when I slam the door on her.

I'm savoring it for just a little bit longer.

My hand glides from his shoulder, up the side of his neck, and cups the nape, my breathing steadying almost instantly. The hand caressing me stops, then his thumb is under my chin, lifting it to witness firsthand the broken shards of me painted within my irises.

Somehow, the sorrow I feel is mirrored in his expression. The last thing I want is for my pain to bleed onto him. I want to rid him of that look with a desperation that shocks me. I don't understand why anything saddening his heart calls me to action.

My voice is a whisper in the wind as I tighten my hold on him. "Don't be sad."

Yet, a solemn smile lifts his lips as he scans my expression. "I'll stop when you do."

I'm shattering. And he's trying to let me, but not without some pieces cutting him, too. No one should have to mend me. That's my job.

I don't know why my sadness affects him so much.

My eyes search his, then rise to the furrow between his brows. My hand follows suit, with gentle fingers smoothing away the creases. "I'm okay." I try to sound convincing.

Before he can reply, my thumb slides across his cheek and slowly skims over his lower lip. The delicate sweep causes his eyes to drift shut like heavy drapes.

His breath warms my thumb as he speaks against it. "Are you ready to talk about it?"

My stomach drops.

No.

Feeling the way my body becomes rigid, his eyes open to find mine. Heat, wanting, and worry coexist in harmony deep within them.

I ignore his question, asking one of my own. "When I thought I was dying and went to kiss you..." I pause, trying to summon the confidence to finish my sentence. "Did you really lean in only to encourage more secrets from me?" I swallow, looking down at his chest. "Was it really all a test?"

He's quiet long enough for my heart to sputter wildly. But then, his hand skims over my ribs, caressing my side with a promise etched into his touch.

"No." His voice is firm, confessionary.

No? I knew it. The insatiable tether between us couldn't have existed only in my mind. *Then why did he act like I was the bane of his existence?*

Another question shoots at him. "You've been angry with me from the start, so why are you being so kind to me now?" A spark of familiarity wraps around me just as his arms tighten around my waist.

He looks at me with such tenderness and longing as he admits, "Something changed the moment I walked into that hut to interrogate you. It's been driving me crazy that I can't figure you out. My anger came from not understanding what's happening. I'm sorry."

The anger... I get it. I lashed out for the same reasons.

This strategic interrogator would mask his confusion with resistance to me. The eyes that pretended to look at me with hate—now they display something I understand. *Recognition.* A frustrating tale between us that we aren't privy to.

It drives me insane as well. But right now, we aren't pretending, or consumed by the uncertainty. Not with his want so clear in the way he holds me.

Trees rustle around us and crickets chirp relentlessly nearby, as if nature is shouting for this to happen. Or it's warning us to stop.

I tell myself it's okay to forget everything except for him. That I can give in to the pull.

Just for another minute.

My focus hones on his lips, then drags slowly back up to his eyes. I lean in half an inch, scared that he'll pull the rug from underneath me like he did last time. Nerves and desire rise into my breathless voice. "Do you want this?"

The question snaps his restraint like a rubber band as he divulges one word, straight from the core of him. "Please."

His lips crash into mine.

CHAPTER 13
FUCK IT

He steals my breath with the firm press of his lips.

The hairs on my arms rise as his fingers brush against my cheek, slip into my hair, and pull me deeper into the kiss. I could groan at the relief. Maybe I actually do.

Our lips part for a breath, only to layer once more. The kiss is nurturing. Healing.

My minute is up.

Slowly, I start to draw back. But all my body will allow is an inch.

With his hand still cupping my cheek, his forehead rests against mine gently. His other hand is a complete contrast, desire and need clear in the way his fingers tighten on my waist.

Tilting his head, he tucks my hair behind my ear gently. A silent question lingers behind his eyes, asking if I'm okay—asking if he did the wrong thing by kissing me in my fragile state.

Letting the weight of my head rest in his palm, I drop another piece of armor, letting him see the yearning etched in my features.

The delicacy in his touches, in that kiss—you'd never expect it by looking at him. I drink in the sight of him greedily, placing my hand over his racing heart.

I feel it. The pull.

The curse rips from me. "Fuck it. One more minute."

My lips collide with his.

I wasn't prepared for this. Yet, something inside me stomps its feet in primal celebration.

The kiss... It's pure need. His tongue finds mine. The fluidity and sureness of his movements combat against my mind—wanting to control and please. I'm too rigid. I'm fumbling the kiss, I'm stuck in my damn head.

Somehow reading my mind, he slows his pace, trailing his fingertips along the length of my arm in a silent suggestion: relax.

I get out of my head and into my body, letting our mouths meld in a harmonious flow.

Shit.

My body is on fire, something deep within me ignited, and it guides my hands to his shoulder, pulling him to face me more. *Closer.* His hand squeezes my hip in response, a low rumble in his chest beckoning me to surrender whatever shred of self-control I have left. I demand the same of him, and just like that, we become passion embodied.

My lips, my wandering hands, a sound from my throat—it all tells him exactly how much I need this kiss. Without a second to process, his hand is behind my knee, pulling it until I drop into his lap, straddling him.

Shock stutters my kiss, a gasp slipping through my lips. He pulls away immediately, hands spread across my ribs as he surveys me head to toe. "Did I hurt you?" Concern laces his voice.

I shake my head, skin flushing.

Creations, I've kissed before. But that's it. How do I tell him that I'm mortifyingly inexperienced? That I've never even straddled anyone? That I've never wanted to more than I do right now?

A nervous laugh escapes my lips. "No, you didn't. Sorry."

Suddenly, I don't know where to put my hands, and I ball them up against his chest. My heart picks up as the overwhelming need to impress him inadvertently makes me look like an idiot. *I just need to get on with it. I'm too old to be this fucking frigid.*

A scorn slices through me from the words I spit at myself, knowing better than that. *Breathe. It's okay.*

He doesn't dare to move, reading my tense body language and avoidant eye contact. His kindness envelopes me when he asks, "What are you sorry for?"

We lock eyes, both lost in completely different ways.

I explain, "I'm not—I want this. I'm just... new to this. Sorry." Unsureness etches into my voice and features.

Then, I wait with crushing anticipation. Wait for him to tell me he doesn't want to hold my hand and walk me through this. For him to tell me to get off so he can go find someone who can please him. Or for him to urge me along impatiently. I'm waiting for him to come up with an excuse to leave instead of directly telling me that I'm not worth going slow with.

Nothing new for me.

What I didn't expect was for him to smile at me, close-lipped and gentle—in a way that puts me at ease. A smile that says he'll stop the world if it means I'll feel comfortable.

So, I guess I'll give us another minute.

Slowly, he wraps his fingers around mine, placing them flat against his chest. "I don't accept the apology that you don't need to give."

My heart clenches at his words. Goosebumps wake as his fingers leave mine to skim down my wrists, over my elbows, and up the backs of my arms.

I swallow, my eyes closing as I confess, "I can't get out of my head. I just want to let go."

His fingers draw a line down the sides of my torso, and I shudder, with his heart racing against my palm. *We're both nervous.* I relax at the thought.

A soothing, low voice beckons my eyes to lift to his. "There's an art to letting go. To be present with someone—it's vulnerable. Intimacy is attunement. We read each other's bodies, listen, and do what you want to do, not what you think is expected of you. Your instincts will grow with time."

His hand lifts to my chin, angling it so he can press a featherlight kiss just under my jaw. I arch my head back further, balling his shirt in my hands as I pull him closer.

I feel his smile against my throat. "Just like that..."

He trails his lips lower down my neck, and I gasp, his warm breath hovering above my skin and leaving goosebumps in its wake. "It's a shared experience of what you want, and what I want—finding out how to honor and respect. But to do that, you need to take your time to learn about each other."

The words slip past my guard. "You're the only person I've kissed who thinks that."

The avidness in his eyes is obscured by my words, clouding with something dark.

Before he can reply, I run my hands up and down his chest, soothing myself and reassuring him at the same time. "You're not like that. Thank..." I try to hide my smile as his expression lightens.

"Hmm?" he asks with a reverberating sound.

I mimic it, feigning ignorance. "Hmm?"

His chest rumbles against my palms when he blesses me with a low chuckle. The sound is debilitatingly addictive. "So this is going to be a thing?" he asks. "Your unwillingness to thank me?"

I point a finger at his chest. "You made it a thing by mocking me for thanking you. Naturally, I'm not going to just give you what you want."

He watches me, a smile lifting his lips. "Good. I only ever want what you want to give."

Well, shit.

At that, heat coils in my stomach. His patience, kindness, care, and the fact he's undressing me with his eyes—all of it has me leaning even closer.

"Hypothetically," I start, and he's fighting a smile, "if I wanted to thank you for your wisdom, would you tease me for it?"

His hands stroke up and down my sides. "Hypothetically?"

I nod, tucking my bottom lip between my teeth.

His voice is akin to silk when he speaks. "I'd say it was my pleasure."

I squint at him, knowing he's not done.

"Then I'd say that's five times now."

A laugh bursts out from me. "There it is."

He smiles brighter in response, seemingly struck with the sound.

How is it possible I feel so close to him already? I want to let him see me, and I hope he lets me see him.

Letting my body relax a little bit further, I decide to share one more thing for him to hopefully understand. "I've always seen intimacy as something sacred—an energy exchange that I've protected from men who don't value it." My eyes glaze over, remembering times where I felt like nothing more than a used, warm body. Hands roamed up my legs before they bothered to caress my cheek. It all moved so fast that I knew it wasn't from needing me, but rather, to fulfill a need for themselves. Male friends or colleagues would be a distant shadow until a few drinks kicked in. Only then, I'd become what they wanted. I wasn't truly, though. I could feel it. I was something to be conquered, my heart a factor unconsidered.

Unease curdles in my gut as I wonder if what we are doing now is reflective of the zero to one hundred I've come to expect from men. I've only known experiences where I'm a thing of the moment and not a person to cherish.

I lean away from him slightly. *Am I not worth the gentle and gradual peeling back of layers?* Am I... just a body to Orion?
Orion.

His name in my mind summons a shiver down my spine, and suddenly, I have an answer. *He's different.*

Dipping his chin, he requests for my benefit, "Let go of the shame. Whether you lay with one hundred bodies or zero, it must always be an intuitive choice."

Worrying my bottom lip, I gingerly whisper, "It's not just that. Sometimes hands find their way onto you, and you don't want them there. It made me very avoidant... I don't give myself to people, because—I, uh... don't feel safe to be vulnerable."

He's silent, a shadow slipping over his features as if seeing the unwelcome touching that haunts my skin.

"I'm sorry." Pain lances through his tone. Empathy glints in his eyes as if he wishes he could've been there all those times. To stop it. To tell me it's not my fault. That I did nothing wrong.

I shrug with one shoulder, unsure what to say.

He carries on. "You never deserved to be treated like that. And I know you know that, but I want to say it anyway. If I'm making you uncomfortable or rushing you..." He lightly runs his hand over my hair until it rests on the nape of my neck. "Please don't let me move in a way that you don't wish for me to. I'm sorry for how I've acted until now, and I hope you know that I see you as someone to care for. I'm so sorry if I resembled any of those men who didn't earn the chance to be this close to you."

A crack in my chest splits further in two, but not in a way of heartbreak. Rather, in a way that feels mending, as if the guard I've fortified around my heart wants to let him in.

I don't want to talk about the dark. I just want to show him why he is the light.

His eyes drop to the smile blooming across my face.

"At risk of being teased, I offer you a sixth and final thank you," I offer.

A hint of light nudges away the shadow I cast in his eyes. "For what?"

I look down at his hands resting on my hips. "For being patient, because that's what makes me want you. I want your hands on me, your lips against mine..." My words trail off as I cup his cheek, running my thumb over his lips.

They lift into a smirk as the next word leaves my mouth. "Badly."

I lean in, our chests flush. Confidence encourages my hands to slide down and caress his jaw. He leans into my palm, closing his eyes. "It might kill me, how much I want you," he replies.

When his eyes lock with mine, I see a question in them. Waiting for my say so—the green light. And that's exactly what has me pulling him in, binding our lips.

The earth might shatter around us. His mouth claims mine, strong arms tightening around my waist, pulling me impossibly closer. My hand runs through his hair, a fiery need pulsating through me.

His lips travel to the side of my mouth, my jaw, moving lower in tantalizing and soft pecks. When he finds the spot between my collarbone and shoulder, a small moan escapes me. Then a rough sound comes from his throat in response. Incarnate heat radiates from us. It's scorching in a way that makes me feel drunk. Dizzy.

He pulls back, only to crash against my lips again, the need between us palpable.

"Beautiful." The word leaves his lips between his heavy breaths and deepening kiss. He leans back to look at me, hands roaming my body as he admits, "It's not enough to describe you."

His words stun me—roll through me in a shiver. Then his lips are back on mine. *Where they damn well should always be.*

I praise, "You're showing me better than you could tell me."

He smiles against my mouth, our teeth clashing for a beat before we dive deep into each other once more. *Wild.* That's how I'd describe this feeling. Insatiably wild.

His hands squeeze my thighs before running their way up and down my legs, my hips. The force of my desire urges me to shift forward in his lap as the kiss becomes more sensual. Exploratory.

He lets out a low moan of agreement as if he feels exactly as transcended as I do.

I admit against his mouth between kisses, "I feel like I can't breathe right now." I might actually combust after all.

Regretfully, I pull away, trying to catch my breath. Our chests rise and fall against each other as he tries to do the same.

He studies me, and I study him.

What rattles me senseless is his soul, his emotional maturity, his masculine, yet nurturing energy.

Disbelief courses through me at meeting someone like him—that he's *real.* "Fuck's sake."

He lets out a low chuckle, like he knows exactly what I'm thinking and it's both shocking and pleasing to him.

The fire slows to a simmer as he loops his arms around my back, idly stroking his thumb up and down my spine. My fingertips are featherlight as they skim down the frame of his face, absorbing every detail through my tactile sense, as if visually isn't enough.

Swift and subtle as a whisper, he presses the world's softest kiss on my lips, pulling back to catch my cheeks going pink. *Of all things, that's what makes me shy?* A smirk lifts one side of his mouth when he notices.

My flushed skin welcomes the waft of cool air that slinks over it. Sliding my hands to rest on his shoulders, I turn my burning cheeks toward the sudden breeze, but it's gone too quickly. All that's left is the starlit forest, wild animals, and the chatter of insects.

Like a ton of bricks falling onto my head, I remember why we're out here in the first place. My muscles tense and I lean away from him. *Orion.*

Time's up.

CHAPTER 14
JUST A STORY

Time halts, my stomach hollows, and I study his expression, seeking something. I look for any hint of confusion behind his eyes, or a question for why I'm suddenly in distress. But that's not what I see.

His relaxed features, and the way he watches me speaks volumes. It's as if he was waiting for it to dawn on me. He's either relieved or petrified that it's finally come. I can't tell.

My face falls. "Orion?" I say his name low and prolonged, a warning and question in my tone.

A deep breath fills his lungs as he nods, the rest of him unmoving as if any sudden movement will spook me. *He's right.*

"You know." I say it as a statement, but doubt creeps in. *He couldn't.*

I don't even know. Not really.

When he looks blankly at me with a deflating spark behind his eyes, I know the air will not meet a denial from him. What he does is rest the back of his head against the tree, watching me process with a familiarity of someone who's known me far longer than a few days.

The vivid vision, the undeniable connection... I feel it, but I don't understand it.

A thousand questions rattle inside my brain, fighting to be the first one asked, but then something clicks. Something that's bothered me in quiet moments.

"What does my name mean?" The question is firm, demanding.

His forehead furrows in the middle, lips pressing into a hard line before slightly parting.

"You can say it," I whisper, giving him access to my name. I know what it means to *him*, but now I need to know what it should mean to *me*.

"Stella…" His jaw clenches as if he's bracing himself, and all I can do is hold my breath. "Your name means… from the stars."

I lose my stomach at those words. The speed of thoughts forcing their way through my mind opposes the deathly stillness of my body.

In a blink, I'm faced with the vision again, of an intertwined flash of stars. Then it's gone, leaving me to face what's in front of me.

The words feel like gravel up my throat, but I make myself say them out loud. "Both of our names—they're dedicated to the stars." He watches me closely, delivering a slow nod.

My processing consists of nonlinear words spilling out of my mouth as I try to piece everything together. "The trail, the barriers, the pull between us… The feeling that I fucking know you."

His head tilts, barely perceptible, as hope hides behind his guarded expression. "Do you?"

Memories surface from when we first saw each other—the day I was captured.

"I know you."

"*Do you?*"

Except this time, the words feel heavier.

He whispers, as if gently prompting me, "Why are you here, Stella?"

A bolt of electricity courses through me at the question. The way his voice lilts around my name.

"I'm not sure," I whisper back.

But the truth is, I might not think it's a coincidence anymore.

When I was sitting at my shitty desk at my shitty job, something inside of me finally broke. I couldn't keep up the act—going through the motions, day in and day out, as a barely-conscious submissive. A product of people's expectations.

That's what it was. The catalyst. The fact I didn't even know who 'myself' was. I just knew I lived a life so far removed from her.

I could've kept going—slice another piece of my mind away to appease and fit in, but on my walk home, I saw a weed sputtering through a crack in the concrete path. A wave of awe struck me. The strength it took to force its way through something so solid and grey stunned me. This little pop of color dared shove its way through its restraints as an unapologetic fern-green, with a bright yellow flower bud. Right then, a whisper caressed my mind.

Break through. Find yourself in nature.

The next thing I know, I'm quitting my job, deactivating all online presence, and telling the people I know that I'm leaving for a while. Then I'm on a plane. On a trail. Off a trail. *Here.*

My throat tightens, but I manage to confess, "I'm not here by accident."

He dips his chin slightly, responding cautiously, "No. I don't believe you are."

We stare at each other, his silence encouraging me to keep going. Keep thinking. So, I do.

Running my hand over my hair, I scan the forest as I process.

Exhaling a shaky breath and without meeting his gaze, I tell him, "I saw something earlier, when you said your name. A flash of... galaxy. Entwining celestial forms. I think they were souls."

His fingers gently caress idle circles on my hips, and I'm afraid to admit something else—to him and myself. The second it came to my attention, I suppressed it, fear of the unknown, the inexplicable, causing me to stuff it deep within me. But I find myself saying the words now. "My favorite book, the first I ever remember reading, was about the stars. About Orion. That's where it all started. No matter how desolate and insufficient life felt, Orion promised more for the world. To watch over everyone, with the help of a star that came with him. It inspired me." My attention drops to my ring. *I promise to find more.*

I glance at him, his expression unreadable as he asks, "What was it called?"

He didn't know about that.

My voice is laced with reluctance when I tell him, *"The Keeper."*

I think he stops breathing.

A gnaw in my stomach has me pressing for his thoughts. "What?"

Instead, he asks, "Tell me more about the book."

I shrug with both shoulders. "It's a kid's book. I used to borrow it from the library and read it over and over. One day, I hid it in my bag and took it. As wrong as it was, my kid brain believed it was mine. The story awakened something in me, and I felt... hopeful reading it. As I got older, I couldn't bring myself to take it back. Even when I was seventeen, I remember clutching it against my chest while contemplating the job at my dad's friend's company I was to start the next day. Years later when I moved out of my parents, I left it in my old room, because the hope it used to give me stopped feeling possible.

Orion's hand seemingly moves without him knowing, caressing me as he absorbs each word. I watch him with the same fervor, wondering what about this book has struck him.

"It was a farfetched fairytale," I add, trying to convince him. When he stays silent, somehow reading that I don't believe it myself, I can't help but slip into a fawning, nervous laugh. "It's not possible—stop looking at me like that. You believe a kids book that says the universe gives each constellation a purpose, a planet to look after, that the cluster of stars has a soul? Come on, Orion..."

A shiver runs through me, my breath hitching as the coincidence of the children's story, his name, and how I looked up to Orion as a protector barrels into me.

His voice is a low and gruff rasp as he asks, "How did the story end?"

I bite my bottom lip, not wanting to answer.

"Stella." His voice is gentle as he prompts again, "How did the story finish?"

War wages within me, where half of me wants to understand, and the other half refuses to accept the implications that might come from understanding.

Shit.

I tell him. "The constellation was assigned to Earth with the purpose of ensuring justice, joy and peace. When Earth was nearly too far gone, the essence, or the soul of the constellation, came here to restore the planet, and another Star Soul came with him to help. Orion held the star as they flew over cities, and it would sprinkle glitter from its fingertips, letting it settle into everything. And when you turn the page, it went from black and white to color, bright grins across their faces as they'd emerge from buildings. Holding hands. Basking in sunlight or dancing in rain. Riding bikes, waving their hands to the sky or embracing each other. Then, the Star Soul and Orion went home..."

My voice trails off at the way he's hanging off every word, chin dipped and eyes piercing through me. "What else?" he asks in a whisper.

Looking away, I throw the words at him. "I don't know. It was just a *story*."

He leans in closer to me, the roughness of his palm resting gently on my cheek. "Was there anything particularly strange about it? Something that stood out?"

"Fuck." Rubbing my eyes, I try to focus—to understand why I feel so nervous to tell him. "I thought it was weird that the book had a dedication. It's unusual for kid's books. And..."

He presses on. "And?"

A shudder rolls through me involuntarily. "It wasn't in English. I only really noticed it when I got older. But nothing came up when I tried to translate it."

"Stella." Thinking my name aloud, he asks, "You said the book is at your parents house?"

He can't be serious. He can't actually think this story has any weight to it. Yet, my heart thrums relentlessly like a hummingbird's wings.

A humorless laugh leaves my lips as I stare at my balled hands resting against his chest. "Why?" I try to sound dismissive, but the undercurrent of a bite speaks volumes.

He places a hand atop mine, and suddenly, I'm lost in the pages again, thinking of Orion—the reason I started looking up to the stars. I swallow down the overwhelm that has gnawed its way into my chest. *It was nothing more than a children's story that I read. Stole. Kept.* I repeat that to myself for the millionth time tonight. I don't want this to mean more.

Dammit, I am barely functioning as it is. I'm a shell of a person, and I don't want to be tied up in whatever this is. I can't handle the inference of it.

Writing him off, my tone is flat. "It's a strange coincidence."

He rests one hand on my thigh, the other gently stroking over my hair. "There's more you don't know—about the village, me, the universe. *Yourself.*"

A small gasp pulls through my teeth as he voices the words I desperately don't want to hear.

His throat bobs, the lines of his face serious. "When I saw your birthmark, your face, it started unravelling answers to questions I've had for a long time. The blank spots in my mind—I need you to help me fill them." I stare at him blankly as he adds, "Face it with me."

"No." I snap the word out.

Lifting my ring between us, he encourages me. "You promised... you've been called to—"

Ripping my hand away from his grasp, I interrupt him with a voice louder than I intend. "I can't." I scan his face, frozen. "Stop." The word is a plea.

Arms slide gently around my waist, as if he's scared that I'll slip into a shadow and dissolve spontaneously.

I might wish for that.

"Stella, we—"

My hand shoots to his mouth, covering his lips with my palm. Shaking my head, I whisper, "I'm not ready. I don't want to hear any more."

Rough fingers close gently around my wrist, slowly pulling it away from his mouth. I try to lean away from him, but his imploring expression pins me to the spot. "Please, Stella, just listen—"

My voice cuts through the air, enunciating each word. "I can't do this."

A stuttered breath drags through my lips as his face crumples. Pain lances through me as I deny every cell in my body, resisting how it yearns to lean into this absurd prophecy. *To him.*

A birthmark, a sprouting weed in concrete, a secret village, my ring, his energy—they're all crumbs and signs that connect me to a larger destiny that I don't have the capacity for.

Strong hands rest on my hips, affliction present in his voice. "Why are you so afraid? Why are you rejecting this?"

I practically yell, "Because I'm broken, Orion! How can I have some altruistic calling, and be this force, be with *you*, when I *loathe* myself?" An empty smile touches my lips before turning down at the corners.

I try to explain, "You said I don't know you *or* myself, that there's other things I don't know. You're right. But I'm *not ready*. It's like..." I scan the canopy of trees above us, exhaling as I try to find the words. "It's like telling someone what the color red looks like because they don't know how to open their eyes and look for themselves."

He scans me thoughtfully as I continue. "You can't tell me I have this destiny, this connection with you, when I don't know how to be open to receiving it. That's why I came out here—to learn to open my eyes. But you can't force them open. It's not that simple.

"To know there's more is one thing, but to believe I'm worthy of it..." I scoff. "That's a whole other thing." Fiddling nervously with his shirt, I admit, "I need to learn how to not be my own enemy. Maybe then, I'll see red."

Gnawing at my lip, my eyes drop from his. Then, his warm hands pull me closer to him, wrapping tenderly around me.

He asks gently, "I don't understand why you can't have both. Why can't you work toward your future, while healing in the present with my help? Isn't it easier to find red if I'm telling you how deep the shade is, or how vibrant it can get?"

I think over his words before replying, "I have this incessant buzzing that lives beneath my skin, razor sharp and refusing to let me believe that I can be someone important, have a life of meaning, leave the world better than I found it. That's what I'm fighting.

I can't just have you do the work for me, tell me exactly what to do, help me feel all the things I long for, and say all the things I wish to hear from myself. Because then, I'm still walking around with my eyes closed, wondering what the color red truly looks like."

The atmosphere bends around us as he takes in what I'm saying, seeing exactly how terrified I am.

In that hypnotic voice, he soothes me. "I'm sorry you're hurting, and I want to help, but I can respect what you want." His eyes trace over me, like he's memorizing and savoring every detail. "I won't pursue you or persuade you further until you come to me, wanting it. But can you promise me one thing?"

The question is as gentle as the fingers he skims over my hair. I nod, fighting to reign in the well of tears threatening to fall.

Hope casts a glow behind his eyes before he asks, "Promise me that you won't shut me out completely. You take all the time you need, and I'm so proud of you for what you're setting out to do, but please don't put all your walls up again. Leave a small crack open for me."

Dipping my head down, I fight the flurry of panic that urges me to change my mind. All I want to do is say yes—to lay in his arms and tell him everything he wants to hear. But I have to do the difficult thing, because it's what I need.

When my eyes lift back to his, I catch them glistening in the moonlight. He doesn't hide his feelings. He's not ashamed. Unapologetically vulnerable.

Hating what I'm about to say, I force it past my lips. "That crack will break further and further, because you have the power to crumble all my walls. You have the power to consume all my thoughts. I can see it happening. I will lean on you to fill the void of darkness within me. Your smile *alone* makes it easier for me to breathe. So, I can't Orion. I can't have you as an option to run to, or have you remind me of this looming destiny."

Pleading with my eyes, I beg him not to make this harder. "I know that this is fucking insane—how I already feel about you, what it could turn into. I need to cut it off at the knees before it grows."

I could fall for this man, dangerously fast. Impossibly quick, I could yield all my guards to lay at his feet without so much as a push. There's something here, where if we spent more time getting to know each other, I could let him save me. But it would be at the expense of being my own hero.

His hands grip my thighs like something inside him is urging him to try again. He says, "We all need someone to lean on. We're designed for companionship. You don't need to do this completely alone—"

I interrupt, "Yes, I do though. Because I won't go as deep. I won't learn to sit with this pain inside me, knowing how easily you could soothe it—distract me from it."

One hand lifts to hold my jaw as he assures, "I won't. I'll give you space when you need it..."

Fuck, this hurts.

Even so, I speak my truth. "I won't *want* space—I'm weak. I won't ask for it. I'll depend on you instead of myself. Please, just..." I groan at the words before they come out. "You have no idea how long I've waited to feel chosen. To have someone fight for me. To feel *this*. I'm realizing that the only way I can learn to heal myself, and feel love, is to deny looking for external sources of it. I have to choose me, and figure out what that looks like."

He thinks this over, and then responds carefully, "You can choose yourself at the same time I choose you. People work through their pain together all the time. You don't need to cut me off."

Sending a silent plea to the sky, I ask for the clarity to say this right. "I escape my emotions by depending on people, places, and dreams to distract me. I'm extremely good at cutting corners. I'm smart in a self-sabotaging way, where I half-ass my healing so it looks good from the outside. But when something happens, and I don't have those people or things to depend on, I crumble. I implode. I don't have the internal foundation to be okay on my own. I'm asking you to let me implode, and not help me cheat when I'm trying to rebuild."

Defeat and understanding crash together and paint itself on his face. The image sears into my mind, even though I only see it for a second before he drops his forehead against my shoulder.

I'm an inch away from caving, second guessing myself, but a raw thought drives itself into my consciousness. *Sometimes, showing up for yourself means letting someone else down.*

"Fuck," he murmurs. He's fighting to give me what I ask for. He doesn't entirely agree, but he accepts it. I can tell in the way he gently squeezes my hips, as if it's a goodbye. In the way he lifts his head and reveals that indifferent composure.

With a single nod from him, I know all the masks I tore down have been resurrected.

A sickening feeling of loss prickles my heart, and I try not to panic as I search for the man who's disappeared before my eyes. *He's doing what you asked.* And I miss him already. The fondness, the way he looked at me like I've been his for a thousand years.

Without warning, he hooks his fingers behind my knee and lifts me off him as he stands. "We should get back. They'll wonder where we are."

Bewildered and in a disheveled mess of dried tear stains and shock, I stare up at him. "Orion..."

Almost imperceptibly, he flinches at his name—the newfound weight I'm forcing him to endure alone pressing in on him. But he quickly recovers.

I can't hide the sadness in my voice as I ask, "Do you hate me now?"

He clears his throat and announces, "You said what you need is to be completely alone—that you don't want to lean on me.

That you want to learn to console yourself and love yourself. That you don't want it halfway, or even a piece of me. I'm giving you what you asked for, right now. This is what that looks like, Stella. Don't ask me if I hate you, because you know I never could. Either way, for you to do this, how I feel about you has to be irrelevant. So, console yourself, pull it together, and let's head back."

Dammit. He's right. Swoony and soft Orion is gone. And that's exactly what I need.

I absorb the punch in my gut and take some deep breaths. Wiping my face and sweeping the dirt from my knees, I force myself to stand with my shoulders back.

Once I've collected myself as much as I can, I meet his eyes one more time. A tick in his jaw urges me to walk past him, to not draw this out for both of our sakes.

When I don't hear his footfalls behind me, I peer over my shoulder to find him staring into the distance.

"Thank you," I whisper, and I don't wait to see if he hears me.

Our first step back into the village beckons TG's attention. He inclines his head, and I realize it's a response to a signal Orion must've given him.

Through the heaviness of puffy eyes, I watch as he strides toward us, the jaded fog of numbness settling over me.

Orion instructs TG, "Take watch of her."

"Of course?" His voice raises at the end of the word, negating the diplomacy of his response, and letting confusion bleed into it.

My eyes become unfocused, trying not to react to the flat and apathetic tone Orion speaks with. "Thank you. Set up post outside of the hut. Someone will relieve you in a few hours."

He isn't going to be my guard tonight. Doesn't want to be in the same room with me. Good. This is good. *Console yourself.* Even if my fortified walls are crumbling to dust and I want to throw up.

TG nods, but there's something behind his eyes showing concern. *What can he see? What does he know?* Without another word, Orion walks away. My eyes betray me, watching his retreating form just before he slips into a hut and takes my stability with him.

A coldness spreads through me, craving to go after him and let his warmth revive me. But that's not fair on either of us.

TG clears his throat, gesturing for me to lead the way back to my hut. On floating legs, I walk straight to the bed and pull a pillow against my chest. My fixed stare only strays to TG as he inhales like he is about to say something. I fight tears from welling up, begging him not to ask. To not make a joke or tease me.

He looks away, grabs the chair, and starts to move outside, but he pauses in the doorway. "I hope you can get some sleep." The loaded statement is thrown over his shoulder in a tone one could mistake for compassion. Then, he's gone.

Sleep is a taunting beast, dragging my lids shut, then filling my mind with images that force my eyes to open wide. *Over and over.*

I realize Orion set TG's post outside of the hut to give me privacy. To give me space to sit with my feelings. *Sweet, thoughtful bastard.* I squeeze my eyes closed at the same time my heart clenches.

This time, I keep my eyes shut, refusing to open them until morning. Eventually, through tossing and turning, sleep overcomes me, but I dream of him. Kissing him, losing him, being stranded alone. I wake up only to find the same is true in my reality.

CHAPTER 15
LIGHT AND DARK

I'm not proud of it. In fact, I feel quite pathetic that I spent the entire next day in the hut. My mind swells trying to contain the racing thoughts. *The book. My journal. Our connection. The fucking stars I—*

I shut down where that thought is going.

I only leave the hut when my bladder is near bursting, holding off as long as I can because I'm afraid I'll run into him. But I'm desperate to see him at the same time.

Fuck!

The new guard escorts me to the bathroom and back, my eyes staying glued to the ground the whole time. I crawl back into bed, wearing the same clothes as yesterday, and stare at the bowl of food that's now sitting on my bedside table. I'm hungry but also not, deciding in favor of sustenance. I pick it up and mechanically chew the food. That is, until the flavors become less and less distant in my awareness, and thus, I polish the bowl.

The day feels both eternal and evaporative as the sun sets and the nightlife chatter roars outside. TG comes in to swap out the dish from lunch with dinner, taking a seat as guard. In my peripheral, I notice the way he eyes me wearily as I stare blankly at the wall.

I wonder if Orion told him. They seem more like friends than leader and subject.

TG's voice breaks through the dark cloud over me, asking, "Do you need anything?"

His voice is too friendly, and I eye him skeptically. *What's the catch?*

Raising his hand and leaning back, he says, "Just checking."

The way he taps his fingers on his knee, throwing glances at me—I know he wants to say something about me and Orion. Only the universe knows why he seems to care.

Before he can confirm my predictions, I plead, "Don't." My voice cracks from unuse. "I know you know something. And I just..." *Can't talk about it.*

It's not just about Orion. It's everything. Years of feeling unhappy, ugly, weak, inauthentic, scared, lost, alone—every part of me that has ever been broken burns my blood like dry ice. I so desperately just want to feel like enough. And I have to be the one to decide I am. *I just don't know how.*

He hesitates before nodding, and I'm grateful when he looks away and leaves me alone. Immediately, I shove my face into my pillow.

The distance I feel from myself is chasmic. I know this nothingness well, but I've always had something that needs me to bury it deep and get on with my day. Here, I have no choice but to endure it. It's a feeling I want to escape, but it's also a familiar place I go to because I know what to expect. I could ponder on how it's a self-preservation mechanism to deny myself of positive feelings because the fall is further when I inevitably find darkness again— that rather than sadness or joy, I choose nothing, because that's all I feel worthy of. But I can't be fucked to unpack it further.

With red-rimmed, puffy, and sore eyes, I feign reprieve when sleep starts to tug at my consciousness.

Chirping birds and distant laughter fill the air, rousing me from my restless sleep. First, I roll my eyes, scowling at their joy. But then, I decide that today I will try. I will go outside.

Images flash of what my day could entail, but when I come up blank, I suspect it's because my movements have been dictated and shadowed. But with a sliver of trust from the village, I'm less guarded and might actually have some leeway.

Pulling my dry lips between my teeth, I get to my feet and stretch my arms above my head. I don't know why I feel the need to be quiet, but I walk on the balls of my feet across the room to peer outside. An unfamiliar guard sits at the post, looking over her shoulder at me.

"Oh, sorry." I startle, skimming my surroundings for someone I recognize. *No luck.* Stifling the urge to retreat and crawl back into bed, I push the words past my lips. *Be brave.* "I was wondering if it would be okay to go to the stream?"

The guard seems to take me in: wicked bed head, two-day-old stench, swollen-faced, and dirt under my nails. I expect her response to be curt and flat, but it's surprisingly delicate and chirpy, paired with an easy grin. "Sure, let me go check."

She's very happy for some reason.

Must be nice.

"I'll be right back. Wait here," Happy informs me, and relief gusts through my lips in a swift release.

"Thank you," I call out to her as she walks toward a hut.

The hut I was interrogated in.

Still clutching the fabric of the door in my anxious fists, I think over her words. *Wait here.* Only then does it occur to me that I didn't consider running.

The sight of Sage emerging from the hut and walking toward me with her infallible grin has my whole being relaxing.

"Well, if it isn't the smelliest woman alive." Her voice sing-songs the abominable nickname.

"I'm working hard to maintain my reputation." I throw her a lopsided smirk as I cross my arms.

She waves me off with a huff. "Get some clothes, I'm taking you to the stream."

Taking me there. Not escorting. Or guarding. Whether the word choice was intentional or not, a swell of gratitude warms my chest. She has no idea what that means to me. To feel included and safe with someone. I barely know her, and I don't want to be hypocritical and find someone to lean on instead of Orion—or myself. But her kindness is a glimmer of light through the dreary rain within my mind, and I bask in it long enough to feel a semblance of footing in this foreign place.

I open the draws to my bedside table, and grab the flowy olive-green skirt, holding it to my waist as the length kisses the tops of my feet. A beige, thin-strapped tank top looks like it would pair nicely with it, and as I pull it out, I run my fingers over the faint, twisted vines embroidered along the scoop neck, a smile crinkling my eyes. *Beautiful.*

Slinging the bag Sage gave me over my shoulder, I walk outside and see her talking with TG and an elderly lady who seems to be one of the cooks.

Her? I would bow to.

Like a hammer on my senses, I notice the wariness in the way some people look me up and down, my muscles tightening in response. I try not to pay attention to it, instead focusing on the sleeping Okah, noticing Divy isn't amongst them. Two men strum these small, infinity-shaped guitars, their gazes unrelentingly locked—unveiled before one another in a way that makes me smile.

Feeling like I'm intruding on something private, I turn my attention to children weaving flower crowns from fallen foliage on the ground. The short distance lets me hear the boy giggling when he finds a large leaf that's almost completely intact. We lock our eyes, and my bones turn to liquid when he holds it up to show me, with a grin splitting his face. He looks proud, displaying it like it's priceless.

My face breaks out into shocked awe, silently mouthing a 'wow!' to him. Just like that, he offers a parting giggle before his attention returns to his friend. But the bliss of what just happened lingers in my soul.

Mid-exhale, my eyes snag on a group, their deft fingers carving pointed triangles out of some kind of dark and solid material. Only once they pick up a whittled stem do I realize they're making arrows. I rub my arm absentmindedly, picturing the knife and spears, trying to understand why they have all these weapons if no one else has ever passed the barrier. They're protected, so… why? I suppose if I can enter, others can too, and maybe it's more of a preventative measure.

Cutting across my vision are two women jogging to join a group that's now swallowed Sage. But she slips through them, waving me over. *They're all coming to the stream? Awesome. round two of scrutinized judgement while I prune like a prude.*

Subtly dying inside, I take two steps toward the group, bracing myself.

That's when I feel him.

That invisible force alerts the cells in my body of his proximity. As some kind of a cosmic magic trick, he suddenly appears in the group next to Sage.

Do not falter your steps. Keep walking. Breathe.

Obviously my body can only manage two of these things, because my lungs refuse to cooperate the second his eyes find mine. Though, the eye-contact is fleeting, barely half a second before he looks away. No reaction, no tensing of his jaw or muscles. No acknowledgement. *A stranger.*

Ah yes, a nice sucker punch to the gut. The sting of rejection makes my eyes water.

I recall the words in my journal. *You're not the emotion you feel, you're the observer.* The observer in me pinpoints the feelings of his rejection—a craving for his attention and affection, and anger that I brought this on myself. Inhaling a deep breath, I reframe. I want his affection because I crave connection and intimacy. Validation. Subtly, I lock my fingers when pressing my palms together. I let the warmth seep deeper than the surface of my skin as I move toward them. *Giving myself the affection and validation I crave is how I connect.*

Begrudgingly, the crackle of angst in my chest quiets. I give a silent thanks to myself internally, and a small smile touches my lips in response. *I did it.*

Sage waves to me, warm and vivaciously, enticing TG to look my way too and mimic Sage's gesture. I don't know if he's making fun of her or me, but there's no malice in it. Like a ton of bricks slamming into me, Orion looks my way next, but there's a coldness about him I try not to shiver against.

Part of me is turned off by how quickly he could be so callous, after not getting what he wants. But then I remember I asked him not to leave even a sliver of approachability open for me to abuse.

As I close in to join their group, I offer a courtesy smile, awkwardly saluting with two fingers when it's silent for too long. I've never in my *life* done this gesture. *Why would I choose right now to experiment?* Orion's eyes trace a line from my hand, to my strained smile, and back to my eyes, holding there firmly. Completely composed. Unbothered. *But lingering.*

Sage sing-songs, "Are you ready?"

Near sagging in relief at her taking the attention, I exclaim, "Let's go!"

I try to sound happy, but when Sage flinches, I know I was too loud.

Flicking my eyes between TG and Orion, I lower my voice to an appropriately casual level of noise. "You guys coming?"

Please say no, please say no.

TG answers, "No, uh..." He looks to Orion, as if checking to see how much he should say.

They're hiding something. I try not to assume it's about me.

Orion finishes, "Sage will accompany you." He gives TG a look, and they both start to turn away in departure.

Orion throws a look over his shoulder as if a last-minute thought needs to be said. "Have fun." He pairs it with a quick smile that doesn't quite reach his eyes.

A few days ago, I'd never laid eyes on this man. Now, his hurt reflects my own. A hurt that feels unwarranted, given the short time we've known each other.

But has it been a short time?

I open my mouth to say something, but nothing comes out, knowing whatever I pursue with him will be at the sacrifice of addressing the shitstorm inside of me.

For too long, I haven't had a choice or say in my life. I go where society needs me, like a sheep being herded through a small gate. Here, now, even as a prisoner, I feel free to be an individual and separate from influence. I have time to figure out who the hell I am. For once, I choose me first.

Sage fills my line of vision, announcing with a grin, "Come on." She pulls me forward a step by tugging at my wrist, before looping her arm through mine. As we start into a steady stroll, I marvel at how the gesture feels like the most immanent thing we could do. As if it's the first of many times she'll wait until no one is watching before giving me a look of suspicion, trying to coax information from me with a simple phrase. "Well, that was fascinating."

Glancing around nervously, I relax when I notice the group is far enough not to eavesdrop. Divulging into an exasperated groan, I stumble over my words. "He... Yeah, I—uh..."

Trying to find a way to describe the situation in summary is impossible.

Sage laughs, her forehead furrowing in sympathy as if she completely gets it. "I know he told you about me and my abilities. I can pick up enough from the two of you that you can speak your truth."

Relief eases my shoulders away from my ears even more. I speak quietly, "He did mention that you were a Seer." A red blush creeps over my chest and cheeks as I ask, "Wait, so did you see us? What happened? Exactly how much do you know? "

A devious smile lifts her lips. "No, I didn't see whatever is making you fidget." She watches with a mischievous narrowing of her eyes as I pick at the hem of my clothes. "But now I'm curious, and it's incurable."

I roll my eyes. "Sweet Divine. Please, Sage, have mercy on me."

She laughs deep in her belly, and it vibrates through me like a melody. "To see something as if I'm there, I have a process. I

can't do it whenever I want, endlessly. Nature must check my intention and purpose, and I use the ability wisely—with integrity. Nature needs balance, and the more I see, the more I need to rest after. So, I didn't use it to spy. But I can feel and pick up on emotions anytime." She clicks her tongue. "But that, too, has a cost."

I stare at her blankly. "You can just feel what someone is feeling? It sounds intense, like if they're feeling something bad, you would feel it, too. Is that the cost?"

She inclines her head. "Well, you can lose a sense of what feelings are yours if you don't know what you're doing."

"Can you block it out?" I ask.

She purses her lips in thought. "It's like asking me to look in your eyes but not notice the color." She releases a long breath. "I try not to notice people's feelings, because they belong to them. And I might see something they want to stay private."

I nod, thinking over what that might be like—always working to ignore an inherent part of yourself. Then I laugh internally, because the kettle has met the pot.

I ask, "So, if someone's angry, do you have to remind yourself that you're not angry? Wait. Does their anger feel different to yours?"

She chuffs. "No, the way I can see is through a picture in my head. I pick up their emotion, it shows me an image, then I process what they feel through the image."

I prod nervously, "So, my emotions are playing like a movie in your head? Or, are we talking more like a scrapbook of my emotional misfortune?"

Her focus becomes distant, as if she's looking in her mind and not at the forest in front of us. "I am not familiar with movies or scrapbooks," she answers, a smile tugging at one side of her mouth. "But I can feel a longing between you and him. I also feel the resistance. This push and pull. It looks like... two fires, with a brick wall assembling between them. It's built, then it cracks, crumbles, and does this over and over."

She looks over to me, watching my reaction as she finishes, "I sense regret. Stubbornness. Longing."

I scoff at her, the words pinching my heart. "Completely inaccurate," I drawl. "You could use more practice."

"Of course. I'll do better," she promises, sarcasm thick in her voice.

With a light smile, I keep my eyes to the vines snaking the ground, thinking out loud. "You haven't seen a movie or scrapbook before?"

She is silent for a few seconds, her steps losing some of its buoyancy. Then she simply says in a recluse tone, "No."

I don't have her abilities, but I have enough common sense not to keep asking when that question clearly made her uncomfortable.

Trying to side-step, I ask, "So, you have superpowers... That's slightly insane to think about."

I scan her features, perplexed, then nearly lose my stomach at a memory. I remember how she watched my escape, and how I somehow knew it was happening before even learning about her. Then I remember how we first met, and I chose to let her in to see my very soul. My mind races as I process this unique thing she does, but for some reason, I don't panic. Curiosity out rules any rising shock of this place and what I'm learning about her.

Pondering my reaction with a smile playing on her lips, she explains, "You know of a world where what I can do is believed to be a long-forgotten myth. Where anyone who might mention these abilities are humiliated, hurt, or hidden. But there is a world within a world, Stella. Right under our noses."

Swallowing the lump in my throat, I glance around. *Why am I getting emotional at this?* I've questioned if I'm dreaming a few times in this conversation.

I ask, "Is it just you? What is this place? What do you mean a world within a world?" Curiosity forces the questions to fly off one after the other, leaving no room for explanation.

Tightening her arm around mine, she swiftly directs me away from a giant spiderweb I nearly walk straight into.

Inhaling with wide eyes, I thank her with a sound that's more guffaw than human-like. *What a nightmare that would've been.*

Through a chuckle, she answers, "No, it's not just me. Humans have all sorts of abilities. Have you ever heard of the term 'Activ'?"

I gawk at her. *Activ.* I have heard of this. My breath slows as I search deep in my mind for the memory.

"I remember seeing something about it online," I think out loud. "It was everywhere for a couple of weeks, years ago. People with powers, like those you see in films." I cringe, remembering she hasn't seen one and not to mention movies. "But I wrote it off as some conspiracy. And then it just kind of disappeared."

What I don't tell her is that I longed to believe it was true. I fantasized a different reality for so long, losing myself in made-up stories, but I couldn't envisage this to be something that exists. *Something that happens to me.*

She watches me carefully. "I'm half-surprised you've heard of it at all." Her voice sounds gentle, easing the information from her lips. "It's true."

My feet stop moving, but she gently coaxes me along with a tug.

"Once Activ, you can train your abilities like you would a muscle, or your brain."

I gasp. "Yes, I remember. Something about these abilities being a natural and heightened attunement to an intelligence?"

She nods. "We have nine intelligences as a species. The type is based on the person."

I rub my eye with the base of my palm, processing. Turning to her sharply when a question pops into my mind, I whisper-shout, "Wait. How does someone become Activ? Can anyone have these abilities?"

She thinks before responding, as if deciding how much to say. When her eyes meet mine again, her voice is as sure as the sky is blue. "Not anyone, Stella. *Everyone.*" The words are delicate as silk, yet firm as rock.

I gulp like a dramatic cartoon character before repeating, "Everyone."

Me too?

My heartrate spikes, while an eagerness to ask more questions claws at me.

Sensing the way I'm hanging off her every word, she shoots me a look. "That's enough for today. I've already said more than I should have."

Gawking at her once more, I deny her words. "You can't be serious. You basically just ripped reality from me and then said 'hehe, oops.' How long have we had abilities? How do we know if we have them? Wait. How did we lose them?"

She hesitates for a second, but then lowers her voice as she tells me, "We didn't lose them. Discon took them. Long enough ago that most people living now weren't around when they were taken. But if someone does manage to become Activ, it's not a gift—it's a death sentence."

Sucking my bottom lip between my teeth, I physically have to bite down on it to stop from imploring her to continue.

Discon? What is that? Sage is an Activ. The myth is real. What. The. Fuck.

A shiver runs down my spine. "How did they take them?"

She stays firm in her boundary, patting me on the shoulder in consolation of her secrecy. "Oh look, we're nearly there!"

Rolling my eyes at her playfully, I mutter, "I won't push for more today. But don't think I'm just going to drop this."

She clicks her tongue. "I don't need to hear those words to know there's questions festering inside you." She releases my arm to grip my hand, pulling me into a sprint and racing ahead of everyone else.

Laughter bubbles up my throat instead of the question I want to ask. *What do my festering questions feel like? What image does it conjure?* If I wasn't frantically scanning the ground, trying not to trip over these bulging roots as she drags me along, I might've asked her.

Finally, she slows when we're way ahead of everyone. I thank Creations that I can speak freely in this village place, but moreso, that we've stopped running.

"I thought I was the only one who noticed—that it's wrong that the world is nothing but tech and cement," I admit between wheezes.

Maybe I'm not crazy. *There is more.*

She stops, turning to face me. There's not a single drop of sweat on her skin. "You're not."

Putting my hands on my hips and doubling over, I plead with my heart to calm, knowing my face is red as a tomato. *How she's not cackling at how unfit I am is a true surprise.*

Speaking to the ground, I groan out, "I can't take it out there. Everything feels artificial..." When I stand to face her, I stop mid-sentence, realizing she's smothering a laugh at the disheveled mess before her. *There it is.*

"Not one word," I warn, tipping my head back, gulping in air. "As I was saying..." She raises her hands in innocence. "I just felt like I was always competing against everyone for a right to be alive. Trying to convince those in a position of power that I have worth by giving them all of my time. I'm so sick of the 'do it all and do it alone' mentality that's so *championed*."

My breathing slows as I pace back and forth in front of her. "I don't know if I'm making sense. I'm trying to say, we don't know what we're truly here for. *Alive* for. I sure as shit don't think it's to suffer. To not have enough time to express or discover ourselves. We're kept too busy to take a second and realize that there is something very wrong. Sure, I'm spiraling that there's this whole other world—" I gesture back in the direction of the village "—but more than that, I'm relieved."

Scraping the tip of my boot along the loose dirt, I draw little swivels.

She asks, "What do you think we're truly here for?" as she tosses her braids over her shoulder before linking her fingers behind her back. *She's not asking to challenge me, but to gauge me.*

Tracing the swivels, I absentmindedly begin drawing crisscross lines to join them.

What are we here for? Could it be as simple as... "To live."

Her stare bores into me. "For what? For who?"

Lifting my arms outward and shrugging, I exclaim, "I don't know. For the sake of it?" I laugh. "If I wasn't consumed all the time with responsibilities, maybe I would have a better answer for you."

Resting her hand on my shoulder reassuringly, she says, "Well, here? You have time."

Her words hit me like a freight train, even though I thought that exact same thing when I spent the entire day in bed yesterday. My nerves are on end about what I'll find behind the curtains I drew closed a long time ago. But also, I'm enthralled. This place validates a quietly burning part in my soul—one that was dampened and muffled before I came here.

Picking up on what I'm feeling, she reassures me. "You're a lot further in your awakening than you give yourself credit for."

I sit down to take my boots off. "Thank you. I'm trying." The laugh that follows is fueled from equal parts hopeless and hopeful.

She looks down at me. "I have a question for you."

I halt midway through taking off my sock to look up at her. "Creations, you're giving me that face. The one that tells me you're going to dig deep into something I'll feel uncomfortable talking about, but you're going to ask anyway."

She smirks at me. "Smart, Smelly Stella," she remarks.

Before I can chide her, she cuts in. "You said before that everyone is 'do it all and do it alone,' but you spoke of it like you don't agree with living that way. Is that not what you're doing? Building a wall between the fires, to do it all and do it alone?"

I freeze, realizing she's somehow picked up on what I said to Orion last night—that I'm refusing external love because I need to feel it myself first.

Clamping my jaw shut, I try to find the right words. "I can see how it seems like I'm embarking on the very quest I condemn... but with Orion, it's different."

Does she know about how deep our connection might go?

Thinking about what I said, she purses her lips and plops down next to me. "We need community. We thrive in connection.

To self, yes, but also to others. Can you not see him as useful to your growth?" Her tone is genuinely curious.

I lean back on my hands and place my bare feet atop the damp dirt. "It's not that I want to do it alone, it's that I don't think I can. Which is exactly why I need to. If I throw myself in the deep end, I'll have no other choice but to swim, right?"

She picks up fallen leaves and starts laying them out in a spiral, starting at the center and working her way out. "You want to take all options of love away and find it in yourself?"

"I never said love," I say through a scoff, eyes widening.

She glances at me side-long. "Right."

Reaching for a small, yellow leaf to add to her design, she muses, "But you did find him. Us. Can you learn to *like* yourself while letting me and Orion be your friends? But, you can be your own *best* friend."

I roll my neck out. "With you... I'm not opposed to having a friend. But me and Orion... We can't just be friends." I face her, staring at her profile as I claim, "Even with you, I'm nervous..."

She turns a questioning look on me before asking, "Why?"

I admit, "Because I don't trust myself not to seek out either of you, or anything I can get my hands on really, to do the work for me, or distract me from it."

Processing, a deep hum emanates from her chest as I marvel at the creation she's made. I've never seen art like this, nor someone take something from the ground and order it in a way that sings.

Her voice grabs my attention. "If you were the only person on this planet, do you think you'd grow more than someone on another planet who had a community?"

The question pinballs through me, and the answer comes out in an unfiltered blurt. "I already felt alone on this planet, knowing I was surrounded by people who were too busy, trying to get through their own shit. The world is incredibly individualistic. Coming out here to be physically alone—that was something I chose. I guess it made the loneliness hurt less if I was controlling it."

She nods, standing up and reaching her hand out to me. I take it, rising to her eye level as she pulls me to my feet. "I believe through companionship, storytelling, and letting people be there for you, we can reach enlightenment. There's taking time to be alone, and then there is isolation. Only one of these is healing."

She sounds like Orion.

A flurry of fear and pain spurs within me as I question my choice. But just as I banish the thought, she carries on. "Learning to love yourself is a path you take forever. Why deprive yourself of people to journey with?"

Pressing my lips to my teeth, the urge to suppress my vulnerability burns like acid in my throat. Somehow, the courage to speak finds me. "Because I run from the black pit inside me, and when I can't, I stuff it full of things that have color. That's not fair to Orion, or you, or anyone, and I don't want that to be my journey."

My journey is going to be finding peace in those idle moments with myself. Not sorrow. I need time to integrate what I've learned.

She watches me while I stare at two birds who land on a low-hanging branch, one after the other. I never knew being in nature could feel so... right. I see myself in everything around me, like the veins of the leaves matching the ones beneath my skin. I can breathe clearer, and my shoulders relax from years of being pushed up near my ears. My mind isn't being penetrated by artificial lights within four walls. The rushing sounds of business conversation and cars and city noise...

I'm afraid to admit how much I like it here. Because I can't stay.

Sage's long, rough fingers wrap delicately around mine, and I turn to see her blink with glistening eyes. *I made her cry. Why?*

A bucket of ice water is thrown over me, realizing how much of myself I laid out before her. I overshared. Schooling my features and drawing away from her, I force a smile. "That's life."

Part of me wants her to empathize with me, but just like Orion, I get sympathy.

I'm making the right choice. I know I am.

In the next second, the first of the group breaks through the dense forest and approaches the stream.

In a light tone, she affirms, "You will find what you're looking for. I believe in you." Facing the water, she suggests, "Let's go enjoy the stream?"

Thankful for the change of energy and conversation, I relax a little.

The lilt of my voice is teasing when I ask, "But what will you call me after I'm all fresh and clean?" Feigning panic, I add, "Wait, how will you even know if it's me?"

She barks out a laugh, reaching out to touch my face. "I'll have to follow your voice."

A chuckle breaks free from me as the back of my fingers knocks her hand away as. At the loss of contact, she gasps, turning and waving her arms in the air. "Where are you?"

I step further away, putting on a low and echoey cadence to my tone as I say, "Follow my voice, Sage."

She yells out, far louder than I can ever forgive her for. "Smella!"

I snort, hushing her and pushing her arms back into her sides.

Fighting my hold, she slips her arms out and clasps my face in her hands, calling out, "Smella, is that you?"

Glancing around, I watch as more people approach the stream. The few stray eyes watching us are paired with confused expressions. "Alright, people are staring, stop."

Mouth open, she sucks in a heap of air as if preparing to yell it louder, and I give her a pointed look and stifled smile.

"Fine," she relents reluctantly.

With a hearty laugh, I shake my head at this wonderful, caring, certifiably-insane person.

Without any warning, she turns and starts toward the stream, my focus sliding from her as all the undressing people inform me of the grave error I've made. *I didn't bring the cloth.* The grimace on my face spreads over my body, horror filling me like a cup of water.

More people strip down to their skin. It's a sight of nothing but nudity. *Everywhere.*

Attuned to me, she turns back and states firmly, "Honor your body."

Without any warning, she pulls her top off, and my eyes shoot upward. "Creations, Sage!"

Listening to her voice receding towards the water, she proclaims, "You're free. Act like it." The splash of water tells me she's emerging into the crisp and clear stream. She calls out, "Are the trees and birds and butterflies wearing clothes?"

I groan, but I'd be lying if I didn't feel the nudge of her words, coaxing to life a wild and feral part inside me. A gleeful mischief guides my next moves, and suddenly, I'm pulling off my clothes like ants are crawling through them.

My feet pound the earth, a thrill buzzing inside me like fireflies. Strutting toward the stream in jiggling, glorious nakedness, a new mantra bounces around my skull.

I'm free. Act like it.

Yes.

CHAPTER 16
BEAUTIFUL EXPANSION

I am a lily pad in the water, floating about like my only purpose is to be held weightless by the liquid's embrace—glimpsing a sunny day through the thin veil of my closed eyes, the sun kissing my cheeks. The water covers my ears, isolating the sound of my steady breathing.

Despite how relaxed I should feel, the brain likes to stay busy. Unmonitored, it can stray into thoughts born of unhealed wounds. Productivism is one that's deeply ingrained into me, evident in the guilt I feel right now, and the need to get up and do something. Anything. To earn my place in society. *But I don't need to earn my existence.* The reminder sinks me an inch when I forget to inhale again.

Refilling my lungs and floating higher to the surface, I think about how my body is on display. I'm so *visible.* I don't like putting myself in a position to have my body judged, criticized, fantasized about by people with ill intentions. The urge to cover myself right now is like a vice around my throat. But I clench my jaw and resist it.

Opening my eyes against the beams of light, I seek my comfort. *Trees.*

I half-turn my head, letting the cool water swallow my cheek, and the array of forest foliage fill my vision. The stars and the trees have always been something I sought to feel nurtured and recognized by, for who I am. Or really, who I wish I could be without the layers of external expectation. They take me just as I am, and I want to learn from them—because only something that's so unapologetic in their existence could grant me the same gift.

Trees started as a place I'd go to placate my body image. They weren't like humans, who were so quick to comment on the thickness of someone, or their thinness. Their smoothness, or the texture of appearance. The bumps and imperfections.

We marvel at the trees with heavily-lined bark and call it a beautiful pattern. We have those too, but they're called *wrinkles*, and we're convinced by the Elites to hide them at all costs. Billboards, media, magazines, social media—I mean, there's an entire damn industry dedicated to preventing natural aging as if it's a curse. They chase youth as if aging is a sign of failure. They've made us desperate to reverse the masterpiece unfolding over our skin as if it's not a piece of artwork—a representation of our story. I know I'm mostly alone in thinking like this, and it's only recently I've realized it at all. I've learned not to fear my body. I'm trying to learn that how others see my lines and bumps doesn't define how lovable or desirable I am. *I do not control anyone's perception of me.*

With trees, we don't celebrate or condemn them for the color they are. Or assume its rights. Neither do we control who they love. They just exist the way they are, and we accept them.

They don't depend on praise to feel worthy. They don't deprive themselves to fit a box that's sold to them as the ideal. There's freedom in their being that I aspire to reach. There's a composure and firmness in what they are that I think would liberate us, should we decide to learn from them.

Drifting my arms slowly outwards and back, I let the water flow through my fingers. A small smile touches my lips as I realize that I've spent longer than I ever have in peaceful stillness.

I'm not completely healed, though; I can feel pieces of myself missing. A fragmented outsider back home, but I could see myself coming together again in nature.

There's a familiar tapping on my shoulder as angst encourages me to return to my comfort zone. *I made it a few minutes. That's a deitydamn win.* I choose that narrative over the common assumption that no matter what I do, I could've done better.

My feet glide through the loose weeds that shoot up from the stream's floor, until I meet their roots with a squish between my toes. As I emerge from the water and head toward my clothes, I peer around subtly, looking for Sage.

A giddy flutter is born in my stomach as I notice that everyone isn't so dispersed from me like last time. But, I'm at war with two feelings. The thrill that I don't feel so intolerable to the village people combats with the insecurity that they can all see me naked.

Amongst a group of people near the falls, I catch sight of Sage's braids. The ease of their conversation while vulnerable and exposed inspires both envy and awe.

Exhaling through my nose, I finish dressing and lower myself to the ground, practicing the art of sitting still in observation.

It's boring as fuck. Or maybe I'm just not doing it right.

No one tells you that forging a friendship between your body and mind is like trying to tolerate that overbearing friend who always complains about the same things without doing a single thing to change their circumstances. But I am trying, and I will eventually become less overbearing.

The sound of voices nearing breaks through my meditation as they approach, but it's a welcome gift. I'm done working on myself for the day.

A satisfied hum sounds from Sage's chest as the other girl speaks her mind.

"You know? The rainbow, for example, only exists in complete contrast. Gloomy rain and bright sun—you need both at the same time to create something phenomenal."

I thought I was done with introspection for a minute there, but class is still in session, folks.

Sage's enthusiastic nods and the high pitch of her voice is so cheerful, and I can't help but crack a smile. "Yes!" Sage gestures to me. "We were just talking about this before! Nature requires balance. Equal and opposite. The truest moments in life are when we surrender to that balance of light and dark."

The words entice a question to sprout like a flower in my stomach, and I wonder if Sage can feel it. The subtle raise of her brows at me is indication enough. *She does.*

Hesitation looms over me as I worry that this friend of Sage might hate me. *Ignore me.*

Releasing my bottom lip, I ask anyway. "How do you stop fighting the dark? I only know a world where I'm desperate for the light, but stuck in this void."

The girl locks eyes with Sage, and then turns to me. My mouth dries out in the two seconds it takes for her to respond.

"Well, I think that fighting the dark, wishing for only light, means you'll never get to see a rainbow. You'll never get to witness your authentic self."

Sage carries on from that thought. "Lean too much into the light, the dark will come to swallow you whole when you least expect it. Stay in the dark too long, and you might stop believing in the light."

The girl answers my question. "To stop fighting it, maybe we need to find reasons to be grateful for it."

I stare at her, the epiphany hitting me so hard it knocks some weight loose from my chest.

The girl giggles, the sound sweet in comparison to my hearty chortle.

Outstretching both hands to help me up, she whispers like it's a secret just for me, "The answer to so many people's problems are in nature."

Annoyance flares through me like a bolt of lightning when I realize the first thing I do when we return is involuntarily look around for Orion.

Notice the thought and let it pass.

Sage runs over to help the older woman who's carrying a heavy harvest of vegetables from the gardens. I run over as well, picking up a full basket from the floor and following them. Awe would be the best way to describe the feeling I experience walking into this structure. It smells of earth and warmth—something so foreign to my home. My feet halt as I crane my neck upward.

Not a killing shed, then.

It's huge—organized into sections of storage based on vegetation and materials. Work benches are filled with kitchenware and spices in stacked jars. A gasp rips through me as I turn, taking in a viscerally unforgettable sight. The barn is built around a tree, littered with branches that concave around shelves stacked with books. Plush, egg-shaped lounges decorate the library corner of the—*not*—killing shed. I'm convinced if I sink into one of those coffee colored lounges, I'd only get up if I were being dragged out, mid-tantrum.

"Get. Fucked," I utter in promise of transcendence, levitating toward it without hesitation.

Sage calls out, "Ah, I see you've found our Hermsa."

I turn to her slowly; a great effort is used to peel my eyes away from it. "Hermsa? Does that translate to 'where I'll be buried'?"

She smiles. "You and me both, but no, it translates to 'the beautiful expansion.'"

The translation prickles my scalp with jubilation nearly as much as the Hermsa's very existence.

I tilt my head to the side, waiting for her to elaborate.

She explains, "We learn of the world, and the people within it. Worlds inaccessible to us. Worlds we wish to escape from, ones we yearn for, ones were in without noticing. The great expansion is a place to get lost, and to be found." She looks over to it, with sparkles unmistakable in her eyes.

Her words settle beneath my skin as I imagine how incredible draping across that lounge with a book would feel.

Something clicks in my mind, an answer to a question. I've wondered for a while why her accent sounds like her mum's at times, and switches to another on certain words. If English might be her second language, when did she learn, and how?

I ask her, "Do you speak another language besides the one of... here, and English?"

The question catches her off guard, stealing the spark from her eyes just as a throat clears behind us. We both turn to see the Elder Chef, and she answers my question. "We learned English because Discon stripped us of all we were and forced us to speak in their preferred language." The Elder Chef's eyes dazzle at the sight of the forest library, "But these books are in many languages."

What the fuck do I say to that? Despite her smile, there was a bite to the first part of her answer, and I wonder if I've offended them, or triggered them somehow. *Shit.* I struggle to find the words that convey the taste of bile in my mouth from the fact they were forbidden from their native tongue.

My thoughts dart to who these Discon people could be. We have the front face of governance at home, but I would be lying if I didn't wonder about the power that sat behind closed doors, pulling the strings. There has to be. Governance seems, logically, the people who would move in a way that is for the people's highest good, so why does everything outside of here feel so wrong? It's a testament to Orion's leadership, because the more I see, the more I recognize what the world could be if the one leading us cared about our wellbeing.

Only those who sell their soul to the system will receive security of food, housing, employment, and medicine, as if this is a gift they're giving us and not an inherent right for being alive. But here? It's more than that. The leaders care if you're *happy*—feel a sense of belonging, purpose, and value.

Placing Discon as the faceless power... It's like a curtain has been pulled back, but somewhere deep down, I knew something devastating to the people was standing behind it. I can confirm now that the world runs with black oil in their veins instead of blood—incongruent with our species and what it means to be human. What has felt broken in me for so long, is the world I lived in. Why I felt so alone, is because I was trying to exist as an outsider within it. Maybe, what I have been trying to heal in myself is a matter of the world I reside in, and not the world within me.

My pain, my shattered soul, is slowly being reassembled with golden glue as I find peace in knowing the way I feel isn't entirely my fault.

Sage snaps me back to the conversation as she elaborates, "I was a prized possession of Discon, and I stopped cooperating until they let Mum teach me my native language. No one else knew, because they were scared more people would demand things. So, I'd speak to myself in my cell constantly, and write letters to practice the language. Only in testing would I have to speak English. But something good came from it." She looks over at the Hermsa. "I can read many books."

I fight the swell of raw pain in my chest, pleading it not to reach my eyes and make this about me. But, Sage being Sage, picks up on it. She inclines her head, a promise within her smile as she tells me, "It's okay, it's in the past."

But it's not. Not really.

I don't say that, though; instead, I hug her, squeezing so hard I hope the meek value of love in my heart reaches her.

The Elder Chef insists, "Ease up girl, or her eyes will pop out with the force you're squeezing with."

Sage laughs, and I'm right there chuckling with her as I reluctantly release her from my hold.

Before my greedy eyes can absorb any more of the Hermsa, more people enter the barn, speaking to the Elder Chef in the village language.

Easily, they all slip into conversation, which I assume regards the spices, because they're pointing at them. A swell of gratitude breaks loose in my chest when Sage switches to English for my benefit, but I also feel a bit of guilt in making them do so. I don't have time to learn their language before my trials, so I choose to focus on the gesture in acknowledging me. But, if they allow it, I'd love to try learning some basic words at least. To acknowledge them.

"And turmeric," one of the male cooks says.

"Is your back still inflamed?" Sage asks.

A nod follows in response. "Three days now. I might ask…" The male cook looks to me, as if catching himself before he accidentally reveals something.

Might ask who *what?*

The question never leaves my lips, and they carry on, leaving out names and whatever they nearly disclosed.

Someone here can help with injuries. Why is that a secret?

I follow them outside, watching as they add the turmeric and other ingredients to start the sauce base for the meal in a pot. Everything here is so intentional. Everyone is too… just in their being. They have this air of confidence. The longer I stand here awkwardly staring, the more it becomes increasingly obvious that I lack that in essence.

I start back to my hut and offer a wordless goodbye to Sage, but her surprise causes me to stop walking.

"Where are you going?" she demands.

She knows the location of where I'm going, but not my intention.

Unsure of an alternative that she might be alluding to, I stutter, "I—uh…"

She smiles at me and outstretches her hand, the gesture squeezing my heart. "I have a surprise for you."

A prolonged and unsure hum leaves my throat as I take her hand. "Will I like this surprise?"

She chuckles, and I realize right then how quickly she has become one of my favorite people.

"Hopefully," she sing-songs.

I scoff, letting her lead the way.

We approach a group around a fire, instruments close to them as they speak in their language.

She turns to me. "While lunch is prepared, we're going to give thanks to our Mother with some melodies and chants. Join us?"

Surprise flitters through me for two reasons. One, that she's asking, and two, that her mother is here.

With a toothy grin, I nod. *I haven't heard music in such a long time.* A yearn for it is already itching under my skin.

Looking around, I seek someone who resembles her. "Wait, who is your mother?" I ask.

When I turn back to her, she looks confused, then rolls her eyes in realization. "Oh! No. Not *my* mum. *The* Mother. Of nature—Creation itself. Our *collective* Mother."

An eagerness bubbles in my chest. "You believe our creator is a woman?"

She finds a seat on the log, patting the spot next to her. Hiking my long skirt up, I swing a leg over to straddle it and face her.

"Our universe, Creation, the Divine. Whichever term, I don't think it has gender. And to me, Mother isn't a woman. It's feminine. Some mistake the two. Mother Nature is just one manifestation of the universe—Earth's physical representation. But all of it is love. We descend from love, and that's what we return to. While we're here, we experience it in music, food, art, friends, a kiss, an argument, a revelation... All acts in the name of love." Her voice is laced with a fervor that makes each word sound certain.

Glancing languidly away to find the trees, all I can manage is a hum from deep in my throat.

If we come from love, does that mean we don't need to seek it, but instead, be it?

Sage's bright voice pulls me from my thoughts. "So today, we connect to the source through music." She looks around the array of people and their instruments. "Through chanting, melodies, singing, and dancing."

A tinge of amusement in my chest has the words slipping past my lips. "I'm in. It all sounds *en-chanting*."

I curl my lips in, trying to smother a chortle as her chin dips and she swings her head to me, looking at me through her lashes. I'm genuinely not sure if she wants to throat punch me or laugh.

She rolls her eyes at me dramatically, groaning. "Mother Almighty, *no*," she drawls, but a smile creeps onto her face as she starts to mock me. "Why can't I feel your regret from saying that? You do not wish to take it back?"

My jaw drops open, and I shove her playfully. "No, that was funny."

She throws her head back, laughing so hard that the only sound coming out is compressed air.

Pointedly looking at her, I chide, "Not funny, eh?"

This is one of those times you take mental images of. Fuck, I didn't realize how much I missed the sensation you get in your chest when you make someone laugh. My mind floats to Orion, looking around as if I might catch a glimpse of him laughing, too. But he's not here. *I miss him.* The thought entices a sensation similar to someone beating my heart like a gong, the feeling of longing roughly rippling through me in vibrative waves, rattling my core.

The yearn I have for him collides with the gratitude I have for Sage, and it makes me want to weep. I struggle to get the words out without my voice faltering. "Thank you so much for your time and the lessons on... everything. I can't explain what it means to me. What *you* mean to me. Thank you."

Seeing the abrupt change in my expression, her forehead furrows as the corners of her lips dip downwards. Wordlessly, she hugs me tightly, and I squeeze back with just as much enthusiasm.

The full weight of my presence sits in my body instead of living inside my mind. I'm aware of the soft slide of fabric on my skin as I pull back from the hug—the soft pulse in my feet as they rest bare on the grass.

As if in slow motion, I watch everyone with fresh eyes. Someone adds herbs to the large cooking cauldron, and another person leans over it to smell the alluring aroma. The men and women all contribute and work together as a kind of... organism. I wonder how long this village has been around, and how Sage feels about growing up here. Did *she grow up here?*

I turn to Sage as she picks up a stoker and nudges the logs in the fire. "Were you born in this village?" Realizing I've never asked if they refer to this as a village, I ask, "*Is* this a village?"

My stomach dips at the slight tensing of her body. *Shit, what did I do?*

Without facing me, she replies, "I have lived here for a few years, but no, I wasn't born here."

She feels an entire world away, and it pinches my heart.

In a flash, she seems to regain her bearings, and I'm left wondering if I imagined her eyes glazing over.

Facing me, she gestures around us with her hand. "This... is our Juf'ua." A tranquility overcomes her features as she adds, "It translates to 'safe place for the spirit.'"

"Juf'ua." I close my eyes as warmth settles over me.

When I open them, she's looking at the fire, and I decide not to prod further on her story if she's uncomfortable. So all I say is, "That's cool."

When she glances back at me, something crosses her features, as if she's weighing a decision.

Bringing one of her knees to her chest, she rests her chin on it, exhaling through her nose. *She's about to tell me something that's hard for her.*

I stay quiet, ready to listen.

Staring into the flames like the story is within it, she begins. "I have to start with my mum's story. She was taken to a place called Discon. Anytime someone is discovered as being Activ, they get taken there. They were told that the Activs were being studied—held there—to help people. Activs weren't treated as humans, they were there to experiment on. It doesn't make sense to this day how people so cruel can exist.

"If you're not being *studied,*" she says in a voice too calm, "you're in your cell. One meal a day, everyone would be together in a common area. And that's where she met my dad. They fell in love instantly. One night, they were whispering about wanting to leave together when someone else had the same idea across the room.

"A powerful Activ wanted to leave, and attacked the guards while trying to get out. They calmed him by telling him they would take him to get his things and sign some paperwork before letting him go free. Mum said she had never felt fear like that for another person before, as she watched them escort him away. The next night, he came to join everyone at dinner, and he..." A solemnness enters her tone. "My mum said he was broken. He never spoke again—just sat there, hollow, staring at his meal, night after night. He became the example for anyone who thought to leave." Her tone carries an undercurrent of sorrow, and my face can't help but reflect it back to her.

I twist my ring around my finger, the unease of this story making me gnaw at the inside of my cheek.

She carries on. "With the whispers spreading that they might never be let out, Discon brought in many things to make it an ideal place to live. But putting a bird in a cage made of gold, doesn't mean it's no longer in a prison. After being there so long, my mum and dad found ways to get time alone, and eventually, she fell pregnant with me."

My stomach drops. *No.* The feeling of wrongness goes far beyond bone deep. What this place is, what it does to people... It's no place for a baby. A child. *Anyone.*

The pained look on Sage's face makes me clench my jaw, holding the swell of emotions at bay.

Straightening her spine as if standing up to the memory, she continues. "Discon was... thrilled to study an individual with no outside world conditioning."

My eyes squeeze shut at the pain in her voice. "After I was born, I spent a lot of time in those testing rooms, or alone. I was an anomaly. A test subject, protected from variables. They wanted to see if this would make my abilities more potent."

Why would they want that? Confusion spins me until I'm dizzy, my mind reeling with questions I can't bring myself to ask. *What is Discon really doing with these people?*

Sage chuffs, pulling me back to my body. "My mind and my body belonged to them. When I was just old enough to speak in full sentences, I watched behind a two-way mirror as they pinched my mum roughly on the arm, testing me—examining my brain's responses. Then, I'd have to identify the emotions she felt, past the cloud of my own. That's my first memory of my mum, actually. Not her holding me or singing to me as I fell asleep."

Even though she says it as if she's processed it already, I can see her light flicker out. She picks up the fire stoker, mindlessly scraping it through the dirt back and forth, as if she can't stay still, or it's soothing her somehow.

A compassion for her so overwhelming spills over the edge of my tongue. "I hate this. That you went through that. A child, alone. Kept from your parents. Forced to... I'm so sorry, Sage." Reaching out to clasp her hand in mine, she squeezes my fingers tight.

Shrugging with one shoulder, she says, "I saw my parents at the minimum to form attachment. But, I grew up alone. Only when I was older did I grasp how much planning my parents put into it, when we escaped." Just like that, her face transforms from an icy glaze to a spring meadow.

A tear escapes and rolls down my cheek, speechless.

She playfully nudges me with her shoulder. "We got out."

I nod, offering her a weak smile. Reaching out to play with the end of her braid, I tentatively ask, "Where are your parents now?"

Her lips lift into a bright grin, and she straightens to look around for them. *They're here! Have I walked past them and not even noticed?*

Her eyes halt their sweep of the crowd, and her face relaxes affectionately. She inclines her head, raising a finger to point them out. "There they are."

Twisting to follow her eyeline, I turn to stone when my eyes lock on her parents. The dots connect in my mind, catching the small details of resemblance as I stare at them, mouth agape. *I'm an idiot.*

Turquoise and Spearman.

Slowly turning to face her, I plaster on a smile, desperate to hide the swarm of shock and fear torpedoing through me.

Seeming to take in my emotions, she levels me with an empathetic look. "They are very powerful. But you don't need to fear them anymore."

I choke out, "Anymore?"

She laughs. "Well at first, we thought you were a spy from Discon, so yeah. At that time, you were right to be afraid of them."

A nervous laugh escapes me, and I nod slowly. "Awesome. That's... so cool that they thought that."

"But..." she drawls, summoning an optimistic sputter within my chest. "They see you in a different light now. Trust is not given easily by us, and I'm sure you can imagine why. But when they trust, their loyalty knows no bounds."

Looking over my shoulder, I can't help but see them in a different light, too. Respect and awe fills my heart—for the couple who fell in love and escaped that awful place with their daughter. *Sage's parents.*

Still unsure about the connection to the village—*Juf'ua*, I ask, "How did you three get *here?*"

Leaning in and lowering her voice, she informs me in a way that tells me this is a sensitive topic. "Orion."

CHAPTER 17
INTELLIGENCE

To no success, I try to ignore the falter in my heart's next beat. His name *is* impactful, as he warned me it might become.

I ask, "He aided them in their escape?" This time, I can't ignore the way my heart sinks slowly, like a leaf falling from a tree.

Her tone is somber when she explains, "Even though Orion was like a son to my dad, he always thought of him more as a friend than a father. As I got older, my parents became more desperate to get me out of there. It nearly killed my mum to override the suppressants they were feeding the Activs to dull their abilities—but she did, and used her telepathy to help their escape."

I gawk. "Telepathy?"

"Well, a form of it," she explains. "Mum can put thoughts into someone's head, make them feel like it is their own, but can't read their mind. Her intelligence is a thread of linguistics—the Lings."

Blowing out my cheeks, I observe the loose dirt and fine tips of the grass beneath my tapping foot. How does one process the heaviness of all this? By saying, "This is crazy."

She rattles off information as though it's not earth-shattering to hear. "It took them months to plan the escape, and once they did, Orion brought them here. Told them its name is Juf'ua, and what its purpose would be. See, he'd already made a home for himself here before going to Discon the second time."

Whipping my head to Sage, my voice is too high when I ask, "He *went* to Discon? A second time?" I wave my hands in front of my face. "Wait, wait, wait..." I whisper, "He was living here by himself?"

Pressing my fingers to my temples, I scramble to piece her words into a timeline. Her voice stays low, slowly clarifying, "When he was twelve, he heard about Discon from someone he knew at the orphanage and snuck out to see it for himself."

My forehead furrows at the words orphanage, and she nods with a sad smile before continuing. "Some guards from Discon found him spying. And when they saw how quick he ran, they knew he was Activ. More guards cut him off and eventually caught him. He spent five of his teen years at Discon."

I can't help it. I look around us, searching for him as if he were a part of the conversation, and I could... *What?* What would I do if he were the one telling me this? *Would I hold him, scream on behalf of the injustice dealt to him? Or would I sit with a blank expression curated by sheer horror?*

I ask, "Do you think he'd be okay with me knowing this? I feel like... I don't know." I rub my chin, feeling strange as if I'm invading his personal space without permission.

Picking up on my emotions, she assures, "Orion and I are like brother and sister. He tells my story, and I tell his—because sometimes, it's easier that way. It's okay that you know. He wants that."

A swirl of mixed emotions course through me at the surety in her voice, but still I ask, "He would? Why?"

She glances at me, considering me in a way like I'm missing something. "He just would. And there is a lot more to his story that he can tell you one day. This is part of my story, too."

The tightness in my chest loosens. "Okay, so how did you all get from Discon to this place?"

She picks up where she left off. "After half a decade at Discon, he found a way to escape through the infirmary vents, after pretending to go unconscious from a test. When he got out, he came here. Said he was called to it by this invisible force."

A shiver runs down my spine.

It called to him.

Like it called to me.

I swallow, both desperate to know and anxious to find out more about this brave, lonely boy. "Then what happened?"

She looks up to the sky, as if the rest of what unfolded is scrawled in the clouds. "He wanted to find a way to free everyone. He lived here, built a lot of this—" she gestures around us "—while learning everything he could about his abilities. About Discon. Then, he staged his second capture."

I stare at her with a slack jaw, my heart cinching at the thought of him taking on this evil by himself.

He went back to Discon knowing he'd be tortured. To save people.

A flash of his scars in my mind shakes me to my core, stilled with the threat of emotion burning behind my nose. *What did they do to you?*

"That's when he met your dad?" The unease subsides a fraction, remembering her saying he wasn't always by himself.

She nods. "Well, they didn't know each other when he was there the first time because Orion was always kept somewhere else. Wasn't allowed to come to shared meals because he didn't cooperate. The second time, he had to.

"I was already in my twenties by the time I met him. On one of those days, I was allowed to eat dinner with my parents. My dad strategized the day, time, and path to escape, when they knew I'd be with them. My mum fought the suppressants until she collapsed, but managed to plant thoughts in the guards' heads to leave certain doors unlocked. Since the suppressants didn't quite hold Orion's level of abilities—even though Discon believed they did—he was able to get them out quickly, carrying my mum while my dad ran hand-in-hand with me."

The image of them running from this place stirs a fear within me until it feels like a crushing weight. But at the same time, pride torpedoes through it, lifting the hairs on my arms as I imagine how free they felt when escaping.

She continues, "Orion brought us here, and we agreed to join him in his mission to save everyone, one by one, from Discon, and bring them here where they could be free."

I can't shake the feeling that there's more to the story, and more to the mission. But as more people gather around us, I notice Sage hold back and start to fidget. *Not everyone is okay with me knowing all of this.*

Running my hands down my face, I take it all in, my words muffled as my hands cover my mouth. "That... is terrifying and incredible." Shock washes over me in waves as I recount pieces of what she's said.

Discon. Orion alone. Sage's isolation. The mission. Orphanage.

I look to Sage. "Orion, your parents, and you... made what you went through mean something."

Her eyes glisten, seemingly against her knowledge. "Thanks, Stel. One day, our pain will be the thing that changes the world."

Studying her, awe causes goosebumps to spread over my arms, then an understanding startles me. *Everyone here has a story.*

I've been so consumed in my own life, I never considered that everyone here has their own pain. Their own history.

These people were rescued from Discon, and the fifty shades of hair and skin and accents make so much more sense now. They were taken from all over the world and brought to this prison for Activs. My mind reels as I try to understand how such a horrid place like Discon exists in the world, run by these terrible people. I wonder if they sleep soundly at night.

Fingers raking through my hair, I see the people around me with fresh eyes, begging to know how they're so strong after what they've been through. Where I am isn't just a village living outside of society, it's a refuge for survivors. That layer of perspective pulls my heart into my stomach, also knowing they, too, have pain and chasms and are healing from what life did to them—made to feel as if they didn't belong and something was wrong with them... until they came to Juf'ua. Suddenly, the name takes on a whole new meaning.

A safe place for the spirit.

With bated breath and eager eyes, I watch as people settle the small, infinity guitars into place within their arms as others gravitate to the edge of their seat and straighten their spine, positioning themselves in front of xylophones. A collect these thin, cylindric, wooden cans.

Leaning into Sage, I whisper, "What sound do those things make?"

She follows my subtle pointing and replies, "The zaggies make a *whoosh* and *fizzle* sound, like waves crashing on a shore."

As if summoned, they make the sound, and everything changes. The atmosphere encircles us, as if turning their undivided attention to the musicians.

It does sound like the beach. I've been a few times in my life, but looking around at the surrounding forest, I find this landscape far more compelling to me. Maybe it's because in a strange way, the forest feels like it's mine, and I like the idea of someone understanding what I mean by that. I ask her, "Do you prefer beaches or mountains? Which brings you more peace?"

She winces near-imperceptibly, as if in order for the answer to be voiced, a memory has to puncture through the forcefield she's hid it behind.

"Sorry, you don't have to tell me," I say quickly, unsure why the question hurt her so badly.

"No, it's okay," she assures me before answering.

"The beach. I've never been, but after hearing a story about what it's like, my second and final request at Discon was to have a sound machine play the soundtrack of the ocean for me to fall asleep to. I sat, unspeaking and unwilling to participate in testing, and they said I was asking for too much—that if they gave this to me, I could consider it a gift that did not come without strings.

"They didn't outright threaten me, but with a smile on their face, they gently reminded me that I'm lucky to have visits with my parents. I knew they meant that if I were to ask for something else, they would take what meant the most to me. It scared me the first night I used it, because now the 'gift' was something that made me think of losing my parents. But over time, I let that go, and the simple and soothing sounds saved me on my darkest nights."

Another dagger to my heart.

I don't know how, Sage, but I'm going to take you to the beach one day. I promise to find more for you, too.

Drawing both of our attention, the next sound of a gentle, picking pattern on the guitars begins. The melody ascends high, then descends low, and my breathing mirrors it, connecting me to it.

Around us, I see people nod, tap their feet, and close their eyes as they dive into something otherworldly inside themselves.

I nearly turn to liquid when the drums join, the evolution of the song unfolding in this unspoken conversation, feeding off each other. Some hit their instruments in fast motions, others in steady pulses, the rest matching that of the heart inside my chest.

Without access to the forests and having most of the stars hidden behind light pollution and buildings, music is the only thing from back home that felt like it existed outside of the societal constraints. It was playful and innocent, yet powerful. It spoke as if expressing everything I couldn't, or didn't know how to. Just as the sounds of the beach saved Sage, a composition by certain artists would do that for me.

Receiving the musically beckoned call, the xylophone joins, then the long, eloquent notes of a fiddle find its place seamlessly.

An urge to close my eyes and tune deeper into the song is overpowered by the necessity to observe it all unfold.

What starts as a synchronized introduction melts into a heartier version as a guitarist strums, seemingly being guided only by intuition.

My hands wrap around my knees, my breath stuttering on an inhale as the music builds to a crescendo. Then, just as it reaches its peak, everyone stops.

I blink back to reality, as if coming out of a spell. Then, those remaining in the group introduce the final piece to the song.

Their voices. A low hum vibrates the air in isolation, until the instruments join once more. The sound is a force that slams into me.

They find a rhythm, the singing and playing melding like a lively conversation with a loved one. The tip of my spine feels electric, sensing something buzzing between each person, connecting them.

Connecting me *to them.*

The singers take the melody for a ride, the instruments chasing after them with gleeful skips. One singer hits a high note, and I can't feel my legs or my skin. *What is this?*

A memory of Orion, on the morning I tried to escape, flashes in my mind. He'd said, "The music itself is something else entirely." *Creations, he was right about that.*

The thought has me scanning faces in search of him, and a piece of my heart chips away when I can't spot him. *I'd love to see his reaction to this.*

The melody elevates, a playfulness enriching it, forcing my foot to tap along, and my eyelids to slide shut. Tilting my chin up slightly, I let the tip of my nose guide the sway of my head left to right.

Hearing the movement of steps and friction of clothes, I open my eyes to see people get up and start dancing. They weave around each other, arms outstretched from their bodies and flowing with a freedom guided by the invisible prompts of the song.

Sage turns to me, pulling me to my feet and twirling me around. Pure joy escapes in the form of laughter. I watch her and the people around me dance until I cautiously start to move, too. She nods with encouragement, then lets my hands go, slowly as if she were a mother bird watching its chick learn how to fly. Tentative and hopeful.

Nerves prick my scalp as I glance around, feeling watchful eyes. Dancing isn't something I'm used to doing in front of people. It requires a lowering of your guards, a sense of emotion to move through, which is something I turned off to get through my days. Angling my head back toward Sage, a surety settles over me. *What matters most is what I think about myself.* Right now, I don't care if I dance weirdly. I care that the music is putting a spell on me, and I want it to take me somewhere.

I let it.

I dance with abandon, swaying my hips and turning on the tips of my toes. I arch with the long notes of the fiddle and quicken my steps with the drums. Pressing my back to Sage's, we lift our arms above our heads and link fingers messily, flowing our arms side to side with the strum of the guitar.

When I turn to face her, we are mirrors of each other. Sweat dots our faces as glee roams through our expressions. *Well, I'm really the 'sweat' factor in this scenario.* A wild smile splits my face as my heart pounds against my chest wall.

She bounces with the drums, leaning in to be heard above the music. "This... is how we flow through our emotions—express ourselves."

"So, you don't lay in bed all day feeling sorry for yourself?" I'm only half-joking.

Laughing, she replies, "I should've said this is *one* of many ways."

I give her a look that says 'checkmate.'

She tells me, "Dancing is also our way to rebel against people who have tried to take our joy."

With that, we continue to lose ourselves in the sacredness of the next song. And the next.

Thinking no one can hear, I start humming the tune. Soon, I feel the attention of Sage and the other girl from the stream on me, encouraging me to hum louder with them. This time, I don't hesitate. I'm in a whirlwind of freedom I didn't know existed, and I ascend to it.

When the song starts slowing, my hips sway gentler in return, the muscles in my cheeks hurting from smiling so damn much. Gratitude fills me as I look around the group, swiping the sweat-soaked strands off my face like a child on a playground. They didn't have to invite me into this melodic and euphoric bubble.

Catching movement in my peripheral, I realize we're being watched by Sage's parents. In half a second, thoughts race into my mind. *They're just watching their daughter have fun.* Because even though it looks like Turquoise is looking at me, she can't be. Her expression holds something like fondness, which can't be right. Her dad has his arms crossed, a stern expression on his face as he looks between Sage and I with a hint of disapproval. *Yeah, that's more like it.*

When a group half in front of them parts, my steps waver at the sight of a pair of eyes locked on me.

Orion.

He watches me with the focus of someone desperate for water, and I'm a cup full of it. *Overflowing.* As if he hasn't known warmth in months, and I am a scorching fire. *Blazing.*

Swallowing hard, I'm unable to drag my eyes away from his scrutinous stare. It's filled with need and wonder, but in the next blink, it switches to indifference, just as he slips from view behind another group of people.

Sorry, Interrogator, but that image is burned into my mind. A small smile touches my lips at that.

A hand lands on my shoulder, and for a second, I foolishly think it's Orion. But it's Sage, standing with the girl from the stream today, another girl, and a male—who speaks first.

"Your energy... I think I speak for a lot of us when I say it's beautiful to witness. You're different than we expected, opening up like a flower blooming."

Their words find their way into my heart like a cat who's nuzzled into a comfy spot in the sun.

The people here might be welcoming me, and I could burst from my own skin with joy at the thought. "That might be the best compliment I've ever received."

The girl from the stream giggles and adds, "It was special to watch you surrender to yourself. It's not an easy thing to do." She looks around, and I follow her line of vision to see the bright smiles aimed at me. "We respect people like that."

My hand flies to my heart, forehead furrowing. "Thank you. Shit, I should be thanking you all for letting me join in. In the small time I've been here, I feel different..." *Or should I say,* "I've become more of myself."

I recognize the male as one of the drummers, and we speak about how talented he is, how he learned, how he knows when to speed up or slow down. One of the guitarists comes over to the drummer, and he gives me a rich smile before taking his hand and leaving our little group.

The girl from the stream watches me with eyes that are infinitely kind, then she says two words. "I'm Sloane."

She gave me her name.

Then we're embracing, her hug like butter on warm pancakes.

"Hi, Sloane," I say with my chin resting on her shoulder. Pulling back to meet her eyes, I offer my name. "It's so nice to meet you. I'm Stella."

She beams, looking at the girl next to her who hasn't spoken yet. Sloane rests a hand on her shoulder, and they seem to have an unspoken conversation.

The other girl seems standoffish, but not in a timid or rude way—more like someone who is guarded. *Coming from Discon, I can understand that.*

Then, the girl's fingers move in a swift dance, or pattern. I learned the basics of sign language when I was younger, but I don't recognize the way her fingers and hands move.

Sloane explains, "Her name is Rainer."

A smile fills up my face, but I don't embrace her, noting the micro-step back she takes when she sees me light up, as if anticipating a hug.

Is she deaf? Or unable to speak? Will I offend her if I say my name vocally? Can she lip read? I don't know if she understands my sign language.

Picking up on my festering questions, Sage jumps in. "That's Juf'ua's sign language. She can't hear or talk, but she can read lips."

Nodding in thanks, I introduce myself. "Hi, Rainer. I'm Stella." Gingerly, I add, "Can you show me again how to say your name?"

She looks to Sloane, as if checking she read my lips correctly. When Sloane communicates something with her hand gliding through the air, Rainer turns back to me with a shy smile. Watching as her hands move, I study the shape and copy it. After correcting it slightly, I grin at her when I think I have it perfect. A light shines through her features, and I take that as confirmation that I did it right.

Locking eyes with Sloane, Rainer's one-sided smile grows wider as they entwine their fingers. The love in the look they share... I realize with shock that instead of wishing I had what they had, I can just be happy for them. *Their victory is not my loss, because I'm starting to feel my own love.* A new, strange feeling of bliss springs through me.

Taking in the sight of these three women, a sense of glory runs laps around my heart. *I have friends.*

But as precious as this point in time is, I become hyperaware that none of us knows what to say next. Sage, being Sage, breaks the ice and drags us over to where dinner is being served. "Let's eat," she chimes.

On this night, I go to bed with a full stomach and a slightly-fuller heart.

CHAPTER 18
I'VE NOTICED

The next morning, I lay sprawled in bed, half-covered with a thin, burgundy blanket as I wipe sleep from my eyes.

Either Orion or Sage's parents gave the command, but my guards have been lifted. During the day, I still get escorted if I want to leave for the stream or aimlessly wander the forest, though. But it's by one of the girls or TG, and it doesn't feel like I'm a prisoner—but a guest now. Not to everyone, which I understand. They've been through so much and haven't been a part of conversations that allowed others to see me differently. I can't expect them to trust me when people outside of Juf'ua have been so cruel to them. I'm still a stranger they don't know. But I try not to succumb to the intermittent glances that hold inspection and wariness. I focus on those who I've built relationships with, and hope that in time, I can earn their trust. If not, then maybe the Trials will show I mean no harm.

I fidget nervously at the reminder of them approaching.

Awareness of the Trials nags at me, with the uncertainty of what to expect leaving my nerves on edge. Late at night, I wrack my brain, trying to figure out what I'll have to go through.

One day, the thoughts pressed against my chest and I asked Sloane, Rainer, and Sage to come with as I attempted to go for a jog through the forest. The youngest Okah trotted alongside us. I noticed that they come and go as they please, always roaming freely. Trying to distract myself from the myriad of reasons I wanted to stop running, I asked, "Where do the Okah come from?"

Sloane explained it without a single wheezing breath, as if running was as simple as strolling. "His name is Yellow, after Rainer's favorite color. She's rarely out of his line of sight, since the day the Okah were brought here. They were created at Discon, planned to be controlled and used as the Watchers' beasts."

I shivered at the name 'Watchers,' unsure if I even wanted to know. Curiosity won me over as I asked, and she gave me a regretful look.

She wasn't meant to tell me that last word yet, until I had earned more trust.

Yet, she bravely shared a small piece of information that spun me for a loop. "They were rescued from Discon and brought here. For some reason, they trusted Orion's scent—or his spirit, I'm not sure—and didn't attack when he let them out of their cages. They followed him here, and I always think about how they knew they'd be safe with him—that they were being taken somewhere better. Any trace of how they were created was destroyed so more couldn't be made and turned into vicious enforcers."

An image of Divy when I first arrived filled my mind, and I couldn't help but picture a city full of these bear-sized, wolf-faced hybrids—how terrified everyone would be. But seeing her with Orion, I've come to learn that she's misunderstood. Her purpose was to be a weapon, but I don't think that's the summation of her. The Okah are worth so much more than for being used solely at a human's will. They're a living being, and not to be reduced to a tool. Divy, the alpha, has incredible emotional intelligence, and I love that she and the others knew there were more out there. We aren't so dissimilar. Even days after my first encounter with Okah, I repeatedly got lost in their beauty. These creatures were unlike anything I'd ever seen in the outside world.

I sputtered between deep breaths, "Yellow and Divy, all of them—they have this magic about them. The fire of survivors, like all of you."

Sloane signed to Rainer, bringing a tender smile to her lips as she signed something back. Sloane translated, "Did you know Divy is short for *the Divine?*"

A honeyed warmth filled me. The fact that Orion named her that—I loved it.

I signed it back to her, and when she smiled even brighter, I knew I got it right and committed it to memory.

I asked, "Do you know his meaning behind the choice?"

Rainer signed her response, and Sloane translated, "To give her power back. A symbol to show that her creation is beyond Discon's will and that of something good, from the Divine."

The thoughtfulness, his heart, I nearly tripped over my own feet as affection rolled through me in warm waves. That, combined with the fact my face felt like it had a heartbeat, stopped me in my tracks. I let my hands find my knees and gulped air into my lungs that felt pea-sized. I might've imagined it, but I swore that Yellow huffed his amusement, also noting that the others barely broke a sweat compared to my disheveled panting.

The next day at the stream, Yellow came up to me curiously, inhaling my personality in small bursts before sitting next to me. Craning my neck at the small, horse-sized Okah, I physically restrained myself from running my fingers through his chestnut fur. *Don't spook him and stunt the progress of his affections.*

Progress seems to be a theme. Over the last couple of days, people were relaxing more around me, with their wary glances dissolving into curious or placating. Where whispers were shared or groups snuck away from my curious eyes, there's now people openly speaking and practicing this yoga flow. Well, they don't speak English, and it's not technically yoga, but I admire the slight unveiling of their norm. I'm falling in love with this place, and my heart aches knowing that even if the shift of energy makes me feel partly welcome as a visitor, that's all I am here. A prisoner, to an observer, and finally a guest, all whilst awaiting my trial. *To leave.*

I close my eyes against the rush of angst that spirals through me at the thought.

A memory of yesterday afternoon rushes back to me, where I found myself mesmerized by their flow once again. They moved as if slow dancing, striking invisible opponents with calm and practiced movements. Their hypnotic focus was pinned on something I couldn't see, and suddenly, that familiar pull started dragging my focus like a magnet. Toward... Orion.

Heart plummeting into my stomach, I caught a rare glimpse of him. Since what happened with us under the tree, he'd either be in that hut, off somewhere with Divy, TG, and small groups, or across the field looking away from me as soon as I noticed him. *What I'd give for five uninterrupted seconds of his eyes on mine.*

My jaw threatened to unhinge when TG tried to catch him off guard with a sucker punch from behind, but Orion dodged it easily, falling into a light-hearted spar together. Weaving movements and strikes were graced with a nuance that's earned through years of knowing each other. Then, they were laughing and grabbing a piece of fruit from a basket, Orion laying a brotherly slap on TG's back. Then, there it was. That carefree smile, the centerpiece to an affectionate expression on his face. Forcing myself to swallow the lump in my throat, I reminded myself that before I can even dream of his affection, I must dream of my own.

Sloane's throat cleared, anchoring me back to the conversation, which meant I'd rudely ignored my very sweet and perpetually-serene friend.

"Who do you keep looking at over my shoulder, Miss Stel?" She surprised me with a cheeky and knowing look. *She's been spending too much time with Sage.*

Avoiding her question, my eyes dipped to her deft hands working leaves around each other. "How are you already on your sixth woven basket and my first is halfway done?"

Sloane smiled, perfectly tranquil. "I can imagine it's because your eyes and your mind are on him. Not the task."

Without permission, my line of sight was pulled over her shoulder, and I watched the fluidity of him. The sure steps he took, the quick correction he gave to someone's form as they struck the air. Every bit the confident leader he doesn't like to be referred to as.

A thought flitted through my mind at the time: *I'd like to learn how they do that.* An urgent bubbling inside me demanded that I find a way to aspire to their level of mind, body and soul connection.

My next thoughts were voiced aloud to Sloane. "I've noticed..." I forced myself to stop looking at him and focus on her, willing myself to continue. "His power. Since learning more about Sage's abilities, I've been curious. The way he moves..."

Fast. Strong. Powerful.

Sage said everyone has the Activ gene, but how does someone become Activ? I don't know why it took me so long to think about this, but if I were able to become Activ, I wonder what I might be able to do. The thought alone had my foot tapping with possibility. Maybe I avoided thinking about this because I wasn't ready to recognize there might be this power within me. Partly because of what it means to be Activ with Discon hunting them, and partly due to fear of being more—even if that's what I left everything for, and have engraved in my ring. Scratching my head, I closed my eyes at the fighting emotions. It was not the physical manifestation of the way he moved that I resonated with, it was the source of it. A knowing deep inside called for my attention. The harder I slammed the door shut, the more fierce the electric force slammed back.

Sloane observed me, voicing the hunch. "You're afraid of it."

Without warning, Orion's eyes pulled toward mine, and stayed there. My breath caught in my throat as this charge of energy between us solidified instantly. "I am." My reply came out slightly strained.

Two, three, four seconds... Then he severed the eye-contact. *Ouch.*

I explained to Sloane, "There is this *aliveness* in me, and I get the sense it's bottomless."

I genuinely wasn't sure if when my consciousness peeked into the chasm within, I would imagine the power blinking an eye open to look back at me, as if we were both noticing each other in the same instant. I tried to lay it back to rest, but it knows that I know of it now.

I whispered to Sloane, "Everything scares the shit out of me. The power. The truth. Myself. Him."

A different recollection of Orion and I takes place of this memory. Images of starved kisses and wandering hands, conversation from the depths, being consumed and lost in each other. *Well, it was more like finding ourselves in one another.*

The blush that crept up my neck and cheeks was kindly ignored as Sloane asked, "What's scaring you right now?"

Groaning, I admitted, "That I won't learn how to not be painfully aware of him. That I'm failing. I work through my thoughts, I meditate, I keep my distance. I'm applying what I learned, and I can feel my healing slowly taking place, but I miss him. I yearn for his proximity and attention, as one does for each new breath. So right now, I'm scared of how pathetic I am, and that I'll never learn to love myself above all, and that this new world I'm in is too good for me."

She put down the basket and turned her full attention to me. "The other day, you said you had a list, right? When you got like this, you would read it and see what you needed in the moment. So, what do you need right now?"

I pulled my bottom lip between my teeth and shook my head with closed eyes. "Yes. Thank you, my list." I drew out an 'um' before speaking out loud to her. "Self-validation, reassurance, quality time. That's what I need. So..." I spun my ring around my finger. "He's not avoiding me, he's busy and respecting my wishes. I'm taking time for myself. Wanting to be close to him, yet choosing myself, takes strength, and I'm proud of myself for doing it. But I also yearn for him. Both can exist at the same time. It's okay. I'm okay."

My heart's racing pace started to slow, and she nodded for me to continue. "Okay, great. Validate and reassure. So, what about quality time?"

Blinking at her, I couldn't help but smile with gratitude.

I counted on my fingers. "I have been letting my feelings in, practicing healthier internal dialogue. And I've protected the warm feeling of getting to know myself by choosing to spend time alone."

Squeezing my eyes shut, I murmured more to myself, "I'm choosing to create a life that feels authentic, and I'm scared. I don't know how to navigate my feelings for him and this power inside me while learning to love myself. But I'm figuring it out."

My words echoed into a silence that lingered. When I looked up, I saw Sloane's beaming grin. "I'm so proud of you, Stel."

Flashing a bright grin back at her, I proclaimed, "You're so fucking sweet, and gentle, and... Just, thank you. Truly."

She put the basket back in my hands in silent instruction to continue, the cutest smile ever reaching her glittering eyes as she does it. It stayed there, even as she began working again.

Guilt ate away at the swell of gratitude inside me, because I said I would do this alone. But I haven't been. Not completely. He sees me with others, letting them in. *Does he think I just don't want to let* him *in?*

I trust he understands that there's a difference for me—between platonic and romantic connection. Romantic love consumes me, and they become my priority. But in a sisterhood, I don't shapeshift trying to impress them, or to feel worthy of their love.

I wish I had my journal. The complete mess of my mind is desperate to be unleashed on the pages. Knowing I don't have that option to divulge it feels a lot like a knife through my heart. Instead, I try to navigate it all through talking to myself or by using the tip of my fingers to trace the words onto my pillow with invisible ink.

I'm interrupted by the sudden sound of commotion outside. Sitting up in bed swiftly, my heart quickens its pace as I try identifying what I'm hearing.

Joyful cheers move my feet across the space in a hurry before I shove my head out the door with swiftness.

A growing crowd forms near the treeline, enthusiastic conversation crashing over each other as the air tingles with excitement.

What's happening?

Answering the question in my mind, an Elder claps their hands, announcing, "They're back!"

Who?

Glancing over the crowd for people I know, I see Sage's parents are amongst the group, along with Sloane, Rainer, and Sage. In the next breath, I watch as Orion and TG exit the main hut.

Quickly throwing on some shorts to pair with my sleep camisole, I make my way toward Sage, who's standing at the edge of the commotion, speaking with someone I don't know. But as I approach, the morning dew on my feet isn't the only thing I soak up. I absorb pieces of conversation as I pass, some of it in English.

"I thought it would take longer!"

"They're all okay..."

"They brought how many?"

"Three new cast iron pans!"

Reaching Sage, I rest a hand on her shoulder, bobbing my weight from side to side as I try to peer through the gaps in the crowd, realizing everyone is surrounding four people I have never seen.

"Who are they?" I ask Sage loudly enough to be heard over the excitement from everyone.

Whatever she responds falls on deaf ears as I watch the crowd part for Orion. He's warm with everyone, but guarded— only at ease with TG, Sage, and her parents. Now? The smile on his face is tender and welcoming. It's slightly shocking to see him physically affectionate as he embraces the three men, one by one, with a swift clap on their backs. But that's not what has my ears ringing, or my throat closing up.

It's the woman.

She embraces him by pressing her *whole* body flush with his, wrapping her arms around his neck. *Clinging* to him. The fact that he doesn't immediately recoil, gag, and yell 'ew' in her face has my blood heating up.

Taking a steadying breath, I try to let the overzealous expectation slide off my back. Instead, I mutter through a clenched jaw, "Finally," when he steps away, and their *hug* is over.

She looks up at him with a jaw-dropping smile. She's stunning, with a disposition that carries a casual confidence.

Good for her. I force a smile.

Then, she presses her hand to Orion's chest with a flirty chuckle. My smile drops and something like nitric acid floods my veins.

I hate her.

No. I don't know her. Comparison is the thief of joy. She is a woman, and we build each other up, not compete. We empower. I scramble for other affirmations I've recited when feeling insecure and pitted against another woman.

No one pitted you against her. She is not your enemy. He's not yours. You made sure of that for a reason.

Pulling my lip between my teeth and biting down on it, I try to reign in the swarming thoughts born of jealousy and reason, who fight like siblings in my mind.

Closing my eyes, I focus on the slight tickle of damp grass between my toes and the morning sun on my cheeks, trying to dull this rage simmering under my skin. But when I open them again and see how he offers her an easy smile in response to hers, I nod to myself internally. *I'm done.* I'm checked out, numbly watching this woman and the other Gatherers haul their bags of stuff into the main hut alongside Orion, Sage's parents, and TG.

Sage's delicate touch on my arm startles me, and I turn to see her eyeing me with a worried furrow forming on her forehead. I do everything I can to feel nothing for her to pick up on. Only an empty white page will her mind conjure when seeking my emotions.

With a blank face and muzzled jealousy, I ask, "Sorry, what did you say?"

Considering me closely, she repeats, "The Gatherers left a few days before you got here. We weren't expecting them for another day or two."

I parrot, "Gatherers?"

She nods. "They went to get supplies for things we can't get, grow, or make here."

Confused, I sift through my mind, trying to recount what they were wearing, what they hauled into the main hut.

Ankle-length cargo pants, T-shirts... *Shoes.*

"They went into civilization disguised as... what? Trekkers? Tourists?" I ask.

She looks ahead of her as if seeking the words to answer with. "They need to blend in. It's dangerous for the people of Juf'ua to be recognized by anyone from Discon."

Thinking over her words, I recognize the risk they take going out to gather. *But how do they get it? From who?*

"If there's no money here, how do they get these things?"

She laughs. "You don't miss a thing, do you?"

The laughter that emanates from her lightens my frown, but it quickly returns at her vague answer. "We have our ways of getting what we need."

I squint my eyes at her. "How ominous."

Her returning smirk does little to evade my curiosity. Quite the opposite, actually. But she raises her hand as my mouth opens to speak.

"You know I would tell you everything. I've already told you more than I'm supposed to. There is too much at stake here, and the leaders need more time before you're allowed to know more." An apologetic, yet firm expression fills her face.

"Fine," I drawl, slouching to exaggerate my disappointment.

She chuckles. "*Don't* do that, Smella."

Laughing, I falsely concede, "No, it's fine. Really. I'll just go on living, clueless."

She rolls her eyes with the start of a smile on her face, but before she can annihilate me with her wit, I raise my hands. In a serious tone, I assure her, "I understand. I do. Thank you for sharing what you could, and I won't ask for more."

She eyes me skeptically, a hum vibrating in her throat. "That was almost convincing."

I gape at her. "I was sincere!"

She places a hand on her hip. "Then why can I feel the questions growing in you, trying to crawl up your throat?"

I lick my teeth, eyes drawn to the hut they entered.

"One more question," she says. Then, as if she's getting herself excited, she wags her shoulders up and down. "Make it a good one."

Trying to look like I didn't already have one ready to go, I look up and 'ponder.' "Well..." I start. "It's..."

"Yes?" she encourages, drawing out the word when I trail off.

I huff a laugh. "I wasn't even going to ask, because it's such *useless* information to me. But since *you* asked, I was just wondering who the Gatherers are." I plead to Creation that sounded as nonchalant as I intended.

She watches me, smothering a smile.

"Or don't tell me, I don't care." I lift my shoulders in a shrug, displaying false nonchalance.

She shoots me an incredulous look. "Stella. I say this with care. You are as subtle as an Okah walking past the left-overs table."

Digging a hole deeper into this facade, I press, "What? I don't know what you're referring to. I'm just a curious person."

I know she can see the lie splayed over my face, not even needing to read my emotions. She shoots me a look that says 'oh, you're going to keep pretending we both don't know what you're actually asking?'

I shoot her one back that says 'obviously.'

Stifling her amusement, she answers, "The four people, as I said, are our Gatherers. They're trained and excellent at stealth.

They've all been here for different lengths of time and selected for specific *reasons*." The wink she gives me translates specific 'reasons' to specific 'abilities' in my mind.

She carries on. "For no apparent reason, I am going to focus on just *one* of them. The woman."

Swallowing the mortification, I shrug again. "If that's what *you* want."

She chuckles at the ground, and I playfully shove her away.

"Okay, okay." She straightens, taking on the demeanor of 'enough joking around.'

Her tone is laced with caution, as if she's handling a delicate flower. "She isn't committed to anyone. Although..." Her voice takes on a tentative cadence as she adds, "She has shown interest in Orion."

A wave of spikey pins rolls over my skin, my nerves exposed and raw.

Hurriedly, she explains, "But he hasn't returned her affections."

I sigh. "I see the way the woman looks at him, Sage. And I saw her with him just now. It's okay for him to return their affections, it has nothing to do with me," I lie straight through my teeth.

She huffs. "He's been wanted by many, but I don't think he's gone as far as to love or become serious. We're close, but we don't speak about that stuff together. Since Juf'ua, I can't say that I've seen him do anything but keep to himself. People kind of know that he is unavailable."

I tense at the thought of others touching him. Him touching others.

He's not mine.

"Well..." I look away from her and toward the treeline. "He's friendly with her. Maybe she likes a challenge."

"I suppose. But..." The apprehension in her voice is what piques my curiosity, turning me back to face her.

"But what?" *Do I even want to know?*

She purses her lips. "I've never seen him look at her, or any other woman, the way he looks at you."

I cease to breathe. My ego is satisfied, thrilled. But my higher self asks me to question why I react so deeply to this information. *Is my sense of worthiness still tied to an external source of love?*

Words from my therapist echo in a far place of my mind. *It's a powerful place to be in, if you're okay that it happens, and okay that it doesn't.* Wanting a minute to myself, my eyes slide to my hut, a tightening of my chest resisting the small space right now. The forest is where I can breathe.

Orion's presence crosses my eyeline as he exits the hut in a purposeful stride, his expression sharp and focused as if many things consume his thoughts. The group follows behind him, making their way toward the food and water, loading up after their long journey. Without time to look away, his head turns to me, our gazes slamming into each other. The remnants of my distress linger in my expression, and from across the field, he picks up that something is off with me. His steps slow to half their pace, and his firmness dissolves into a look of inquisition. The stupid invisible string between us is an unbreakable tether that constantly sells me out.

Quickly looking away and schooling my features to amiable, I force a calmness to my voice. "I see." I don't want to lie or hide, so I confess. "The idea of them, it affects me. And it doesn't matter how he looks at me, because he's better off with her." I groan. "I hate that I asked, but I'm glad that I know."

A plea glistening in my eyes is mirrored in the words I lay before Sage. "Do you think I could go for a walk in the forest, alone? I hope somehow you can read my honesty when I say I will come back. I don't have anywhere to go, and I don't think I'd want to, anyway. But just for a tiny bit, I want to be alone in nature."

She watches me, compassion and understanding pulling at her features. "Let me get it approved. Wait one minute."

Tapping my foot and gnawing on my cheek, I watch as she walks over to the leaders, a pep in her step disguising the urgency I know she feels to get me the space I need. She only speaks to Orion and her mum, and I feel their eyes on me. Forcing a small smile, I try and fail not to linger on Orion.

He looks worried. He's not going to let me go. My heart sinks. But then, a swift nod, his eyes never leaving mine.

Breaking the eye contact, I watch as Sage bounds over to me with a smile, maintaining an 'everything is alright' expression much better than I am.

She exclaims, "You have an hour. All to yourself!"

Relief pours over me like the first fall of rain after a crash of thunder. My gratitude leaks from my skin, and I know she can feel how thankful I am for this trust and time alone.

Recalling how Sloane taught me to read time here, I look up at the sun's positioning to mark the start of an hour.

Hugging her swiftly, I turn and stride into the forest, begging it to encase me like the sanctuary it is—a safe place for me to fall apart and learn to pick up the pieces.

CHAPTER 19
STAR CHILD

Without eyes on me, my body relinquishes all pressure to be anything but frayed nerves personified. Tears slide down my cheeks in silent streams as I weave through giant trees and their less-than-humble roots.

My shaky steps guide me without aim, and my chest loosens with each trunk I skim my fingers over. The burl on a tree holds the shape of a spiral, reminding me of my lesson to learn—that I will be faced with the challenge of self-love over and over throughout life. Each time I reach the center, I'll be faced with a new obstacle that takes me right back to the beginning. But each time, I'll be more equipped. That's where I am now: in the early stage of supporting myself through this self-doubt. But I feel different facing it. Stronger. Safer. Willing to endure it in order to get through it.

Stopping in front of one tree that would take five of me to wrap around it, I notice the small plants around it, holding clumps of tiny red berries. I mentally note to ask the Elder Chef what these are.

The untouched nature of this forest awes me, and I marvel at the way some trees started as one, and at some point meshed with another tree, sharing the growth of new branches.

Whispering, I ask the forest, "Is that what we are supposed to do?"

Are we not supposed to learn to grow on our own?

My attention catches and holds on one tree in particular. Something about it feels youthful. It's smaller than the others, branches growing out wide as if reaching for connection. *Me, too.*

Walking over, I plant my feet as close as I can to the trunk's base, throwing my arms around it in a hug. *Can you feel my heartbeat?* Smiling, I lift my head and rest my chin on the trunk to gaze up at her. I look at the blue sky through small bursts that are framed by her dark green leaves.

"You're something, aren't you? Beautiful," I croon.

Inhaling deeply, I rest my forehead on the tree and close my eyes, absorbing her strength and offering any scrap of love in my heart I can offer in return.

"Hmm." The gratified sound has my eyes shooting open and spine stiffening. Releasing the tree, I turn and let my focus pierce any gaps in the forest around me, seeking the person of that sound—the source.

I rasp out, "Hello?"

They saw me crying, sobbing, and embracing a tree. My shock morphs to embarrassment, slowly introducing anger. I hate that they saw me vulnerable when I thought I was alone and safe to feel openly.

"Who's there?" I call out. The only sound that meets my demand to reveal themselves is the crunch of leaves under my bare feet as I take a step forward.

Did I imagine it? Shaking my head, I realize I probably made the sound myself.

"Hello, Star Child." I freeze mid-exhale, the blood draining from my face. Spinning around, panic seeps into my mind, telling me all the reasons I'm in danger from a voice I can't place.

If it were someone from the tribe, they wouldn't be hiding.

Masking the tremble in my hands, I clench my fists, repeating, "Who's there?"

Another moment of silence. Then the voice shatters my reality. "Look behind you, Star Child. We just met."

Turning slowly and tilting my head up to the tree I hugged, disbelief comes out in the form of a panicked laugh.

Great. I've officially lost it.

Digging through my mind, I scour for any proof that I might have fallen and hit my head. Or that I'm dreaming. Because there is no way that tree just spoke to me.

When I come up short of explanation, I glance nervously at the marble-like pattern of bark, then up to the branches. *Where do I look? Where would its eyes be?*

Pinching the bridge of my nose, I lean into the crazy. "Um, are you talking to me?" As my whispered question hits my ears, I go to roll my eyes at the impossibility of it all—until I *feel* the tree nod.

The tree's energy reaches out and pulls at the air around me, and somehow, I know that translates to a cheeky and knowing grin. Frozen still, my body seems to abandon the idea of breathing.

"I wasn't supposed to talk to you yet, but I felt it necessary. I wanted to meet you. The other ancients are curious about you, too, so I think they'll forgive me." Her voice embodies self-assurance and mischievous energy, wrapped in a bow of wisdom.

In a monotonous daze, I echo, "You wanted to meet me..."

I'm talking to a tree.

The leaves slightly rustle, as if she's amused. "Star Child, please do breathe."

I oblige.

Then, I forget again when she adds, "You don't have to speak to me with your voice."

She may as well have slapped me stupid. "I don't have..." Curiosity restarts the sentence in my mind. *"I don't have to speak out loud? You can hear me?"*

I feel that *nod* again, from deeper than my physical body—that chasm of winking power I try very hard to ignore.

Pacing back and forth, I only pause long enough to face my palm to the sky, elbow bent. *"This is wild. You know that right?"* Resuming my steps back and forth, her patience settles in my stomach. It feels like a duck floating in a pond. Like a flower waiting to bloom. *Organic.*

"The Ancients," I venture, *"who didn't want you to talk to me yet. They're here, too? Can they hear me?"*

Another nod. *"We have waited a long time for you. And then again for you to be alone. We had to bide our time for you to learn and process the true state of the world and human abilities before approaching you, so that we didn't frighten you."*

Pressing my lips into a wry smile, it's my turn to nod. *"Yeah, no, definitely not frightened. This is very casual and normal."*

"Funny, Star Child." The leaves rustle in what I'm now sure is amusement.

A tickle up my spine feels like a huff of annoyance to my right, directly before I sense an amused eye roll from behind me. My own eyes widen at the sensation as I turn to scan the other trees.

"Such wise words, Little One." A baritone, male voice penetrates my mind, startling me.

Whipping my head towards a humungous tree, I stare at the roots that wrap around the trunk's base in tall walls before thinning out to spread across the ground. Letting my head fall back, I can barely even see the tree's leaves above the rest of the canopy.

Whispering to myself in a string of curses, I push my fingers through my hair and step back.

The deep, baritone voice introduces themselves. *"Hello, Star Child. I know this can be overwhelming. You are doing well."*

I choke on a laugh. *"Am I?"*

He replies, *"You have not fainted. That is good."*

I snort. *"The bar is pretty low for me, then. I appreciate it."*

Little One's leaves rustle as I ask, *"Are you one of the Ancients? And why do you both keep calling me Star Child? Oh, how do we understand each other? Am I sleeping?"* I need information to be able to piece this together, so the questions keep piling, quickening in delivery.

Silence follows. I scared them off—came on too strong. Or they never were there.

Then a third voice comes in, beckoning my focus to another tree too tall to see the top of. Her voice is sweet, empathetic, and quiet like a soft breeze. *"We call you Star Child because that is what you are. We are the Ancients. You can communicate with all of us, and us with you. The draw you feel toward trees is not arbitrary, but I don't believe you're willing yet to know the details. The truth is there for you when you are ready to face it."*

Attempting to gulp is futile with such a dry mouth.

"How will I know when I'm ready?" I ask as a headache starts to pound lightly behind my eyes from processing.

They speak in unison. *"When you realize you don't need to be."*

My brows scrunch. *"What does that mean?"*

A pause, but then Little One speaks. *"Tell us, Star Child. Before you learned of us, what brought you out here in such distress?"*

The question is laced with such earnest compassion. A lump forms in my throat, as if I'm a lost puppy starving in the streets, flea-ridden and trembling at a hand offering me food. But I tentatively take that shaky step forward, trusting the outstretched kindness.

I can't stop the tears lining my eyes. "I'm scared." The rasping confession meets the air, before I finish in my mind, *"Of life itself. Of my potential and not having what it takes to meet it. Of getting the love I've always wanted and not believing I'm worthy of it. Of how much work it takes to pretend I'm okay, and that I never truly will be. That I'll never know peace in my own heart, or silence in my mind."*

I *feel* their empathy as my chin wobbles against the harsh reality of this pain inside me.

Looking up at the tree, I reign in the disheveled mess my body wants to crumble into. *"I'm terrified I'll always feel like... this. A shell of a person."*

Little One's voice comes to me like wind, promising hope. *"The human experience is complex. Emotions are abundant. But we can see you're trying and working tirelessly on your development."*

A wave of exhaustion slumps my shoulders as a montage of images flashes through me, consisting of the last few years, and especially the last week of trying to heal.

"I am." My lips kick up in the same second a tear slips down my cheek.

The baritone voice reverberates inside my mind. *"Take the time you need. Know that your pain, and the efforts to heal—it is part of your journey."*

What is the point of suffering, happiness, or life? This is all so damned stupid.

Somehow reading the spike of anger and resistance in me, the voice adds, *"Try not to get lost in what pain is fair to experience, or reason with the hand you're dealt. It won't vanish; it can only transmute."*

Inhaling a shaky breath, I close my eyes and let the words settle into me.

Little One speaks with unbridled conviction—unlike the caution one might take with the state I'm in. *"There is a fine line between taking time to prepare for your destiny and running from it."*

A slap in the face. One I might've needed. Still, it stings.

The baritone voice follows with more sensitivity. *"Something for reflection, Star Child... What happens in the moments of waiting? When you're* waiting *to be ready, to be ready.* Waiting *to be healed, to be healed.* Waiting *to be loved, to be loved."*

My brows pinch in confusion. *"I don't understand. Why are you repeating yourself?"*

A soft fluttering of sparks under my feet steals my attention before the voice brings it back up. *"I'm not, Star Child. See, in the time it takes to get to where you want to be, you're stuck. You're caught in this vicious cycle of loathing your past self and idolizing your future self. This leaves you to be one thing while you're waiting: a broken present. You've already started making decisions that are ending this cycle—taking the uncomfortable and uncertain leaps toward love and healing and rising. You have started to accept who you are now, instead of wishing you could skip ahead to embody the person you want to be. You're no longer waiting, but doing. We just ask that you continue to prepare for your destiny, even when fear shackles your heart. Even when you feel the urge to run from yourself."*

Standing suddenly feels too much to ask for, so I crouch to the balls of my feet, hanging my head between my shoulders. *"But how can one prepare for a destiny so beyond what they think they're capable of?"*

The question washes a swell of pride over me like a soft breeze would. Recognizing her energy, I look over at Little One, confused.

She supplies, *"That question sounds like someone is willing to work and not wait."*

Hoping they can feel the roll in my eyes and the smile on my lips, I quip, *"Whatever. Let's say I'm contemplating this destiny."* A seriousness laces my next words. *"All I've ever wanted was to get from stoic to feeling normal, but now this..."* I pause.

Sass crashes with firm reverence in Little One's voice. *"You were never meant to be ordinary. And you know that."*

A gear switches inside of me, born of determination. I stand up tall and ask, *"I'm broken. So, how do I get from here to where I'm expected to go?"*

Silence.

All three of them answer in unison. *"Believe."*

They don't elaborate.

The forest around me—black at the edges of my vision before—becomes whole and vivid. Birds and bugs and lizards coo their native chimes while that presence inside my mind slips away. Just like that, I know the conversation is over.

So, when I hear a soft crunch of twigs and an unfamiliar voice come from behind me, I know it's not them.

"Kehsa," the female voice says in a familiar lilt of Juf'ua's language, but their accent is thick and from elsewhere.

Spinning to face the voice, it makes sense suddenly why she spoke to me in their language, knowing I wouldn't understand. The stern lines of her face, crossed arms, dipped chin, and unwelcoming ire in her expression tell me all I need to know. She was told I was here, knows I only speak English, and she wanted to make sure I knew I didn't belong—that I was not one of them.

From the second I saw her lay a hand on Orion, I didn't like her much, either. This Gatherer Girl hated me for some reason beyond being an outsider; I could tell by the way she dragged her eyes over me, unimpressed. Unfortunately for me, she's even more beautiful up close.

"Hello." I feign confidence, praying to Divine that the tears from earlier haven't stained my cheeks.

Refusing to take the bait she set for me with her greeting, I smile politely. Her jaw ticks in response. The air around us grows taut, something ugly and unspoken emanating from her. I try to shake off my vulnerable state and recent discoveries, readying to shield.

As an egoic compromise for submitting to speaking English, she makes a point of reappraising me, the scrunch in her nose conveying she's unconvinced of something.

"I heard you were out here, and even though they may feel comfortable with you being unattended, I think that's giving you too much credit." Her tone is just shy of biting, as if sliding a finger along a knife's edge without drawing blood.

The insult finds its mark against my will, the anger in me yawning awake. *The way she held Orion. The look she's giving me, interrupting something sacred, and interfering with my hour alone.* The anger argues to be unleashed, rising in plumes of smoke within me, but I keep it steady at bay.

Plastering on a polite smile, I reply, "I can see why you'd think that, with not having the slightest idea who I am. How wonderful of you to be so protective of Juf'ua, even if the concern is wasted and misjudged." The distaste in my tone couldn't completely be filtered out. I'm only human.

Surprise lifts her eyebrows half a fraction before the corners of her eyes close in a brief squint. "Yes, you are a stranger. To Juf'ua. To *my* home. A captive, waiting for the Trials of Trust to commence. I am here to check on the imposition, and what it does with its time alone."

Seething rage clouds my mind. *This bitch called me an 'it.'*

Without catching it in time, my reaction splatters across my face, showing in the stiffening of my spine. She smirks at me like a wolf spotting a lone sheep.

Smack that smirk right off her face.

No. Control.

I refuse to sink to her level of unsolicited judgment and animosity, reasoning with myself that she's on some kind of power trip.

"I believe your free time is up now," she snaps.

A wave of fury crashes over me as she speaks to me like I'm a petulant toddler whose play time is over. But this time, I catch my rage before it slips onto my face.

Instead, my eyes lift to the sun, and I check the shadow with a finger as I was taught. Confirming my suspicion, I still have roughly twenty minutes left.

When my focus slides back to her, she's daring me—no, *begging* me—to argue.

She's not worth the battle or spent energy. I want this conversation to be over so I can gawk at the fact I can talk to trees. And I'd love for that reasoning to be the sole deciding factor in my next words, but it's not. Knowing she wants me to push back is exactly why I don't. *So, not completely evolved then.*

"Fair enough." My voice is overly chirpy, and so are the light steps I take past her, back toward Juf'ua.

Always one step behind me, I can feel her glare blazing into the back of my skull on our silent walk back. Being hyper-aware of breathing steadily and keeping my appearance unbothered are my main focuses.

But I am pissed off.

We cross the treeline, and like lightning to thunder, my eyes find him in a flash. His crash into mine a second later, the bowl of food in his hands forgotten, the people he's talking with abandoned. Whatever grievance he feels toward me slips from his features as he somehow reads the quiet fury behind my eyes. Inexplicably, I relax at the very sight of him.

Before I know it, he's closing the distance between us, assessing me and Gatherer Girl. My muscles tighten in anticipation of his proximity, coiling with each approaching step, and then he's in front of us.

I forget all about my rage and the woman standing next to me until he questions, "You're back so soon?"

Plastering a close-lipped grin on my face, I pointedly look at Gatherer Girl, then back to him. "Yep."

Try as I might to look unbothered, he knows something isn't sitting right with me, and for some reason, this causes a slow drag of his eyes over to Gatherer Girl in wordless accusation.

She speaks as if he'll hear her reasoning and undoubtedly agree. "We can't put everything here at risk for a stranger. I don't trust what she will do with her alone time."

The sweet blink of her doe eyes acts like they can, and have, swayed his opinions before. *I hate it.* But when his face embodies indifference, I can't tell if I imagined the tensing of her shoulders and the nervous tap of her finger on her thigh.

His eyes are pools of warmth begging for me, boring into mine as if asking me to stay staring at him forever. I've been deprived of basking in their glory for days, and I'll be damned if I don't let them swallow me whole. Right here. Right now. Creations, I forgot how breathtaking his presence is.

Lies.

Without looking away, he informs Gatherer Girl, "She has earned the time. It's not your call to take that away."

His self-assurance, comfortability in his own skin... His intellect, and the way his composure breaks for me—a heat spreads through my chest, expanding my very essence.

Caught tracking my roaming eyes, I blink away the moment, breaking the spell—just in time to catch Gatherer Girl's reaction to his words, his attention to me. Hurt. Disapproval. But this doesn't make her shy away. I watch her morph into this seductress, claiming his attention as if it belongs to her.

Taking a small step toward him, her hand reaches to graze his forearm. The notion is so seamless and natural that I nearly flinch at the implication. Turning that glorious smile on him, her voice is smooth like velvet. "You're right. I should've listened to you, Ry."

Slow motion is how I watch this unfold, my ears hot and ringing after hearing the nickname slither from her lips, waiting to catch a glimpse of her forked tongue.

He is not mine.

She inclines her head. "You always make the right choices."

Bright sparks of lava set off inside me, something feral and wild buzzing beneath my skin at her layered comment. The audacity. The urge comes to me in a hopeful shrug, suggesting we could just shove her across the field.

No. What is wrong with me?

When her hand squeezes his arm gently, a thumb stroking over his skin, I know the chip it bites into my shoulder is permanent.

Bite back. Bite that fucking hand.

Stepping back, surprised by my violent need, I level with myself. *I don't want to be like this.*

Any man would swoon at her attention, and I don't even look to see Orion's reaction. I can't bear it.

Nonchalantly, I start to walk away with ease in my steps, throwing over my shoulder, "Thanks again for letting me wander around! I'm going to take a nap." Smiling the most brilliant beam at Gatherer Girl, I add, "It was so nice to meet you."

I think I hear him say the word 'don't' amongst a sentence, but I'm not sure who it's directed at, and I don't turn back around to find out.

Once I'm in my hut, I promptly slump onto my bed and bury my face in the pillow.

CHAPTER 20
I'M SCARED OF YOU

I murmur my muffled dismay into the pillow as if it has sentience and interpersonal skills. The only time I lift my head is to take in a full breath before dropping my face back into our therapy session. Even though it's ninety percent unintelligible rambling, I don't think it minds.

I can't focus on anything other than wishing I could disappear somewhere and hide, but where is safe? My apartment? It feels wrong to picture going back there. But I'll have to when I leave here. I have to pass the trials first. How am I meant to convince them I'm trustworthy? Sage told me her parents first thought I was a spy from Discon, and I wonder if others still think that. I wonder if that Gatherer Girl thinks that, and that's why she was such a—ugh. Picturing her with Orion is like gluggy dough being churned in my stomach. I won't have to see them together when I leave. Less than two weeks before my trials, now.

The thought is meant to be soothing, putting a timeline on the end of being here, dealing with him, with Gatherer Girl. Instead, it rings a bell of panic inside my mind, now knowing more about the oppressive and chaotic world I'm returning to. Being *here* has brought me closer to myself in ways I didn't think possible. And two weeks is not enough time to fix myself. Two weeks, and then I have to go back. But now that this Gatherer Girl is here... I don't know if I'll survive the bombs dropping on what I know as reality whilst watching them fawn over each other.

On the count of three, I'll turn into a spray of mist. One.
Two.

Nothing happens.

Dammit. Why can't I ever get anything I want?

Knowing what I need to do to heal, and having a higher perspective, somehow makes this harder. If I over-react, fail to console myself, let my emotions rule me—I'm hyper aware of what my enlightened self should do instead. That's when the shame comes, and this crushing weight of pressure on my chest. Then comes the confusion.

My therapist's voice fills my head, role-playing a conversation we might have. *But are you not dismissing your authentic reaction by shutting it down and expecting to be okay with everything?'*

I reply to the imagined version of her mentally. *'Anger, worry, and panic do not serve me—they only show how weak I am.'*

Then she replies, *We are not the negative emotions, we are the response to them. Have you tried accepting, and loving them? It might be worth trying to hold yourself through it, instead of resisting it. If someone you loved came to you about something that upset them, would you simply reply that being upset does not serve them?'*

And I reply, *'No. I wouldn't. I would want to be someone they could feel free to express themselves around.'* And then she'd nod slowly, as if she isn't internally screaming at me to realize that I need to do that with myself.

Having self-awareness is one thing, but embodying a healed response is something I can't figure out in the next few fucking days.

The sound of approaching footsteps pulls me out of my spiral. Ones I've come to recognize. My stomach drops to the floor.

"Can I come in?" I hear the amusement and concern in his voice, no doubt by the sight of me, stomach down and face smooshed into the pillow.

The politeness in his question has me turning my head toward Orion. *The face of an angel has popped his head into my hut to torture me further.*

Lifting to rest on my elbows, I eye him skeptically. "You're *asking* to come in?" I scoff, "No one *asks* to come in..."

When did the shift happen where I earned a bit more privacy?

Without moving an inch, a smile kicks one side of his mouth up. "Is that a yes or no?"

Curse that beautiful smile. My own meets it instantly. That is, until I picture that look on his face aimed at Gatherer Girl, and suddenly I'm a goblin wishing to wreak havoc on a small town.

"Are you alone?" I ask. The edged words drip with jealousy and accusation before I can clamp it down.

His smile falters as he scans my features with a veiled emotion behind his eyes. "Yes?" The word is more curious than curt.

Looking down, I respond, "Come in then."

When I'm graced with more than just his floating head peering through the door, I notice he's holding a bowl of food and a cup of tea. I sit up and cross my legs, watching as he places them on the bedside table. I realize how hungry I am the second the sweet scent of chopped fruit fills my nostrils.

Looking back at him, I fight the grin trying to bust past my bottom lip that's being chewed on nervously. *He brought me food.*

"Thank you." Tingles prickle my scalp in worry that I've misread the situation. "Unless... you brought that in for yourself and you're just resting it there. I don't want to assume you brought it for me. That would be really awkward." I grimace and gesture between us. "Or am I making it awkward by streamlining every single thought I have? Just... If it's yours, I'll go get my own, don't feel obligated—"

I stop short as he offers me a close-lipped grin, air escaping through his nose in the sound of amusement. "It's for you. It was always intended for you, so don't worry."

Sighing in relief, I don't hesitate, gulping down half of the tea. *He even knows I like my tea lukewarm.* My eyes flick up to him as I pinch a piece of apple with my fingers and pop it in my mouth.

"Thank you," I repeat. The memory of our conversation days ago floats between us, where he teased me for thanking him. I promised him he shouldn't get used to it. *Little did I know that meeting him might be the thing I'm most thankful for, even if I won't see him again after I leave. Ugh, I'm not meant to attach to him...*

He moves to sit on the edge of the table, ankles crossed and watching me silently with an interest I can't decipher. His presence fills the room effortlessly, dipping his chin in place of saying 'you're welcome.'

Continuing to pick at the fruit bowl that's now nestled in my lap, I break the silence. "So, how are you?" I glance nervously at him, then down again.

His voice is rough, low. "I came here to ask you the same question."

Instinctively, the mask slips over my features, the words sliding out in passive cheer. "I'm good."

Seeing right through the lie, I can't tell if his expression is of offense or understanding. *A mix of both?* Looking down at the ground for a second, he pushes off the table to stand tall. "That's good. Enjoy your breakfast. You're welcome to eat it outside with the others, should you feel like it."

A fist closes around my heart, gripping tighter with each step he takes toward the exit. He's been so kind, so considerate, I don't want to appear ungrateful for him checking in and bringing me food. *And I just don't want him to leave yet.*

"Wait." The word leaves my mouth in a hurry.

When he stills, facing the exit and waiting for what I'm going to say next, I realize I hadn't planned that far ahead.

"I—uh, fuck." Putting the bowl down and scratching my forehead, I scramble for words. *Say something.*

He turns to face me. The need I feel in getting him to stay is mirrored in the etching of his features, silently hoping I'll ask.

"Please, sit with me?" I ask.

As he watches me for a moment, unreadable, I can't help but fiddle with the blanket. Powerful legs stride across the room, taking a chair from the table with him and sitting in it close to me.

Struggling to maintain eye-contact, I instead trail the little scars along his neck. "I'm grateful for you sticking up for me out there. And for the meal. Oh, and for coming to check on me."

The safe option compared to what I really want to say.

"You're welcome, Stella." The way his mouth delivers my name may as well have been a caress along my cheek. I close my eyes, all too aware of the crack already forming in my armor for him.

What is this connection we have, and why is it so fucking potent?

In the silence, I seek him, but the fervor in his gaze—the unabashed, shameless weight of scrutiny in it—has me looking around the hut. Anywhere but him.

Staring at the slant of the leaves that reinforce the roof, I sigh. "I'm struggling, Orion." The confession leaves in a whisper.

Somehow, his attention becomes even more undivided, honing in on me. I don't need to look at him to know that the only thing that exists to him right now are the next words that leave my mouth.

"This self-love journey, meeting my destiny—it's turning into an impending responsibility, and it's stressing me out. I wanted this journey to be freeing for me, but it doesn't feel like that. I mean, taking this time has made me practice managing my emotions, prioritizing my needs, and being more vulnerable—kinder to myself. Unravelling me in a way, so that I'm less of a mystery. But..." I pause.

My internal world feels like it's been put in an incubator, forced to endure a level of growth that feels accelerated. Everything here is moving so fast that I can barely keep up. How quickly everything you know can change baffles me to stunned stupor as I consider the severity of revelations since being here. *Our connection. The trees. Abilities. Activs. Discon. Juf'ua. The trials. Leaving soon, if I pass. Never seeing him or Sage again. Losing him to the girl. Losing myself when I go home.* The pressure dunks me underwater, and I'm thrashing to get afloat.

The trees—*Creations, that sounds so strange to think*—told me not to run. Not to disguise my flee from my destiny as some chivalrous self-love quest. *Because they are interconnected.*

Baby steps. Prepare in baby steps.

Unsure of how long I'm lost in my own thoughts, a rough-textured hand lays gently on top of my knotted fingers to bring me back to my body. The contact is so soothing I could wince. So natural, I could float into the bliss of it.

Running my thumb up the side of his, I hope it somehow conveys what I'm struggling to voice. To reveal. But that's a lot of pressure to put on such a small movement.

Opening my mouth to speak, all that comes out is a sigh. Slipping a hand free, I pinch the bridge of my nose.

The internal war between volleying arguments rages inside my mind, too fast for me to process. I distantly notice his thumb entwining with mine. I had a plan: learn to self-regulate and love myself, and figure out what kind of life I wouldn't mind living. *But can I lean on others while I learn? Is that picking the easier way, or is it the right way?*

"Hey." He runs his fingers over the back of my hand, ducking his head down to try to meet my eyes. "Talk to me."

Finding the concerned expression he wears has the potential to melt the icy barricade around my heart. But the numbness has already taken effect. I've started shutting my emotions down.

Sliding to the edge of his chair, he takes both my hands and encases them in his. He squeezes gently, as if physically asking me not to slip away. "Stella." He says my name like he's restraining himself. "I know you want to do this alone, but there's nothing wrong with talking to someone."

Barely above a whisper, I admit, "I want to open up to you... I just can't."

If a real emotion slips past my well-practiced mask and someone asks me what's wrong, I'm so used to regurgitating 'oh, I'm just tired.' I don't know how to be real with someone... Talking about what's bothering me is not normal. *I did it with Sage and Sloane.* That was different. It's easier to be vulnerable and share things you've already processed. At this moment, I'm discomposed, unprepared, I don't know what will come out when I speak.

But I need to try, so I force the words past my lips. "I don't want to be this broken burden that's thrown into your life. Emotionally inept. You, having to sit here and try to pry information out of me—that's not fair on you. Why can't I just... Fuck." The frustrated groan tears through my throat.

He waits patiently for me to finish, and when he realizes I'm not going to elaborate, he asks, "Will you look at me, please?" His voice is gentle, but I still go rigid in anticipation of our eyes meeting—scared to show him my pain, and for him to recognize I'm not worth the effort of holding space for it.

My heart thrums against my chest, and I slowly track my eyes up. I see his chin. Lips. Cheeks. Finally, the windows to his soul in the form of attentive and soft eyes. The tension in my muscles loosens, as if sensing the safety of him.

He offers me a sad smile. "You're the furthest thing from a burden. Whatever is going on with you, I want to hear it, no detail too small."

I tighten my grip on his hands, easing the nervous biting of my bottom lip. My chest rises and falls in quicker breaths. Angling his head a fraction, I know he's seeing my desire to talk, encouraging me to push past the hesitation of setting my thoughts free.

I whisper the confession. "I'm so scared."

A relieved, deep inhale expands his chest. *Not because I'm scared, but that I'm opening up.*

"Okay." I hear the undertone of eagerness in his voice, but he's fighting to stay nonchalant—which I appreciate. The last thing I need is pressure or to be rushed.

"What's scaring you?" The way he observes me with patience and genuine interest—I don't understand why he's so invested in what I have to say.

But I tell him anyway.

My voice is small, but I manage to share part of what I told the trees in an unfiltered confession. "That I'll always feel like my destiny is too heavy for me to carry. That this darkness inside... will consume me, to where I won't know a life of escaping it. That I'll question my worth until my last breath. That I'll always be an imposter."

I try to slide my hands away, the fierce urge to run and hide guiding the movement. But he gently holds on, trying to anchor me, running his thumb over my knuckles in wordless reassurance that it's okay, to keep going. Creations, how quickly I can feel comfortable in his presence is terrifying.

Face it.

I let the words fly. "And I'm scared of you."

Losing myself in you before I get the chance to discover who I am, alone.

Silent and devoted to the words weighing in my mind, he just absorbs it all. Listening with intent, his empathy coats me like a warm blanket. "I'm sorry you're going through so much."

I know, undoubtedly, he means it.

The weight lifts ever so slightly from my chest. The pain is still there, the problems are still there, but saying the words out loud feels like a bit of a relief. Plus, someone else knowing what I'm going through helps in a weird way. Except the longer we sit here in silence, I'm convinced he doesn't know what to say. He didn't ask about *why* I'm scared of him, because it would open up the conversation of *us*. And maybe he doesn't want there to be an *us* anymore. I feel suddenly annoyed that he asked and got me to open up, only to acknowledge that yes, in fact, I am going through a lot. *That's it?* I just laid it all out there, and I don't know what I was expecting as a response, but that wasn't it.

Looking away, I pull my hands from his slowly, and he doesn't stop me, which only confirms my theory. Now I feel like an idiot. "It is what it is," I offer with a polite smile.

A frown creases his brows. "No, don't do that. Don't dismiss your feelings. And don't feel shame for having them."

I laugh uncomfortably. "Yeah, no, I know. I just mean I'm used to these feelings. *I* didn't dismiss them."

His look of confusion is hued with hurt, so I explain. "Talking helps a little bit, saying it out loud, and I'm grateful for you listening. But I meant, it is what it is because that's the reality of my situation. And if what I said made you uncomfortable, I apologize." I rub my forehead, whispering to myself, "Dammit, why did I open up to you?"

I notice him stiffen slightly. Realizing he heard what I said, I try to backpedal. "I don't want your pity—that doesn't help me. I guess I hoped for you to say what I needed to hear. Advice, action, strategies. I don't know. Either way, I shouldn't have put that kind of pressure on you."

When I venture a glance at him, the squint in his eyes tells me he disagrees. "Saying it out loud does help—"

I interrupt him, arguing, "So, you're saying that I feel better and that it helped when I'm saying the pain is still well and truly there?"

Levelling me with a look, he adds, "I have been where you are, and shutting it all inside doesn't work. Feelings are energy. They need to flow. Keeping it inside makes it stagnant. Your feelings need an outlet, it's just about finding ones authentic to you. So no, I'm not saying your pain is gone now, I'm saying this is a start. Now you just need an outlet." He reaches for my hands again, leaning in closer, scanning my face. A horrible memory dawns on me.

Confiding in a friend I thought I could trust turned into an excuse for them to come onto me. I was having a bad day, my sadness and loneliness piercing through the veil of my everyday composure. He had asked me if I was alright, and I tried to express the source of my sorrow at that moment, hoping he could offer advice or tell me I'm not the only one who gets like this sometimes. Instead, he used it as a way to shatter the vision I had of him and push himself onto me, telling me all I needed was an outlet. That he could help me forget for the night. I shoved him off of me, getting as far away from him as possible. Another male who saw a woman as something surface-level and existing for their benefit. He didn't care about the black holes in my heart, or what I had to say. He used my vulnerability and tried to sneak past my guards while they were down.

I blanch away from Orion in disbelief. *Is he serious?* Striking when my defenses lower? This is a firm reminder of why my guards stay up: because he wants to use my body for *his own* outlet.

"I don't need an *outlet*," I seethe. "If you want *that*, go and have an *outlet* with Gatherer Girl."

The second it leaves my mouth, he recoils like I've struck him. Regret trickles through me as I realize I've lashed out at someone who's proven time and time again he's not like that. I might've read the situation wrong. Maybe I did it on purpose—to push him away. Maybe I'm valid in wondering if he is going to turn out like every other guy I've had the pleasure of being fucked over by. *Fuck.*

Still as a statue, the fine hairs on my arm threaten to rise as he speaks in that firm voice. "You think so little of me? Of yourself?"

It's my turn to retreat, struck by his words. But he doesn't know what I've—

"I have reasons to be wary, Orion." I finish my thought out loud.

He thinks over his words before voicing them. "I know what you're doing. Trying to deflect what's between us by accusing me of taking advantage of your pain to get in your pants. Is this the part where I get pissed off and confirm that all guys are pieces of shit? Throw my hands up and leave you here for *Gatherer Girl?*" His expression softens as my face contorts into distress at his tone, and at his words.

Called out, I exhale sharply with a scowl plaguing my features. Admitting to myself that I was wrong and self-sabotaging feels a lot like bile rising in my throat. *But he's not my punching bag.* The thought that I'm treating him as such sweeps my feet from under me.

My eyes trace the sternness of his mouth, his hardened eyes. Wavered words spill from me, my hummingbird heart racing. "Dammit. Orion, I'm sorry. That was mean. I recognize that the unhealed parts of me are taking it out on you, and I don't want to do that. I never wanted—" I gesture between us, referring to the unsettled tension "—this. Us to fight. I'm sorry. You have every right to be mad at me."

Studying me for a moment, his mind works until his shoulders relinquish some of the tension it holds. "I'm not mad, Stella. I'm constrained. Walking a tightrope. There's what I *want* to do..." He says the word with a longing to support me. "And then there's what you're *allowing* me to do. And I'm trying to navigate."

Offering a few quick nods, I whisper, "Okay." My tone is gentle, understanding. "I don't want to make this harder for you."

Straightening his spine, he suggests, "Let's try this. You're upset, overwhelmed, scared, angry, jealous—"

Gaping at him with cheeks turning red, I start to protest, "I'm not jealous."

He tilts his head at me, his voice even and smooth when he asks, "You're denying that you felt jealousy?"

Running my hands through my hair, I let out an exaggerated grunt. "No. But do you have to address *every* elephant in the room?"

Everything feels confusing, and also right. Which just adds to the muddle of emotions I can't make sense of. *Does growth have to feel so putrid?*

Staring at my fingers as they pick at loose threads in the blanket, I concede. "Fine, let's talk about the stupid elephant." Quieter, I mumble, "Actually they're not stupid." Looking to the roof, I add, "I didn't mean to say that. Sorry, elephants," as if they can hear me. I slowly bring my focus back to his expression, only to see he's suppressing a smile like his life depends on it.

He looks up, playing into my delusion as he says, "Smart elephants."

Now *I'm* suppressing a smile. Even if it seems illogical to feel guilty at insulting an animal who can't hear us, he appeases me by helping me make amends, anyway. And now more than ever, I want to kiss him.

Managing to refocus and finish his thought, he asks, "So, you're needing a way to let these emotions out. How would you do that normally?"

Narrowing my eyes at the wall, I think about his question. "I would... go for a walk. Lie down and think about it. Sing or write. Cook. Read..."

My words drift off when I see the start of his smile forming.

"What?" I blurt out, a hint of amusement in my tone.

Intrigue softens his face. "I'm just picturing you doing all those things, and it made me smile."

I roll my eyes at him. "What did you think? That I only cry and brood and lash out at people?"

Warmth spreads through my chest at his answering smirk. "Kind of."

I give him a flat face and pointed look, which only amuses him further.

He asks, "Which one do you feel like doing now?"

"Brooding. Definitely," I answer without missing a beat.

A low chuckle rumbles in his chest, but his eyes tell me it's with fondness.

I know what he meant, so I answer again, "I think I just need music right now."

Without hesitation, he's standing, and I'm craning my neck to look up at him.

"I'll be right back," he announces.

Without time for me to even question him, he's gone. I'm twiddling my fingers, laughing to myself at how abrupt my emotions can go from spiraling to smiling, and now reeling over how good I feel in his presence. How safe my darker thoughts are when voiced to him. How quick I can lose all composure and sanity at the mere thought of another touching him. The image of Gatherer Girl hugging him makes me angrily snatch the bowl of fruit and bite into an apple piece—*hard*.

Minutes later, he reenters with an eager swipe of the door. I don't even look to see what he's carrying, because he has that grin on his face. The one that makes me forget I have to breathe. That I have knees that don't buckle. That makes me grateful to have sight.

I tease, "You're weirding me out, smiling so damn much."

He quips back, "Well, I don't just cry and brood and lash out at people."

This time, I can't fight the grin or the laugh that bursts from me. *Cheeky bastard.*

Mid-step, he pauses, his smile faltering for a beat. I blink, watching in slow motion as his eyes graze over every inch of my face like he's savoring the sight—committing it to memory.

Only able to do one thing, I choke out the word, "What?" Then, I promptly look away.

The soft swish of his pants tells me he's striding towards me. "Nothing." Then speaking so low I don't know if he means for me to hear it, he claims, "Everything."

Crouching to the floor, he places the items down, beckoning me with the incline of his head to join him. Shifting to the edge of the bed, I slide down to the floor to sit cross-legged opposite of him, leaning my back against the frame. Scanning the items he brought, I physically feel my heart swell. *A notebook, two colors of what looks like pens, an infinity guitar.*

Shock meets gratitude and etches itself through my unhinged jaw and furrowed forehead. I turn wide and awestruck eyes on him, and I think I see the corner of his mouth lift when he sees my reaction.

Explaining what he brought, his voice is lighter than I've ever heard, as if trying to compete with the way a morning sun makes water sparkle. "So, the notebook is for writing, journalling, whatever you like. And I brought this because if you're up to it, I can play, and you can sing?"

My stomach drops. *Sing in front of him?* I meant sing in the shower, the car, in stolen moments alone.

Nerves take root in my chest. "I'm not a good singer, I just love to sing."

Reading the panic sprinkled over my face, he states matter-of-factly with an amused expression, "I didn't say 'sing really well.' I just said to sing. If you'd like."

I run my tongue over my teeth with a crooked smile "Can I just make it clear that this isn't going to be one of those moments where I'm being modest, and then I sing and you're mesmerised at my Divine-given gift, and I'm brushing off your admiration, and you're saying 'no you're really good...' You get where I'm going with this, right?"

He ducks his head, a whisper of a chuckle escaping him.

Lifting a hand before he can reply, I add, "I just do it for fun, so don't expect anything special."

"I promise to drastically reduce my expectations." He leans back on his palms, responding in such a serious tone that I can barely detect the sarcasm.

Narrowing my eyes slightly, I consider him. "Good."

Straightening my spine and looking up at the ceiling, I let a playful expression drift over my features and a teasing lilt guide my tone. "Can you play something that reminds me of the beach? The power of the waves, the softness of the sand, the smell of salt, the expanse of it all making me feel small and introspective?"

This time, he doesn't hold back his smirk, not even as a laugh of unfettered joy escapes his tough-guy facade. In this moment, he's just a man. And I'm making him laugh. The sound is unequivocally eclipsing.

He takes the guitar into his arms and bobs his head from right to left, as if weighing something up in his mind. Then he does the impossible—his fingers move, and they take me to the beach.

A lightness overcomes my entire face, and then I'm half-laughing in disbelief, half-gawking.

He raises his brows, damn proud of himself. "Something like this?"

Absorbing everything about this moment is a drastic need. The exact spot he's sitting in, the soft glow of light casting half his face in shadow. The creases around his eyes as he smiles at me. The song. The fact that it's mid-morning. The exact shirt and pants he wears. The faint scent of the chamomile tea we both had with breakfast. I grasp at every detail available to me and create a file in my mind, just for this moment.

His voice startles me. "Is that look on your face just from the song? Because if it is, I'll play until my fingers bleed. Maybe even then, too."

My entire being hones in on his, the want in his eyes taking me from the beach to an inferno.

No, *it's not the song.*

I clear my throat, snapping out of it and making it clear to him with a look that I know he knows, but this elephant will remain unaddressed.

Undressed.

Should we get undressed?

Stop.

"So, just like that, you pick up the guitar and play *this?* You're the guy at a party that takes metaphoric requests of transportive melodies?"

A half-smile lights him up, and he adds to the complexity of the song. More picking and less strumming, never breaking the eye contact. "I don't go to parties." With a tilt of his head, he teases, "Plus, you'll eventually learn there's not much I can't do."

"Creations," I mutter, groaning at his arrogance.

Truthfully, though, I know he's joking. In the same breath, I also don't doubt the truth of it. But I'm not letting him know how irrevocably impressive he is.

I tease, "Oh, duh. You're far too cool for parties."

Something dark shadows his features, eyes glazing over a fraction. *Shit.* Sage told me of all the time he spent at Discon. When would he have gone to parties? *Idiot.* No matter how much I want to talk to him about his life, I'm scared to bring up the tragedies he endured and remind him of something he'd rather not think about right now.

"I'm a busy man," he answers simply. But I know how layered those four words are.

I answer, "I've noticed."

"Have you?" He shoots me a coy smile, his fingers stilling against the strings of the guitar. I realize my mistake too late—I've just admitted to paying much more attention to him than I care to let on.

Reaching my arm out, I tap my fingers on the guitar softly in gentle instruction for him to continue. "I'm still at the beach."

His eyes darken at my playful tone, obliging me. But not before he can quip, "Is your singing as delightful as your deflection?"

A hearty snort-laugh escapes me. "I think we've established the need to reduce expectations when it comes to me, yes?"

He gives me a pointed look, one that promises me something I'm scared to want. With his eyes still saying one thing, his lips form the opposite. "I'm thoroughly ready for you to underdeliver. The floor is yours."

I clear my throat dramatically, and he huffs a laugh. Closing my eyes, I wait for that internal cue. *There.* The hum starts in my chest, the sound reverberating. Attempting to find the notes that feel like the song, I try too hard, and it doesn't fit.

Creasing my brows and watching his fingers, I try again, getting closer to what kind of sound matches the song.

His light-hearted teasing breaks my focus. "I must say, your version of singing is very interesting."

I shoot a glare at him. "Give me a second. I'm warming up."

A smile tugs at one side of his mouth. "Of course. Ignore me."

"I will."

I can't.

When I stop thinking about trying to fit into his song and only focus on what I enjoy, a tune comes to me. When he starts the song again, I feel comfortable with the flow, and my place in it. I add my flare—holding some notes longer, going higher or lower when I feel the call.

The song shifts slightly, slowing down, and I flick my eyes up to him, stuttering my voice.

He nods in encouragement. "Keep going."

Smiling softly, I relax further into the slower version. His guitar starts to meet the deviations of my voice, the song becoming *ours* in equal parts.

When the song ends, we do it again, and this time I've found my rhythm. I well and truly surrender to the song. Looking back to him, something clicks into place as we share this wholesome, artistic expression—taking a silent hut and filling it with something beautiful. Creating something from nothing, together. *Magic.*

The song ends, and I hold a note as long as I can, breaking into laughter when my voice cracks with the last bit of air leaving my lungs. He licks his lips, and his smile grows until he's beaming at me. I'm returning it tenfold. My chest rises and falls. His fingers hang loosely over the guitar. As he watches me, I see something like awe fall over his features.

"You absolute *liar.*" He draws out the last word slowly, mischievously, like he knows a secret about me.

I roll my eyes in response. "Way to ruin the moment, Orion."

When he opens his mouth, I warn, "No. Stop it."

He taps his forefinger on the wood of the instrument, a smile touching his lips. "Okay."

We stare at each other for a beat.

I whisper with a clasp of my hands, "That was so fun."

Searching my eyes, he responds just as quietly. "It was."

Squeezing my knees and propping myself up taller, I joke, "So, the beach was amazing. Tomorrow, we can go somewhere else? A volcano... Or the top of a mountain!"

When I see the hope etched in his eyes at the word *tomorrow,* I realize that my joke is unkind. Pulling him in, pushing him away, pulling him back—it's not okay.

As if reading my thoughts, he schools his features and plays along with the non-committal joke. A small smile, a simple nod, and a single word. "Anywhere."

Why does this feel like goodbye all over again? *Maybe we can be friends?* No, it wouldn't be like me and Sage. But I can try, if he's willing.

I open my mouth to ask him just that, but I change the words at the last second. "Can you teach me the easy version of that, in case you're busy and I want to play?"

He pauses a moment, then shakes off whatever he was thinking about. "Of course."

He teaches me, laughing at how serious I look as he tells me to relax. Once morning crosses to afternoon, he assures me I've got the song down, and that he has to leave soon and tend to a few things. *The hours went by so fast.*

First, he checks in with me. "How do you feel? Better?"

Better? My heart might just burst open. How do I resist the rising tidal wave of longing that's plotting against me? How do I stay away when it hurts to neglect the magnetism between us? But how could I ask for him to be close when my own journey to self-love will cease?

He watches me closely, and I force my desire to simmer. "I feel much better. Thank you... for everything."

He swallows, and I can't explain how I know that he understood what *everything* means.

Placing the guitar down, I spot the notebook, a thought hitting me like a freight train. *My journal.*

Gasping, I snap my eyes to him. "I've been meaning to ask. I had a backpack, and there's a journal in it that helps me. Could I... have it back?" Clasping the notebook to my chest, I amend, "I'll still use this one, and I'm grateful for it, but there's something in the other one, and I need it."

If I wasn't so attuned to him, I might've missed the brief pause in his breathing. "Of course. I'll bring it to you." He doesn't even look surprised. When he looks away from me, I know. My stomach hits the floor.

"You read it." The words are barely audible.

His eyes drift back to mine—not quite remorseful, but not proud of it either. "I did."

I'm completely and utterly exposed.

My skin warms as he searches my eyes, explaining, "I inspected your bag and its contents upon your arrival because you were an enigma. You found us, got past the barrier, were unreadable, a potential spy from Discon. When I couldn't find a code within the wording, and once we spoke in depth the night we…" He cuts himself off, derailing that train of thought. "I understood that it was just your personal journal. I'm sorry, Stella. I didn't mean to invade your privacy."

The look on his face is definitely guilt, pleading for me to see his reasoning. And I do.

Unable to look at him with my face so red, I sigh. "I get it, you had to." When he stays silent, I flick my eyes up to him. Seeing the devastation on his face pulls at my heart strings.

I assure him, "I would've done the exact same thing in your position. I'm not mad, I'm just a bit embarrassed." Scowling at him playfully, I proclaim, "But just because I understand, doesn't mean I won't give you a wet willie when you least expect it."

Stunned to a blank expression, he chokes out, "A what?"

I raise my brows, scanning the confusion and general shock of his expression.

"What? Do they not have those universally?" Surely, licking your finger and shoving it in someone's ear is a petty, disgusting, and hilarious joke no matter where you are in the world or how old you are.

He scratches his head, staring at me, "I can't say that I've heard of it."

Why does he look so bashful and taken aback right now... Does he know what I'm talking about? I mean, if he doesn't know, what does he think I'm talking about?

"Oh, fucking Creations, no!" I wave my hands out in panic, wide-eyed as my voice jumps two octaves. "That is not what you think it means." I cover my face, humor finding its way up my throat and into my tone. "When I said I'd give you a wet willie when you least expect it, this is what I meant," I explain as I suck the tip of my finger and pull it out with a pop. "Now, I put this in your ear." I move to poke his ear with my saliva-coated index finger, but he catches my wrist in a firm grip.

I watch the very moment he breaks into a grand smile and barks out a surprised laugh.

"You will never successfully perform a wet willie on me."

My eyebrows fall flat, but I can't hide the amused slight of my lips. "You were expecting it. That doesn't even count as an attempt."

He teases, slowly lowering my hand away from his ear, "You can definitely try."

Pulling my hand from his grasp and waving him off, I try to put on my best attempt at indifference. "You're right, I'd never succeed. I won't try again."

He smirks at me. "Not falling for it."

I shrug. "It's far too childish an act for me to partake in. You have nothing to worry about."

He chuffs, "Perhaps I will wet your willie first..." Before he finishes, we both scrunch our noses up into a grimace, knowing that it didn't come out the way he wanted it to and burst into laughter.

Pushing him playfully, I instruct, half-laughing, "Go on, grab my journal, you weirdo." I smirk when he covers his ears with his palms, turning to shoot me a warning glare and wicked grin.

I dip my head in his direction, mouthing the word 'scaredy-cat' at him. I can still hear him chuckling to himself just after he exits the hut.

I use the time alone to collect myself, standing up and shaking out my hands, because it feels far too good to laugh with him. I peek over the guard I have up, due to the fact he's let his down first. Something between us today feels easy. Playful. I adore it.

When he steps back inside, I'm sitting on the edge of my bed, holding the notebook in my lap and loosely biting on the back of the pen.

My eyes flick to his hands, one holding my backpack and the other holding the palm-sized, almond brown, hardcover journal that takes me to a million moments at once. The lowest of my lows are shoved in my face as I recall the pained and scribbled words. Then, that familiar feeling of something more flickers when I remember what graces the last page.

The list.

Nervously glancing at him, I watch as he drops my backpack at the end of my bed and stretches the journal out to me, his grip soft as if it's sacred and fragile. When my fingers graze along the soft fuzz of the cover, I visibly relax, taking it from him and clutching it against me.

"Thank you." The words are entwined with a breathy exhale of relief.

Tucking it under my pillow, I notice him go to speak, but hesitate for a moment. Cautiously, as if I might spook, he starts, "I was wondering..." A pause. My heart speeds up. "I have an exercise I'd like to share with you, something you can do to help the flow of your emotions."

I watch his throat bob as he swallows, shifting his weight as he waits for my reply.

The Chief of a rebellion. Of Juf'ua. This powerful man... is *nervous.*

Just as nervous, I say, "I'd love that."

He exhales sharply, his lips twitching into a smile. "I want you to put your right hand on your heart. Your left hand goes..." He helps position it as he explains, "Palm facing up and open to the sky."

He steps back. "Perfect."

I wait for the next instruction, weirdly excited.

"Close your eyes." His voice is low and sure.

After a moment, I let them drift shut.

He continues, "The left hand in the air channels from the Divine Source, and the right hand directs the energy. The intention is something you set. So, for this, it's to cycle out the energy around emotions you wish to let go of and bring in new energy from Source."

Without moving, I ask, "But how do I set the intention? Do I think about it or speak it out loud?"

I hear the smile in his voice when he answers, "Whichever feels right for you. But I do think with conviction in your voice, it can send that frequency out to the world, and make it clear to Source to reflect that back."

"Okay," I answer with a curious incline of my head. "What do I say?"

He's quiet for a moment, but then he responds, "Repeat after me, alright?"

Biting my bottom lip, I dip my chin, letting him know I'm ready.

His voice is firm, confident, when he says the words, "I love myself."

My eyes shoot open, my whole body faltering at the words. But he doesn't flinch as I scrutinize him. He stands before me, the picture of strength.

He dips his chin, a wordless question in the movement.

Will you utter the words that torment you?

I clench my jaw, closing my eyes and putting my hands back into position. It takes me a moment, pulling on the words that dig into my throat, wanting to stay unspoken. "I love myself."

When I open my eyes and look at him, currents of pain flow through his features, as if it hurts him to see how hard it is for me to even say the words. But he reigns it in quickly, the sternness of a leader returning to his features.

"Close your eyes." The instruction is gentle.

Fighting the part of me that wants to pull the blanket over my head, I sit here, closing my eyes through the uncomfortable opportunity for growth—itchy under my skin.

His voice sounds closer as he says the next words for me to repeat. "I accept and cherish all my emotions." I repeat this, then he adds, "And I release what no longer serves me." I repeat that, too.

"Again," he says.

My teeth grind. "I love myself. I accept and cherish all my emotions." He prompts me when I forget the other part, and I finish with, "And I release what no longer serves me."

This time, I hear his rough voice, lower, his clothes rustling as he crouches before me. "One more time."

Inhaling deeply, I push the words past my lips, slightly easier than the last time.

The vice on my throat loosens, the weight on my shoulders lifts, and my stomach muscles relax. I'm aware of my breathing, and a strange, yet welcoming tingle of aliveness spreads through me. *I'm calm.*

His hand gently wraps around mine, still held up in the air. Placing it on my knee, he informs me, "You can open your eyes now."

Slowly blinking against the light, he comes into focus. The world has stopped spinning for this very moment. Nothing else matters, except for being where I am right now. The present. The gift of five seconds, with nothing to do but look in his eyes.

A slow smile tilts my mouth, watching as his focus drops to witness it, enticing one of his own.

"You're so beautiful." He utters the words swiftly, as if not wanting to get into trouble but needing to say them.

He doesn't wait for a reaction, and pushes past the moment before I can process the fluttering in my heart. Standing up and walking backwards toward the exit, he suggests, "You can make up your own versions of the exercise."

Rushing my words as he starts to leave, I stutter. "I—yes. I will, thanks—thank you."

He pauses just before the door, getting a final look at me with a subtle, crooked smile blessing his face.

I fight the urge to crumble from how much it means that he cared enough to teach me that. How much he means to me. The prospect of him walking out that door right now spins me around with a blindfold, disorienting me.

"Wait." *That's twice now.* Twice I have asked him to wait before leaving today. Without hesitation, he does.

I get up without thinking, and before I know it, I've crossed the space between us and wrapped my arms around him in a hug. Tight, swift, barely giving him time to react. I don't even know if he had time to wrap his arms around me in return before stepping back a few paces from him.

Hooking my hands behind my back, I bob my head to the side, my expression conveying the words for me. *Sorry, I had to.*

He just stands there, his face unreadable.

Then, he takes a slow step towards me.

My breath hitches.

He takes another step, and the uncertainty of what he's going to do coaxes nerves to prickle my scalp.

But then, his arm weaves around my back while his other hand cups the nape of my neck, and he pulls me into his strong embrace. I wrap my arms around him, feeling his back rise and fall with his steady breathing. Against my will, I take in the familiar scent of *him*. Everything slows. I surrender, and his hold on me tightens as I nuzzle into him. Fireworks. A still lake. He makes me feel both at the same time.

Being his friend is hard. Not being his friend is hard. Either way, he's capable and manages to adapt while I flail in his proximity *or* distance. The new sensation of craving time alone with myself is a gift I wouldn't give up, but I also can't get him out of my damn head.

I need to know how he does it so I can learn.

My question is half-muffled with my face pressed into him. "How do you do it?"

CHAPTER 21
WANT

Leaning back just enough to see me, the perplexed expression on his face is reflected in his response. "Do what?"

Hesitating, I fiddle with his shirt behind his back.

"Just *be*. Not think about me. Go about your day. I mean, maybe you don't even have to try." A fervor finds its way into my voice. "Sometimes, I get so mad because I want you to give me my mind back—the space in my brain which you didn't occupy before. The dreams I had before you came in and refused to leave. This is exactly what I didn't want. But I can't be mad at you, so I get mad at myself."

His lips part slightly, brows pulling together as he listens intently.

"I can't make it stop." The words start pouring from me like I've broken the dam, but I look anywhere but him as he holds me steady. "If you have ever felt even a sliver of this, how do you do it? How do I not look at you and see if you've laughed when something funny happens? Not look for you first in any room? Not seek out any excuse to talk to you or about you, or wonder if you liked dinner, too, and what you liked most about it? I have to *work* to not let you consume me."

Seconds from pulling away from him, I'm stopped by the way he grazes his fingers along my skin, gently resting it between my shoulder and neck. His eyes peer deep beyond the surface of me, as if barreling through any line of defense I have. He stares directly at *me*, shaking his head at something I said.

His voice is rough when he speaks. "Do you really think you've not consumed me—mind, body, and soul?" His laugh holds no humor as his gaze pours over me. "Do you truly think you aren't my waking thought? The subject of all my curiosities? Can you honestly believe that your voice, your smile, your tears, mind, strong will, tender heart—all of you—isn't completely capable of unraveling me?"

I blink at his confession, balling his shirt into my fists.

He runs his hand through his hair, staring at me as if he can't believe I ever thought he didn't feel this way. His voice is deep, resonating with the intensity he speaks. "There's a difference between us, Stella. You fight your thoughts of me, and I welcome them. You're my checkpoint. You've carved out a space and settled in my mind. But I want that—to let my thoughts wander as I go about my day, and keep returning to my checkpoint. I'm always coming home to you."

My stomach dips and back flips, disbelieving in his affection for me. Stuck in a state of stupor, I just stare at him. The intimacy of this conversation starts to feel like hands pressing down on my lungs, and I step back. I keep stepping back until the backs of my knees hit the bed, and then I sit.

I don't get it. This man? This magnificent, composed, intelligent, calm and collected, Chief *Orion* is consumed by me?

"But, why?" I ask, dumbfounded.

He moves, sitting next to me on the bed with space between us, which I suspect is to not overwhelm me.

I clarify, "It makes perfect sense that I would want you. Anyone would. But the way you... It's hard to believe." My face slackens in realization. "It's like new-toy energy, right? I'm just new, and that's interesting."

His face pulls into something offended, but I don't realize it's on my behalf until he says, "You asked me how I don't think about you. Well, I do. You want to know how not to be consumed? I can't help with that, because I am. I'm trying to understand if it's my feelings that's upsetting you, or if it's that I don't have a secret way to be devoid of feelings. And what's confusing me the most, is why you're hoping that my affection for you is a novelty that's going to wear off... Why would you want that?"

Before I can process the rest of what he says, I fixate on the last part, snapping, "I don't want that, I *expect* that." Looking down at the ground, I fight not to cry.

"Please... Look at me," he urges, reaching out, then stopping himself. "Why would you expect that?"

Facing him, I shrug, as if the answer is obvious. "Orion. You're proving to be different from a lot of men. But out there, women aren't empowered. I don't see myself as desirable, valuable. I'm expendable. Not worth your devotion."

His face hardens, a cool rage slipping over him. "Who made you believe this?"

I can't help but laugh nervously, the seriousness of this making me itch to move. Walking over to the chair, I lean against the back of it, facing away from him.

Picking at the wood with my thumbnail, I push past the angst trying to seal my lips. "I seem to receive the same lessons in different skin. Wanting someone, and that being unrequited. Or someone convincing me they want me, but not to date me, care for me. Just to fuck me. Sooner or later, you realize that you're the common denominator, believing you're not lovable. So, I guess *I'm* the idiot that made me feel this way, because when you're not wanted by the people you care about, you stop wanting yourself." I brave a look at him over my shoulder. "I'm still not sure if you're another lesson. If your feelings will fade the second I decide it's safe to lean into them."

My words have struck him. I can't tell if it's contained rage, sorrow, or dispute. With a tense jaw, he speaks the words as if they're burning his throat. "They were not meant for you. Be thankful they moved on. It's less painful than treating yourself as a forgotten and unwanted toy."

My face contorts into unconcealed shock and anger. Aghast, I sputter, "Be thankful?" Turning around to face him, I snap, "I should be *thankful* I got played like a fucking fiddle until I finally lost the last piece of self-esteem?"

Holding onto his composure, he somehow keeps his voice low and measured. "No. That came out wrong. Even if they had no idea who they had in front of them, they let you slip away. And even if it hurt, they were part of your development to who you are today. *They* weren't for you, Stella."

I blanch, "Is that supposed to make me feel better?" I shake my head, astounded. "Thank you so much, I feel so warm and fuzzy inside now, knowing that all of it was to bring me here— to an untrusting, cynical, fearful, conservative person. Nothing of who I wish to be."

Standing up, he strides over to me, and I press my palm on his chest, the lines of my face stern as I keep him at a distance. Slowly, he lifts his hand, wrapping it around my wrist. Gently, he lets his fingers glide over the back of my hand before pressing his palm against it. "I'm not explaining myself properly. Who you are today, who I see, is someone hurt, but filled with light. The sun herself. And the sun burns in order to be bright, Stella."

I scoff. "I'm not bright, Orion. It's like we are talking about two different people."

Venturing a step closer to me, he tucks a strand of hair behind my ear before resting his warm palm on my shoulder, and I don't stop him. He looks at me with a focus I struggle to stand up against. "Just so you can have a counterpoint to the narrative you believe about yourself, I'm telling you that you are desirable. I want you. I don't just want your body, I want your innermost thoughts. I want to see you laugh and dance around with Sage. To sit across from me and sing. Make that pissed-off expression at me when I've annoyed you, even though I know you're trying not to smile. I want to be there when you cry, so you can climb into my lap and ask me to hold you. I want us to agree, and to disagree. I want your nervous glances around an open space when you can't look at me, like you're doing right now."

My eyes crash against his, and I soften into him, putting my hands on his stomach. Without pause, he responds, his thumb caressing the spot between my collarbone and neck while his other hand finds my back to pull me closer.

"Orion." His name, both a whisper and a plea on my tongue.

He implores me to hear him as he speaks. "I want to watch you close your eyes and look transported when you smell dinner being cooked. And when we eat, I want to tell you what I liked most about it. I want to see you stand frozen in awe at the sight of a tree or a waterfall. I want you to say unhealed and obnoxious things because you're scared. I want you to challenge me, call me out when I say things that aren't helpful, or if I haven't given you the reassurance you deserve. I want to be better for you. I want to watch when you decide to open up, or when you decide not to, and I'll wait until you change your mind. I want your honesty, your bravery, your transparency. And I also want you with all your walls up. However I can have you, I'll consider myself lucky. And more than that, I respect you. Because I know that you want me too, and you chose yourself. That only makes me want you more."

Clenching his shirt in my fists, I drink in the sound, the sight, the heat of his conviction. I want to believe him. But this could be lust that ends when he's had enough. *Don't trust it.*

The thought is either on my face or accidently said aloud, because he's answering, "I mean every word. Believe me."

Undeniably, there is something between us. So, when my bare feet guide my body away from his hold, it's not because I believe him to be lying. I just think it's a misguided and short-lived infatuation. *I'm nothing. Not yet.*

My whole body stills. The trees told me about this. *What happens while you're waiting to be loved, to be loved? The time in between feels broken. I'll feel broken. The only way to get to the point of being loved is to* let *myself be loved. It's not going to just happen one day, zero to one hundred. The time in between is the small chances we take on ourselves, which leads us to it. And that ensures the present doesn't feel like a gloomy cloud of waiting. They wanted me to take the leap, and warned me not to run from my destiny, but prepare for it.* Fear slices me in half at the mere thought of surrendering myself to him. But what about my relationship with myself? *Maybe when it comes to learning to love, there's only so much you can do alone.*

Taking the final step before slipping from his hold, I'm all too aware of the loss. There's been a concern bouncing painfully through my conscience, and I decide to unearth it, let it spill from my lips. "Perhaps you're just used to the women here, and you're interested in something different. Would you not rather spend your time with women like Gatherer Girl? She's a clear reflection of what I can't give you."

Pushing his hand through his hair roughly, he stares at me incredulously. "Stella, stop. Stop it." Closing his eyes and turning his head away, his voice sounds like it's being dragged over gravel. "I can't endure the way you speak about yourself..."

My arms cross over my chest. "You stop! Don't make me open a window of my soul to you and then force me to slam it shut because you don't like what you see. I am trying to believe you, and to do that, I'm voicing my insecurities. If you refuse to comprehend my pain, then don't lie and say you want all of me."

He's closing the distance and cupping my face in his hands before I finish my next shaky inhale. "I do. I'm sorry. It feels like a knife in my gut, knowing you don't see what I see. But I'd rather you twist the blade than stop telling me exactly how you feel."

Closing my eyes softly, I lean my cheek further into his palm.

A shiver dances up my spine when he takes another step closer, his soft exhale skittering over my skin. "Exactly as you are now—that's enough. Loving yourself isn't the destination, it's every moment leading up to it."

Arms falling slack at my sides and dropping my head to his shoulder, I groan. "I'm fumbling in the dark, patting the ground for broken pieces of my heart and trying to mend it whole. You telling me all the reasons why I'm worthy illuminates the whole room, and every tiny shard I long abandoned *glows*." I lean back to see him and watch as he realizes that I don't mean that as a good thing.

His face falls, but quickly embodies that stern mask.

I whisper, "How do I light up my own heart?" Fighting the tremble of my bottom lip, I add, "I don't think someone is supposed to convince you of your worth."

Looking to the side, he thinks over my words, skimming his hands down my arms until loosely entwining with my fingers.

Squeezing his fingers gently, I ask, "How do you feel all those things? You're so fucking whole and perfect—I just want to be like you and Sage..."

I pull my hands free to rub my eyes, and my feet tug me in paces back and forth, unhinging the bolt on my innermost thoughts. "I'm begging to understand how everyone seems to have this code to existing, and I'm on this fucking scavenger hunt, turning over rocks to find clues!" I laugh so I don't cry.

Welcoming the soft pinch of the floor on my knees as I drop to sit on my heels, I croak out, "I'm this jagged and rusty knife in a drawer full of perfectly-stacked silver cutlery."

He lowers himself to balance on the balls of his feet before me, and I tentatively meet his eyes. *The way he looks at me.* The calm in a storm.

Taking a deep breath, he seems to choose his next words carefully. "I'm not perfect. I bear scars far deeper than the ones you see on my skin."

My heart sinks to my stomach. A window to his pain is revealed to me, a raw unveiling of all the carefully-placed masks he wears. It instantly makes me want to sob. Apology coats my features, for too many reasons to count—that he's seen me looking, what they represent... My throat constricts, preventing any words from leaving my mouth.

There's no tension held in his face or shoulders, reassuring me that it's okay with a tender caress along my cheek. "There's no secret everyone's figured out. We're all healing, and that looks different to everyone. One day, you'll believe all the good things you are." His face relaxes in understanding. "But you need to believe it for it to feel real, like you've been telling me."

Relief seeps into the marrow of my bones, physically sagging my shoulders and closing my eyes. "Yes." I blink at him. "Since leaving home and coming out here, every tiny remnant of ache inside me has rushed to the surface. The deepest parts of me have finally been acknowledged and felt. It hurts, but it's working." A hopeful smile graces my lips. "I do have love for myself, otherwise I wouldn't be trying so hard." *Holy shit*. The weight of that sobers me.

Looking at me tenderly, he stands to his feet, reaching out to help me up. "Those remnants are hauntingly beautiful. Your light is just as stunning. And I think you're starting to see that."

Without thinking, I wrap my arms around his neck, puffy-faced and beaming at him. "There's a middle ground," I whisper, narrating the realization as I'm discovering it. "Where I'm not chasing euphoria or running from misery. There's a place where both are welcome, and no matter which way it tips, I'll just... surrender to it?"

A close-lipped grin lights his features, and he wraps his arms around me. "Sounds like you just found a clue."

Committing it to memory, I whisper, "Don't resist."

His voice is like hot syrup pouring over freshly-made pancakes. "That... is how you be still with your emotions."

I let my eyes wander over this incredible human—taking something complex and helping me reframe it in a way that feels achievable. He's inspiring. The way his mind works, his wisdom, his care... The way he's attuned to my words and body language. Even the deitydamn way he's not fixing my problems but supporting *me* to solve them myself. I'm just impressed with him in every sense of the word.

He murmurs, "To what thoughts of yours do I have to thank for making you look at me like that?"

My smile shifts from wistful to playful as I shrug. "I was just thinking that you're quite clever for a brute."

He chuffs, dipping his head to the side as if he's weighing up the validity of the statement. "Hardly," he says with a smirk. But it's the wink that does me in—shoots through me like a missile. My scoff is a poor excuse of covering up how severely impacted I am.

Loosening my locked fingers behind his neck and sliding them down to his chest, I feel the way his heart beats. Quick like mine. The urge to press my lips where my palm is... is distracting. I want to thank his heart with a kiss, for carrying such heavy scars. Letting my eyes roam up, I want to lean my forehead against his and run my hands through his hair. To pull him in and press my lips against his, ensuring they know how thankful I am for the thoughtful words they spoke, just for me.

His breathing hitches as he stiffens. "You're doing it again," he warns in a breathless voice.

Doing what? Inhaling sharply, I squeeze my eyes shut, trying to erase my thoughts. "Fuck, I'm sorry."

When I deign to look at him, his gaze is raking over me, torturously slow, a spark igniting when our eyes meet again. Then, the bastard smirks. "Let's not start something we can't finish." A pause. "Yet."

Laughing nervously, I don't trust myself to be so close to him, so I step back a few steps. "Right." Clasping my hands behind my back, I admit, "I forgot about the whole 'touching without touching' thing." Then, I mumble light-heartedly, "An embarrassing and inconvenient ability."

Frozen still at the last word, I repeat in a croak, "Ability."

As if plucking the thought from my mind, he asks, "Are you Activ?"

Shaking my head furiously, my mind starts to drift— kneeled over a cardboard box, reaching in and pulling small memories from my brain. I was content to forget about it until a later date, but it's getting harder to ignore.

I rasp, "I don't know. I only really know about Sage's abilities, so I can't say I have any idea what, or how I do that. Outside of here, people with abilities are imaginary, a loose what-if written into fiction. Here? I'm still trying to wrap my head around it."

Crossing his arms, he's morphed into the hardened militant man. Problem-solving mode. "Sage has briefed me on what intel you have."

Gauging my lack of reaction, his eyes search mine, lips parting as if stopping himself from elaborating. A question lingers behind his eyes: 'Would you like to know more?'

Answering him aloud, I plead he understands my meaning. "I do, but I've had a *day.*" I let my neck roll out as I decide if I have the energy to face the next blow to my brain.

The low warning in his voice is prodding. "I'm worried that if I tell you, and we unpack any more right now, you'll get overwhelmed and shut down."

He knows me.

My skin was burning too hot, but knowing I don't have to learn any more today—it's like plunging into a cool stream, the relief immediate.

Rubbing my hands over my face, I tell him, "It's not like last time. I'm not shutting it all out. Or you. But, can we come back to this? I just can't today."

A hint of a smile slips through his firm expression. "Of course. I'm going to dig around, so when you come to me, I'll have some answers. I just—" He pauses, hesitating.

Picking at the skin near my thumbnail, I ask tentatively, "What is it?"

Shaking his head, he mutters in a throw-away comment, "I'm just not sure what your ability falls under."

My head draws back, confused, but then exhaustion has me shrugging it off and sarcastically mumbling, "Comforting."

Swiftly lifting my chin by the crook of his fingers, he promises, "We'll figure this out."

We.

Then his hand drops, and he's walking toward the exit.

As he pauses in the doorway looking back at me, the air around us holds its breath, as if it too can see the affection, pride, and relief etched through his features. I interlock my fingers behind my back, whispering, "Bye," before a grin plasters itself on my face.

"Bye," he replies, and then he's gone.

I didn't tell him about the trees.

CHAPTER 22
RICH LAYERS

I have my fucking journal back!

Scurrying across my bed on all fours, I gasp as I rip it out from under my pillow, and run my fingers over the worn cover. In the next heartbeat, I'm flipping through the pages greedily. Skimming over the entries, I cringe at the knowledge that eyes other than mine have read this. Interestingly though, conflict wages inside me, between the wince of exposition and the lightness of being seen in my unfettered rawness.

Whether he likes it or balks at the darkness within me, the black oil of my pain will remain slick, coursing through my veins alongside the hope of regenerative blood. It's part of me. And *I* need to accept that. I don't need to be pretty, pleasant, and perfect.

Rolling onto my back, I scan the roof as I consider a life where I walk with steps unadulterated. Purely *me.*

Right now, that's someone who's intense. Wild. Sad. Happy. Complex. Sometimes rational. Sometimes lazy. Smart. Sometimes too hyper-focused. Strange. Occasionally outspoken. Sometimes introverted. And sometimes, I'm dancing with strangers in the middle of a secret village. I laugh at the duality of everything I am.

As easily as the clock ticks over to a new minute, I can shift who I am.

A thought rams into me, and I gasp, sitting upright.

What if I stop putting so much pressure on finding out who I am, and free myself to discover who I'm *not*? Experiment with living? *That's how I'll find my authenticity.*

Pulling the book open and scrawling a title above the list, I write and underline: <u>Living Authentically.</u>

Inhaling deeply, I slowly glide my finger down the course texture of the worn page, reading my list.

<u>Living Authentically</u>

A guide to loving myself

- Point number 1: I feel seen and understood

- Point number 2: I feel reassured, validated, and considered

- Point number 3: I feel desired and wanted

- Point number 4. I feel safe and secure

- Point number 5. I love quality time with myself

- Point number 6 – My affection is welcomed

- Point number 7 – My love is healthy

- Point number 8 – I use comparison only to connect, not to shame myself or others

- Point number 9: I honor my complexity

- Point number 10: I surrender control and find flow

- Point number 11: I'm curious, engaging in deep conversations with myself and asking questions

- Point number 12: I challenge myself

- Point number 13: I express myself organically

- Point number 14: I keep promises with myself

- Point number 15: I manage the way I think about myself, and it's filled with compassion

- Point number 16: I know how to come back to my body when my emotions try to rule me

Finally emerging from my hut, I avoid Gatherer Girl and her group of friends. I catch two straying looks of disdain in my direction before I decide to pretend they don't exist.

No.

With the list fresh in my mind, I challenge myself—*Point 12*—to reframe with compassion and say something nice about them.

I—*hmm.*

The seconds pass by as I near Sage, laying on her back across a log, her head in Sloane's lap.

Oh, okay. I believe that behavior has an underlying reason. Perhaps what appears rotten is just *pain*. Like me, maybe she's on her own journey. Maybe the fact we are mutually a nuisance to the other serves a purpose? There's something magical about that...

A bubble of laughter wants to rise, as the unhealed part of me scoffs 'oh, really?' in response. Internally rolling my eyes, I whisper 'shut up' to the void.

Sage sits up when she notices me, a grin perking up her whole demeanor. "Hello, Smella."

Rainer draws her head back an inch, looking at Sloane and signing something. Sloane mirrors the confused expression, signing back whilst saying the words aloud. "Yes, I heard 'Smella'?"

I ask Sloane how to sign 'don't ask,' and they chuckle when I shoot daggers at Sage.

Within a few minutes, we're passing around grazing plates with fresh vegetables, dipping sauces, and mini hot balls of flavored rice.

The food here in Juf'ua is unlike anything I've had before. The simplest things taste so fresh and delectable. The shapes and sizes are odd, having grown with the purpose of nutrition, as opposed to being aesthetically pleasing. Holding a lumpy piece of steamed sweet potato in front of me, I wonder if it all used to look like this before growing your own food became outlawed.

Popping it in my mouth, I scan the faces around me, indulging in the atmosphere. It's warm, open. The steady glow of their solar lights romanticize the space, and the open sky starts to reveal the first stars of the evening. The temperature drops and the Okah play-wrestle—which is far more terrifying to watch than it sounds—or they nap to the sweet droning of nearby conversation.

When Sage rolls over to her side, laughing so hard it's silent, I realize I'm the luckiest captive, and I will never be the same after knowing her. After finding this place. Here, I've become more comfortable in my skin than I've ever felt. My mind feels as if a cloud has lifted from it, and everything I longed for quietly in the back of my mind... is real. I have true friends that care about me. Orion is here. The Okah's majesty I marvel at never gets old. Juf'ua's intentionality and philosophy of finding ways to simply exist is a reprieve from constantly trying to prove I deserve a spot in a society that takes all my hours. It's slower here—natural, aligned in a way that feels like flicking off a fluorescent light and sitting with the subtle radiance of candlelight. Mind, body, and soul, I'm closer to feeling 'okay' than ever before.

A pang of sadness sucker punches me in the gut when I realize there's not long until the full moon, and I'm tried to leave. To go home—*not home*, back where I came from. Nothing but greyness and concrete.

I don't want to go.

The glance Sage flicks at me is knowing, and I watch as she goes to say something, but stops herself when noticing people will hear. A shared look conveys what words don't need to. But after a moment, she speaks softly just for me to hear, "Tomorrow morning, let's rise with the sun and talk."

"Okay," I manage, knowing she feels the way my heart swells with appreciation for her friendship. She drops a hand on my knee and squeezes before we return to the conversation with Sloane and Rainer.

My focus drifts, pulled by that tether until I see Orion and TG speaking with Sage's parents and one of the younger children. Their idle conversation is sweeter than the corn I bite into, until Gatherer Girl leans over her friend to speak to Orion. I can't hear them, but I can see his indifference. Short, polite responses, while she's turned her charm up to ten.

Let it go, let it go. Look away.

Letting my eyes drop down, I see Divy asleep at Orion's feet, curled in on herself and far less intimidating—until her eyes open to lock with mine. I pale until she blinks sleepily, but still alert to my attention. Awkwardly, I smile at her and offer a discreet wave. *I might even miss you, too. Loyal and majestic Okah, I know you'll look after him.* Suddenly, her ears twitch, something shifting in her expression as she watches me. I wonder if I said any of that aloud, but I shake the thought off as quick as it comes. Then, she stretches out to rest her head atop Orion's feet, blinking at me once more before falling asleep.

She's got him.

I'm already awake and dressed when Sage pops her head in the next morning. The first brush of dawn dances along my skin as I meet her outside, the birds welcoming a new day in their songs they sing.

I'm marveling at the long stretch of clouds, and the faint yellow kissing their undersides when I notice Orion exit his hut. I fight the shudder as he stretches his arm across his chest, showing me his back. The soft light touches his skin, lays over his shoulders as I wish my hands could freely...

Shit. Did I do the thing?

He turns to me, the look of surprise melting into one of knowing when our eyes lock.

Yes, I did.

In my peripheral, Sage crosses her arms, and I turn my head to face her—wishing I hadn't. She wags her brows at me with a cheeky smirk, and I chortle while rolling my eyes.

Turning back to Orion, I wave goodbye quickly and his mouth kicks up into an easy smile. Sage takes it upon herself to mimic me, waving at him and whispering like a ventriloquist, "I love you." Even knowing he couldn't have heard that, my eyes still widen. I loop my arm through Sage's and drag her away.

The touch of sadness from knowing this is one of the last mornings I'll see him falls away as Sage's shoulders shake with laughter.

"Tell me why I'm convinced you're the mature one." I bite through a stifled grin.

Leaning all her weight against me suddenly, making me stumble, she claims, "Being mature doesn't mean I can't tease you."

Shaking my head at her doesn't seem to affect the smile on my face.

We fall into a silent walk, letting the sounds of the forest's awakening speak in place of us. Our bare feet transition from dewy grass to damp earth, and then to rich layers of crunchy leaves.

When we don't turn toward the stream, and she ducks under a tangle of vines to the left, my feet halt. As I watch her step over a fallen log, she throws me a glance over her shoulder, somehow knowing I'm not following.

Perplexed, I ask, "Isn't the stream this way?"

Mischief gleans in her eyes. "I have a surprise."

I groan instantly. "It's so early, Sage…"

"Just a bit further." She drawls the assurance. "I want to show you something."

Thirty minutes later, I surmise that we have different definitions of 'a bit further.'

Finally, she stops walking, and we stand in front of the largest tree I have ever seen in my life—bigger than the baritone tree. Its branches start low, and the more I crane my neck to look up, I see them start to entwine with the neighboring trees, creating a pattern like ripples in water. Its aliveness pulsates with a power that awakens a deep and primal part of me.

This tree is definitely ancient.

A prickle on my scalp precedes a voice in my mind. *"Excuse me?"* A warning comes from the tree, and I flinch. *I forgot how weird that feels.*

I reach out tentatively. *"Is something wrong?"*

It pauses. *"Ancient?"* I *feel* its raised brow.

Sputtering, I rack my brain. *"Not ancient as in old! You're… very youthful looking. The other trees said—"*

The bubble of laughter drifts past me in a soft breeze. *"I know, Star Child. I was attempting humor. You seem fond of sarcasm and teasing. I apologize for being quite out of practice."*

I grin up at the tree, a laugh bursting from me. *"Oh! No, that was funny."* Cautiously, I add, *"And that's an example of sarcasm."*

A strange vibration nudges my chest and somehow, I know that the tree is laughing. *"Little One was right about you. And if I may, I'd never consider being called old an insult. Not everyone is afforded the gift to get there."*

Before I can ask what they mean, I feel the weight of scrutiny and slowly turn to a very-confused Sage. "Mother Almighty, I might get whiplash from all the emotions coursing through you."

I pull my lips between my teeth in a stifle. "Sorry. So, you wanted to show me something?"

Deciding to let it go, she faces the tree again, pointing with her finger to the top. "It's up there."

I bark out a laugh. "Okay, tell me about it when you get back."

She wags a finger at me. "Oh, you're climbing. Trust me, it'll be worth it."

Two things. One, she's done it before, at least once. So maybe it's not as impossible as it looks. Two, now that I can talk to trees, I feel very strange climbing them.

Pulling my hands into hers and luring me closer to the tree, my mouth drops open. Speaking to Sage first, I argue, "No, no, no."

Then to the tree, *"Do we even have your permission to climb? I mean, if you were a person, I wouldn't just jump on your back or sit on your arms..."*

Sage drops her head to the side, forehead furrowing in a plea. "Just put your feet and hands exactly where I do. This tree is special to me. Please, Smella."

Groaning in the start of concede, I get my response from the tree. *"It's honorable you ask. You and Sage are always welcome."*

At the same time, Sage and the tree speak five words. "*I won't let you fall.*"

Blinking at her, I wonder if she can hear the trees, too. But the longer I stare at her in shock, the more her brows pinch together, bemused. *No, she can't.*

It's something that feels just mine, in a way that is sacred. Special. Shielding. They're a confidant, a guide, a fucking miracle. Gratitude inside me jumps up and down on her toes with a beaming grin at this gift I've been given.

Tapping my finger against my leg in rhythm with my racing heartbeat, I stare up at the top again. "Go on then, before I change my mind."

Squealing and jumping into action, she begins the climb, and I follow her footing exactly, trying not to look down.

CHAPTER 23
WHAT IF I

We reach a stupid height, my knuckles white with the grip I have on the branch. Trepidation has my muscles tense and shaking, while Sage literally leaps from one branch to the next.

Scowling, I mock her earlier words under my breath. "Just put your foot exactly where I do. Trust me." I burn a hole into the back of her adept frame.

Do not look around. Not down, not anywhere but exactly where my hands and feet go.

Sage calls out, "Okay, I'm at the top!"

I reply through a clamped jaw, "Hopefully I don't accidentally push you when I get up there."

She chuckles. "Come and get me." Leaning over the branch with a recklessness of someone on the ground, she leans and points. "Go to that branch next."

My heart stops beating. "Will you *please* hold onto something?"

She rolls her eyes at me, watching my footing. "So, now you *don't* want me to fall?"

My leg muscles burn, my breathing is ragged, and my fingers are near numb. I give her a flat look. "This is so much fun. I'm having a *really* good time."

She states, "You will be thanking me when you finally get your wheezing behind up here."

I carefully step over a branch and weave around the last tangle separating us. "My wheezing behind?"

Shrugging, she asks, "What?"

I let out a short-laugh. "I get what you were going for, but that doesn't put a pleasant image in my mind."

She waves me off with a huff as I duck through the tangled branches and step up another rung. I notice where she's sitting and how the interwoven branches hold her in a cradled seat.

I finally reach her resting spot, plopping down next to her and trying to catch my breath.

With a grin spreading over her face, she sweeps her hand out—here it is. I follow her eyeline, and I'm suspended, frozen between breaths. The canopy rolls on for as far as I can see, breaking in spots for waterfalls, streams, and hilly expanses.

She leans in, pointing. "There's Juf'ua."

It takes me a second to find what she's looking for, and my mouth drops open. "You can barely notice it with how well it's camouflaged. And it's so much bigger than it feels when you're in it."

She chuffs her agreement.

The bright yellow orb has risen just above the horizon, and it lights up the baby blue sky, pouring over the array of flowers and trees within the thick forest, welcoming a new day.

The aliveness of the forest prickles my skin, as if collectively acknowledging me, as I do them. Inhaling sharply, a shiver rolls up my spine.

"Well..." I might have had more to say, but it never comes. I'm utterly smitten and speechless by the sheer divinity of nature. The rarity of this moment. How many people will go their whole lives without being able to see this? Such few can afford the time to escape the concrete cities.

Sage states bluntly, "No one can hear us. Tell me."

No one except you and the entire forest. A wave of assurance caresses my heart, and I know my secrets are safe with them.

She bends a leg and rests her chin on her knee, ready to listen. Knowing she can read my emotions, I decide to give her my mind as well. Unfiltered.

With a long exhale, I look out to the view.

As soon as I start, it's impossible to stop. Sage listens as I share that me and Orion kissed. Goosebumps trail over my arms as I remember the feeling of being in his embrace, his body pressed against mine, our lips desperate for each other.

She gasps. "I knew something happened, I just didn't know what!" But her enthusiasm simmers when I look down at my tangling fingers. "What happened after?" she prods.

I worry my bottom lip before letting her know. "I told him I needed space. That I couldn't... explore things with him. That I wasn't ready."

She watches me with a soft smile and a hand on my leg, letting me know she feels how hard that was for me. "I saw him go into your hut after the Gatherers came home.

"Yeah." The tension in my face relaxes, the corner of my mouth lifting as I replay it in my mind. "He gave me back my journal, and we made this wholesome song. We talked too, and I told him how difficult it is to stay away, asking him how he does it. Part of me freaked out, that I had just assumed it was hard for him too, and that maybe it wasn't at all..."

"And?" she asks tenderly, encouraging me to continue. Her question is simple, but the weight of it sinks into my chest.

"We have this connection that neither of us fully understands. I told him I hate how it consumes me. He told me he feels it too, but he *welcomes* it." I turn to her. "Sage, he called me his *checkpoint*."

Her chin lifts, pushing her bottom lip out. "That sounds really sweet, I'm not sure I know exactly what that means though."

"I've got a permanent spot in his mind, like I live there. No matter what he does, or where he goes, he always wants to return to me. His checkpoint."

She presses a hand to her mouth, her eyes widening as if she too, gets swept away in the tidal wave of emotion.

"He's incredible, Sage." Awe and grief thread through my tone.

She gestures with her hands as she speaks fervently. "Is not being with him really what you want?"

I tell her about the list. How I'm closer to myself than I've ever felt, and that if I pass the trials... "I feel like I'll be leaving with unfinished business."

My hands drag down my face.

I tell her about the touching without touching, and she gapes at me, looking off into the distance and suggesting the ways she'd use it with mischief in her smirk. A deep belly laugh rolls through me.

But the humor slips into sorrow, because I'll miss her and her cheekiness. "If I pass, then I leave here... I'll never see you again." My chin trembles, eyes locked on hers, memorizing every detail.

She pulls me into a hug, whispering as if she isn't sure she's allowed to say it or if it will upset me and make this harder. "I don't want you to go."

A tear runs down my cheek unceremoniously and unforgivingly as I squeeze her back. *I don't want to go either.*

Pulling away, her bottom lip quivers as she battles to keep it together. "Stella, I can feel how confused you are. Tell me what you're thinking."

How can I walk away from one of the first people who listens to me like this? A true friend. I want to be as good a friend to her, as she has been to me. I need more time to repay her for the care she's so generously given when I needed it most.

I wipe my tears, raking my hands through my hair. "There's so fucking much, Sage. Are you sure I can just dump it all on you?"

Her voice is filled with sincerity as she answers immediately. "Tell me everything."

I do.

Painting the picture in its entirety, I have to start with what it was like for me back home. How lonely I've been. How different it is to Juf'ua. How I don't think it's a coincidence that I came here. I tell her every detail, except the gravity-altering epiphany of Orion's name, and the children's book, wanting to make sure Orion would be okay with that first. It feels... private and unprocessed—a tied destiny that feels ethereal. When the trees don't chime in to tell me otherwise, I stay quiet about the absurdity of my conversations with them, too.

I turn to gauge her expression, and see empathy exude from her. She shuffles closer to pull me into her side, my head resting on her shoulder in response. "Oh, Smella..." she says while stroking my hair. Affection from her feels like home, or what I imagine that to be. Besides Orion, Sage is the only person who's held me when I needed it, and now she pulls me even closer. I relish in the comfort, and we just stay like this for a while, watching as the landscape below us drifts gently with the wind.

"Sage..." Her name on my lips sounds choked as emotion punches through me. "I don't have anywhere I belong."

"Uhi bergano tsui et hera swoar, e tsui et dask. Uhi bergano tsua et belesah et dre's du," she says in their language, emotion thick in her voice, too.

Lifting my head to look at her, I wipe my face and sniffle. "What does that mean?"

She looks out over the view, explaining, "It's Juf'uanean, translating to 'You belong where your heart can soar, and where it can rest. You belong...'" She pauses, searching my eyes. "'When you believe you deserve to.'"

Juf'ua is somewhere I can rest, and maybe soar. Believing I deserve to, it's a process of unlearning. Maybe it's not entirely a place she means, but a state of mind that I can take with me anywhere, no matter what life has in store for me.

Hope rises within me as I squeeze her hand. "Thank you." I don't need to say more—I know she can feel it by the way her watery eyes stay locked on mine.

The sun has slowly sailed higher while I've been spilling my guts to her, and now, she shifts to face me more, a focus in her tone. Determination. "What would be your greatest outcome?"

Pondering on her question, I turn my attention to the lush expanse before me, a small voice coming from the chasm within. When I turn my mental awareness towards it, the intensity of it grows, jumping up and down and waving its arms.

Surrendering, I let it rise. Guided by rightness and laced with fear, the words fall from my lips. "I'd stay here."

She's silent. Shooting a side-long glance at her, I pause at her expression. This is the first time I've seen her so serious. "Face me," she asks gently, and I shuffle carefully to do exactly that. "Why do you want to stay?"

Tipping my head to the side, I shrug as if I don't already know. But I do. "I'd learn about this way of life. About myself. My connection to Orion, and why it already feels so profound. I'd train to inherit that mind and body connection you all have. I'd climb trees with you." A smile spreads over my features as I look up at the sky, even though I'm scared shitless. "We'd swim in streams and make clothes. I'd spend more time with the cooks. I'd learn about my ability. I would want to learn more about the Activs, the world, Discon. I—" I stop the words from leaving my mouth, a familiar sense of fear pricking up.

"You what?" she prods, not leaving space for me to deflect from saying the words.

Admitting this for the first time out loud, I confess, "I want to learn so I can maybe do something about the state of the world outside of here. But first, I need to be okay with reaching my potential. I'd stay, because this is where it'll happen. I just know it."

Judging by the awe and pride coating her features, I know she understands how deep that statement runs. It's an acceptance—to leave the nest of familiarity and fly into the unknown.

I'm ready to discover the truth of why I have these abilities, and why my name is from the stars, right alongside Orion's.

CHAPTER 24
FOR A CHANCE

After I make it back to the ground with shaky limbs and abundant curses, we start our trek back to Juf'ua.

Quietly, the forest recognizes me as I pass, whispering in collective, but I can't make out any words. The steady hum of all living things around me jostles my senses, my core. The forest I walked into two weeks ago—I felt it like an overview, whereas now, I feel the sum and all its parts. I'm hyper aware of each tree planted, feeling the network of roots webbing beneath my feet.

I've been asleep my whole life.

As we approach Juf'ua, a sharp gasp fills my lungs. I can feel the grass and the imprint of people walking over it. I feel the people. Not their physical body, but the spaces around them, the air, energy—interacting with their movements *through* the space.

Putting my hand out across Sage's chest, we stop walking. "Wait." The word is barely audible, but she does.

Across the field, I see Rainer reach over and pet Yellow. As her hand moves through the air, I can feel it divide as she cuts through it. The second her physical body moves an inch into the next space, the air starts reforming back to its whole. It's like dunking your hand in water and removing it; the body of water remains, but it ripples with the memory of your interaction with it.

My brows scrunch as I think it over. I can't feel her actual hand, whereas with Orion, he could feel my physical touch. One is energy, and one is physical. It doesn't make sense.

Experiment.

Honing in on her hand, I watch the gentle stroke of her palm over Yellow's fur. Imagining I'm the air around her, I mimic her movement, petting her hand. She flinches, drawing her hand away and staring at it, perplexed.

My eyes go wide before looking away. I scramble for the ability, shoving it back into that cardboard box in my mind. It fights me, wanting to unleash after finally being tapped into. Fueled and eager, it whispers to me. *I'll wait, but just know, you can't take it back now.* I feel it calm, the heightened awareness of everything less overwhelming.

Sage pulls my attention to her. "You okay?"

Clearing my throat, I admit, "Yeah. I think my ability is... It's just intense."

Concern sits in the creases of her face, but I assure her. "I'm okay."

Laying tender fingers on my forearm, she checks. "You sure about this?"

My mouth curves into a satisfied smile, even though my heart pumps wildly under my skin. "Let's go."

Striding toward the main hut, I think over the words again. My mind pulls the sentences apart and restructures them in different ways until the very last second.

Sharing a look of determination, Sage gestures for me to go in first.

I hook one side of the door—with only a slight tremble—and draw it open. Entering the hut with Sage in tow a step behind, I stand before them, chin raised with the confidence I don't feel.

As expected, there's Orion, Sage's parents, and TG. They're deliberating over what looks to be a map. In half a second, I notice more of the same size and color of that paper, rolled up and to the side of the desk. They sit upright in a cylindrical vase, like a bunch of flowers. *What's on those maps?*

The chair nearly tips to the floor as Sage's dad rises, swiping the map from the table. "What is she doing in here?" His voice is lethal with the accusation of someone who hates being caught off guard.

The hairs on my arms threaten to bristle, but before Sage can even think to respond, Orion's somehow between Sage's dad and me in a blink. The way he stands casual and relaxed impressively masks the warning flickering behind his expression— sending a message to Sage's dad without being aggressive.

Sage's mum speaks calmly and quickly in their language, and Sage replies in English for my benefit. "Stella has something to discuss with you."

Five sets of eyes land on me, and I summon the courage to step forward. *Wait. Who do I look at when I speak?* Instead of panicking, I decide to try to spend equal amounts of time with each set of eyes.

I start with addressing Sage's mum, her curiosity lifting a brow. "I know the full moon is in two weeks..."

My attention drifts to Sage's dad, trying my best to hold my own against his scowl. "When the Trails of Trust will begin."

His words rush over mine, impatience clear in his disposition. "What is your point?" I swallow down the fear that feels thick in my throat, looking over to Orion just as he tilts his head at Sage's dad, something stern in his expression. Sage's dad exhales, crossing his arms and shutting his mouth. He nods for me to continue, expressionless.

I shift my weight, rolling my shoulders back an inch. "If I pass, I'll be sent home." I swear, on the word 'home,' Orion stops breathing for a count of one.

Creations, he's making me more nervous.

Focusing my attention on TG, I continue, "I've been having realizations and growth." Against my will, my eyes flick to Orion. "I've made connections I didn't ever expect..." *Look away, keep your focus.*

A distracting amount of adrenaline starts to rise in me. Something about what I'm saying, what I'm about to ask, is eliciting that aliveness I'm still familiarizing myself with.

Quickly looking over to Sage, I'm encouraged by her smile.

Addressing her mum, I claim, "I'm in awe of the way of life here. I've evolved, and I couldn't have done it anywhere else."

I'm so nervous that I feel out of breath, but I seek the eyes of the Chief.

Licking my lips, the announcement is finally released from the grip in my throat. "Instead of the trials testing whether I can leave, I want to be tried with the intention of staying here in Juf'ua."

His eyes pierce into me, but every inch of him remains unflinching.

Distantly, I notice TG nodding with a smile. Sage's parents engage with her in Juf'uanean conversation. The tension in here thickens as their tones sharpen, a clear predicament I've put them in fueling the style of vivid gesturing. Orion doesn't say a single word. Does not look away from me.

Locking my fingers behind my back, I fidget nervously out of sight, hoping they can't hear my pounding heartbeats. My eyes wander around the hut nervously, my bare feet pressing against the woven floor as I tell myself repeatedly not to chew on my bottom lip.

Sage's mum steals my attention. "It is understandable that you are fond of life here. But the truth is, this is not somewhere you vacation. There is much you haven't witnessed. Things on hold and hidden while you have been here. There are..." She looks up as if searching for the word.

Looking at her husband, he provides, "Pre-requisites."

She turns back to me, continuing, "*Pre-requisites* to being here."

TG adds in, "This is our life's purpose."

Sage's dad looks bored as he adds, "This is bigger than you having some realizations and making new friends. Unfortunately—"

I interrupt, knowing where the sentence was going, and that it is definitely not unfortunate for him. "I'm sorry to cut you off, but this is not a vacation for me. It's an awakening."

Standing straighter, my legs prickle with goosebumps when I hear the clarity and conviction in my voice. "I am not what I thought I was. It's not just me who's evolving—it's everything that I thought existed. Reality itself. I know there's more to Juf'ua, I know about the Activs. I know about Discon. Juf'ua is a place that smiles at me with challenge in its eyes. I've been dared to rise, and it needs to happen here."

Everyone stares at me, and I don't dare shiver under the weight of it.

Sage's father surprises me with a softer tone, his expression hinting at contemplation. "The trials will not be simple. Juf'ua... is a movement. What dedication do you have to being here beyond reasons that only benefit yourself?"

I had been quietly filing away things I observed, noticing their training, meetings, their fiery passion, and sense of seeking justice whenever speaking of Discon. How Sage told me that Orion had helped with their escape and brought them here. That it was once just him, and now there's a village full of people. I wondered if he helped them all escape. Orion told me this is a sacred place, and the haven I've known it to be had something simmering underneath it, like a charge. A currency of secrets. Hearing them call it a movement, I'm shocked but not surprised.

Glances from everyone find their way to Orion, expecting him to chime in, but he stays silent. Listening. Assessing. Calculating.

The hut is silent. The distant sound of movement and chatter is all I can hear.

Shit. I haven't considered how I can benefit them, only what I'd gain from being here. Then, like a ton of bricks, I remember something.

I was called here.

"You're right," I admit.

Sage whispers to me out the side of her mouth, "What are you doing?"

Looking at her, then addressing the others, my voice never wavers. "I may not know exactly what the movement plans to do, or the true state of the world, but I know enough to say, without a doubt, that I am not here by coincidence. If you cannot trust my words, trust the force that called me here. The barrier that welcomed me."

My eyes flick to Orion, the hint of a smile flashing for a beat before it's gone. Next thing I know, he's up and standing, slowly closing the distance between us. He stops in front of me, and it's like he's the blade and I'm ice, sharp and unrelenting alone, but something beautiful when put together. His stance, his power, makes every molecule of my being stand to attention. But I don't cower. I don't move. I don't succumb to the pressure of everyone's scrutinous attention on me. No, I only focus on Orion, and give him time to deliberate.

I've said everything I could. Now it's up to them. To him.

But really, it was always up to me. Lifting my chin, I let the determination rise within me and paint itself on my face. My disposition entices one corner of his mouth to lift.

He finally speaks, his voice low and commanding. "You're ready—" he inclines his head "—to stop hiding?"

I swallow, but my attention is unflinching, fixed on him. "I am."

He watches me like the weight of the world is on his shoulders. That I might be the thing that'll finally break him, if he's wrong about me. Taking another step forward, his power pushes against me, trying to intimidate me. His voice is a deep purr. "No more running?"

The corners of my mouth tugs up, my eyes roaming over his stern expression. "No more running." Dipping his chin down, he challenges, "Are you ready to look in the mirror and let us see what stares back?"

The question catches me off guard, but I still answer. "Yes."

His next words have an undertone of something I can't place. Something raw. "You will be seeing the truth of what we do, and we do not welcome those who hide from darkness. We run toward it, a blazing light."

With a body still and sure, I tell him, "I am unfinished. Unhealed. Uncertain of so many things. But what I know is that I will crawl through the depths and claw my way back out for a chance of liberation. For my life, and every life."

Orion's eyes darken, that militant focus slipping into something wolfish. Something promising to swallow me whole if I'm not careful. I look back at him with promises of my own, the small space between our bodies crackling. I might've underestimated him—his power and leadership. He's been holding back in my presence. But as I meet this version of him, I know in my bones he will not go easy on me.

"Very well," he says simply, but the barely-contained energy flowing from him is anything but. The invisible waves stream from him, entwining around my limbs, my waist, beckoning me to come closer.

Sage clears her throat, and the color drains from my face. *We are not alone.*

I try to piece together an unbothered expression, even though I'm sure my face is tomato red. I nervously glance around the room, seeing the sly grin on TG's face and Sage's cocked eyebrow. Sage's parents are thankfully expressionless, despite their focus swiftly darting between Orion and I, *quietly calculating.*

"Your Trials of Trust begin tomorrow morning." The announcement has my eyes whipping to the source. Orion doesn't step back or relent the intensity of his presence, not caring nearly as much as I do with the fact they all just watched us practically eye-fuck.

Sage seems to read my surprise and asks, "Why tomorrow?" She doesn't seem upset, just curious.

Orion shrugs, looking at her, and allowing me a full breath as he addresses Sage. "Why wait? If she's ready."

I ask, "Don't you need the full moon for... its power or something?"

He looks back at me. "No. We usually do trials on the full moon because it symbolizes endings, beginnings, and marks a time of transition. But it's not necessary. You seem eager, so why wait?" He slides his hands into his pockets. "Will that be a problem?"

He's testing me—seeing if I crack under the pressure. But I won't with this hum of power waking in the chasm, teetering eagerly underneath my skin.

Tongue briefly swiping across my bottom lip, then biting it to stifle a grin, I state, "Not a problem at all." My voice is firm, and I do not falter.

His smile broadens at my acceptance of his challenge. By the flicker of relief I see in his eyes, maybe a small part of him expected me to pull away. But I'm tired of being tired. I want to wake up.

Tilting my head to the side, I ask pleasantly, "What time should I be ready?"

I scan the group. Sage's mum observes me, fingers interlocked in front of her. Sage's dad stands with crossed arms, a brief narrowing of his eyes. Sage moves next to TG, and they nudge their shoulders together, mirroring each other's saccharine grins. Then Orion—taking a step back so we stand in this wonky circle, with an electricity fluctuating in pulses between us. I get the distinct feeling of readying for some kind of battle.

The tension snaps like a rubber band when Orion starts giving orders. To me: "Be up at first light. Dressed and fed." To TG: "Spread the word, and ensure everyone is ready on time tomorrow."

To Sage's parents: "You're with me, and we'll outline the trial stages."

To Sage: "You'll prepare the elixirs."

The what?

To everyone: "We as a collective will assess..." *I figure that doesn't include me.* "And I will make the final call," he finishes.

I watch them as they take action, not hesitating a second once receiving their task. Then, my eyes are on Orion, conflicting emotions coursing through me. Fear taps me on my shoulder as he orchestrates the test of my life, but heat coils lower as he looks so damn hot while doing it.

Sage huffs a laugh under her breath, and my skin warms. I forgot she gets wafts of my emotions, and I make the wise decision not to look at her.

Orion commands my attention, a final attempt to scare me off. "Tomorrow, everyone will discover you, as you discover yourself. An exposition of what you conceal."

This is the first time I've hesitated. Panic snakes its way up my spine as I picture in what ways I'll be unveiled. *But what's the alternative? A grey life?*

Folding my arms, deliberate and slow, I answer with as much surety as I can muster. "I'll see you all at first light."

Looking at them one by one, I finish on Sage, who turns with me as we stride from the hut like we own it. Once we're far enough away from the hut, we look at each other side-long, and I snort-laugh. She grabs my shoulders and squeezes, jumping up and down with a celebratory laugh.

"Deitydamn, what the fuck just happened?" I beam through a chortle, my hands pressed to my temples.

She whistles, impressed. "You did so well." Gasping, she turns to me as if recalling something important. "And you and Orion, Mother Almighty, that was some serious foreplay."

I cackle, then look over our shoulders as I hurry her towards my hut, chiding, "Fuck, Sage. You can't just announce that for anyone to hear."

She skips next to me, lifting my shoulder with each leap as I do not join in. Lowering her voice to a whisper, she sing-songs, "You love it."

Shaking my head at the memory, I blow out a breath. "He's an intense man."

When we get inside my hut, the reality of it all sets in, and we just stare at each other for a moment. Shock, nerves, and absurd amusement takes my stomach out for a spin.

Sage's features mellow into soft lines as she offers me a small piece of insight. "You must go into the trial unaware of the stages—just remember to stay open." She pauses, narrowing her eyes with a smile. "My Smella... If I was to bet on anyone, it would be you."

Her arms wrap around me so tight that I can barely breathe.

Resting my chin on her shoulder, I squeeze her back. "Thank you for believing in me." *From the very start.*

Pulling back, she gives me a scrunch of her nose and a close-lipped grin. Then, she's gone.

This feeling I have... It's strange. Nostalgic. It starts in my chest, as if this small ember of light is expanding slowly, creating a steady, swirling vortex. It sucks in thoughts like 'I'll be alone forever,' 'This is not a world I want to live in,' 'Nothing will change,' and suddenly, they don't feel true anymore. The vortex inhales the jittery, black smoke in my stomach that visits me every time I feel astray, and it leaves me with...

My eyes glisten. It feels like breathing through your nose after a long stretch with the flu.

I didn't recognize it at first, having been without it for so long.

But the sensation... is hope.

CHAPTER 25
FORGIVE ME

Nerves fester incessantly within my limbs the morning of my first trial, as it marks a historical moment in my life, knowing that whatever happens, things will never be the same. But for that same reason, I also feel hope and thrill, as today could shift the course of the emptiness I envisaged my life would encompass. *But that's if I pass.* I promised to find more, and the first trial looms over me as a taunting carrot on a string, wanting me to jump for it. I'll try my best.

Hoping no one can see the shake in my hands, I interlock my fingers in front of me. I watch with bated breath as people find their spots, either sitting or standing in a large circle around me. The intensity of the growing crowd makes the spotlight feel brighter until my eyes burn. Finally, the leaders arrive.

Sage, her parents, and TG sit down at a large table. Orion stands in front, with a wide stance and hands behind his back. The five of them form the panel of my fate, and I skim over their expressions, from person to person until I can't go another second without seeking *his*.

I try not to balk under the heaviness of everyone just staring at me. Waiting. The steady hum of the forest reminds me they're watching, too.

I can take my first steady breath when Little One's energy floats through me like a feather in the wind, planting unwavering confidence in me. I close my eyes briefly, wishing for it to settle into my bones. When I open my eyes again, they're filled with unbridled resolve, seeing that Orion is the epitome of unparalleled focus. There's a question in his eyes. I tip my head in response. *Yes, I'm ready.*

Orion scans over the faces in the crowd, calling out so everyone can hear. "Mihl'e Dahn, Ghana. Thank you for being here, as we trial her—" his eyes meet mine "—to see if she can be trustworthy of joining us."

He's keeping my name private until I choose to share it.

My heart clenches in the millisecond pause between his words, watching as he turns back to the crowd.

"You've all been through a version of this. You know what she's feeling on some level. We will be respectful, and any energetical support of encouragement you wish to extend to her, feel free.

The crowd is silent. All I can hear is the soft thuds of Orion's footsteps as he moves toward his seat. But just before sitting, he announces, "The first part of the trial begins now."

Speaking directly to me, a string of silk threads its way into his tone, and I wonder if he's aware of it.

"Sage has prepared an elixir. This will be to test your tolerance to yourself. If you don't trust yourself with your own shadows, we can't trust you with ours. If you decide not to show up for yourself when things get hard, we cannot trust you to show up for us. The pain in the world..." A heavy pause. "It's a mountain we climb willingly. To endure all that comes with it, we require people brave enough to face darkness. And it starts with your own."

Are they going to torture me?

My stomach drops at the same time my mask slips for a micro-second. But of course, Orion catches it. "The elixir will bring forth the dark parts of you, and you will face them, inside of your mind."

In front of everyone? Will I just look like I'm sleeping? I chew nervously on the inside of my lip while he explains.

"Sage will consume an elixir as well, which will allow her to relay what you're experiencing. But you will not know we are there." Leaning forward on his elbows, he asks with a rumble in his chest, "Do you consent to the first trial, where you will confront your shadows?"

To the last second, he wants to make sure that this is what I choose, reminding me I have freewill and can still walk away.

Fuck that.

Inhaling deeply, I straighten, my eyes dropping to the murky green elixirs in front of Sage, then back to his.

"Yes."

Orion raises his brows, as if he needs me to say it all.

I quickly add, "I consent to the first trial, and I'm ready to face my shadows."

Something like pride sweeps across his features, then it's back to his muted militancy. But it was there long enough for my heart to flutter.

Sage approaches me, handing me one of the elixirs. The small glass vial lets me see the faint layer of floaties on the top. My lips curl downward at the sight, and I shoot her a look. She stifles a smile, and then knocks hers back in one swallow like a shot. I don't hesitate, throwing it back right after her. Swiping the back of my hand across my lips, I shudder at the taste. Sour, citrusy, earthy.

The elixir whooshes through me instantly, widening my eyes, making me lightheaded. I stumble back slightly, and something hits the back of my legs. I turn, blinking as my vision goes fuzzy. *A chair.*

When I sit, it's lights out. I don't know if my eyes are closed. They feel open, but I can't see even a hint of light coming from anywhere, veiled in pitch black.

My fingers squeeze the wooden armrests of my chair, my breathing coming in shallow breaths.

A tug of energy, of presence, has me stilling. When I angle my head left, towards it, I think it's Orion I can sense. His proximity.

Exhaling in relief, I assure myself that this is the elixir. I'm still in Juf'ua.

"There are two types of pain." I flinch at the closeness of his voice, not expecting it. "One that hurts you, and one that changes you."

How close is he? How can it be both spoken right behind my ear, and with the echoed vibrato of someone far away? It warps my sense of reality.

Gluggy glue holds my mouth shut, and I have to force my jaw to release so I can speak. "No," I argue, "one cannot exist without the other."

There is no response, and I think it might never come, until he finally speaks again. "In a way. But what I mean is one pain is good, leading to growth. The other is bad, keeping you confined to the depths of despair. Bad pain comes from blame, shame, stagnation, and resistance of self. It hurts you. Good pain is befriending your shadow. You can learn from it—choose to work together to propel forward."

I struggle to swallow, the air getting thinner as my hands start tingling.

The glue starts to spread through me, immobilizing me as if something is trying to tear out of me, and I'm denying its release—forcing it to stay hidden. But the harder I push, the more paralyzed I feel.

I gasp for air again as I feel this weight over my shoulders, my chest... I'm sinking.

Orion's voice sounds far away. "This is where you make that choice."

In the pitch black, a sudden spotlight shines on me, and I blink against its brightness until the little spots fade from my vision. Then all the blood drains from me when I see something forming into a figure in the distance.

What the fuck is that...

The figure refines itself, forming a silhouette of a person. Leaning back in the chair, I pant silently as panic takes over me. As it starts approaching me.

"What do you see?" Orion's voice is an echo.

Prying my mouth open to form the words, I whisper, "It's a person." My heart stops. Widening my eyes, the first hint of light hits the figure, and I recognize it. Her. *It's me*. But she holds no love. No patience. No compassion. She is wrath embodied. Hate, trapped inside skin.

I blanch, "She's me."

He pauses. "What does she want from you?"

Shaking my head, I try to figure it out, but each step she takes towards me is a promise of pain. Revenge. She's a predator.

My knuckles turn white as I grip the chair, nails digging in with a pressure that might break them.

A snarl rumbles from her chest, further enraging that vicious promise in her eyes. She's going to kill me.

Whipping my head away, I can't bear to look at her.

Go away. Leave me alone. A whimper slips from me.

Wake up.

"Please," I beg. But to whom, I'm not sure.

Even squeezing my eyes shut, I feel her take another step toward me, her arms at her sides, fingers half-pulled to a fist with rage.

Opening my eyes, I look around for somewhere to escape to, but all I see is black.

How am I meant to get away from her—to fight her when terror plagues every muscle in my body?

Orion's earlier words roll toward me as a cloud does in a storm, a warning in the overcast. *Good pain is befriending your shadow.*

Gritting my teeth, my attention slowly inches toward shadow-me. I catch the tail end of the pain in her eyes, my rejection burning her like a scathing wound. But once our eyes lock, she releases a hateful sneer. *Shit.*

A realization falls heavy on my heart.

"I—" Pushing the words out is like trying to swim with gallons of water rushing against you. But I unlock my jaw.

Try again.

I gasp. Those two words... They came from her. But her lips didn't move.

Pressing my toes into the ground, I push past the frayed angst shooting up my spine, finally managing to speak. "I'm sorry."

Shadow-me halts—shocked. The apology is like a wrecking ball to her anger. We just stare at each other, and I notice something about her eyes. There's a faint pink ring encircling her irises, soft and delicate against the black she wears and shadows under her eyes.

Nausea unsettles my stomach, but with each inch I move toward her and further from resistance, it eases. A slight reprieve allows me a deeper breath as I insist, "I'm so sorry that I turned away from you, that I always..." She swings her arm towards me, and a gust of air slams into my stomach, forcing me to heave over, winded and coughing against the force.

Shadow-me takes another step, then another, and my instinct is to throw out my hand and shield myself, protect myself. But then I think about her. Who protects her? *Is that why you're mad? I left you all alone, in this dark place. Are we in the chasm?*

She bares her teeth at me, her body vibrating with rage, as I feel invisible hands close around my throat. *Shit.* I fight to get air into my lungs, fear consuming me, until a spark of another emotion pushes against it. Empathy somehow finds its way in because I know how severe loneliness can be. How ugly it can make you. Cruel, even.

"You're terrified," I choke out. She's in survival mode, and I'm the threat, caging and abandoning her. I need to get her back to her emotional brain so she can hear me.

Forcing my limbs to move, I release the death grip on the chair, slowly. Resting the back of my hands on my knees, palms up, I relinquish any sense of control. Sitting square with her, I straighten my spine and take a stuttering breath, softening my features.

Her steps falter, the vice on my throat easing just as her scowl slips for a second, allowing her pink-hued eyes to assess me.

Her jaw drops wide, and she screeches at such a pitch that I flinch to cover my ears, but I override the instinct. The hairs on my body rise, and I choke back the sob that wants to tear from me, hearing the agony in her scream. She pants, wrath making her shake as she stares at me.

"I just left you here. I hid you in such a dark place. Rejecting you. Letting you believe I hated you. That you were a monster..." Her lips curl back, fists clenching. But I see her waterline brim with tears.

You hear me.

She takes another step toward me.

"I ran from you... like you were the problem. But it was my choices, and the choices of others who hurt me, that created you. Each painful thing solidified you. You're a part of me, and I treat you like you're the bane of my existence, desperate to get rid of you." I gasp as something dawns on me. "But that's not what you do with your shadow, is it?" I ask her, my curiosity genuine.

Without warning, her feet boom with each step as she storms towards me, determination in her eyes, torment etched through her whole being.

The words rush from me as I brace internally, not moving a single inch as she closes the last bit of distance between us. "Everything I learned about the light was because of the dark. I put the light on a pedestal, and damned you. I need both to balance me out. I need you." I look into the face of fury—my pain, my shadow—and I make a promise to her. "I love you."

She's a few meters away, then in a flash, she's standing still in front of me, taking full breaths from her exertion, fighting me with a look of confusion and loathe.

I surrender to her. "I thought that to be happy, I needed to get rid of you," I whisper, "but you're my compass. You drain me in the company of people I shouldn't be around. You spike my panic when something is wrong because you want to protect me. You pulled me away from that life I hated by filling me with misery so powerful I had no choice but to leave. You saved me... and I *left* you."

She leans down, placing her hands on my armrests and caging me in, inches from my face as she stares into my soul. But I don't fear her. I want to hold her.

Forgive me.

With wide eyes searching my features, her lip starts trembling, and her forehead furrows in sorrow. Then, she crumbles at my feet, digging her fingers into my legs and drawing blood as she clings to me. I wince at the sting of broken skin, but the way she claws onto me, I know she's worried I'll abandon her at any moment.

I release a shaky breath. My voice breaks as I assure her, "I'm not going anywhere."

My heart cracks when she looks up at me, her sobbing so agonized, so loud and broken, its potent anguish. I cup her face, tears sliding down my cheeks at the sound and sight of her wailing despair. "You burned everything in my life down, and paved a pathway for me to find the light. For *us* to find the light—because you're coming with me."

The promise barely has time to leave my lips before relief has her leaping into my lap, balled up, her side pressed into me. She pulls on my shirt with tight fists as she buries her cheek into my chest.

I wrap my arms around her, stroking her hair, guilt eating me alive from the core outwards. "You're not alone anymore, I mean it. When I go to the stream, we'll watch the tiny black and white butterflies float past, and the little fishy's swim close to us curiously... I want you there for all of it.

"When I need to make decisions, I want your opinion. Because I know now that you fill me with fear when I leave my comfort, because if I get hurt, you're the one who deals with it alone. But we have light too, and we have each other. So we can take risks now, because if it hurts, I'm coming to sit with you, and we'll face it together. Okay?"

Leaning back, she scans my face, the frown and slight bare of her teeth telling me she's unsure if she can trust me. Telling me not to lie to her.

"When I laugh or feel joy, I want you to remember that it's because I know you're with me. You're the yin. The light is the yang. And I can't have a meaningful life without both of you. You're my greatest asset." I put my hand on her cheek, wiping away a tear.

The void we're in starts to slip, the sound of nature puncturing a hole in my semi-conscious state. Her grip on me tightens as she looks around frantically, turning wild eyes on me, her breathing quick and unsteady.

"Hey, hey," I croon. "It's okay here." I look around the pitch black that exists beyond the spotlight. I think of when I feel the least amount of pain, and then I lift my finger, dragging it down slowly. As I do, the darkness fills with pinks and oranges, lighting up the void as clouds kissed by morning light illuminate us.

She gapes, watching, her breathing slowing down.

Next, I add luscious green grass, dandelions popping up alongside tiny purple weeds.

She smiles.

I hold back a sob at the sight of it.

She faces me, and I smooth her hair off her face, running my fingers over it and turning her slightly to tie it back. I hum the song me and Orion wrote, of the beach—deciding I'd add one into the vision, for her to watch the waves crash.

I pull her into a hug, the elixir continuing to fade away. When I lean back, her eyes drift sleepily, as if she's exhausted. So, I add a comfy hammock off to the side, with a blanket and pillow. The sunrise glows against her skin as I place her hand over my heart. Repeating the process, I place my palm against her steady heartbeat.

"This..." I gesture to our hands. "This is where we find each other. Let me take some of your pain, and you rest. When you're ready, come and find me, and we'll dance. It's us against the world."

She holds me tightly, whispering, "Thank you."

I can't hold back the sob when she speaks. Guilt pierces me, as I know it's only because I gave her voice back. "I was so mean to you. I'm so sorry. I love you."

We had a whole lifetime of feeling alone, when the truth is, we had each other the whole time.

Placing her forehead against mine, she whispers, "I love you, too."

When I open my eyes, I blink against the light returning, my hand slipping from her chest as she dissolves. So, I place it over my heart. *Ours.*

I'm still here.

Me, too.

My lips quirk into a sad smile when I feel the tingle run up my back.

When my vision clears, I see faces all around me. Some with tears staining their cheeks, hands clasped over their mouths in shocked awe. Others stand tall, pride in their expression, resolve in their eyes. Then I face the panel, empathy and satisfaction sweeping over their features. Even Sage's dad might've been moved, his scowl barely perceptible.

I finally look over at Orion, and he stands. I don't wipe the tears from my face. I don't look away. His compassion for me and the authority of his role clashes in the way he carries himself as he walks towards me.

He steps to my side, facing the panel and casting his focus over the people of Juf'ua. The effects of the elixir roll over me in waves of exhaustion. Everything Pain and I just went through... I can barely keep my eyes open, but I watch, as one by one, the people of Juf'ua lift their hand and place it over their hearts.

They see you, Pain. We all see you.

Even Gatherer Girl uncrosses her arms, placing her hand on her chest, her face unreadable.

I smile through the tears that fall, once again. As he turns to me, I look up to him.

"We as a collective, have deemed your first trial, passed." His voice booms, and the people of Juf'ua applaud, Sage whooping louder than everyone.

I exhale through a tired smile. "Nice," I announce, giving a shaky thumbs up.

His eyes glint with something akin to joy, but heavy lids prevent me from inspecting it further.

I'm lifted to my feet and my arm is thrown over broad shoulders. Orion holds half my weight as we walk. *Damn, why do I feel like jelly?*

He leans close to my ear, speaking low so only I can hear. "I'd lift you into my arms and carry you if I knew you wouldn't hate the public display."

I scoff, amused. *He's right.* It'll give people more reasons to gossip about me. Forcing one exhausted leg to move after the other, I allow my eyes to drift over the faces of strangers looking back at us. I don't know if I'm imagining the pinched brows and quieted conversations as they watch the village's Chief personally escort me. Imagine if they were to see him carry me to my hut. Based on Sage saying she'd never seen Orion with anyone like this, I wonder if they'd approve or hate the idea. Especially with me, an outsider. Not that I'm anywhere close to being with him like that, but I can't help the spiraling thoughts born of what-ifs.

I stumble, one foot catching on a rock, and Orion steadies me before I fall. Electricity races through my skin where he touches my waist, a shiver running up my spine.

Glancing over to Orion, I contemplate what I would do if I didn't let what they think make decisions for me. Softly pressing my hand against his stomach, I anchor myself until the presumed whispers fade away. He's so close that I can see every eyelash encasing those earthy eyes. The ones that seem to only be for me. Somehow, he knows what I'm about to say, because just before the words leave my mouth, his kicks up on one side.

"Maybe, just this once, you could carry me?" I ask.

He stops without hesitation, readying to bend and hook one arm behind my knees, but I pause him with a firm hand on his shoulder.

Meeting his gaze through half-lidded eyes, I warn him. "Listen up…" The bastard is already smirking at me. "If you make a single hint of a grunt when lifting me, I'll put you in a chokehold…"

He stifles a laugh. "I would never."

Pursing my lips, I bob my head to the side in acceptance. Looping my arms around his neck, I offer a small smile. "Then proceed."

In the next breath, I'm in his arms, forehead pressed into the nook of his neck as he carries my drained body and overextended mind toward my hut.

Trying not to look anywhere but forward, I whisper against his skin, "Will the people of Juf'ua hate seeing you carry me?"

I can't see his expression, but I feel the tightening of his grip. "They'd be surprised, but I can't say that they'd hate it."

The question I don't ask afterwards: *what about if they saw you care for me?*

Instead, I simply nestle against his neck, a yawn stretching my jaw.

The walk isn't far, but I've somehow nearly fallen asleep twice. I realize it the second time as I blink my eyes open at the sensation of the soft mattress beneath me, and how I melt into it. They close again, my powerfully-heavy lids demanding to stay shut. A thin blanket is laid gently over me, and I distantly feel a soft stroke from a rough hand run over my hair. *The smell of him.* Four sweet words slide through my daze. "I'm proud of you."

Then, his absence.

Just before sleep can take me, the forest lets celebratory droplets fall over my skin, feeling like the sprinkle of rain. Baritone's voice, rough and soothing, enters my mind as I drift to sleep. *"Well done, Star Child."*

To say I'm shattered from today is a vast understatement. Muscles throb, and my mind is hazy, even after sleeping the entire day. Sage woke me when the sun went down with a bucket and washcloth so I didn't have to go to the stream to bathe. She also informed me that my next trial is tomorrow.

After eating dinner half-asleep and barely participating in conversation, I plop back in bed, shoving a pillow between my knees and nestling into comfort.

Groaning, my bladder presses into me with an apologetic 'we need to pee.' *Can I hold it a few more hours until morning?*

No.

Grunting, I push myself up and grab the sunlamp on my bedside table.

Trying to be quiet, I tiptoe out my hut door, and gasp at the giant figure curled up in front of my hut. Bringing the light closer, I blink against the dark, seeing... fur. Then it moves, and bright yellow eyes turn to look at me. *Divy.*

Surprise flickers through me, and I scan around for Orion. But everyone has gone to bed, and the Okah are most likely in their giant hut, which is at least ten times the size of mine. They're protected from the sun, rain, and the occasional storms. Sage told me it's lavished, with each having their own bed and fresh water in their bowls.

"Hey," I say, not sure why I'm talking to her like a person, but continue to do it anyway. "I need to pee."

Watching me, she blinks slowly, her tall, pointed ear twitching toward some kind of critter in the forest before returning to face me.

"I'm just going to step around you, okay?"

Please don't eat me.

My heart ticks faster as I move a foot sideways, sliding along my hut so I don't accidentally step on her. But then she huffs an exhale, getting up to move out of my way.

"Oh." I swallow. "Thanks."

Why is she here?

Starting to walk toward the Terf'gs, I look over my shoulder when I hear the precise thud of four feet on the ground, following me.

Tilting my head at her, I inquire, "Are you coming with me?" I know that she can't respond, but still, I ask, "Did Orion put you on guard duty?" I tsk playfully. "None of the humans wanted night shift, eh?" Nervously making conversation with an Okah might be in my top ten weirdest moments.

She comes up beside me, and we walk together, her back in line with my shoulder.

It's so quiet, except for the crunch of leaves under our feet, and the literal crickets making this feel even more awkward.

I purse my lips, sneaking a glance at her side-long. "Girl code. Never let a friend go to the bathroom alone in a dark forest. I respect that."

With the moonlight and stars illuminating her, she turns those yellow eyes on me—watching me.

I pull my lips in. "It was the word 'friends,' wasn't it? Too soon?"

Walking closer to me, her chin dips, and an expression lingers behind her eyes—one I've only seen her give Orion. It's claiming. Affectionate.

I smile tentatively. "Friends, then."

Looking away from me, her eyes sweep across the forest, her prowl relaxed but her proximity defensive. My brows scrunch. Surely, I'm misreading everything.

When we get to the Terf'gs, I speak quietly to her. "So, I won't be long. Please, make yourself at home." I gesture to the landscape around us.

I'm definitely imagining the flat look she gives me, because that was funny.

I make my way into one of the small rooms, looking around in the dim light of the sunlamp, contemplating what kind of art would look cool on the back of the door.

Once I'm done, I step out to see her sitting with her back to me. *Keeping watch?* Something in the tree has caught her interest. Her nose points at it, fixed to sniff greedily.

"Good smell?" I ask her with a baby voice.

She slowly turns her head to me, pinning me with those glowing eyes as her ears twitch backwards.

I raise my hands in surrender, quickly correcting myself. "Not a dog. A *lady*. Fierce. Scary beast. Got it."

After a moment, she rises to walk, my amendment seemingly exonerating me.

We walk side by side once again, and I might have a death wish, because I whisper to her out of the side of my mouth, "It was a good smell though, wasn't it?"

She ignores me.

When we get to my hut, I stop myself from reaching out to stroke her fur. Clicking my tongue, I speak softly, "Well, goodnight." Just before the door closes, I see her lay down, with her back towards my hut.

The rest of the night is spent tossing and turning, thoughts of my first trial coming in flashes.

I see Pain.

And she is red.

Like a strawberry.

She's every moment that's ever hurt me, in a form—stored in me, somewhere in the chasm of my soul. I wonder if my Light also lives there, and what she would be like if I met her. I scoff. *She's probably elegant.*

Not only do I have every version of myself condensed into two forms... but I have the physical me. And... I have the cells of every ancestor before me, watching over me from the sky, twinkling and bright blazing balls of fire.

I have an army behind me. Within me.

The fact I ever felt alone... It's the greatest illusion of all time.

CHAPTER 26
CONFESSIONS

On the morning of my second trial, tension curls through me in an unruly whirlpool, threatening to bring my breakfast up.

The encircled crowd is strewn over chairs, tables, the ground, or standing. The panel is assembled, and Orion stands in front. His wide stance, and hands loose in his pockets, project the picture of informal leadership. This feels just like yesterday, and I wish I could say I'm less scared because I've already done a trial, but I know today will be different when I spot the elixir in front of Sage. The cloudy, burnt orange colors promise a tangy aftertaste. I decide there and then, I'm not going to smell it first.

To my shock, Divy prowls over to lie beside the table, and my pattering heart slows slightly in her presence. People turn to look at her, Orion included, as gasps come from everywhere. By the tender and surprised expression Orion turns on me, I wonder if I'm crazy for believing she came as support for me. I try to distract myself from the next rise of angst by focusing on her.

Orion projects his voice. "This next stage is a trial of your ability, and what you can bring to Juf'ua. We are aware you are still discovering your ability, and you're not able to demonstrate as we usually would. Yes, you could tell us. However, to avoid any speculation of its legitimacy, we have prepared a truth serum."

I almost burst out laughing. Truth serum? So, I have to tell them about the 'touching with no touching'? *Fuck.*

His eyes lock with mine. "Everyone here has their own story that led them to joining Juf'ua. No one has to prove their worthiness to live here, but only their trustworthiness. This is a safe place, and for us to share our abilities with you is no small thing. You must be willing to share yours with us, too."

He walks over to me casually, still addressing the crowd. "It's a sacred thing to be open about being Activ. We know many who have lost their lives—their freedom—and had things taken from them for simply being themselves."

When he's a few steps from me, he speaks low and quickly. "What's wrong?"

I reply with my lips barely moving, panic surging through me. "I don't even understand what my ability is, and I have to, what, explain that I can caress people with my mind? What the fuck am I doing? Why did I think I could be of any help to Juf'ua? This is mortifying."

Determination glints in his eyes, a nearly-invisible nod that speaks for him. *Trust me.* In the next breath, he turns to face the panel, shifting his weight but gently brushing my shoulder in the process.

He announces for all to hear, "To let you in, you will let us in."

The crowd gives their agreement, sharing thoughts with each other and watching me with eagerness.

Sage brings over the elixir and hands it to me gently, eyes searching mine. *She can also tell something is off with me.*

The cloudy orange drink sits in my fingertips numbly as I look over to Orion. A question is evident in my eyes. *What do I do?*

When our eye contact lingers, the crowd murmurs. Can they see our connection? *Creations of all fuck, our connection.* I look up at the stars that exist behind the light of day.

"*Star Child, breathe.*" Baritone's voice fills my mind, causing me to flinch and nearly spill the elixir.

Sage and Orion share a glance, clearly unable to hear the intrusive thought from the tree that made me react like that.

"It's okay..." he assures.

"Do I tell them?" I yell the question at Baritone in panic.

I tap my foot, anxiously waiting for guidance from the forest. I want to throw up.

The only response I get is a soft rustle of the trees behind the panel, only for my eyes to see.

I remark with an internal grunt, "*Just so you know, that's an incredibly unclear answer.*"

Orion speaks low, stealing my attention. "You have no idea how capable and valuable you are. Let yourself discover that today. Speak your truth. I'll step in if I need to."

His words put a focus in my mind's eye, sharpening my senses. *I'm doing this to find out what I can do. Who I can be.* My shoulders drop an inch from being tense and raised.

Orion projects his voice again. "Do you consent to the second trial, and to sharing your knowledge on your abilities?" The look he gives me, the way he spells out the last words... He worded that carefully. Relief courses through me, my chest loosening and a soft exhale sliding through my parted lips.

Knowledge is subjective, so I could interpret it as having information that's certain to be true. So, if I'm not sure, then I'm not bound to share it. The abilities they have a right to know about, but the connection I have with Orion... I can keep that between us.

I declare back to him, "I consent to the second trial, and to sharing my knowledge of my abilities."

All eyes are on me as I lift the glass to my lips, the crowd falling silent as the elixir slides down my throat.

I was not expecting it to be sweet like peaches. Another small mercy is that this one doesn't have tiny lumps in it, just finely dusted grains.

Orion and Sage walk back to the panel to take their seats. By the time they get there, it's kicking in.

Deitydamn, my internal monologue slurs. I can practically feel my pupils dilating. Everything is so clear, so exposed. Any fidgeting in the crowd, an absentminded pinch of the brows—I can see it all... And then a sound of chains... like the steady tick, tick, tick, of letting a draw bridge lower. Looking around, I can't find the source. It dawns on me that the sound is in my mind, and my lungs expand in a sharp inhale. Invisible, deft fingers are prying my chest open.

My wide eyes drop down, my hands flying to my chest, expecting to see a gaping hole. But the forest green tank top and the skin beneath is perfectly intact. It's my energetical body—the formless being beneath my physical form. The chasm has cracked open, primed to reveal. And it feels... *good*. My mouth opens slightly, a shiver running up my spine as self-consciousness is at an all-time low.

Flicking my eyes up at Orion, I tilt my head at him with one hell of a smirk. He stiffens, keeping his expression carefully neutral. I look over the crowd, hearing whispers and seeing speculative expressions. Sage covers her mouth with her hand, pretending to scratch above her top lip. *But I can see everything, Sage.* I can see your cheeky grin, the glint of mischief in your eyes.

Don't worry, Orion, I'll be more subtle.

A giggle works its way past my tongue when I get the feeling of my heart being tickled, coaxed into a bold undraping.

"Woah." I draw the word out, unable to bite back the grin on my face as I turn in a slow circle, appraising everything with child-like awe.

A wave of awareness comes through, sobering me like an ice cube sliding down my spine. *Conceal.*

Orion speaks. "We'll just give it one more minute for it to take full effect. How are you feeling so far?"

My attention crashes into him, and whatever I was going to say dies on my lips. *Creations, he is so fucking handsome.* Look at him. The comfortability he has in his skin, the way his authoritative posture melts so seamlessly into his casual confidence. His effortless attunement to me is *sexy*. I drag my eyes over him, wanting to memorize every inch of his body with my lips.

He straightens, and if I wasn't on this super heightened truth-trip, I might've missed the sharp inhale, or the way his eyes darkened.

"I feel wonderful." My voice feels like it's lagging a second behind when it meets the air.

He stretches out his neck, impacted by the scrutiny of my attention. *How the tables have turned, sir.*

When he gives me a warning look, I address the crowd as if they're my dear friends. "Does it make sense if I say the sensation of speaking... feels like clumsy dancers stumbling late on a stage, as if they've missed their cue in a big performance?"

The people of Juf'ua laugh, some turning to the person next to them and speaking softly with smiles on their faces. Some nod like they know the exact feeling I'm talking about. But my eyes don't linger on them—they return to the panel, as they announce we're ready to begin.

Orion's voice is direct and to the point. "Tell us what your ability is." A simple question, requiring a complex answer.

I bite back the urge to tease him, to lift a brow and prompt him to say 'please.' But a stronger voice silences the urge, not wanting to undermine him in front of his people.

Without a second to heed the voice hushing me, the clumsy dancers slip from my mouth. "Well," I start, putting my hands on my hips. "I don't really understand it yet. But it seems to be some kind of energy thing. I can touch without touching."

Well, that didn't stay in for long. I snort-laugh.

Some gasps scatter around me, and I address them with a dramatic shrug and lift of my hands. "I know, right?" When I see the perplexed expressions on others, I add, "It's pretty fucking wild."

I sit on the ground cross-legged, leaning back on my hands and scan the sky in thought. "I've been thinking about it... a lot. And it might be some kind of heightened awareness of living things?"

Shifting so my legs lay flat on the ground in front of me, I address the panel. "When I give my full attention to something and interact with the energy, or the air around them, I can create that contact, without needing my physical body to do it. It all happens up here..." I tap against my temple.

Sage's mum speaks to Orion, but loud enough for everyone to hear. "As some kind of telekinesis?" She turns to me before he can answer. "Can you move objects?"

I think about her question, then laugh to myself, trying to imagine moving Orion with my mind and how much he would loathe it.

She clears her throat, pulling me from my thoughts.

What was her question? "Right, sorry." I pick up some dirt and rub it between my palms. "I haven't tried, so I don't know."

She raises a brow at me, narrowing her eyes slightly, and suddenly I mimic her expression—just to feel the sensation of it on my face. Sage nearly laughs, but catches it after only a single sound escapes.

Her mum blinks slowly, choosing to ignore it. She asks, "Then, how exactly do you know you have this ability?"

Fuck. My stomach drops, and I move uncomfortably, crossing my feet underneath me and staring at the ground. The words want to rush from me, and I physically bite my lip to stop myself from speaking. I manage a shrug.

"How can you say you have abilities, and this knowledge, without any experience to back it up?" Sage's mum presses on.

Oh no. The longer I go without answering, the more the serum starts to burn in my chest. I rub my knuckles over my heart in small circles, trying to soothe the acidic demand, wanting to let the words out. Instead, I come up with a solid plan to get out of this.

I call out, "Everybody, watch this!" I lay down on the ground, sweeping my arms out back and forth to make grass angels, hoping to distract them long enough to forget I owe them an answer.

I don't hear anyone say 'wow,' so I must not be going hard enough. I swipe faster, prompting them as I yell, "Wow, right?" But you know what, the longer I do this, the more I'm just impressing myself. I get lost in how nice the grass against my skin feels, and how good it is to move my body.

"Stella, focus please," Sage says, nearly choking on amusement, while people in the crowd outright laugh.

Dammit.

I pick my head up and scan the panel, locking eyes with TG, who has his hand over his mouth, his shoulders moving up and down as he tries to restrain himself. I squint at him, suspicious that he might know how I can do what I do, but will cop it from Orion if he ridicules me.

Orion.

Getting to my feet and dusting off my pants, I focus on the man who's the picture of calm. Fondness is laced through his features, but with a subtle lift of his chin, I know he wants me to answer their question.

Easy for him to say, he isn't the one who——

"I do have experience." The words rip from my mouth without any prewarning. I practically shout, "I wanted to be the water drop falling down his back."

My fingers curl loosely over my lips as I watch the crowd. An array of confusion and snickering blanket the people.

Sage's mum and dad seem devoid of humor, unlike TG and Sage, who really should excuse themselves at this point. They are not helping.

Orion does not flinch, clarifying for me, "At the stream, I felt a brief touch from her, but she was far from me physically. I asked her about it, but she had no idea she was doing it."

The crowd starts speaking over each other, sharing their thoughts and theories on what my ability could mean, when Sage's mum silences them with a question for Orion. "You didn't tell us?"

"I wanted to know more first. When it happened again..."

"Again?" Gatherer Girl interjects herself. Her friends scowl at me, offended on her behalf. "How many times has this happened to you?" She asks Orion the question as if she feels sorry for him, for ever being sullied by my touch.

I think, matter-of-factly, *he didn't seem to mind.*

Her face scrunches in rage, some people bow their heads in a collective 'oof,' and others look between us, ready to wage war on her behalf. That's when I know I said that out loud. By the looks of it, others seem to know she has a thing for him. Maybe even expected their inevitable partnering.

Nope.

Orion redirects the attention to him, addressing the panel members as he answers, "I've been looking into it, however, I'm not certain yet on which intelligence she has."

I purse my lips, wanting to add to the conversation. My cheeks redden slightly, but a larger part of me doesn't have time to feel embarrassed in my next words. "When there is a moment, and I visualize myself reaching out, like when I traced my finger down his back, somehow the energy actualizes it. I don't know if it's *my* energy extending out to touch him, or if it's me influencing the energy closest to him to do it for me."

Sage asks then, "How long can you do it for?"

I cock a brow, and Gatherer Girl draws my attention, clasping her hands with a sharp look in her eyes.

Sliding my attention from hers to Orion, I answer with a slight tilt of my lips, "So far, only in short bursts."

He nearly smiles—it's right there before he pulls a mask of indifference over his features. Although, his gaze speaks two words of amused reprimand to me. 'You're trouble.'

Sage's dad moves right past the comment and puts his cup at the edge of the table. "Can you sense or interact with this?"

My eyes drop to the navy blue clay mug, and I focus on it, noticing the energy around it, but when I imagine lifting it, the energy bounces off like it's hitting a wall. "I don't think so," I mutter. "Even though I feel it has energy and matter, my ability doesn't seem to mesh with its kind. I think I interact only with living things."

Sage's mum leans back in her chair, curiosity taking her deep into her mind as she stares at me.

TG then asks, "Is this the full extent of your ability and its development?"

"Yes," I reply. "Well, of *that* ability..." I slap a hand over my mouth.

We were nearly done, why would you say that?!

Reaching deep inside of me, I search desperately for the version of me that doesn't say whatever she's thinking.

I call out to the trees. *"I don't want to tell them about you. Is it okay if they get it out of me? Help, please!"*

A soft rumble beneath the soil calms me, so subtle it's nearly imperceptible. The Ancient that Sage and I climbed answers, *"Star Child, you may let them know about how you can communicate with us. They have good intentions. However, you're not ready yet to know more, and you must know your truth before they have a right to it. Tell them that you are under no obligation to share what we have spoken to you about, without our consent. If we tell you something in confidence, they must respect that."*

The pressure eases from my chest in their presence.

Sage's dad declares, "Speak the truth—finish what you were saying."

The confusion planted on Orion's face spurs guilt in me.

Sighing, I scan the trees around us as I release the secret I've been keeping from everyone. "Earlier, you said to share with you my ability, but I think I might have more than one, and I don't know if they're separate or connected."

Whispers break out around me. "More than one?" "What is she?"

Orion asks, "What other ability do you suspect you have?" He's trying to hide the surprise, and I can't tell if he's upset or not that I haven't told him.

Nervously glancing between his eyes, I confess, "I can— uh... talk to trees."

Silence.

Chaos erupts.

People speak over each other, some wearing shocked expressions, some still as statues.

Lifting a hand, Orion calls out, "Silence." The chatter dies instantly.

His command runs through my veins, a smile lifting my lips, until I see the look on his face. *He's... angry with me? Suspicious?* I'm not sure, but I don't like it.

I dip my chin and stride toward the panel. To him. By the looks of their faces, I'm not supposed to approach. They glance at Orion, waiting for him to stop me. But he doesn't. He leans back in his chair, head inclined. My hands land flat on the table as I stare him down. "And what exactly has you looking at me like *that?*"

I *feel* the crowd lean in to hear Orion as he speaks just for me. "And how is it that I'm looking at you?"

I search his eyes. "Cautious. Mistrusting. Pissed off."

He leans forward, resting his elbows on the table, and lists an expression I hadn't considered. "Worried."

He's worried. *Why?*

But before I can ask, TG utters, "You can talk to trees? Since when?"

I stand back a couple of steps from the table, looking over to TG as I answer him. "Since the morning the Gatherers returned."

Sage's dad asks, "And you told no one?"

I quickly glance at Orion, then back to him. "I hadn't processed it. And it felt... private. But I just asked them before, and they said I could tell you now."

TG asks, "And what did they say to you? Why have they contacted you?"

I honestly keep waiting for someone to tell me I've gone insane, or question that I'm making this up. But the truth serum confirms the reality of it.

My stomach flutters in the presence of Little One. *"Tell them what we said to you, Star Child."*

I take a deep breath and picture her standing right next to me, chin raised. "They said that if they tell me something in confidence, you must respect that, and not push for me to speak it... And..." I scratch my head. "This is awkward," I say to the treeline.

Sage encourages me to continue at the same time Little One does.

I push on. "I can share that I've only spoken to them a handful of times... So I think they mean, in the future, you have to receive consent to know what we speak of."

That was uncomfortable, setting that boundary, but when I finish speaking, all the trees in the nearby canopy start rustling their approval. I feel a swell of pride rush through me, and I smile up at the trees.

The crowd lifts their eyes to follow the sound and the sight, as does the panel, gawking as if witnessing something extraordinary.

When my attention returns to Orion, I can't read his carefully-concealed expression. He replies, "We will always respect the wishes of Mother Nature. We will not pry where we are not given access."

I can't focus on anything but him right now. His lips are in a tight line, the warrior ever-present, and the man who softens around me feels closed behind a wall. That last sentence feels layered. *He's not mad that I haven't told him yet, is he?*

I try to think about it from his perspective, and maybe he wishes I did. A thought slackens my face muscles. *He wants what he has since our night under the tree, where we had our first kiss. He wants me to lean on him.* I didn't—not with this. But I needed time to process, and to do this alone. With the middle of my brows rising, I plead with my eyes. 'Please understand.'

A crack in his rigidity responds to me, scanning my expression and softening his own a fraction. I forget that he has a war within him, too—combating emotions when it comes to me, And I know from firsthand experience that it's like digging through the trenches.

He picks up his water, takes a drink, and then stares into the empty cup, lost in thought.

Sage's voice is devoid of any lightness that I'm familiar with when she addresses me. "You can talk to trees, and engage with the energy of living things... Would you say your ability feels rooted in nature?"

Orion stiffens. Something has fallen over the people, as if I've summoned dark clouds over the village, and Sage's question is the boom of thunder.

I think about this, then comment tentatively, "I'd say it does. I'm not sure how, but when you asked me that, it felt right."

She smiles at me, but I see the worry cross her features. "Okay."

Sage's dad is thankfully far less sorrowful-looking as he asks curiously, "How do you hear the trees, exactly? Can you share with us what it sounds like, and what the limitations to it might be?"

Closing my eyes, I tune in, trying to find the best way to describe it. "You know, I think they communicate with me in a way I understand."

I recall how one of the Ancients said she knows I'm fond of sarcasm and light-hearted teasing, and so she tried to embody that.

Opening my eyes, I tap my finger against my lip, eyes on the ground as I pace slowly. "Maybe, if I were an Okah or a bird, the way they communicate would shift to accommodate. I don't think they have a language, but they adapt to the recipient's language."

Stopping my pacing, I turn to face the panel, fidgeting as one does when deep in thought or conversation. "I tried speaking to them aloud, and they heard me, but I only really speak to them in my head now. It feels like they're omniscient. They can tap into what I'm thinking, feeling, doing... and I can reach out and speak to them, in this uncharted void in my mind. They're a mix of male and female voices, different ages... but I don't think they actually have genders."

I check to see if the panel is waiting to ask me something, then I sift through the faces of the crowd, to see if they're bored of me rambling yet. But the expressions around me only reflect enrapture. They're listening.

I press on, "I can feel them, too. For example, if I'm panicking, I hear their comforting words, and then this flutter of warmth spreads in my chest—as a soothing hug would make you feel. If they want to encourage me, I don't actually feel the pat on the back or see them smile. I would sense the energy that comes with the gesture, and it'd float through me in a way my human body can receive it. Does that make sense?"

The panel shares glances, the people of Juf'ua wearing looks of captivation.

Orion seems less in his head when he addresses me. "Yes, you explained that incredibly. Are you open to exploring this more in the future, with the consent of Mother Nature?"

I check in with the trees, and then I give them a thumbs up. "They said yes. I'd like to know more, too. And there's a lot for me to learn about the world and being an Activ. I still feel kind of protective over the bond, so it might take me a minute to open up. But if I feel comfortable, and they give the green light, I'll share everything I can with you."

The panel all give their own versions of approval and understanding.

TG clears his throat, leans forward on his elbows, and tucks his chin into his palms. His voice is playful, a smirk teasing his lips. "I have a question."

My own smile meets his as I lock my fingers behind my back. "I'd be surprised if you didn't."

He chuffs a laugh, and then something more serious falls over his features. "What brought you to Juf'ua in the first place? Before you found us, why were you in the forest?"

I stare at him. My smile slips. The atmosphere shifts around me—colder. I place my hand on my heart. *Pain.*

His eyes drop to the gesture, and empathy coats his features.

Inhaling, I admit, "One day, I looked at my life, and just asked myself, 'what the fuck am I doing?'" My laugh is humorless. "I had no idea how to make a decision for myself, because I've been living under other people's thumbs. Under their influence. Their ideals. So, coming here, to this forest—that was for me."

TG prods, "I can respect that. But why *this* forest?"

I shrug, glancing over to the trees. "I was led here."

Everyone is silent as the weight of that settles in.

TG asks, "To embark on a self-discovery quest?"

"That's how it started, but as to how it'll finish? That's up to how long I get to spend here." My voice has never been so steady.

I look up to the sky, a smile lifting my lips. "I'm just trying to find meaning in life again. And now I know I'm not the only one."

Throughout the crowd, I hear mixed responses, but the common theme of it all is resonance. The air suddenly feels less sharp. Less segregated.

The panel shares glances, and one by one, they tell Orion they have no more questions.

Orion stands, stepping out from behind the table, and inspects the people. Juf'ua's approving nods have my heart quickening, my shoulders relaxing. Their welcoming warmth drifts over me. My time as an outcast is fading to reveal blue, like dark and heavy clouds do after rainfall.

Without any objections, he turns to me, announcing, "You have passed the second trial. Thank you for your honesty. The third and final trial will commence tomorrow morning—"

"Wait. I have a question." I blurt the demand, urgency in my tone as I remember something.

I study his schooled neutral expression, straight shoulders, and the way his lips move when he says, "Yes?"

"Earlier, when I first mentioned the trees, and Sage..." I look over to her. "You asked if my abilities revolved around nature. Everyone seemed..."

Orion told me he was worried. Sage looked concerned.

I think for the right wording. "I can feel the weight of what's not being said. There's something I don't know, and I'd like for you to tell me."

A sheen of caution slides like shadows over his eyes. Everyone and everything becomes eerily still. The hairs on my arms bristle with the tension in the air.

Orion walks over to me, swallowing something like fear before making eye contact. "There are nine branches of intelligence that our abilities fall under. Activs specialize in one, and it manifests based on our purpose and the type of person we are."

He pauses, searching my features as he jumps the hurdles in his brain.

I whisper, "Orion, you're freaking me out. Please, just skip to the part that you're trying not to say, and I can learn all about the intelligences later."

He licks his lips, dropping his head for a moment. When he looks back at me, something like valiance coats his features, as if he's trying to inspire it inside of me. "I think you're a Natura."

A bell of awakening alerts my senses. A rightness. *Yes,* the chasm says. *We are.*

"Okay," I prod. "And why does that make you all look so sullen?" Then, I whisper for just him to hear, "You had fear in your eyes, Orion. Are you scared of me?"

Without pause, without that worried look anywhere in sight, he tells me, "Naturas are rare. They scarcely exceed the ability of herbalism, botany, and base-level physical interaction with nature's network. They don't speak with them. They don't... You have only just Activated, and your abilities far exceed this."

TG adds, as if Orion can't bring himself to finish telling me the truth. "You are of high value to Discon."

The blood drains from my face. "Why?" I rasp the words out.

Orion remains steady, the grounding force in a building tornado. "Because you are a useful rarity on their side, and dangerous if opposing them."

I blink at him. "Okay, I might need some of the history lesson, not just the scary part."

He rests a hand on my shoulder. "We don't even know what you're capable of yet, but by the sounds of what you can already do..." He trails off, his lips twitching and brows scrunching in a flash.

He doesn't finish the thought. Instead, he says, "They've been using Activs, seeking the most powerful, and gradually refining the suppressant that makes the Activ gene lay dormant. They spread it through our food, water, air. That's why you've

Activated, because you're inside the barrier, unexposed to the suppressant.

I swallow, my eyes darting around as I process. "Can we taste the suppressants? How have people not noticed?"

"It doesn't have a taste or odor. The suppressants work on the majority, but it does fail sometimes. They've been seeking an infallible suppressant, one that can't be overridden."

I ask, "What happens if it fails?"

His jaw clenches, pausing before answering. "It rarely happens, but they have systems globally set up to extract anyone Activ and bring them to Discon."

I don't know if he's aware that he steps closer to me, or that his features harden in a way that feels protective. "With you potentially being able to influence and interact with all living things, your Activ gene might be the difference for the suppressant."

I'm sucked into the vortex of power he exudes, his low voice as he tells me, "I'm not scared of you, Stella." He searches my eyes, gazing upon me as if I'm something precious. "I don't like the idea of you being important to them."

"You're scared... *for* me?" I whisper the question, feeling the urge to rest my hand on his chest—stopping myself right before I do.

With conviction in his voice, I can't help but believe him when he says, "I'm not going to let anything happen to you."

Sage interrupts us. "Let's dismiss everyone."

He waits to be sure I hear him, and I nod, before he turns to address everyone. "Thank you for your time."

Without another word, I watch as people start getting up to leave. One of the last people to move is Gatherer Girl, and her inner circle. She glares at me, despite her approval of my passing.

Keep an eye on her.

Sage's parents call Orion over, and his promise to me lingers in his eyes before turning to walk toward the main hut, TG in tow.

Answering my unasked question, Sage provides, "They'll be going to revise tomorrow's trial with this new information."

Sage flicks her attention to the left, and I follow her line of sight toward Gatherer Girl. *Does she sense something in her emotions?*

"Mother Almighty," Sage exhales. "She does not like the way Orion looks at you."

I scoff, "Well, maybe we should be adults and talk about it."

I take half a step towards them before Sage is redirecting me.

"Um, maybe don't talk to her while on truth serum." Then she hooks her arm through mine. "I nearly wet myself when you called her out, though." Mimicking my accent, she says, "He doesn't seem to mind." Her head falls back as a laugh bursts from her.

Gaping at her, I claim, "I forgot about that, and I definitely need to sleep with one eye open from now on. Though she can try to intimidate me all she wants, I won't stop believing that he's mine."

She stops walking, and her neck nearly breaks as she swings her head around to me. "Oh..." She draws the vowel out. "Is that right?"

I press my lips against my teeth before turning wide eyes on her. "I said that last part out loud, didn't I? Awesome." She grins at me mischievously, and I cut her off before she can speak. "No, don't enable me. I'm not ready for him."

Pulling her back into a stroll, she remarks in sing-song, "Whatever you say."

"Hey," I drawl. "I'm trying really hard not to hate myself for how much I want him. Please, support me to focus on me, and not on *me and him*."

She runs a hand over my hair. "You're learning to love yourself, and what's meant to be yours won't pass you by. There's no rush. Okay?"

We enter my hut, and I collapse on the bed, drunk on the truth. "Am I selfish? Denying him, denying what I feel for him, and also denying her? What if they'd be happy together? Ugh, that makes me sick." I rub my stomach soothingly.

She fluffs my pillow and sits down on the bed. "You make your choices. She makes hers. He makes his. You're only in control of how you conduct yourself, and how authentic it feels. The rest isn't up to you." She grabs my chin and shakes my head gently.

I laugh and wrap my hand around her wrist, stopping her playful assault. "I never imagined a friend like you even existed." My eyes glisten as I watch her through the haze of exhaustion weighing on me. "You make me feel safe. And I love the way you carry yourself. So brave. So honest, you don't even need truth serum. You're *my* hero. After everything you've been through, *because* of everything you've been through, you..." I wave my arm out like a rainbow. "Shine."

She giggles, placing her hands under her chin, looking up. "Who, me?"

I squeeze her cheeks. "Yes, you!"

She chortles, tugging me in as she says, "You're my best friend, Stella."

Picking up on the well of tears building from my heart and making its way to my eyes, she squeezes me tighter.

"I love you," I whisper in her hair. Then I gasp. "I've never said that before. Well, out loud, to someone else. I said it earlier today, to Pain. I actually really like that the first person I said it to was *me*."

She pulls back, beaming at me. "What I hear is that besides yourself, I am the greatest love of your life?" She cocks a brow.

I push her shoulder, laughing. "Way to ruin the moment."

She stands up, laughing. "I love you, too."

I push my bottom lip out. "So, what now? Do we just forget about Orion and run off together?"

Nodding as if the answer is an obvious yes, she claims, "He'll understand."

I laugh, nuzzling into my pillow.

Exhales, she says, "Alright, you have a relaxing sleep, and I'll come check on you later. The serum will last a few more hours, and you'll just get sleepier. You might have weird dreams."

I speak through a yawn. "Oh, yay. You go relax too, friend." I give her a knowing look. "*Best* friend," I amend.

She winks at me, a beam plastered across her face as she turns and leaves me with the dissipating effects of my truth.

I roll onto my side, tucking my hands under my pillow, then feel something there. Lifting it up, I see my journal, and on top of it, a tiny, white, velvet pouch.

"What are you?" I groggily ask the pouch, pulling on the little bow securing it at the top. I peek inside and frown. *What is that?* Tipping it upside down, a folded up piece of paper and a stone falls out.

It's a clear and rich yellow stone, patterned like marble. Running my thumb over the smooth surface, I hold it up to catch the light. *This is stunning.*

A gasp rips through me the second I recognize it. This is the stone that was attached to Orion's knife. *He's giving it to me?*

I open the paper that's folded up and realize it's a note.

"Stella, this is called a Golden Citrine. I've carried it with me for a while. You asked me why I had it, and I never answered you. It was a gift, and I held it close as if the sun himself warmed it for me when I felt cold. Its purpose is to support you, transmuting negative energy into joy. It's an aid in finding peace. I want to give this to you, and to Pain. Keep this under your pillow or carry it with you. Let it be there when I can't, if you'll allow it. Yours, Orion."

I don't know when the tears started falling, but they do it one after the other, without missing a beat until it's just a solid stream.

He sees us, Pain.

I read the note again and open my journal, tucking it in with my list. This man just hit four points in one gift.

- *Point number 1: I feel seen and understood*
- *Point number 2: I feel reassured, validated, and considered*
- *Point number 4. I feel safe and secure*
- *Point number 9: I honor my complexity*

The urge to go to him is profound, imposing itself beyond any rational thought to stay away. The only thing that convinces my feet not to haul me over to him is realizing he's in the main hut with the other leaders.

Clutching the citrine tight in my fist, I press it to my heart. *For me and you, Pain.* Unsure if it's me, her, or Light that encourages it, but my body hums with that familiar feeling of hope.

CHAPTER 27
LREMI

Blinking my eyes open, I wake up feeling both fully rested and completely disoriented. I push off the bed and peek outside, seeing that night has befallen. I've slept through dinner, and everyone is well and truly asleep. *What time is it?*

My mouth feels very dry, and I turn to grab my cup of water on the bedside table, seeing a covered bowl of food. Someone brought me this in case I woke up hungry. Clutching the citrine to my heart, I tip my head back as I struggle under the weight of gratitude. *Whoever it was, thank you.*

Drawing my lip between my teeth, I close my eyes, wondering how much longer I'll be under the effects of the truth serum. It's not as forceful as before, but I still feel the urge to reveal. To unveil. And there's someone in mind I feel pulled to do that with. The citrine is still clasped in my hand, things I've buried ready to tip over the edge of my constraint when I stride out of my hut.

Stopping abruptly, I stare at the giant fur lady sleeping outside of my hut.

I gape in glee. "Divy!"

She lifts her head, seemingly assessing me like something is off.

I inform her in a whisper like we're old friends, "I'm going to go visit Orion quickly. There's something I need to say to him." Then I ask, "Do you want to come with me?"

Rising to her full height in her way of agreeance, I have to resist the urge to reach out and run my fingers through her fur. Apparently the serum still allows me to maintain some semblance of self-preservation when it comes to not petting the Okah.

Not a single anxious thought exists in my body or mind as we stroll side by side toward Orion's hut. *I love truth serum.*

I stop outside his hut, only knowing it's his because I've seen him enter and exit it.

I wonder what it looks like inside.

Seeing the light is on, I blow out a thankful breath. "He's still awake," I announce to Divy quietly, as if it's not completely obvious to the Okah with senses far beyond that of a human.

I wanted him to be awake, but also, I want him to sleep soundly. He deals with so much, he needs rest. I decide I'll make this quick.

Divy lays down and watches me stand just outside the door. I whisper to her, "Good idea, you wait here. Might be a bit squished with all of us in there. I won't be long."

When I turn to knock, I remember its soft fabric.

"Stella?" His tone tells me he knows it's me, but he's wondering what I'm doing here.

Drawing the material back a few inches, I reply, "Yes?"

He's laying on his bed, ankles crossed, and whatever book he was reading lays flat on his chest.

Confusion coats his features as he looks at me. "Come in."

The door falls closed behind me as I take one step inside and plant my feet, my hands tucked studiously behind my back. I offer him a small smile. "Hey."

Letting my eyes wander over his hut, all I see is a bed, a table, chairs... It's just like mine, but with a stack of books. He's been here so long, and it's so bare—as if he's a guest.

Creasing my eyebrows, a pang of surprise muddles my mind.

"Where are your decorations?" I ask him.

Placing a bookmark in his book, he sets it down on the table and sits up. Concern rakes through his features and stiff muscles. "What's wrong? Are you okay?"

Knotting my fingers behind my back, it crosses my mind for the first time that I've just entered his space, and he might not want me in here. "I'm sorry. Please don't be angry with me. I just wanted to say goodnight. And I wanted to see how you decorated your hut." I scan the room again. "But... you don't."

He softens, exhaling as he stands and walks over to me. "You're still on the truth serum, aren't you?"

Narrowing my eyes at him, "What's that got to do with anything?"

A smile teases his lips. "I'm not mad at you. I was just taken by surprise. You've had a big day, and you really should be resting for tomorrow." Then, he looks around, addressing my concern. "And I don't like decorations."

"Oh." My eyes rove over the hut again, picturing him in different spots around the room. I've wondered so many times what he's like in his own company. *Just Orion.* But I heed his dismissal. I must've thought he'd be happy to see me. This is definitely not what I imagined I'd be feeling when I came into his hut for the first time.

Looking away from him, I force a cheer to my voice. "Okay, I'll leave you to it."

I turn to leave, but his hands rest on the outside of my arms. "I'll walk you to bed," he offers gently.

"Wait." My feet are rooted to the ground as the lingering serum urges me to stay and say what I came to say. "I don't need you to walk me to bed. I'll go in a second, I just... Can we just wait one second?"

My heart is racing. The burn in my throat is heavy with the suggestion of freeing the words I want to speak.

So, I do. "I just wanted to be close to you. And I know that's pathetic. And unfair to you. And lacking willpower on my end. But only for a minute, I want everything to fall away, and it simply be me and you. Just Stella and Orion."

His hands skim down my arms before dropping back to his sides. A shadow crosses his features as he soaks me in from too far away. When he looks at me like that, I can see the man beneath all his obligations.

Taking a small step in, I drop my forehead to his shoulder. "Can I make a wish?"

His chest rises and falls with steady breaths, and I hear him swallow. "What do you wish for?"

Without moving, I close my eyes and tell him my wish. "For you to dream of wonderful things, and your sleep to take you somewhere so blissful, that when you wake up tomorrow, the burdens you carry don't feel so heavy."

His breathing holds for a moment, and then his hands are cupping my face, bringing my gaze to his. I'm struck with his beauty, his proximity, and his voice when he asks, "Why are you worried about my burdens?"

I admit, "I want you to be happy."

His eyes search mine, a tender smile lifting the corner of his lips before he says, "You wish for me to have a peace that I don't get in this lifetime. And I'm *okay* with that." He tucks my hair behind my ear.

The serum forces out, in a whisper, "I'd like to be your peace."

His lips part slightly, but I fill the silence. "But as good as it feels to be close to you, even just for a minute, I'd sooner turn to dust than have my presence add to your burdens."

He sighs, running his thumbs over my cheeks. "I know the feeling of wanting to steal moments with you. But you're on truth serum, Stella. I don't want you saying things you wouldn't say in the light of day. Things you might regret."

I frown at him, placing my fists on his chest gently to stop him when he tries to walk out the door with me. "This isn't the same as being drunk, where you don't know where the words are coming from. Anything I say is certifiably true. So, wouldn't it make sense—" I eye him with a smirk before continuing "—that I wouldn't regret it because the only things I can do and say are aligned with what's most true for me?"

A playful edge dances in his features as he returns my smirk tenfold.

As if I'm troubling him, he tsks. "Nice try. There is sound logic in that, but still, there's a part of your freewill not present. Yes, it might be the truth, but would you feel compelled to share it with me if not for the influence of the serum?"

His smile is prideful and arrogant when I lick my teeth, seemingly outwitted.

Squinting at him, I press a finger to his chest. "Was it not you that said it's okay to lean onto things when I need help opening up?"

He beams that show-stopping smile at me before throwing his head back in laughter. "Don't twist my words to convenience yourself. This is different."

Stifling a smile, I try to conceal the annoyance of losing this argument. But the words find their release. "Dammit."

Under my knuckles, I feel his chest rumble with amusement.

Looking into his stupidly mesmerizing eyes, I admit, "I can only hope then, that when I'm not on truth serum, I'm still brave enough to tell you how unforgivably handsome you are, and to do the many things I want to do to you."

His smile falters, his whole body stilling, and his eyes darken so fast it's as if he had no choice in the matter. Groaning in warning, he closes his eyes as if trying to reign in the montage of images I subliminally planted in his head.

I smile slowly at his reaction. "What, you're not even a little curious?" I ask, letting my eyes prowl over his face, lingering on his lips before meeting his eyes again.

Lips parting slightly, he voices the word that his eyes convey when he looks at me. "Trouble." A warning and a plea in one.

I roll my eyes. "Fine." Stepping away from him, I straighten my spine. "I really like how respectful you're being, and I realize that I'm being unfair to you right now, so I'll stop." More to myself, I mumble, "I'd probably just make a fool out of myself anyway."

Pausing at my confession, he treads carefully. I can tell he doesn't want to take advantage of my honesty, but he wants to address it. "Stella, you could never be considered a fool to someone who basks in everything you do."

It's my turn to still. My heartrate picks up, and I groan as I step back. "You're right, I should leave." My eyes convey that's the last thing I want to do, but we both exercise restraint to its capacity.

His chin dips and the masterfully-designed bastard smirks at me. "We can come back to this conversation another day."

I counter, "I might not be here another day if I'm not found trustworthy."

A wave of sadness overcomes me, and his jaw clenches at the prospect. Shaking my head, I backpedal with a sheepish smile. "That was meant to be an inside thought."

Stepping into me, he runs his hands over my hair, cupping my jaw. "No matter what, no matter how many times, I'll always find you." A loaded pause fills the air between us. "Now, go to bed. That's an order."

Grinning at him like an idiot, I step back. When I go to outstretch my hand to shake his goodnight, I nearly drop the citrine. "Oh." I face him, my body melting at the memory. "This is also why I came. To thank you."

He looks almost nervous. It's adorable, the way he rubs the back of his neck. "You're welcome—"

"Wait," I interrupt, putting a hand on his cheek softly. "Can we pause this conversation?"

He creases his brows in silent question, and I continue, "I want to tell you all the reasons why I love it. When I run out of words to thank you, I want to throw myself into your arms and kiss you—show you how much your consideration affects me. How it makes me ache for you with an anguish only described as relentless. But... I can't do any of that tonight. So, please, can we wait?"

He devours me with his eyes, his breaths coming in quicker, jaw clenching as every piece of him refrains from granting me what I told him I want—yearning for it more than I do.

Impossible.

With a softening expression, he takes in the sight of me dreamily. Slowly lifting his hand to mine, he closes my fingers around the citrine. "I look forward to it."

Desire and longing engulf me with a strength I battle to bury. Forcing a small step back, then another, I turn from him only when I'm outside. He's a close step behind me, ready to walk me to my hut.

Then I see the lady beast, her Majesty, waiting for me. Over my shoulder, I speak, "Oh, also, you don't have to get Divy to guard me. I'm sure she'd rather sleep with her kind instead of watching my hut. I'm not planning on sneaking off." I turn, a laugh dying on my lips as I see the bewilderment gracing his features.

Turning slowly, he locks eyes with Divy, who's getting up and making her way over to us.

I croon to her, "You can walk me to bed, angel girl, Orion doesn't have to." But when she pulls her ears back and pins me with a look, I correct my voice from baby speak. Instead, I straighten my shoulders and prime my voice for royalty. "My apologies, Lady Majesty. I forgot myself for a moment. Do forgive me."

I snort-laugh when she exhales in a growl, but I can tell her heart isn't in it. *I'm growing on her.*

Coming closer, she faces the direction of my hut, ready to go when I am, but not before nuzzling her nose into Orion's chest. He wraps his hands around her ears and scratches behind them. "Youhi Rousa." His chest vibrates with the sound. "Rus teyez ug farr."

One of those rare, carefree smiles lifts his lips, the muscles in his face and shoulders relaxing with it. The sight pinches my heart, as if making sure it's not dreaming.

When those eyes find me, I realize he didn't know she was sleeping outside my hut. *She's not guarding me as a prisoner.* Does she do it out of protection, because she cares for me?

The both of them decide to walk me to my hut, and we do so in silence, letting the surreality of everything settle.

Divy curls into a ball and blinks sleepily at us when Orion comes into my hut, staying until I'm snuggled in bed.

Half-turned to leave, he utters softly, "Goodnight, Lremi."

Giving him a close-lipped grin, I contemplate the funny word. "What does that mean?"

I say it back to see how it feels on my tongue. "Lremi."

As I say the word, and he tracks how I clasp the citrine to my chest, an emotion crosses his face with admiration lighting his eyes.

I raise a brow at him, my cheeks warming as my heart swells an inch. "Are you just going to stare at me, or will you tell me what it means?"

His face breaks into a smile that could get an army to lay down their weapons. "It suits you." He shrugs. "But you won't like it."

Mouth dropping open, I demand, "Why call me something that I won't like?"

Scanning my face, he leaves me confused with his departing words. "Maybe it'll grow on you."

I lay, watching the space he occupied, pondering over the secret nickname. My eyes travel to the roof and I stare blankly, the final trial looming over me. Somehow, I start to fall asleep, despite the tap on my shoulder asking me 'what the fuck will you do if you don't pass?'

CHAPTER 28
BETWEEN THE LINES

That night, I'm thrown into a twisted world of dreams. Somewhere in my subconscious, I know that Sage warned me of weird dreams, but I can't shake the feeling that something is wrong.

The gloomy forest fills with mist, coming from every direction, encircling my ankles, then knees, then hips. It feels thick against my skin like water, and I spin in a circle, searching for a direction to run in before I drown in it.

Run!

I push off into a sprint, my feet pounding against the earth as my heart thrums in my ears, sweat rolling down my skin as I try to figure out where the fog ends as it passes my chest, creeping higher. It tries to grab at my ankles, my wide eyes unable to see the hands living in it. A scream tears from me, and I reach out for the trees in my mind, my panic only increasing when I realize I can't sense them. Ice spreads under my skin, and I hear a distant echo of voices. Somehow, I'm certain the trees are trying to reach me.

How am I aware that I'm dreaming, but can't speak to them? Do I only communicate with them in my conscious state? But If I'm lucid dreaming, part of me is conscious...

"How did Little Bird fly when we cut her wings?" The string of words hisses in my ear, making me lose my footing and fall with a loud crack onto my knees. The pain lances through me, splintering my skull. But I scramble backwards, my fingers digging into soft soil until it becomes sloshy mud.

The faceless voice taunts, "We've been waiting for you, Little Bird." Whipping my head in every direction, the voice comes from my left, above me, below me, all at once.

Forcing myself back to my feet, I run with tears falling down my cheeks. "Stay away from me!" I yell to the sky.

Fear tightens its grip on my throat, and I clasp my neck, begging for air that just won't come.

The mud gets thicker and thicker, and I'm barely able to move one foot in front of the other. I start sinking. My eyes zip around me, looking for a branch to help pull myself out, but they're not my trees. They're plastic. And too far for me to reach.

The voice calls out to me, an edge in the way it drops low. "I can sense him in your mind, Birdy. Have you led me to him? Have you found the nest?"

I'm sinking lower, only my chin above the mud now, unable to speak or scream, moving as if my body is foreign to me...

Gasping, I wake to strong hands on my arms, someone above me as I blink against the dim light. Frozen, I stare at the figure, unable to find my voice. Terror seizes every inch of my body, soul, and mind.

"Stella, it's me. You're okay." His voice is rough with sleep, but like a cool balm against the raw burns of my anxiety.

My eyes start to adjust to the light, and I blink at his shirtless frame and disheveled hair, looking as if he got out of bed and ran here.

Throat dry and muscles trembling, I whisper, "Orion."

The mattress sinks as he sits down next to me. "Yes." His voice is low, gentle.

Orienting myself, I place my hand over my forehead, scanning the hut. "What are you doing in here?" I whisper, my hand stilling when I feel the hair stuck to my face and neck with sweat.

He reaches over to get my cup of water, and I push up to rest on my elbow so I can scull the entire cup.

"Divy must've known you were having a nightmare, and she came to get me." Concern laces his expression, and he scans every inch of my face, taking in any information he can along the way.

"She..." Raking his hand through his hair, he looks away, rattled. "When I realized she was coming toward your hut with her fur raised and growling, I—" His eyes find mine again, hoping I'll discern the worry he felt as the words die on his lips.

Knitting my brows, I dig through my brain. "I don't remember my dream." My admission is apologetic.

Wait... Processing the last ten seconds, I ask, "Divy was worried I was having a nightmare? And you came to me?" Forehead furrowing, my smile is slight and eager to grow.

"Of course." The words leave his mouth without hesitation, then he adds, "She was concerned, Stella. People have bad dreams, but none bad enough to get her to come wake me."

Sinking.

I turn my wide eyes on him as a flash of the dream rises in my mind, suddenly feeling as if I'm right there again. The fear crippling me was as real then as it is now, causing my fingers to shake. "I was sinking in mud," I whisper. "Someone was chasing me. I was... lost, alone, suffocating..." Instinctively, I clench my hands, willing myself to breathe.

He dips his head an inch, the movement bringing my attention back to him. The empathy on his face tangles with his power in a way that feels like witnessing fire and ice. I'm comforted by the fact he makes no sense, because neither do I.

Resting a hand gently on my knee, he assures me with a tone that can only be described as solid gold, "You're okay, you're awake now. Not sinking. Never alone." Slowly, I let his words settle over me.

Lifting a hand, he swipes the sweaty, knotted mess of hair stuck to my skin, resting his hand on the side of my neck, thumb lifting my jaw. He moves closer, eyes locked on mine, and I...

I feel his two fingers press into the spot on my neck where someone checks your pulse. *He's checking my heart rate.* Not about to kiss me, then. *Good.*

The side of his mouth ticks, picking up on what I thought, and my skin warms as a blush threatens to spread over my chest.

"Just checking your pulse," he mutters in that hypnotic voice. Then his brows draw together, eyes dropping to my neck. "It's still going quite fast," he says more to himself than to me.

Wrapping my fingers around his, I lower his hand slowly, releasing it when it's placed back to his side. "There." I smile sheepishly at him. "That'll help."

One side of his mouth rises slowly, and that's the exact moment I know *I'm* the one that's in trouble.

A bow is wrapped delicately around my self-control at this moment. It wouldn't require much. You wouldn't even call it a tug. He could draw the end of the tie between his forefinger and thumb, slide it back imperceptibly, barely a hairsbreadth of distance, and I'd unravel before his eyes—*with pleasure.*

I almost dare him to, with the way my eyes trail down to his lips, his chest, his hands—which are gripping the edge of the bed so tight his fingers might go right through the mattress.

My eyes dart to his. *Seems we are both masters of restraint.*

I blink, clearing my throat as he regains his composure.

Standing up, he informs me, "There's not long now until your final trial starts. I've got a couple of things to do beforehand." Running his hand over the new growth of beard, it looks an awful lot like he's masking. "Will you be okay?"

Rubbing my face, I respond, "Yeah. I'll be ready." I look at him through my lashes. "Thank you."

Sliding his hands into his pockets, he stares at me, as if taken somewhere else for a moment. "Remember the first time you thanked me? Look how far you've come. It just rolls off the tongue now…" He lifts his shoulder in a shrug. "With it being so often, and all."

Exaggerating an eye roll, I groan, "Ugh. Remember when you were broody and barely spoke to me? The good old days." I let out a pleased 'ahh' sound, as if those times are equivalent to nostalgic bliss.

A laugh rumbles through his chest. "I'll shut my mouth," he says, his voice lowering when he adds, "You only need to ask, and anything you want is yours."

My heart flutters, my ability to think out of order momentarily.

Finding the words, I remark, "What, and then add another 'thank you' to your tally?" Narrowing my eyes at him, I proclaim, "It's my turn to draw out some 'thank you's' from that brazen mouth of yours.

Because then, I might not feel so indebted to you for your kindness.

He looks down, throat bobbing as he swallows what he wants to say. But when his gaze snaps back to mine, it seems he's overridden the conservative voice in his head. "What if each time I earned your thanks, it's my way to thank *you*?"

Tilting my head at him, I can't help but laugh, disbelief threaded in the sound.

"In exchange for what?" I ask.

I have done nothing but bring stress into his already-overextended responsibilities.

Simply, he shares the world's most cryptic sequence of words. "More than you know."

The gleam of mischief in his expression transmutes into something more serious—grounded.

I curl back into bed and bring the blanket up, tucking it under my chin as I stare up at him. "Well, even if I don't know what that means, I get the sense the feeling is mutual."

Maybe I do know what he means. Maybe I know nothing at all. Or just maybe, both exist at the same time.

His existence, the way we dance around how we feel and the weight of it all...

Not giving him a chance to reply, I ask, "Should I be worried about whatever concoction I have to drink today?" The change of subject slightly unwinds the tension drifting around us.

Shifting his weight, he thinks about my question, opting for cryptic once again. "Fear sharpens you. Wield it."

My mind fires on all cylinders in an attempt to decode.

No luck.

Reading my expression, a hint of amusement nudges his lips into a smirk. "I'll see you soon, Lremi."

He turns to leave. That word, that... name—*where do I know that?* It wasn't a dream. I went to his hut and...

Pausing his exit, he catches the way I go rigid, and how my eyes dart across his face as the memory dawns on me.

He gives me a look—undecipherable. It's as if he's in a limbo, waiting for me to react, so it can guide *his* reaction.

I am uncomfortable. Nervous. Unremorseful. Kind of giddy, which results in a panicky laugh.

With playful accusation in my tone, I ask, "So, the king of addressing elephants in rooms is just going to let that big one walk on by?"

Taking a step toward me, he raises a brow. "When was I supposed to do that? Between your nightmare and final trial? Would that have eased your nerves?" There's a challenge clear in his tone, the way his chin dips as his eyes bore into me.

Sitting up again, I pat the bed for him to sit. "I know you have stuff to do, so I'll make this quick."

Without pause, he strides over and sits on the edge of the bed. "The floor is yours."

A flashback of us playing our beach song comes to mind, when he uttered those same words.

Closing my eyes to refocus, I start, "In case I don't pass and can't find a time to tell you this... I just want you to know that *in the light of day,* I stand by what I said. I have no regrets of a single word, gesture, or second with you. I'm grateful to have gotten it off my chest, but I'm sorry to have put you through it. I never wanted to be the hot-and-cold girl, or bring you stress."

A gentleness softens his expression as he observes me, relaxing his shoulders. He's relieved.

Reaching out, he runs his hand over the top of my head, gliding down in a soothing gesture that feels so natural, neither of us questions it. "You have nothing to apologize for. I understand you need time, and I'm making the choice to be within range whenever you want to reach for me. You aren't distant to hurt me, but to heal yourself, I know that. But, if it gets too difficult for me on the sidelines, I'll discuss it with you."

Inhaling deeply, I feel a piece of rigid guilt fall away like a rock from the side of a mountain, into the vast ocean below. I can't help but be awed by his emotional intelligence. His empathy. I triple check, asking, "You promise you'll tell me if you want me to stop coming by your hut all hopped up on serum? Or if I'm staring at you from across the room, do you promise that you'll give me the finger as a cue to look away?"

He tips his head down in laughter before meeting my eyes. "You do what feels natural, and I'll give you the finger if I don't like it. Deal?"

"Deal." I grin at him.

He continues, "And just so you know, I'm very fond of your unfiltered confessions." A smirk tempts his lips. "But I'm hoping the next one is uninfluenced."

Next one? The choice of words speaks to his confidence in me passing the final trial.

Offering him a dampened smile, I shrug with a contemplative 'hmm' sound in my chest. "I'll take it under consideration."

The other thing I consider telling him, is that if I don't pass, and I have to leave today, I'm grateful to have met him. If I'm sent packing, I'll harbor images of our time together in a locket within my soul. That I'm forever changed, since the moment I met him. That I'll continue to learn to love myself, and as the sound of his voice fades in my mind over time, the mark he made on me will always remain.

Except as he stands to leave, all I do is smile, hoping I'll get another chance.

The people of Juf'ua buzz with conversation, the morning light falling upon some familiar faces, and some still unknown to me. The clothes Sage came to give me after Orion left make soft sounds of friction as I walk toward the center of Juf'ua.

Coffee brown cargo pants start at my high waist and stretch down just loose of my skin until cinching above my boots. They're paired with a thin, long sleeve shirt—an attempt to prevent getting baked by the especially-blistering sun today. The olive green fabric sits fitted above a tank top, beige and already collecting sweat.

Adjusting the tan cap on my head and braided hair underneath, my presence entices a lull to settle over the space. Eyes land on me while mine are focused forward.

Sage's parents, TG, Orion, and the Gatherers converse in what appears to be a terse conversation. Then I see it. The backpacks, bottles of water, and five pairs of feet, dressed in hiking boots like mine.

My heart stops when I get a good look at Orion. Him dressed in casual clothing is a sight to behold—one that inclines my spirits to lift. He also wears long cargo pants, but his are black. Gracing it is a dark-beige T-shirt, and worn-in black boots. Whilst the canopy and evening light consumes us, there's no need for his cap, which means he's turned it backwards. This flips my insides upside-down.

Why is he dressed like that? Also, how is it possible that him wearing more *clothes does things for me? I thought it was supposed to be the opposite? I'm not complaining though, obviously.*

The sight of him and the Gatherers concealing sheathed knives pulls me from my thoughts.

Are the Gatherers going somewhere? Is he going, too? What about my trial?

I blanch. *I'm wearing the same clothes as them.*

In a daze, I stop walking, and they turn to approach me instead. Their proximity sounds the alarms in my mind and widens my eyes in confusion.

Orion addresses the crowd. "Mihl'e dahn, Ghana. Thank you for rising and being here for the third and final trial. We have tested—" he turns to me "—her tolerance, integrity, willingness to connect, abilities, and openness to sharing that with us. Today, we test her dedication and loyalty—to herself, to us, and to the movement."

The people utter their approval and agreement, and my breath hitches when he continues. "Her commitment is a final show of trust. To do that..." He takes one step toward me, then another. "She will join the Gatherers today on a mission."

The wave of dread collides with a fluttering of nerves and excitement, as if coal meets flames in my veins. I'm going past the barrier and into society today. I don't want to leave, but I want to prove myself. But a mission... That sounds daunting. *Am I ready for this?*

Orion turns, sweeping his eyes over the crowd again, his voice projecting for all to hear. "The mission is retrieval. To go out, collect, and return alongside our Gatherers." He inclines his head at TG. "And us."

Fuck. Fuck? Yeah, fuck.

My heart swells when the Elderly Chef steps forward, pulling everyone's attention to her as she shows concern for me. "I don't understand. If she is in danger from Discon, why take her away from the safety of Juf'ua?"

Murmurs and agreement flitter around the open space, and Orion tips his head to her as if approving the value of the question. "That's why I will be joining this trial."

The Elderly Chef steps closer to Orion, lowering her voice so only those close to him can hear—myself included. "Do not let Discon take her."

The urge to hug her overcomes me, but I resist with great strain, settling for a grateful smile. The idea of being taken and tested fills me with such dread that my fingers start to tremble. *Is this a bad idea?* Besides the terrifying possibility of me being taken and what that means for me, I can't help but wonder what that would mean for Juf'ua and the world.

Orion places a hand on her shoulder, looking at me swiftly with a determination that might ease the tension in my shoulders a fraction.

He says to her calmly, "We went back and forth about how to amend the third trial with our suspicions of her Natura abilities, and no matter what we came up with, the trials cannot conclude without a test of her loyalty to the movement." Orion looks to TG. "With us there, we agreed the risk is significantly reduced. We are taking extra precautions with the way we set it up."

Nerves force me to crack all my knuckles, my head facing the ground as I take this all in. I suppose hearing that they deeply considered all of this helps. *Orion and TG are coming.* Knowing I won't be sent off with the people who most hate my guts in this village, now *that* urges me to send a silent thanks to the Divine.

I hear the retreat and soft-spoken acceptance of the Elderly Chef, and I lift my chin to find her eyes. She gives me a smile that holds strength, that might even give me some.

The familiar pull of Orion snaps me back to the moment, just as he turns to address me. "Do you consent to the third and final Trial of Trust? To join Juf'ua and fight alongside us—bringing balance back to the world?

I'm going back into society. Nerves prickle my scalp, but it's quickly met with an aliveness rising from the earth, bleeding through the soles of my feet and filling my entire being.

With a sureness that caresses each syllable, I state, "Yes, I consent to the third and final Trial of Trust. To join Juf'ua and fight alongside you. To bring balance back to the world."

I tense at the sudden sound of yips tearing through the crowd, realizing that some of the musicians and cooks that I've had the pleasure of mingling with cheer. *For me.* For the prospect of me joining them. I can't help it. My face splits into a grin.

Eyes finding their way back to Orion, I see he's already watching me, a smile of his own competing with mine.

Sage squeezes me in a hug. "You will be excellent."

Over her shoulder, I lock on a pair of eyes that harden like steel. Gatherer Girl. She barely even tries to conceal the loathing that runs through her veins instead of blood when she looks at me.

Well, this is going to be interesting.

CHAPTER 29
EARNED

Orion leads us through the forest in a line, methodically sweeping it with his eyes and placing surprisingly-quiet steps one after the other. But, to no one's surprise, Gatherer Girl follows directly behind him, nipping at his heels like a puppy eager for attention.

It's been hours of walking. The skin around my toes clicks its tongue in annoyance, wasting all that time healing my blisters from when I first arrived. This journey threatens, then delivers its promise to make more. At least this time, my socks aren't sloshy from the downpour of rain I faced before my capture.

The setting sun blinks sleepily, easing the thick blanket of heat off our sweat-drenched skin. As Orion leads us, I realize how my trek alone into the forest was so erratic and directionally challenged, because apparently, we're nearing halfway to the town in one day's journey.

In the quiet sound of mismatched steps and minimal small talk, my eyes drift over the Gatherers in front of me. Behind Gatherer Girl is a man with red hair, the color complimentary to his temperament and general scathe when he looks me up and down like a mean girl.

Also irritated by my existence is the older man behind him. He's perpetually silent, barely acknowledging anyone, which contradicts the fact one of his eyebrows is always a little bit

arched—cursed to wear a feature that expresses interest and approachability, when it's more likely he loathes the idea of it.

Directly in front of me is a boy that can't be older than eighteen, quick to placate and always seeking direction from Orion—observing him as if every inhale might be the beginning of a speech laced with wisdom he longs for. These are the Gatherers, who seem to severely dislike me based on loyalty to their *queen*.

Behind me, TG flicks my braid, earning a flat look over my shoulder.

I tsk at him. "Child."

The returning chuckle draws enigmatic eyes from Orion, and vengeful daggers from Gatherer Girl.

Since meeting her, I've noticed how vital she is to the village, and how others seem pleased by her extroverted charisma.

Just me, then, that gives her an attitude. I suppose I'm the stick.

Gatherer Girl takes a little extra step to bring her next to Orion, brushing her fingers gently on his back as she speaks to him. I won't deny that my ego inflates slightly at the step he takes to distance himself from her physical touch.

Lowering her voice, she asks, "Do you not think this is a dangerous risk? I understand it's necessary for part of her trial, but she isn't trained as we all had to be before gathering."

She's an evil genius. A question is soft spoken with big eyes to seem innocent in her query, but it's loud enough that anyone can hear and have doubt planted in their head. Subliminal campaigning. A snake in the grass, slithering by and hissing at me every now and then. If I get too close and step on her tail, she'll bite me with a lethal dose.

Orion looks over to her, expression neutral. Without looking at me, I sense his thoughts—his internal war of wanting to protect me, and the logical concerns of one of his best Gatherers.

"I understand your concern," he says firmly, "and that is why I am here. We've taken extra precautions to ensure everyone's safety. Should things even allude to danger, we abort."

She sighs, a slight clench of her jaw evident. "I don't understand why you're making all these exceptions. Our trials took weeks to plan. She comes here on a day's notice? That's besides the fact that she was even given a trial after her escape." She looks over her shoulder, abandoning the fourth wall she pretended to create and glares at me. I tip my hat to her, a tight smile on my face.

Orion's voice hints at fervency. "We all have our roles. Mine is to make the executive decisions. You're aware of my abilities and instincts, yet you question me on this? Normally, I'd welcome it. Encourage it. But I do question your underlying concern and what kind of impact it has on your skepticism.

Her cheeks heat as he continues, "Trust in me, as you always have, and in the fact that the planning was thorough, in ways you are not privy to."

Watching them, I see something float seamlessly between them—a mutual respect. History that precedes me. I bristle against the sight. My blood boils with envy and unease, but I force myself to breathe through it.

In. Out. In...

She pinches her nose, her expression transforming to one of compliance before starting to walk behind him again.

Orion looks back at me, and I quickly glance away from him. *They're such a good fit. He'll realize that eventually.* I know he feels something for me, but I can't help waiting for the other shoe to drop.

Sensing the lingering tension of the group, he stops abruptly. "Alright. I'm not going to force anyone into thinking astray from their natural inclination. I encourage you to reflect on where the unwillingness to accept these circumstances stems from.

I'm open to your concerns, but I will not stand for unjustified disconnection that can put this mission at risk. We need to go into this with tact, and knowing we have each other's backs." He meets every set of eyes, even mine briefly, before I drop them to the ground. "Understood?" he asks.

We all mumble our agreement.

"Thank you." He turns and continues to lead us.

A true leader. Shaking off whatever bond we may have, I need to see him as only that. I'm on a mission. My final trial. I need to focus, instead of letting jealousy, insecurity, and self-deprecating beliefs deter me from my greater purpose.

Pulling my shoulders back, I forge onwards. Even as darkness is well upon us, we push ahead.

After another couple of hours, I'm grateful not to be nearly stumbling over protruding roots as we stop to set up our sleeping bags. Plopping on top of them to unpack the food we have, we endure the world's most awkward dinner. I'm forced to withstand weary glances, even though they're fewer since Orion's speech earlier.

He hasn't spoken to me and sits the furthest away from me as we form a lumpy circle shape. No stolen glances, brushing of a hand, quick smile... We are nothing more than platonic teammates. *Which is what I need. True independence. Self-regulation.* His attention only takes from that. But why does that thought cause doubt to upset my stomach?

The more I stay firm in isolation being required for self-love, the more I realize that could've been a way to protect myself. Maybe if I did try to let someone in, and they chose not to return the affection, it would confirm every thought I have around it not being possible for me to be treasured. Adored. Cherished. *Loved.* And it would break me. But Orion said he wanted to choose me. He listed all the reasons why.

But he also doesn't really know you, does he?

Well, he did see Pain. But he doesn't deserve to be the one to soothe Pain. That's my job. And I'm working on it.

But won't you always be? Will you always be waiting to live, to live?

The trees... Is this part of what they meant? That I'm ready, only when I realize I'm not, and that's okay?

TG snaps me out of my spiral, pulling my attention from an ant trying to carry a crumb three times its size. "Here." He offers me some of his dates for dessert.

I raise my brows in pleasant surprise. "Thanks." Taking two, I bite into its rich and earthy sweetness. He's always been so kind to me, even when he's being an ass.

"Stella," I say softly with a flash of a smile. It still feels strange, making such a big deal about a name, but there's something in the exchange I've come to love. The vulnerability of it. Something I never thought I'd look forward to. But I trust him. *Here is a piece of me, TG.*

I don't even question it, until he doesn't say anything back. He just stares at me. *Oh, fuck. Does he know what I'm trying to say?* I point to the center of my chest. "Me."

I give him a tight smile and desperately look for where I lost that pesky ant.

I've never been more aware of silence.

As my cheeks warm, I curse the date I chew on for starting this whole thing. *Was this a weird time to share it?*

I glance around, and everyone pretends they weren't just looking at me. Except for Orion, who stares at me.

Taking a book from Orion's page, I address the elephant.

Turning on TG, I ask, "Did I just make this even more awkward?"

"Yes," Gatherer Girl answers flatly. Orion's Biggest Fan chortles and watches with great intrigue as this unfolds.

Observing me, TG puts his hand in the air between us, palm to the starry sky. For a second, I think he wants his date back, but then he says, "Stella."

Looking back at him, I raise a brow in question.

A broad smile overcomes his face, lit up like the small lamp we encircle. "Sorry, I just wasn't expecting that. Thank you for sharing your name with me."

I tentatively lay my palm down on his, and his fingers slowly close around mine. "I'm Cadel—second in charge to Juf'ua and honored to be with you on the final trial."

Surprise drifts through me from him offering his name, and his status amongst the village. I assumed Sage's parents had that role. He's been coasting behind the curtains of charge.

"Thanks, Cadel." I pull my hand from his and drop it in my lap. "Guess I'll have to stop calling you TG now."

He chuckles. "So, you never added to my list of nicknames? I was kind of curious if you'd come up with some to be as colorful as Orion's." He side-glances at the Chief with a knowing smirk.

I lift a shoulder. "I did. But they're not ones a lady should say out loud."

He pulls back, looking at me, his smile growing. "Oh, so it's like that?"

The corner of my mouth lifts, answering his question for me.

Something stands out that I want to ask. "Second in charge? Honestly, I thought that was Sage's parents."

Shaking his head, I feel the eyes on us as he states matter-of-factly, "I can see why you'd think that. I'm not as loud-mouthed as Orion, or as in-your-business as Sage's parents."

How am I meant to respond to that? If he sees the sheen of panic in my eyes, it doesn't stop him from responding with an 'it's true' shrug.

Nervously glancing at Orion, I see the mask of indifference slip into silent rage. My stomach drops.

Placing his hands on his knees, Orion pushes himself to stand. In the next second, he has TG's—Cadel's—shirt fisted in his hands as he pushes him against a tree, eyes fierce and ice-cold as glaciers.

Gasping, I blink wide-eyed at the horror before me.

Needles crawl over my skin when Orion speaks, the lethality of his low voice jarring. "Loud-mouthed?"

Cadel doesn't flinch. He stares at him, his breaths coming in sharp when he retorts, "I said what I said."

Orion's eyes darken, pressing harder against Cadel's chest, and then he drops his head, laughing. Then Cadel's laughing. Orion steps back, releasing the death grip on him, and suddenly, everyone's erupting into unsurprised cackles.

Cadel looks down at his shirt, seeing the wrinkles and slight tearing there. "Asshole, you ruined my shirt."

I stare at them stunned, and Red Hair points to me. "Look at her face!" He guffaws at my expense.

The amused glint in Orion's eyes tenderize with a tilt of his head when he looks at me. He starts striding over with casual ease, and Cadel follows before they sit down on either side of me.

Orion explains, "Cadel and I have been good friends—"

Cadel interrupts, with an exaggerated 'ahem.' "Brothers..."

Orion's lip twitches, before amending, "Brothers." He continues, "For a very long time. Cadel leads from the back, whereas I'm more in front. He's always there to screw my head back on..." Orion stops, looking over when Cadel interrupts him.

"You're making too many innuendos for me not to comment. Are you doing that on purpose? Because it's true, I really am more of a bottom kind of guy."

Orion rubs between his brows with two fingers. "I meant, you're there for me to lean on, and vice versa."

Cadel pats his shoulder. "Well, now we sound like we're in love."

Orion winks at him, and my face turns bright red at the sight. He looks back at me, and if he sees my blush, he doesn't show it. "Let me try to say it this way. As you can tell, he brings a certain lightness to his *leadership*, which compliments my *leadership* when I become..."

Cadel fills the space. "Crabby."

Orion shoots him a look. "I was going to say 'too serious.'"

Cadel laughs. "Yeah, I've got way less responsibility. That's all you, brother. The least I can do is make you laugh when you start sulking."

Orion makes a warning sound in his throat as he stretches out his neck, practicing restraint. "Yes, what would I do without you?"

Cadel leans across me to slap him on the knee. "That's what I'm saying." Then to me, he adds, "Seriously though, if I'm not trying to get under your skin, chances are I don't like you. So, don't take what I say personally."

Red Hair frowns, commenting, "You never make fun of me."

Cadel swipes his tongue across his bottom lip, "Uh..."

Everyone bursts out laughing again, while Red Hair glares at us.

I crack a smile. Glimpsing Orion's bromance with Cadel fills me with such joy that I swear my insides are made of pink flowers and the taste in my mouth is pure sugar. Orion almost looks giddy. I adore it.

Not long after, I climb into my sleeping bag and start to doze off with that smile still on my face. The stars watch over us, and I fall asleep reciting the names I've earned: Sage, Orion, Sloane, Rainer, Cadel.

CHAPTER 30
GREAT PRETENDER

Swiping sleep from my eyes, I sit up groggily to Orion's voice waking everyone up.

Shaking the light coating of morning dew from my sleeping bag, I roll it up and pack it away. We all disperse to change into clean versions of yesterday's clothes and relieve ourselves.

Orion stands with his arms crossed, a weird mix of calming and commanding as he gives us our orders.

"First, we catch the bus." He hands us our bus fares. I jerk my head back in shock at the sight of the gold coins. Surprise shudders through me. I know Juf'ua lives as a secret village deep within this forest, but I can't make sense of why or how he has money. They don't work. *Where do they get it?* He answers my wide-eyed expression with a single phrase. "I'll explain later."

Pinning me with a look, he instructs, "The entire day, you're joined at my hip. Everyone else, disperse on the bus."

Everyone responds with their understanding, then he's staring at me. He lifts his brow slightly, and I realize he's waiting for verbal confirmation. "Oh." I clear my throat, quickly saying, "Okay."

Gatherer Girl rolls her eyes at my ignorance, and I have to stop myself from the strange urge to hiss at her.

Orion points at me and Red Hair, and then states, "We are group one. We get off at the twelfth stop. You four, group two." He points to Cadel, Gatherer Girl, Orion's Biggest Fan, and Curious George. "Get off at thirteen. We'll all go different directions and follow our routes to the warehouse."

With a racing heart, I try my best to conceal how lost I am. *Route? Warehouse? If we get separated...*

Orion looks at me, somehow reading my thoughts. "Joined at the hip." The reminder offers a slight reprieve to the nervous nausea in my stomach.

"Okay," I confirm.

Looking over everyone, he announces, "We meet with Dojo, and he'll give us the package. Group two, take the piece you need, and we'll take the rest back to the apartment."

Part of this must be routine, or they've had a planning meeting before we left, because there's no way they understand these half-sentences with fuck-all context.

He looks at Cadel when he instructs, "While we're waiting, you deliver the package. We'll wait fifteen minutes before heading to the meeting spot."

Definitely left out of a planning meeting.

Cadel asks, "How long do we wait if either of our groups don't show up?"

What? Looking over at Orion, I wait for him to be offended or deny this baseless question, but instead, he simply says, "Five minutes."

Cadel bows his head and says, "Agreed."

Scanning around the group, I see everyone with straight spines, feeling the readiness exude from them—the kind of confidence that comes from extensive experience.

He looks at me, and I fight the urge to gulp.

His voice is unfaltering as he admits, "I've been back many times to the Discon facility since my escape with Sage and her parents, rescuing more people over the years, bringing them to Juf'ua or to return home."

Even though this is the official facility where Activs are taken from around the world and brought to, Watchers are everywhere. Discon is everywhere. The people who run it are a virus on the world, and it's crucial we stay under the radar and avoid the cameras." He dips his chin, as if preparing me for what he's about to say. "Stella, Discon knows about me and what I've been doing. They're hunting me."

My body turns solid as rocks as I stare at him with my heart on my sleeve—speechless. *Why is he here risking himself?* Suddenly, Gatherer Girl's concern yesterday doesn't seem so unreasonable.

I glance at her, and it's as if she knows where my mind goes, because her returning look is half-lidded and bleak.

Orion adds, a false calm in his voice, "It's only fair. I'm hunting them, too."

The only thing I can manage is, "How do we avoid cameras and Watchers? Who are they?" Suddenly, the question feels like the most important one I've ever asked.

Cadel answers, but it takes a second for me to drag my eyes from Orion to him. "The society officials that prevent and manage crime, enforcing its rules... Well, select groups within these officials all over the world are recruited as Watchers. The perfect disguise to be anywhere and take people from the street or their home without question."

I hold in the shiver that wants to wrack my body. What I can't hide is the worry in my expression.

Orion's Biggest Fan has incredible amounts of fervor in his voice as he adds, "We need to avoid them and cameras, because they'll either try to capture him or alert Discon that he's here. So don't draw any attention to him."

I raise my eyebrows, taken aback by the passionate threat. "I wouldn't dare," I reply simply.

Orion gives him a warning look, which earns me an apologetic smile from the Chiefs Biggest Fan.

Orion continues, "What we're going to pick up is high quality earpieces, so we don't need to rely on Sage's mum's ability of telepathy. Plus this way, we can get information returned from the guy on the inside. Group two is going to deliver a piece while we take the rest back with us."

The question slips past my lips before I realize it's coming. "Why is the man on the inside not trying to escape?"

Everyone is quiet for a beat, and I shift my weight, "Sorry..." Before I can finish my apology for cutting in, I'm met with an answer.

Orion's voice has an undertone of sadness, a weight in the air pressing around us as he shares the reason. "His little sister died during a test. Before Sage's parents escaped, he disclosed the story with them. All he was told was 'your sister gave her life trying to help us in the name of bettering everyone's lives. She's a hero.'"

I recoil at the complexity of these sick people. As I gauge everyone's reactions, I see a flame of rage burn in their eyes— myself included.

Orion's jaw ticks. "When we first came back, he was who we came to break out. But he decided to stay, begging we take the elder lady instead, and he would stay and help from the inside—to avenge his sister and all the lost lives."

Filled with sorrow and awe, my heart breaks for the man who undergoes testing and torture as a sacrifice for the Activs. For his sister's memory.

Orion doesn't let the morbidity settle too far before redirecting us back to the mission. He addresses group two, "You're going the long way, through the loading dock, and getting it under the fence. Get out as quickly as possible."

Scrunching my brows, I start, "Where are they going?" What loading dock are they going to? My breath catches, remembering what Orion said earlier, about getting ear pieces to the inside guy. Eyes widening in shock, I blurt out, "Discon?"

When everyone turns to me, their expressions are a mix of determination and concealed memories, and I shut my mouth in response. Going back to that place is already a big deal for them, and I'm not helping. I decide to take on more of a shadowing presence and stop asking questions.

"Sorry," I direct to Orion. "Keep going."

Orion's attention lingers on me, his hand flexing as if he was about to reach for me, maybe in some kind of reassurance. But he decides against it for some reason.

He looks over to Gatherer Girl and Curious George, wordlessly asking them a question.

Red Hair eyes me up and down after seemingly getting a look from Curious George to speak on his behalf. Whether he doesn't want to speak at all, or not to me specifically, I'm not sure.

With hues of reluctance, Red Hair explains, "He's a Natura." My stomach tightens. "He'll work with the soil to move the earpiece under the fence and raise a weed to signal where it is."

Hope lifts the weight from my chest, now knowing he's a Natura too, but both of them seem pissed at the idea of him sharing this ability with me. *What did Orion say?* That I was far more powerful than what they know to be true of Naturas. Do they hate me because they're jealous? Or is it just their loyalty to Gatherer Girl…

As if summoned by the thought, she adds, "And I will be cloaking us."

My mouth drops open, to which she seems surprised by my genuine awe. She looks to Orion before continuing, "Part of what I do is alter the perception of what people think they're seeing. Make them question reality itself."

Scanning between the two of them, I lift my brows, blinking slowly to demonstrate how impressed I am by the phenomenon. "Well, damn," I comment simply.

Orion's Biggest Fan seems to read the satisfied expression on his face as they share this with me, and joins in, wanting to please his Chief. "I'm a Ling. I'll be there to redirect through persuasive speech if we get stopped by an officer. But, just so you know, the Watchers wear these bracelets that make them nearly immune to abilities being used on them, so try not to attract one."

Shit. Okay. I smile at him, to thank him for sharing that information with me. Not that he sees it anyway, since he's watching Orion and basking at the nod of thanks the village leader gives him.

Everyone turns to Red Hair, who rolls his eyes better than any female I've ever known. "I'm a Logma. I'm the person who reads shifts in plans. I can tap into the threads of which motivates someone's decision-making. I get a tinge in my gut if someone veers off course due to my presence, or something close to me. So, if we need to change course at any point based on what I pick up, you're best off listening."

Orion thanks them with a look, and then his eyes are locked on mine. "So, are you ready for the mission?"

Wondering how my abilities come into this, I ask, "What do you want me to do?"

Orion answers, "Observe. Follow. Help us when we ask, and when we don't."

Determination coats my features. The hairs on my arms rise with the ancient power within me. It drums its fingers in anticipation. Eagerness. The leaves on the trees rustle. Warmth of encouragement licks up my spine, and I straighten it, rolling my shoulders back.

"Understood," I answer.

Orion's eyes lift to the rustle of trees that disguises itself in the wind. But he knows. He sees it. *Me.*

Always does.

The first few steps amongst the street feels jarring to all my senses. *The grey.* The speed in which people walk. The cluttered buildings. A car honking nearby makes me jump into Orion's side, the sound so foreign and sharp even after only a short time away from it.

Society. The whole world is like this, and I forgot just how debilitating all this stimulation and clinical landscape feels to exist in. It jars my soul with razor blades.

He looks at me with tender amusement, and I roll my eyes at him as if he was the one who made the car honk. When he laughs low in his chest, I go to storm off as a joke, but an arm is quickly wrapped around my waist, pulling me back the few steps I took and firmly planting me next to him. "Joined at—"

"Joined at the hip, yes," I finish for him, a teasing tone lacing my voice.

Only when he doesn't return my smile, do I see something behind his soft eyes.

"I mean it," he says firmly.

Studying his expression, I assure him. "I will."

Looking around, I vaguely recognize where we are. I was staying close to here the night before I went to meet the hiking group...

Oh, shit. It hits me then...

"Uh," I speak softly to Orion. "So, I'm not sure, but I think people might be looking for me, too."

It's as if he buffers, trying to process what I just said. "What do you mean?"

Scrunching my nose, I admit, "Well, as you know, I came to this forest on a three-day guided tour, and I spent everything I had on it. Pretended to be an Elite. But..." I pull my lips against my teeth before continuing. "I kind of waited for them to fall asleep, and illegally snuck off. A few days later, that's when Sage's parents found me crossing the barrier. So... yeah, they might be looking for me, too."

I expect him to be angry. Frustrated. Worried. But what I don't expect is for him to smile with abandon. I blink at the sight, then my own smile lifts the corners of my mouth.

"You're not mad?" I ask.

His forehead furrows. "Mad? Not even close." His eyes convey something akin to delight. My whole body slackens— *melts*—at the tenderness of his expression.

Lifting his hand to lower my cap slightly, he adds, "But you will need to be extra mindful of cameras, okay? Don't look up... for anything."

"Okay," I breathe.

But in the next breath, I'm cursing. "Shit!" I turn to him slowly, realizing I've been so consumed in myself that I didn't even think of what might've happened after I snuck off. "They would've contacted my parents, my emergency contacts. They're probably worried sick!"

My mind starts racing, wondering how I'm going to contact them. *Can I contact them, or will that put the movement at risk by giving away our location? I'm Activ now—what if they catch me on the way to a payphone and take me to Discon? Or track me to the others and take them? Wait... They wouldn't be tracking me as an Activ, but as a missing person, and if they find me, what if that's when they realize I'm Activ...*

Orion's shoulder brushes mine, "I know you're panicking right now, and I'm sorry, but you need to put this aside in your mind and not let it distract you. We will figure that out when we finish the mission and return to safety."

I scoff, "Easier said than done."

He pauses. "Let it go or let it be the thing that endangers us all."

I grumble, knowing he's right but also feeling nauseated by the guilt. I try desperately to shove the worried expressions of my parents' faces out of my mind.

As we start approaching the market just before the bus stop, group two shifts into tourists. Not high-spirited enough to draw attention, but curious enough about their surroundings to pass as visitors—should anyone be watching.

Gatherer Girl strolls like she has all the time in the world, while Curious George scans a map. Orion's Biggest Fan leans over his shoulder to look as well, whilst Cadel pulls out an apple. He takes a bite and speaks idly to the group. *What is happening right now?* My spine stiffens as fear ricochets through me. I watch them morph into people with backstories, props, and degrees in performance all of a sudden. *What the fuck do I do?* My eyes dart around, suddenly convinced I'm being watched on the cameras, my feet refusing to move.

A throat clears next to me. "You're okay. Just look forward and follow me." Orion's voice is smooth like velvet, his casual smile proportionate to his relaxed disposition. I might be gawking.

The shift in his energy and assuming this easy-breezy character is shocking.

Why wouldn't they tell me to prepare for this? I still feel like every set of eyes are on me. The Gatherers are expecting me to do something. Are the Watchers here? What do they look like? Am I about to give us away? I feel bright yellow in a sea of silver. My pulse hammers beneath my skin, my mouth going dry...

A hand rests on my lower back casually, and I expect to hear Orion, but it's Cadel who speaks, coming up next to me. "You're walking so stiff, it looks like puppet strings are controlling your limbs. Just act *normal*. Slow your steps, relax..."

Orion's voice is lower than I have ever heard it when he commands through a deceptive smile, enunciating each word, "Hands off."

That does nothing to relax me. Quite the opposite.

Cadel follows the instruction, but not before he aims a mischievous smirk at Orion, then winks at me.

Orion adds, "She just needs a minute. Now go back to your group."

Cadel raises his hands in innocence, and in return, I flip him off, which only enables his grin to become more wicked as he turns to join his group.

Peeking at Orion, I catch the way his jaw ticks as he stares daggers at the back of Cadel's retreating form.

We walk behind them, a frustrated sound coming from Orion, and I purse my lips with a question burning in my mind. *Has he told Cadel of what's between us, or is it simply that obvious?*

He slides past what just happened, and asks, "What do you do when you need to calm yourself?"

I blink at the sudden change of thought he thrusts upon me. Inhaling deeply, instinctively, I do the steps. *Breathe. Come back to my body. Positive and reassuring thoughts.*

When I've calmed myself enough, I tentatively ask Orion, "What was that?"

The muscle in his jaw ticks. He knows exactly what I'm referring to.

Adjusting his cap, he says, "That... was Cadel getting under my skin because unfortunately, he likes me."

I incline my head, offering a 'hmm' sound of contemplation. The roguish gleam in his eyes tells me he knows exactly what I'm thinking. *The idea of someone else's hands on me, comforting me, showing me affection... Cadel knew he would react like that. He did it to fuck with him.*

My cheeks heat at the implication. "Seems like Cadel was just trying to calm my nerves."

Orion's eyes bore into me, his expression unreadable.

I can't help it. The words leave my mouth, my tone pairing with a slight lift of my brow. "'Hands. Off.'"

Warmth encases his amused expression, and then he leans closer, lowering his voice. "I don't think he'll make that mistake again."

My insides sing at his closeness. Our eyes stay locked, and any humor that was there fades away with the rest of the world.

Blinking myself back into my body, I focus on walking, and try not to hyper fixate on how I react to him, to these moments. But I just know he saw it in the way I shivered. I put distance between us, and focus on the group ahead of us who are in their roles so seamlessly, while the boldness I had two seconds ago wears off.

"Stella." He says my name, and I just can't look at him. *Why is it so fucking hot today?*

When he says my name again, voice lower and laced with 'look at me' undertones, I have no choice but to oblige. A glint of humor lights his eyes, a grin sneaking onto his lips.

Is he laughing at me? The slip in my bravado? My emotional ineptitude? My unwillingness to hold my ground when I admit I'm worth thinking about in a desirable context?

Frustrated, I shake my head and look forward, imploring him, "Stop looking at me like that."

"Like what?" he asks.

I shoot him a flat look, curtly stating, "As if my nerves and inexperience are funny to you."

Emotions cross his face too quickly to name before he settles on one that's serious. "I'm fascinated—in awe of the way you react. Feel. Think. I'm not making fun of your emotions, I'm just... seeing you. I'm sorry it came across as teasing."

"I'm glad to be your entertainment," I mutter under my breath.

"Stella, did you hear the rest of what I said? Please don't put words in my mouth, or infer that I meant any kind of harm to you."

I wipe my sweaty hands on my pants, absorbing how right he is. "I'm sorry. I was doing the whole self-sabotaging thing again because I felt exposed and vulnerable and then made that your fault." Closing my eyes, I replay what he said about being fascinated, and in awe of me. That he likes to *see* me, unfiltered.

I admit, "It's almost as if I resisted the nice things you said, because it didn't feel true, or earned. I don't want you to get your hopes up, thinking I'm 'fascinating,' and deserving of you being 'awestruck.' I'm actually just filled with terror and poofs of black smoke, which act on behalf of my personality."

He steps closer, inclining his head. "If only you could slip into my mind and see yourself as I do." My attention drops to the long slates of cement beneath our feet—ones I'm familiar with and do not miss at all. *I miss the soft press of my bare feet in lush grass or crunchy leaves.*

"I'd like that," I finally respond.

"The day you realize your worth..." The conviction in his voice beckons my eyes to meet his. "Creations, *that* will be terrifying. In a way that makes me want to beg you to let me be there, to stand beside you and witness it."

Fuck. My body heats and coils, winding around his stupid, little finger. I adjust my cap and clear my throat, nervously trying to cover up the way his words affect me.

"That's very kind of you to say. I would also like you to be there," I blurt out with the single brain cell that's working.

Brushing the tips of his fingers with mine as we walk, I know he hears the truth of what I mean between the clumsy words I managed.

Desperate to change the subject, I say, "I know I kind of panicked before, with not being informed of the performing element of the mission..."

He explains, "That was intentional. Part of the trial."

I give him an inquisitive look, curious as to how it was part of the trial.

He provides, "Would you trust us to have your back? Could you adapt, meld with the team, react at the drop of a hat..."

Pursing my lips, I comment sarcastically, "Cool. I love that. Was the part when I started sweating and walking like a puppet the moment I passed?"

"We have a long way to go before the trial is over, don't worry."

I need to redeem myself... And then, an idea floats into my mind. It has me tilting my head at Orion in question. Intrigue lights his expression.

I tread carefully. "Well, I can still save this. But you might not like it."

"Hmm?" he questions.

I tap a finger to my lips, stating, "It's a loophole."

Before he can add a sentence to the bemused expression he wears, I interlock my fingers with his.

He's a true professional. Not even a flinch in his steps. No tensing of any muscles, only responding with ease, as if we've walked hand in hand a thousand times before. But his scrutinous eyes ask a question. 'What are you doing?'

I explain, "Just for this mission, we could assume the role of two people, in a relationship, just enjoying each other's company. Our *performance*."

I seemed to have convinced myself that this could go without repercussions. That this loophole would allow me to give in to how close I want to be to him without it being *real*. A trial within a trial.

Now? I realize that this probably isn't a good idea, and second guess myself. I wonder if it's unfair to *him*. I start to pull my hand from his, as I quickly say, "But if it's—"

He pulls me impossibly closer, our arms crossed over each other's, his thumb swiping fondly over mine.

A flutter in my stomach rises all the way up, likely making my eyes sparkle as I soak in the sight of his easy smile. Rare. Special. It's on par with oxygen in terms of necessary for my survival.

I lean closer to whisper in his ear. "Pretend I just said something flirty." Then I lean back, my expression unmasked as I admire him.

Tongue briefly swiping across his bottom lip, his gaze threatens to consume me. A low sound comes from his chest before he says, "Something flirty looks good on you."

Would this be us, in a parallel universe?

Sitting next to him at a bus stop, our knees, shoulders, and everything on my left side pressed against the warmth of his frame. My hand is clasped between both of his and drawn into his lap as we watch the city move on without us. The simplicity of presence, and how it can make something so normal, so seemingly mundane, feel euphoric... I beg for a way to immortalize this moment.

Leaning my head on his shoulder, I close my eyes, absorbing the exact sounds around me, how the metal seat we sit on feels cool beneath my legs in contrast to the humid heat coating the city.

Stealing a glance at him, I quickly adjust his hat so it's crooked. He reaches up and pulls mine down so it covers my eyes. When I pull it back up, giggling, I'm gifted with that dreamy gaze and soft laugh of his.

"Bus is here," Cadel says as he walks past us, and then we're up, everyone finding their seats as far away from each other as possible.

Orion skims his thumb back and forth over mine, and I don't think he even realizes he's doing it. His absentminded affection as he scans the area, paired with that near-imperceptible firmness of his features, means he's deep in focus.

Intense admiration expands the cold places in my heart, but I realize the source isn't caused by him. *It's me.* The magic of this moment—I'm part of that, allowing the joy to filter through. But

I'm also firm in the boundary that I need more time before this goes further than a stolen moment.

Surety settles in my bones as the thought flitters around my mind. *I want him, but I want me more.* To know who I'm not, learn my destiny... I prioritize and crave that, more than love from another. *That* is the source of my heart expanding.

CHAPTER 31
A WAKENING

At the twelfth stop, we get off, and I have to force myself not to look back at group two, who stays on the bus. Out of habit, I almost send a silent plea up to the sky, to *Orion*, for them to be alright, but my eyes drop to whose fingers interlock with mine...

Nope. Not going there.

The smell of a bakeshop commands my attention, and I have to physically restrain myself from appeasing the greedy gurgle in my stomach. Even though this isn't my country, it all looks the same, with duplicative threads that run through every city in the world. I wonder, with how unmodified and intoxicating Juf'ua's food is, would their bread be different, too?

"That smells good," I whisper absentmindedly.

Orion laughs low in his chest, squeezing my hand. "Focus."

The mix of freshly-made bread and his affection casts a spell on me, eliciting a groan. "I am, but on the wrong thing," I mutter.

I feel his eyes on me, and I turn to meet them. *Fire.* Ready to turn me to embers.

I echo his earlier instruction. "Focus."

The corner of his mouth twitches upward before we drag our attention away from each other and to the direction we're heading, playing into our roles.

We blend in by matching the median pace around us, with Red Hair walking slightly ahead. *I forgot the feeling of people passing you in a rush, the cramped enclosure that is society. The sullen faces that never turn to greet the one next to them. It's breaking my heart all over again, even if the point is for them not to notice us.*

Taking a sharp turn, we enter an industrial part of town, and I can feel we're close, by the way Orion squeezes my hand, as if in preparation. As we turn down another side-alley, we wait for group two.

When they arrive, Gatherer Girl's laser-focus locks on the joining of mine and Orion's hands. But Orion doesn't seem to notice, as he has a wordless conversation with Cadel before we turn and walk the short distance to the warehouse. Everyone has dropped their assumed personas, but he doesn't let go.

Never let go.

He has to.

I have to. Because then we aren't pretending anymore.

Were we ever?

I slide my hand from Orion's, just as Curious George approaches a door. He doesn't knock, but instead, shows his face to a tiny camera hovering above the doorframe. A soft click, then three more, and the door yawns open.

The person standing there is cloaked in a large hoodie, and they step aside as we walk in.

Darting my eyes around the low-lit space, it's not what I expected. Unorganized parts of tech or mechanics are scattered around, with stacked shelves of mismatched boxes. *Not a rebel's layer, then.* I suppose they're going for inconspicuous.

As we walk toward a large metal desk covered in wires and parts, I tense up at the third look the hooded person gives me over his shoulder.

A tightness around my lungs coils further at his nervous movement, and I glance around the group to see if anyone is seeing what I am—if they, too, feel oddness and uncertainty. But no one meets my gaze. No one is speaking. My lips part, thinking that maybe if I introduce myself to him, he won't feel wary of me, or maybe I might feel comfort letting my voice pierce the snuffed silence of the space we walk through. But I stop myself, wondering if they might be silent for a reason.

Memories of when I first got to Juf'ua and no one wanting me to speak looms in my muscles, my stomach a vessel for unease. Why can't I just know what's going on? Can't they tell me where we are? I remember him saying we are to retrieve something, is this where we are doing it? Or was that a lie, part of the test, and I'm walking into something far more trying than my last two trials? Maybe this one will be physical. Maybe they'll leave me here, lock me up, and I have to figure out how to escape to prove I can help the Activ's do the same.

My mind reels, pulling me into a spiral of overthinking. Orion glances at me, and reading the bemusement in my face, he offers me a subtle dip of his chin in reassurance. A message. *Trust goes both ways.*

Remembering that I'm being tested on my ability to adapt, I allow myself to melt into the shadows, the silence, watching as Cadel steps forward and extends his hand to collect the small box from the hooded man. My stomach lurches, seeing the skin slip past his hoodie sleeve, balancing the box between his wrists. Red, jagged lines scar his skin, a wound still healing as I know there were once hands there.

Don't react.

Flicking my eyes back to the desk, the mechanical parts identify themselves easier now. Fingers, wires... *He's building hands.*

Taking two earpieces out and putting it in his pocket, Cadel then hands the small box to me. I pause, wondering if I'm supposed to also take two ear pieces out. *No.* They're delivering, our team is retrieving. I'm supposed to keep the rest. My fingers hold tight on the dusty cardboard box, as I drop my bag from my shoulders and bury it deep in there.

Hooded Man watches me, and when I rise, slinging my backpack over my shoulder, I incline my head to him in greeting. No sign of anxiety, not a trace of concern readable in my body language.

Orion turns on his heel and moves toward the door we came in. *Joined at the hip.* I make my way next. The slight echo of footsteps falling behind us fills the space, and I know the others are following.

Squinting against the light when we exit, I expect some form of conversation to unfold, planning or something. But group two just continues walking in different directions. Then, they're gone.

Red Hair walks ahead of us, and I remember Orion telling us earlier that we would go from here to the apartment. Leaning into him, he immediately, and naturally, throws his arm over my shoulders.

I ask quietly, "Can we talk yet?"

He speaks low. "Quickly."

Darting my eyes around, I try to think of which question to ask out of the swarming options.

"Was he rescued from—"

Something flickers across his face, an anguish behind his eyes, his lips a firm line.

"Yes." Orion's answer is curt.

I exhale through my nose, the weight of the single word like a punch in the gut. The image of his mutilated skin is forever burned into my mind.

I don't ask anything else, but to my surprise, he offers one more sentence. "His ability was dangerous to Discon, so they removed the parts of him that enabled it when he kept overriding the suppressant."

I still, until a shiver rolls up my spine at the gruesome image that infiltrates my mind. "They took his hands?" I can't hide the horror in the whispered question.

Orion pulls me closer. "And his voice."

My hand tightens on Orion's shirt, acid burning the back of my throat as my body physically revolts the reality of it. But I want to understand the hooded man. If I pass and join Juf'ua, I want to picture him when we seek vengeance.

Orion explains, "His ability is with engineering. A Logma. They took his hands so he couldn't build, and took his voice so he couldn't teach. We don't speak, because that is what he asks of us. We don't sign, because he cannot reply."

"Then how do you orchestrate these trades? How did he build the earpieces?"

"We communicate in other ways. And they didn't take his feet."

I gawk at him. *He built these tiny, intricate things with his feet?*

"He is incredible."

It's on the tip of my tongue, to ask about *his* ability, but I hesitate. *He would tell me if he wanted to.*

He smiles down at me. "He is. A valuable member of the movement." He lifts a brow at me. "No more questions until we get back, alright?"

Offering him an understanding nod, I agree. "Okay."

Sitting at the bus stop, I'm curled into Orion's side, his rough palm pressed against the soft skin of mine, as we wordlessly reassume our roles. Without thinking, I lift my other hand, skimming my finger over the faded white scar along his wrist. Curiosity won out over common sense and sensitivity, and only when he tenses his hand against mine do I realize the error.

I gasp as an icy alarm courses through my veins. I rush the words out, "I'm sorry, I shouldn't have done that."

For a moment, we just stay like this, his expression far removed from what I thought I'd find. It's as if it was relief, shock—not that I had triggered him.

His throat bobs. "When we get back to Juf'ua, ask me about them."

I blink at him, my forehead furrowing at the unveiling that accompanies his words. The willingness to share something so personal. "I'd love to know more about you. Your story." Lifting his hand to my lips, I press a gentle kiss to the scar on his wrist. "I'll ask."

I fear any shred of control will slip through my fingers if he looks at me like this for too long. Like winter turning to spring. Snow melting from the mountains, flowers and green grass springing from the earth, eager to feel the sun's rays. That's how this moment feels. And I don't think it's me that's the thawing ice. I think, for once, I might be the warmth.

A frustrated groan pulls my attention, followed by an exaggerated, "Ahem."

Red Hair is not pleased to be third wheeling, clear in the whine of his voice when he announces with a pointed look, "Bus is coming."

Orion's expression switches from tenderness to the unreadable and armored facade when he turns to face Red Hair. "Thank you."

The bus ride is a blur as I look out the window, only seeing the thoughts in my head. I snap back to reality when it's time to get off. Not long after, we're standing in front of an old-style rectangle building, one of the few left with red bricks. I read in a history book a long time ago that the world was once filled with homes that had character, individuality. This is the first time in my life I've seen a red brick home in person. It strikes me through the heart, wondering what the world looked like a couple centuries ago.

Orion types in a code, and the aged buzz sound is testament to the longstanding building. Taking the stairs up to the third level, I run my fingers over the grainy paint on the walls. A damp, musty, and floral scent fills my nostrils, and I can't help but wonder if it's the tenants lingering perfume or just the aged carpets, holding a combination of everyone's scent.

They've been here before. Many times, by the looks of it, as they both stop in front of a door with this unspoken knowing. Orion pulls a key from his pocket, unlocking the door and pushing it open. Red Hair walks in, but I stop dead in my tracks, and Orion has to usher me inside.

Shock crashes into me, the lounge space furnished in a style I've never seen before. It's like something I read from a novel about a home filled with personality and quirks. *Color.* I'm used to neutral tones, minimal and sleek metal ornaments, glass and Gyprock—high tech and convenience taking priority over the wholesome and intimate spaces. Maybe that's why I was curious about how Orion decorated his hut. I guess I wanted a window to his soul, knowing Juf'ua is a place where you're free to express yourself. Even with the small details like books, blankets, and hand-carved furniture, it still lacked the essence of Orion. This place, though... It drips with the essence of whoever lives here.

Pale green sofas, with faded fauna hand-stitched into it, adorn the space. There's dark oak side tables with quirky ornaments. One in particular captures my attention, as the forearm-sized frog sits in an unbuttoned flannel jacket, legs hanging over the edge and holding a rod as if fishing into the air, smiling with closed eyes.

I jump when Red Hair drops his backpack with a loud thud, taking out an ankle length and long-sleeve navy overall outfit. He slips into it, just on the top of his clothing.

I ask, "Why are you changing into that?"

After two beats without a response, Orion answers, "He's posing as a market sweeper to keep watch for when group two arrives at the meeting spot. He'll come get us when they're spotted, we'll meet up, then head back into the forest. It's not far from the apartment."

"Oh." Looking over to Red Hair, my gratitude for knowing what's happening next falls dead in the air when his grimace communicates absolutely nothing but annoyance at my existence.

"What's your problem?" I blurt out, a rush of bubbling anger rising to defend my outburst.

His response grates on my nerves. "I don't have time for this. I actually have work to do."

Orion moves to step towards him, and my hand shoots to his chest before he can take it. Instead, *I'm* stepping forward, meeting Red Hair's glacial stare with the flames in mine.

I release the lock on my tense jaw as I reply, dismissing him. "Off you go, then."

His lips curl in slightly, eyes hardening—but one quick glance at Orion has him schooling his features to neutral. He bows his head to him before slipping out the door.

Groaning in frustration, I storm over to the couch and plop down. Two seconds pass before I'm restless and standing again.

Trust goes both ways. But they don't trust me. They tolerate me. Barely. An understanding drops on my shoulders of the real reason Orion is here. I thought it was to monitor and assess me, whilst ensuring my protection against being taken by Discon. But beyond that, he must've picked up on the way the Gatherers are towards me, and he's also here to monitor *them*. I was meant to prove myself in this trial—that I am capable of joining Juf'ua. And I think on some level, I wanted to prove it to the Gatherers too, because part of me just wants to be accepted. If I can convince people who don't like me to see my worth, maybe I can convince *myself* I'm worthy.

But maybe I'm not. This whole trial, I've been the furthest from an asset to Juf'ua. I've felt like a lost puppy, using it as an excuse to be close with Orion. To convince myself that I might belong here. But how can I even do that if I'm walking around blind, constantly unsure? I can't plan out my moves, but maybe that's the point. They said that they wanted to assess my teamwork, adaptability, and how I operate under pressure. But, I haven't kept a cool head. I fucking failed. *I'm weak.* Why would the Gatherers ever see me as an asset, or want someone like me to join this movement? Maybe he's right. They're better off without me, and that's exactly why they hate me.

Of course they do. *Even I do.* Or did. *Fuck.* I'm so tired of being a never-ending project.

The uncertainty of my future, the world, these people that suffer under the cruelty and control of greedy people. I just want to be someone who can help—them, and myself.

I want to go home, but I don't have one. I don't think I ever really did. I just want to belong somewhere. I want Sage. I want Orion. But I can't have them without getting better.

What I'd give to crawl out of my skin and escape this feeling.

The floor creaks as I pace around, the skin on the side of my thumbnail red as I bite at it.

Jumping with a gasp, Orion's hands lay on my shoulders, turning me to face him. "What's going on?" His tone is gentle, his focus on me unbreakable as he studies me with the precision of his alter ego: interrogator.

Shaking my head at him, I shrug him off. "Don't," I order.

Stop being the thing I seek.

Without moving a single muscle, he voices what he thinks is the sole cause of my spiraling. "Stella, forget what he said. You *are* working. You *are* helping."

Looking at him, I let him see the seething anger behind my eyes—the way my face holds years and years of torment. "How? I'm a fucking waste of space, Orion, and you're the only one who doesn't think that."

I let him see the resistance I feel toward life. I know my expression holds the rage I feel when I think about how I didn't fucking choose to endure a lifetime of feeling unfinished. Lesson after lesson, I must be better, prove myself. I want to tip my head back and yell at the ceiling, "For who? What's the point?"

"Fuck." The words slip out past my lips as I turn away from him and press my palms to my temples. Tears start to threaten my eyeline. *I'm spiraling.*

I know I look as crazy as I feel.

Feeling the intensity of his inspective stare, I know he's assessing. Calculating. Then, his voice comes in firm and assuring. "I'm here if you want me."

Turning to him, I see he's leaning against the doorframe, hands in his pockets—giving me space.

I want you.

Stepping closer to him with one small movement, I imagine him holding me through the deep sadness. Another step, I picture him kissing away the anger. The ache. One more step, and suddenly I'm in front of him, staring into those eyes that promise to nurture and protect, if only I decide to let him.

Don't be weak. Figure this out yourself.

Nails digging into my palms, I groan as I resist him, taking a step back and staring at the maroon carpet.

I'm the raging force against his repose. The violent waves in a storm, and he's the still sand lacing the ocean floor.

My eyes lift to his chest, his heart. Then my hands are pressed against it, whispering three words between us. "Don't move. Please."

His strong frame steadies me, letting me feed off his calm as I process.

I peek at him, only seeing empathy scrawled across his face. Would he understand the way a claw digs into my heart and rips hope out when I least expect it?

My eyes drop to his mouth. *He could make me forget.* All I'd have to do is press my lips to his. Let him consume me. Let what I feel for him bury what I don't want to feel for myself. His chest rises in a sharp inhale, and I realize I just did it again, and he felt it. "Shit." I clasp his shirt into a fist.

"I hate this." I whisper the layered confession with my eyes squeezed shut.

His voice is rough when he asks, "May I?"

When I open my eyes, I see his hand hover above mine. When I nod, his fingers lay atop mine, my eyes drifting shut once again.

"I'm feeling too much. It's all..." I must be shaking, because I can feel the world around me vibrate, trembling along with my limbs.

In the next second, something falls and breaks. My eyes shoot open, and that's when I see it. The fishing frog has smashed on the ground, and other items in the room have a subtle buzzing sound coming from them as they vibrate.

"Stella." My head whips to Orion when he speaks, his slightly widened-eyes scanning the room, before locking with mine. Determination like I have never seen holds his expression firm and focused. Clasping both my hands in his, he drags his thumbs over mine in a repetitive soothing motion. "Focus on my voice."

Stuttering my words, I ask, "What—am I... Is this me?" Panic grows in frantic bursts, and suddenly, the building trembles with a low rumble.

Taking a step forward, he tightens his grip on my hands, tilting his chin down and sharpening my focus on him in the process. "Your abilities, they're being driven by your internal world right now. Close your eyes, tell me what you feel."

Doing what he says, a tear slips down my cheek, my whole body shaking now. "Um..." I sniffle. "Anger."

"Okay, work with the anger. Find its route."

Rage simmers inside, hot and vile, seeking and attacking the light desperate to shine—slapping the hand away that tries to feed me optimism. My life has been one big blur, rushed and disconnected. Forced to compete against people who could be my community instead. But that's never been society's priority. Eat, or get eaten. Fit this box mentally, or else suffer from falling through the cracks. Now that I'm here, with this ethereal destiny, I wonder if they picked the wrong person. My jaw clenches, the fire inside burning recklessly, consuming me.

"I'm angry that my life still doesn't feel like my own."

I hear the sternness of his voice as he reflects back to me, "Your life doesn't feel like your own. Alright, so you're angry with feeling out of control."

I incline my head with a rigid neck. At the same moment, the light fixtures blow, and I flinch. Orion shields me from the tiny shards of glass that spray over the room.

He watches me calmly and takes a deep breath, giving me a look to do the same.

I do.

Squeezing his hands so tight I might break his fingers, my voice leans over to a plead. "What do I do now? How do I turn the feelings off?"

Searching my eyes, he asks, "I don't think resisting your anger is going to help. I think you need to surrender to it, for it to dissipate. You have all the power here. Right now, your ability is something slipping out of your control, but you can tame it. Choose acceptance of your anger, and this moment, and then let it go."

My list. He memorized it.

I narrate as I process. "Okay. Um. Fuck... Point number 11: I love surrendering control and finding flow."

Think of times where you surrendered.

I believed in the Orion constellation, surrendering control to it. Our kiss under the tree. Talking with the trees. Dancing with Sage. Pain.

I felt safe, because I accepted whatever and whoever I was in those moments.

Letting go of his hands, I feel his fingers slip from mine as I walk slowly to the couch and sit. Wrapping my arms around myself, I force deep breaths in and out until the shudder subsides.

Focusing on my feet pressed against the floor, I go into the chasm, and I talk to Pain. *I know you feel the weight of the world; you feel life is unjust. But that's not all it is. We're learning that. Equal and opposites of everything, remember? You got mad, and then other things started piling on once we opened the door of rage, everything behind it flooded in.*

I hear her voice, replying to me. *I've only ever wanted to be loved by you. Can you love me even like this? The worst version of yourself?*

Shifting so my hands lay over my heart, I recite to her, *Point number 14: I keep promises with myself. And I promised we'd do this together. At our best and at our worst, we've always been worthy of each other's love.*

Her answer doesn't echo in my mind. I don't sense it in the chasm of my being. She answers through the immediate stilling of the world around me.

We did it. I actually self-regulated in real time.

I feel the pride emanate from Orion, which only reflects my own.

Hovering above me though, is the fact my abilities are manifesting. Growing. If I pay close enough attention, I can sense there's more beneath the surface. More power.

In the exact same moment I contemplate the depth of what I might be possible of, Red Hair comes bursting through the door, heaving breaths, as if he sprinted here at full force.

The panic in his voice reflects that of his wide eyes. "There are Watchers *everywhere*."

CHAPTER 32
UNLEASHED

Terror is ablaze in Red Hair's eyes as he comes in and throws his backpack over his shoulder.

Orion switches gears to Chief. "How many?"

Red Hair shakes his head. "Dozens. The earthquake drew out the officials, saying they need to search and scan people to make sure everyone is alright and accounted for. But..." He pauses. "I can tell. This is the Watchers, and they don't think it was natural. They're looking for Activs."

Slowly, I drag my eyes over to Orion, whose stare is already pinned on me while deep in thought. He looks over to Red Hair, only to tell him that I was the one who caused the earthquake.

Red Hair's eyes nearly pop out of his head, "What?" he exclaims.

Orion moves to check out the window, nudging the curtain an inch with his finger.

Red Hair's beady eyes burn into the side of my face, and I turn to meet them head on. They sear into me with a passion of disdain. Touching the tip of his tongue to his incisor, he tells me with a look that I fucked up. My stomach sinks as he makes a sound of frustration in his throat, looking away sharply as if the sight of me is incorrigible to him.

Never mind proving myself to him, I have to stop him from trying to kill me with his mind. My heart beats wildly, a strange and newly-familiar sensation bubbling from inside me.

Protection. Self-defense. If I'm being tested on working as a team, where is *his* sense of teamwork? He's never once made me feel welcome, comfortable, at the very least, respected as a fellow human. *He hates me? Well, I hate him.*

Orion turns back toward us, his strides carrying him across the room with a composure and power that speaks to his unrelenting leadership. The determination in his eyes, the slight pinch between his eyebrows, and the command in his voice puts my body on alert.

"Getting back to Juf'ua without getting caught is going to be harder now. I need you two to *focus.*"

My lips pinch, avoiding looking at Red Hair in case the urge to set off another earthquake hits.

Orion orders, "The chaos outside will help, we'll use it. By any means necessary, do not get scanned. Do not stop for anything. Do not let your emotions waver. Understood?"

I'm not sure if I'm nodding or shaking my head when I ask, "How can you be sure they didn't just think it was a real earthquake?"

Red Hair answers in that tone that reflects his perpetual annoyance with me. "Discon's tracking devices are everywhere—engineered to detect unusual activity and designed specifically to highlight people when using their abilities. They would've already compared it to their earthquake readers, knowing it was from an Activ. If they can pick up on someone composing music with their ability, they'd know if someone threw an energetical hissy fit."

This motherfucker. My fists clench at his words, at the icy contempt in his expression.

I spit my next words at him. "Your asshole attitude was the fucking catalyst—"

"That's enough," Orion interrupts, voice raised. "We have to go."

Looking at Red Hair, concentrated energy ripples from Orion, the air in the room freezing as if intimidated by the sheer power of him. "Watch your mouth," descends from the Chief's lips in a voice I'd crumble against if it were aimed at me.

Looking at me, his expression softens a fraction, his voice taking on that silky element I crave, but relenting none of the authority. "Control your emotions."

Then, he's walking out the door, holding it open so we can slip out after he's cleared the hallway.

"What about group two?" I ask, quickening my steps next to them.

Orion's gaze sweeps the perimeter like a machine. "Cadel will be leading them back to Juf'ua after seeing the Watchers."

Pausing before we exit the building, I go inside my mind, trying to find a foothold to keep calm. An image of the stream floats into my mind's eye, specifically how in the afternoon, the light shines from behind the white wisteria flowers hanging low over the water, framing its edges in a soft yellow glow.

I hold onto that for dear life as we break out onto the street.

Anarchy.

The first thing I notice is news crews setting up. *Stay away from the cameras.*

The next thing I see is the damage. Market stalls tipped, roofs caved, the road cracking... Somehow, the building we were in stands fairly strong. *The eye of the storm.*

Then, I see the Watchers. They're fucking everywhere, crawling between every gap that someone doesn't stand in or run through, these handheld thin rods clasped in their grips as they wave them over people's faces before letting them go.

Orion turns to Red Hair. "Disappear. Use everything you've learned, and do not get caught. Meet us in the forest. Do you understand?"

Red Hair doesn't waver. "Understood." A steely grit overcomes his expression as he turns, and in a blink, I can't spot which direction he even went.

Orion pulls me toward a shattered shop window and leans down to pull his blade from the sheath under his shirt. Then, he puts it in my hand. My heart drops to my stomach. I stare at it.

Before I can even ask, he's telling me what he wants me to do with it. "Cut me." He points to his forehead. "Here. Deep enough for a lot of blood."

I pale, barely able to croak out, "What? No—"

He steps close to me, shielding us as he picks up a hand to caress my cheek. "I need you to do this. Trust me."

The blade starts shaking in my hand, picturing it breaking his skin, and then dragging it across his forehead... "I don't want to hurt you, Orion."

He places a hand on my shoulder. "I would do it myself, but I can sense three Watchers closing in on us. They'll see me do it." I notice the way he's angled himself now, so I could swipe the knife with his body covering the action.

Imploring with his eyes and dipping his chin, he orders, "Now, Stella. They're coming."

Gritting my teeth, I let out a sob as I place the tip of the blade across his forehead, push in, and drag it across as quickly and subtly as I can. "I'm sorry." The whisper is swallowed by the chaos around us.

Blood gushes out instantly, running down his closed eye and through his lashes, streaking his face. *He didn't tense, move, flinch, or react at all.* My eyes trail over his other scars, a nauseating horror dawning on me.

"Perfect." He holds my chin, looking me in the eyes. "Their scanners won't recognize me like this, and if anyone tries to stop us, I need you to be frantic, erratic, seeking medical attention. Do not let them scan you. We're going to keep running until I say stop. Understood?"

I nod fervently, blurting out, "Yes, yes, I understand."

"Excuse me." The world freezes. Fear trails a sharp claw down my spine as I hold Orion's gaze. *The Watchers are right behind him.*

I've got one second to save this.

I gasp at the same time I subtly hand Orion the knife. I scream, "It won't stop bleeding!" while he tucks it into his waist band.

I turn to the Watcher, eyes wild and using my tear-stained cheeks to my benefit. "We need help! Medical attention!" Pulling Orion away, his head hangs low and his hand is pressed to the gushing wound. He feigns not being able to see through the blood, and I rush past the Watchers, guiding him by his elbow. "Baby, don't let go of it! Keep the pressure on!"

We're meters away when I hear that same voice call after us, "Wait! Stop right there!" I shoot a look behind us to see him pushing through the crowd.

I snap back at him with frantic rage, "My husband is injured! He needs help!"

We force our way through the crowd, and I don't look back. Not even when another Watcher looks over to us, instructing, "Stop!"

"Do not turn around. Keep going," Orion instructs, fixing my cap when it gets knocked sideways by someone colliding with me.

We manage to make it to the side road that leads to the forest, nearly at the locked fence. Orion boosts me up to climb first with an ease I am certain should not be possible. I stare at him as I straddle the top, but he doesn't spare a second to acknowledge my shock while he throws the back packs up to me to drop on the other side.

Something in the near distance catches my eye, and my heart sinks. *No.* But then I recognize them, and it's like a defibrillator to my heart. Group two is sprinting towards us, and a smile starts to bloom on my face. *They made it. We're going—*

Fuck. A wave of black uniforms rolls around the corner as a hoard of Watchers chase them.

"Orion!" I yell out to him, pointing so he can see.

He curses and climbs back down the fence.

"What are you doing?" I yell in panic, starting to follow him, but he abruptly stops me.

"Get to the ground on the other side, Stella. Now." His voice holds an uncompromising tone.

I watch in horror as he bends his knees, clasping his hands in front of him.

He's going to hoist them all up? What about him? Razor-sharp talons born of fear tear through my heart, my lungs, arms, legs... *Will he have time to...*

"Stella," he orders. "Control your emotions. Focus on the task."

Shaking my head, I climb down the fence and my feet hit the ground in a soft thud. Metal wires separate us as I stand on the other side, a sickness swarming in my stomach.

Cadel runs so fast he gets ahead of everyone, meeting us at the fence and mirroring Orion's position.

First to reach us is Gatherer Girl, stepping into Orion's locked fingers as he propels her to the top of the fence.

I gasp at the sheer power of that throw, as if she were a pebble.

The Watchers call out, "E-52, stop!"

Everyone tenses at the code, Gatherer Girl visibly turning to stone at the number.

Orion is yelling, "Move it!" Curious George is in Cadel's locked fingers, being launched next. One by one, everyone lands on the other side of the fence.

In seconds, Cadel and Orion are climbing it, dropping from the top of the twelve-foot fence.

How do they move like that?

The Watchers have their batons ready, their faces covered behind masks. The sight screams that we are the enemy. You can *feel* it.

Then, we're running.

After a few beats, Gatherer Girl's voice shudders as she admits to the group, "That was my number. They know it's me."

Orion's voice comes in, calm and comforting. "They won't get you. Any of us. Understood?"

Everyone replies in unison, even me. "Understood."

Every nerve on high alert, I glance over my shoulder, and in the distance, I see the Watchers start their ascent up the fence.

We run deep into the forest, taking the route through thick vines in hopes of disappearing.

I don't know how long we've run for, but my legs threaten to give out underneath me. My lungs are tired and burning, wheezing for air, but I don't stop.

Deep into the forest, we spot Red Hair, who stands abruptly the second he sees us, not hesitating before joining us in our race back to Juf'ua.

I can feel myself start to slow, to drift behind the group, and Orion orders Cadel to lead while he falls behind with me.

"No," I exclaim. "Go, keep running! I'm fine!" I stop, dropping my hands to my knees as I try to catch my breath. "I finally..." I take a deep breath, pinching my eyes shut against the sharp stitch in my side. "Understand those cliché 'go on without me' moments in movies."

He swipes the blood from his eye, stopping to stand in front of me. "Not going to happen," he confirms. Stepping behind me, he slips my backpack from my shoulders, grabbing my water out and handing it to me. I sip it between heavy pants, face throbbing from the over-exertion.

I force the words out, letting them shove past the embarrassment. "Orion, I'm holding everyone back. I can't run all the way back to Juf'ua. I can hide somewhere."

He searches my eyes. "The barrier is closer than you think. We took a very long way out here, using the time to familiarize the others with you before the mission."

I'd gasp in surprise if I wasn't already doing so in desperate attempts to fucking stay conscious. "Okay," I manage. "How far?"

He tilts his head. "Another kilometer or two."

Passing him the water, I interlock my fingers on the crown of my head, expanding my lungs as I try to slow my heartrate—pleading Creation to take my stitch away.

"Okay." I all but cough the word out.

Hearing the collective and approaching thumps of running, I whip my head to the right, expecting to see Watchers, but instead, I see everyone approaching, coming back for me. My skin heats even more if that's possible, and I demand, "Go, don't let me hold you back. Please, I'm right behind you."

Curious George responds, his voice and accent not at all what I expected him to sound like when he scoffs, "That's not how this works, Quaker."

I stare at him, a strange mix of emotions coursing through me at the simple sentence. The nickname—the depths of it being the cause of this turmoil but used in a tone that alludes to endearment.

Cadel comes up to us, addressing the cut on Orion's head. "Are you good?" He scans us both head to toe, looking for more injuries.

Orion claps him on the shoulder. "We're good. You?" he asks, examining him and everyone else. Nods go around the group, and even if I still feel in a bit of a peaked daze, I mimic the gesture.

"Okay," I announce, slipping back into my backpack. "I'm ready. Let's go."

After a brief pause and shared glances, we all turn and run. My mind pushes my body past its limits. We cut through the spaces between long and wide trunks, finding a rhythm as we dart toward the barrier.

We make some ground by the time Gatherer Girl slots herself next to me, and she just can't seem to help herself. "You can't be reacting like that on a mission, it'll get us all killed."

Barely able to spare the air, I manage to retort, "I just learned I have abilities, and they're manifesting. I wouldn't knowingly endanger you all, or do that to the town."

She is ready with a rebuttal. "Oh yes, your abilities. Touching Orion with your mind, earthquake tantrums, and tree-girl adventures. So glad you're here to help us, we'd be lost without you."

Without missing a beat, I reply, "I'm still working out if I can smack you over the head with my mind. That'd be good."

She rips my arm back, jolting me to a stop as she plants her feet. Staring through her lashes at me, she seethes through gritted teeth, "Why do it with your mind? You too pathetic to throw a swing?"

A slow smile tilts my lips upward. "I really get under your skin, don't I?"

Her face contorts in anger. The next second, she shoves me so hard I stumble back a few steps, but she quickly closes the distance until her scowl hovers inches from mine. The energy buzzing underneath my skin awakens, wanting vengeance—*wanting her to back the fuck up.*

I faintly notice the others stop, and Orion's presence striding toward us. "Are you two done? We don't have time for this!"

Rage consumes the logic and reason of his concern as I throw my hand out. "No, let her get it off her chest. I know she's been *dying* to."

Cadel runs his hands down his face. "Seriously?"

I'm not sure who he's scolding, but I don't take my eyes off her as she seethes, "You've been nothing but trouble from the start. A waste of space. We're better off without you."

Nothing I haven't already thought about myself.

But then, she says the wrong thing to me. "Go and cry about your pitiful excuse of pain with your little trees and leave us alone."

When I inhale, it feels as though I'm breathing in the life force itself. Pure power. It energizes me, fills me to the brim with this roaring pulsation that lives deep in my bones. Every fiber of my being hones in on her. *The target.* Pain awakens the chasm, my ability surging to the surface, quivering eagerly under my skin.

I vaguely notice the trees around me start to rustle. I'm barely aware of the ground underneath her starting to pulse, before thick roots emerge from the earth, wrapping around her ankles as she tries to scramble backwards. *Don't let her move an inch.*

CHAPTER 33
STAY

I don't think about what I want to do or try to control the earth. I *will* it, as nature knows my thoughts and intentions in the exact same moment that I do. Maybe even before I do. We're unified. As a lioness approaches her prey, I take a step toward Gatherer Girl. Sounds around me condense into a single, flat pitch. Orion and Cadel's hands are on me, trying to pull me back, shake me out of this daze. I need them off me, and the earth beneath our feet shifts, shooting upwards into a wall, knocking them away and separating us.

"Am I still pathetic, Gatherer Girl?" I hiss through my teeth.

Somehow, Orion breaks through the wall of packed earth and rock, and he's standing between me and Gatherer Girl, hands on my shoulders. I lean to catch the sheer terror etched into Gatherer Girl's face, reveling in it. But Orion leans with me, blocking my view of anything but him.

"Move," I demand. My power sees his unwavering frame as an obstacle between me and what I want, but when he speaks softly, cupping my cheek, I listen. "Hey, Lremi—focus on me."

Something in me remembers the name, the man saying it. *Orion.*

He recites to me, "Rule your emotions, don't let them rule you. We can't draw attention to us, alright?" It's the undertone of urgency in his voice that has me calming. An unspoken communication encourages the vines holding Gatherer Girl to unravel and draw back into the earth. I don't see it past Orion shielding her from my vision, but I *feel* it release her.

Find your foothold. I close my eyes, picturing the white wisteria flowers in Juf'ua, drifting softly in the wind. When I open my eyes and they lock with his, it's almost as if *he* were staring at it, and I was watching the reflection of the tree in his eyes.

All but Cadel surround Gatherer Girl, pulling her along, speaking softly to her.

Cadel steps closer to Orion and I, addressing everyone. "We really need to move. No fucking talking the rest of the way unless it's necessary. It's not safe to stay here longer."

Gatherer Girl doesn't look at me, and a part of myself shrivels at the memory of what I did to her, and the genuine fear in her eyes. I'd had enough, but I regret taking precious time from us all.

We break into a run; the only sound is heavy breathing and pounding footsteps, the eerie silence from the birds and bugs in the forest setting me on edge.

Light fades as the sun starts to indicate evening is coming, and Orion announces we're about five minutes away from the barrier.

I feel a wave of awareness swarm me, followed by a collective announcement in my head.

I gasp, and everyone looks at me. "They said run faster. The trees. Now!"

Everyone exchanges glances and looks around for the threat.

"They're closing in," the trees warn.

I snap at them, "You need to trust me. Move, now!"

Orion repeats the command, and the others go from a run to a sprint for the final distance to the barrier. We're in a close clump, jumping over thick roots and ducking under heavy branches, my legs and lungs begging for me to stop. But I can't, because then they will, too.

My heart constricts in anxiety, as a cry fills the air. "There they are!"

The Watchers found us.

Panicked glances are shared, and the group disperses from the clumped formation.

Looking over to Gatherer Girl, he asks, "Can you cloak us?"

Her features set into firm lines, immediately trying, and I gape when a couple of the others wink in and out of sight. "Fuck!" She tries again, but only a few of us disappear. Seconds later, they reappear. "I've never done it for more than three people. And it's not holding!"

Orion calls back, "It's okay, save your energy. Keep running!"

Orion stays close to me, running at a fraction of his speed to match my pace. Looking over at him, I see the contemplation between his brows, staring back at me, at the Watchers, calculating.

Dread falls through me. "If you're about to fucking pick me up, think again. You'll slow us both down."

His eyebrows raise. "How did you—"

"I can see it on your face," I say through heaving breaths.

He genuinely looks concerned for me, and I'm ashamed at how disheveled and weak I must look right now to earn such an expression from him.

In the corner of my eye, I catch a glimpse of movement that has time slowing. Through the gaps between trees, I watch as Red Hair trips and collides with the ground. Before any of us can react, Gatherer Girl skids to a halt and doubles back. I'm whipping my head between the path ahead of me, and watching as Gatherer Girl hooks her arms underneath his, hoisting him to his feet, and shoving him ahead of her as they push off into a sprint. But those few seconds cost them. Cost *her*.

The Watchers gain on her, and fear twists a knife into my gut. I may dislike the girl, but no one deserves the torture of Discon.

I call out to the trees. *"Can you stop them? Help her?"*

A feeling of resistance hits my chest, and they say, *"No, Star Child. You have to channel our power, we can't act on your behalf or interfere."*

Mentally groaning at them, I ask, *"How do I channel?"*

An overwhelming surety puffs through my chest. *"You already did it. Just will it. Believe it to happen."*

The Watchers are less than twenty meters behind Gatherer Girl now, and I see Orion's entire body sharpen, his focus racing between everyone. His mind works overtime as he battles between an obligation to keep everyone safe, but I'm the weakest. All, or me. I can't force this choice upon him. I have to not be the weakest. At the thought, something moves inside me—yawns wider with sputters of sparks rising to meet the urgency of this sprint to Juf'ua.

"Where is the barrier?" I ask.

A pulsing throb of energy pulls against my skin like a magnet, drawing my focus toward the direction I need to go. The trees confirm my attention caught their signal by spreading the leaves, making way for light to shine on the spot and reveal a sheen of a wall to glimmer mid-air—as if the barrier manipulated the natural light and water vapors to reveal itself to me. It's gone a half a second later, but I saw it.

The searing lick of flame each time I take a breath nearly brings me to my knees, pushing my body too hard. But I can't stop. Less than three hundred meters.

This will be my fault if she gets captured.

Suddenly, I get an idea.

Looking to my right, I try to get the vines to come up and grab the Watchers feet like I did with Gatherer Girl, but it feels like the power rises and fizzles the harder I try to visualize what I want them to do. *Shit, shit, shit, I'm running out of time.*

"I don't know how to do this!" I mentally yell at the trees.

No answer.

I glance at the ground before Gatherer Girl, and remember not to try to control nature, but realize *I am* nature. A faint sense of the power under the ground reveals itself to me. I watch the snaked roots below the soil form an ethereal, luminescent kaleidoscope. A network. The pulsing of their aliveness fires in communication, with raw energy. *I need that.* I am that.

I look over to Orion. "I'm going to use the network, make sure the others get across."

"What?" he barks out, about to protest, but I interrupt.

"I'm going to get Gatherer Girl. See the earth's pulse beneath us? I'll channel it." I stop when his awed and confused expression signals he has no idea what I'm talking about. "Just... trust me. *Please.*"

He pauses only one moment. "Go."

I look over to Gatherer Girl and veer right, keeping my pace as I weave through the trees and cross toward her, adrenaline erasing the surety my legs cannot push any harder.

Her wild eyes search mine, and I catch the panic in her voice as she demands, "What are you doing?"

I don't answer her. I solely focus on the pulses beneath our feet, forgetting how close the Watchers are now. Ignoring the way they yell at each other to hurry.

Please work. Please.

I imagine the electric energy being drawn up in tendrils like smoke, aiming for us like we're magnets. The life force energy that grows these trees, gives them their power, is tangible—transferable. It's the same source that grows us and gives us our power.

I will us to move faster, and the energy transfers through the soil, melding with the makings of our own energy, reflecting the reality of my will. I've never felt more awake or alive than the very second the energy encases me and Gatherer Girl, making us not separate entities, but one. We're propelled forward.

Fuck.

I think about us going faster, and I feel our steps waver, and slow, as if glitching. *Don't think, don't command. Will it.*

Our energy is renewed, our capacity expanded.

I see in my peripheral that her eyes drop down to her feet, then to me, but I don't break focus.

The pulse of life vibrates within us, and we use that to run, instead of the exertion it takes to do it with only our physical bodies.

I'm panting, sweating. Not from the exertion, this time— it's from being almost... too full of energy. *But we're going to make it.*

Our feet barely skim the ground as we soar through the air, closing in the distance. The others wait on the other side, frantically waving us towards them and yelling their encouragement to keep going. *We're actually going to make it.*

In the final seconds of our sprint, I feel something cutting through the air behind us, toward her. I don't have time to look, or to think about what it is. I just react. Pushing off my toes to leap behind Gatherer Girl, I shove her forward with one hand, and she crosses the barrier. Using the momentum of my push, I turn, but only make it halfway through the motion. I hoped I could somehow use my ability and redirect what's hurtling through the air in my direction. I thought that maybe I could summon a wall of earth to rise and shield me. But I didn't have time to do either. Didn't have enough understanding or practice to know where to start. I don't even see what it is before something pierces through the side of my stomach, and I intercept what was meant for her.

The force of it launches me the final steps backwards as I stumble and collapse over the barrier, falling into Orion's arms without a chance to release the scream from my throat.

"No!" He bellows. My breath shudders, knees buckle, and my mind doesn't yet understand why it can't do something as simple as stand up. Orion is the only thing stopping me from falling to the ground in a thump.

From the other side of the barrier, I hear one of the Watchers yell out, "You idiot!"

"Stella." Orion's voice wavers as he says my name. "You're going to be okay." He turns me slowly, a string of curses leaving his mouth as the others form a circle around me.

When I feel Orion press a palm down on my side, I arch away from his touch and scream in agony.

His voice is insistent as he speaks to me gently. "I'm sorry, Lremi. I need to put pressure on it. You're okay. Lean on me. You're going to be okay." Part of me wonders if he believes that, or if he's trying to convince himself.

My eyes glaze over, staring at the ground as I whisper, "I need to sit." And then he's lowering me to my knees, crouching before me, staring at my stomach with a locked jaw and concealed expression.

That's when I look down and see his hand properly, covered in blood. I blink slowly, my eyes tracing the gash on his head—feeling the searing pain in my side. "Is all that blood mine or yours?" I ask, my voice strained.

Before he can answer, that same voice who called the other Watcher an idiot pierces the air, scoldingly furious. "I said do not shoot anyone! We need them alive!"

As they get close, I turn to see them, a grimace contorting my features in pain. Then I see the man yelling. He's wearing a suit, hair slicked back, lungs dragging in labored breaths as he stares at us.

When a few of the Watchers are steps away from us, I see their expressions flatten. Zombified, blank nothingness behind their eyes. They turn immediately, and walk away. When Orion and the others took me to the barrier, they told me it would compel unwelcomed people away, but seeing their awareness drain like that is something else.

The man's face paints a picture of disgust and confusion. "Where are you going? What are you doing?"

They don't answer. They've been compelled.

The rest of the Watchers sprint at us in a pod, and my staggered breaths halt. But instead of continuing their charge at us, the process repeats, each of them turning and walking away. Only the man remains. I nearly choke on my spit, struggling to swallow as his expression lightens, not a single muscle moving as he searches the air in front of him. With a quick squint of his eyes and a minute tilt of his head, he guesses, "A forcefield?"

My insides shrivel up, lips staying sealed and hand locked around Orion's forearm. For obvious reasons, none of us answer the man hunting us.

Closing his eyes, he walks toward us in slow, calculated steps. The way he tilts his head back, lifting his hand closer to the invisible wall, *smiling*—the surety I feel that he'll be compelled to leave slips through my fingers. He stops right before the barrier's brink, somehow sensing the exact distance he needs to be before it would compel him away. I flinch when his eyes open sharply and land on mine. He's completely unafraid and focused on me, even as everyone unsheathes their weapons.

As his focus drops to the puddle of blood forming around me, his eyes widen, forehead furrowing—visibly upset that I've been shot.

Orion pulls me closer to him, a sound of warning coming from his chest as the man lowers himself slowly to his hands and knees before me. His wild eyes bore into mine as he tries to get as close as possible. "I'm sorry he hurt you." It's as if he's speaking to a child.

An unsettled shudder rolls through me, and I scrunch my face up at his disturbing tone and unfaltering attention on me. I'd grip harder onto Orion's arm, but the strength in my hold is waning.

The man whispers, "It was you. *You* made the earthquake." Something like pride and wonder lingers in his voice.

The world tilts underneath me. *How could he possibly know that?*

Everyone shifts toward me, forming a defense line, but as Orion tries to speak, nothing comes out of his strained, taut lips. *What's happening?* I turn to scan their faces, their movements, but everyone is moving too slow. I pick up my hand, moving in a way that is easily five times their speed.

Turning my head towards the man, I demand, "What are you doing to them?"

He lifts a hand to silence me. "The bullet is still inside you. We need to remove it. Come with me, we have excellent surgeons."

A laugh bursts from me, then I'm wincing in pain. "I'm not going anywhere with you psychopaths."

A bead of sweat breaks out on his forehead, as if from exertion. I think whatever he's doing to slow everyone down is taking a massive toll on him, and he's straining to hold it.

He raises his eyebrows. "Psychopaths? I'd prefer you call me Alaric." My stomach drops at having a name so freely given to me, but Alaric just grins, as if his name carries a power I should already be aware of. "Now, I don't know what lies they've told you, but apparently, you're willing to risk dying for *them?*"

I scoff, my lids fighting to stay open. "Yes."

He takes a sharp intake of breath as Orion and Cadel break free from the slow motion. Alaric wipes the sweat from his forehead, pushing the stray hair back that broke free of his slicked back style.

He stands up, breathing heavier as Cadel slides on his knees to be next to me and Orion, dirt thrown forward in the action.

Unmoving and struggling to hold on, I watch as Alaric bares his teeth against some kind of invisible pain. His face turns red as he tries to slow Cadel and Orion, but when I look at their expressions, I realize they're some kind of even match. Until Alaric falls to his side, coughing, as if he's choking on something.

The rest of the group is released from the hold and are next to me in an instant. It must be bad if Gatherer Girl is trying to comfort me. "Stay awake, keep your eyes open."

Then, I'm being pulled up to my feet, and I cry out when my arm is lifted over her shoulder.

Orion is barking orders that I barely register, a hue of panic pricking at the edge of his words.

Gatherer Girl transfers me back to Orion, who sweeps me into his arms. Over his shoulder, I see the others stand side to side, shielding me from him. But Alaric peers through the gaps of their bodies, finding my eyes.

"See you soon, Little Bird." His crooked smile taunts me, the words tapping at the edge of my memory until a flicker of stars line the corners of my vision.

I pick up my shaky fingers and lay them on Orion's cheek. "I think I'm dying."

Orion starts walking, his eyes glistening with worry, but his words are steady and solid—for my sake, I'm sure. "Lremi, I'm going to get you back to Juf'ua, and I'm going to get this bullet out. You will survive this. Say it."

Tears line my eyes, and my lips form the words—for his sake. "I will survive this."

A sad smile forces its way onto his face. "That's my girl."

I don't realize I shut my eyes until he's ordering them open. "Look at me."

I pry them open, instant relief flooding my body at the sight of him.

His voice is laced with quiet urgency. "I'm going to get you back quickly, but it won't be pleasant."

I scrunch my brows in confusion for one second, and in the next, I realize I don't need to know, so my face relaxes. Whatever he wants to do, I'm fine with it. I trust him with my life.

As he gently hoists me higher in his arms, black swarms my vision at the movement. Then, we're moving. The pain knocks me in and out. I see flashes of scenery go by, as if we are flying. But not flying because we're close to the ground, and it feels like turbulence. *Running.* Not me, though. Not even with the trees could I run this fast.

I can't run at all. I just got shot.

My eyes close and I start to slip away again. But something about this time feels final. To my surprise, I don't want it to be.

I hear Orion's tender voice whispering to me. "You made a promise, remember? You wanted to find more. Stay for that, Stella. For *more*." A tear slips down my cheek when his voice cracks.

The last thing I'm aware of is his final words echoing in the darkness. "I just found you." He pauses. "Please... Stay for me, too."

ACKNOWLEDGEMENTS

Firstly, I want to thank my parents. Never did you doubt me. Since I was little, whenever I had the idea of trying something new, or embarking on a difficult journey, you always told me, "go for it darling." Thank you, Mum and Dad, for fostering a belief in me that I could achieve anything I set my mind to. Your support means everything to me. Thank you for trusting that I am worthy of the dreams I have.

Thank you to my sister, who never stops telling me how proud she is of me. Thank you for always making me laugh when I get stressed. Thank you for being excited whenever I ramble on about what ever I'm writing.

Thank you to my dear friends, who listened to me for hours over the years, each time I needed to work through a scene, plot or idea. Belle, Kiana, Naomi, Courtney, Nicole, Catherine, Amanda, Chantelle, Emily, Em, Aleisha... Your support changed my life. You've all played a part in building me up, listening to me when I doubted myself, and then gently telling me why I'm wrong, and why I can do this. You invested your time in me as I chased my dreams, and I'll never forget it. Special shout out to Belle, who is my self-proclaimed biggest fan. I love you so much, and your friendship elevated this whole experience for me. You are the sun.

Thank you to my Betas, Alexandria, Kinsey, Milly Reem, Rosalie, and Alex. Your feedback is what shaped and smoothed out so many moments of tension, and I can't thank you enough for taking the time to share your thoughts with me. I loved reading the story through your eyes. Special acknowledgment to Kinsey, for your online support and making videos and posts, emphasizing how much you believe in this story. You're my Beta angels.

Thank you to Alexandria, my incredible Marketing Manager. My darling friend. You've motivated me, empowered me, helped me, and used that brilliant mind to help me navigate the world of marketing. The amount of stress you took off my shoulders so I could focus on the story made a massive difference in my life. You're a genius.

Thank you to my Developmental Editor, Victoria, for helping me see things that I overlooked, fine tuning the tension, and ensuring that the readers get the most out of this.

Thank you to my Copy Editor, Khyla, for helping me enhance my writing skills, and doing it in a way that had me giggling at the screen. What a gift it is to educate someone and leave them feeling fuller afterwards.

Thank you to Andy, who helped me make the From the Stars Anthem. Your musical genius and benevolent soul made bringing this song to life absolutely magical.

Thank you to my cover designer Melinda, who helped me bring my vision to life, and then some. You're so incredibly talented.

Thank you to my therapist, Merie, for listening, analyzing, and providing such valuable insight towards my mental health. Thank you for the tools and strategies you've equipped me with. Thank you for being a safe place for me to fall apart and for walking alongside me as I rewrite the narrative of what I believed life to be. Thank you for helping me reframe who I believed I was. Thank you for giving me my hope back. Thank you for empowering me, validating me, and most of all, seeing me. You'll find how impactful your work with me has been through the pages of this book and the next to come.

Thank you to my spiritual teachers, Eckhart Tolle and Alan Watts. Your wisdom saved me.

Thank you to my readers, because without you, this is just a story. Each of you that reads this makes it real. Your life intertwining with the narrative is why I do this, because my hope is to make each of you feel seen in one part or another. My goal is to show you how lovable and miraculous you are. So, if you read this, and Stella or one of the other characters resonated with you, consider us now connected. For that's the point of art, right?

Kiki Townley is an author, based in Australia. Her goal with writing is to combine her overactive imagination with her yearn for encapsulating the diversity of the human experience. She has a degree in social work, and the thing that inspired her the most was learning how to empower people to fall in love with themselves. She hopes somehow to reach readers through her characters and stories.

Her preferred genre is Romance, with sub-genres of Science, Dystopian, Survival Adventure, and Fantasy. Kiki blends witty and sarcastic humor with psychological and philosophical depth. Kiki weaves themes of identity and the venturous path to self-love into fictional worlds.

From the Stars is the first in her debut trilogy, exploring love, inherent worth, power, and the anti-hero's journey toward destiny. Her social media platforms are where you can find more information on when the next book will be releasing.